# Sixty Days of *Summer*

Broken Oasis Book Two

**Eve Campbell**

ISBN- 9781923416055

To all the hearts that have been broken,
the walls we build to protect ourselves,
and the courage it takes to let someone
in—remember that sometimes the
greatest love is the one that helps
you rediscover who you really are...

# Chapter 1

## Scarlet

As I make my way back to my apartment after another audition as a drummer for a band, I can't help but feel crushed. I thought I did alright, but that drastically changed when they discovered my brother is Nate Reynolds, the drummer of Broken Oasis.

It fucking stings knowing that every audition I attend, my own identity is swallowed by Nate's fame. I love him to death—always have, always will. But it's disheartening that people constantly see me only as his little sister.

I want to make a name for myself, succeed on my own terms, and not always be in my brother's band's shadow, even if they're the biggest thing in music right now.

It's like a never-ending cycle.

Like today, when I sat down with the band after my audition, the conversation inevitably turned to my brother's band. It's as if I'm just a side character in my own story. Nobody gives a shit about my talent, my dreams, or even the struggles I've faced to get here. Sometimes, I think, is it even worth it? I might be better off pursuing something else where I'm not constantly living in Nate's shadow. But then I remember music is more than just a hobby—it's a part of me. It runs through my veins. It's what makes me who I am and who I want to become. Without it, I am nothing.

Despite being two years younger, Nate and I have always been competitive. It all began when I was six and he was eight, challenging each other to drumming contests, trying to outdo each other with the perfect beat.

Theo, Nate's friend, who has always been like an older brother to me and who I cherish just as much as Nate, was always the unbiased referee, keeping score of our friendly competitions. Deep down, I know I may never reach the same heights of success as Nate, and that's fine with me. The most important thing is that I remain true to myself, my love for music, and make my own path, no matter how small it may seem compared to his.

In our younger years, it was always the five of us: me, Nate, Theo, Bianca - the girl who effortlessly charmed both Nate and Theo - and Quinn, her partner in crime. Those were some of the best times of my life—just hanging out with them, laughing, and making memories. Bianca's tragic passing left an indescribable void that echoed through every one of us. I'll never forget that day—the shock, the heartache, and the suffocating emptiness that seemed to swallow everything. The pain I experienced paled in comparison to the agony Nate and Theo endured. I witnessed how it shattered them, their spirits broken in ways I could never fully comprehend. Despite the passage of time, the memory of that day remains etched in my mind, a constant reminder of how fragile life is and how love and loss can shape enduring bonds.

I jam the key into the door of my apartment, the gnawing worry of falling behind on rent eating away at me again. Despite Nate's wealth and his readiness to give me anything I need, I've always been determined to stand on my own two feet. He'd hand me the world if I asked—that's just who he is. But asking for help has never been my style—not even when he and Theo offered to buy me a place in a better part of town. I'm not one to rely on handouts, a characteristic likely influenced by the constant comparisons to Nate. I want to prove that I can make it on my own. The pressure is suffocating, weighing down on me like a heavy blanket, but my stubborn pride pushes me to keep moving forward, even though the fear of never escaping Nate's shadow lingers.

The moment I push open the door, an eerie feeling settles in the air. Despite the silence and the unchanged state of my small apartment, a shiver creeps down my spine.

As I step inside, my ears strain to detect any sound that might offer an explanation for my unease. Am I just imagining things? I tell myself I'm being ridiculous—that it's just the lingering stress from today making me paranoid.

I turn and lock the door behind me, feeling a sense of security as the deadbolt clicks into place with a satisfying thud. Taking a deep breath, I make my way to the fridge, craving a refreshing bottle of water. As I bend down to grab it, the floorboards let out a loud, ominous creak from behind, making me freeze in place. Fuck, I knew something was off. My heart pounds with such intensity that it feels on the verge of exploding. Stay calm, I tell myself. If it's an intruder, just give them whatever they want. It's just stuff—it can be replaced.

As I close the fridge and turn around, a sudden chill runs down my spine, causing goosebumps to rise on my skin. As my throat tightens and my muscles go rigid, I finally catch sight of him. Beck Wilder—my ex and the lead singer of my former band.

It's been nine long months since our band fell apart, and we each went our separate ways. That day, my heart shattered into a million pieces as I walked in on him fucking Tasha, the band's bass guitarist. Despite ignoring his endless phone calls and the flood of unanswered texts blaming me for his downward spiral, it's clear it's not just about the band anymore—apparently, he can't live without me.

Someone told me two months ago that he's been drowning his sorrows in alcohol nearly every day since. Well, tough shit. I'm sure he didn't give me a second thought when he had his dick inside Tasha.

"Get out," I say, my voice firm, but it falls on deaf ears. I try to move past him toward the door, planning to open it and shove him out, but his iron-like grip on my arm makes it impossible. I try to yank my arm away, but he only tightens his grip.

"I want to talk," he slurs, and I can smell the alcohol on his breath.

"Well, I don't," I snap, trying again to yank my arm free with all my strength. His fingers dig into my skin, tightening even more.

He steps closer. The foul smell of his breath becomes more overpowering, causing my stomach to churn. Despite my attempts to create distance between us, his grip is so tight that it feels impossible to step back. He forcefully pulls me closer to him and clamps his other hand tightly around my jaw. The look in his eyes and the crushing pressure of his grip on my chin sends a surge of panic through me. Still, I refuse to give in to his bullshit any longer.

"Let me fucking go!" I shout in his face, but instead of releasing me, he responds with a twisted, cruel smirk that makes my blood run cold. His gaze drops to my lips, and I brace myself for what's coming next. "Please, Beck," I plead, my voice trembling with fear.

When I try to turn my head away, his face contorts with rage. His intensity terrifies me in a way I've never felt before. Fear washes over me, urging me to take swift action before the situation worsens. With desperation I try to pry myself from his vice-like grip.

With brutal force, he yanks my hair, pulling my head back. His lips crash onto mine with such intensity that I fear I might crack a tooth. I struggle to break free, but his grip remains steadfast. I clench my jaw, refusing to give in as his tongue persistently attacks, desperate to gain entry.

With desperation, I wedge my hand between us and forcefully thrust upward, pushing his head away. He flinches for a moment, but his grip remains firm. I keep struggling, twisting to break free, but then his hand clamps around my throat, pinning me in place.

"Let me fucking go!" I scream into his face. Fury blazes in his eyes as the pressure on my throat tightens, almost choking me. In a frantic bid for freedom, I claw at his hand, my nails scraping against his skin, but my efforts prove futile. His grip only tightens, showing no concern that I'm struggling to breathe.

"You've turned into quite the little bitch, Scarlet," he growls, his spit hitting my face and making me feel nauseous. "You always thought you were better than everyone else because of your hotshot brother. Well, fuck you, Scarlet. You're no better than me. You think you're so high and mighty? Look at you now—trapped under my grip."

Toying with me, he slowly loosens his grip. It's just enough for me to catch my breath, while a menacing smirk spreads across his face. Two years of being with this man have shown me first-hand the extent of his drunken antics—how he revels in instigating fights with strangers just for his own twisted amusement.

He holds me tight, his gaze fixated on my lips once more. I can see the anticipation in his eyes, as if he expects me to surrender to his demands, just like he has cunningly manipulated me to do in the past.

As he moves in for another kiss, my instincts take over. I claw at his face and dig my nails into anything I can reach, desperate to make him back the hell off.

With a menacing growl, he forcefully shoves me, causing me to crash to the ground with a resounding thud. With a sudden impact, my body collides against the hard edge of the coffee table, igniting a searing pain in my side. The vase filled with flowers shatters, creating a colorful explosion of petals and shards of glass across the floor.

As I look up, struggling for air, I notice his towering figure above me, his face covered in scratches, blood slowly trickling down. His fingers drift across the wound, his touch gentle yet cautious, until he pulls his hand back to examine the dark, smeared blood. As he glares at me, his eyes burn with an intense fury.

Before I can react or even get to my feet, he lunges forward with a predatory snarl.

"I fucking hate you, you stupid bitch," he seethes, his towering frame casting a dark shadow over me.

As his voice roars in my ears, I recoil, realizing too late the danger lurking in his clenched fist.

Just as I close my eyes, I feel a bone-jarring force slam into the side of my face. The force of the impact sends a jarring wave of pain coursing through me, shaking my bones and leaving me momentarily stunned as I collapse once more onto the floor.

Through the fog in my mind, I catch the faint sound of his footsteps resonating in the room, yet their exact location eludes me.

The sound of running water brings me back to reality, forcing me to refocus. My vision blurs as I blink repeatedly, trying to focus, until finally I spot him standing by the kitchen sink. Hunched over with his back turned to me, he splashes water onto his bloody face.

My mind screams at me to get the fuck up and get out of there. Fumbling with the front door locks will take too long, and he'll catch me before I can make my escape. The bathroom—it's my best shot. I pat my pocket, and a wave of relief washes over me when I feel my phone still there.

With his back still turned, hunched over the sink, I know I need to act now. There might not be another opportunity later. Desperate to get into the bathroom, I scramble to my feet, my heart pounding in my chest.

The uneven rhythm of my footsteps catches his attention, and moments later, the faucet shuts off.

"Oh no, you don't, you little slut," he growls, his hurried footsteps closing in behind me.

I push harder, feeling my body teeter on the edge of losing balance as my shoe unexpectedly snags on an object on the floor. Dread coiling in my stomach, I stagger forward, bracing myself for an imminent fall. With an effort, I regain my balance, and the force pushes me towards the bathroom door.

Footsteps sound behind me—shit, he's almost on me.

In a rush, I propel myself through the narrow gap in the slightly open door, swiftly turning around and slamming it shut. The last thing I see before closing the door is Beck's furious face looming closer, his eyes blazing with rage.

I stumble back, my heart pounding in my chest, as I watch in terror while the doorknob twists and turns frantically.

"Please, Beck. Please just go away," I plead, my voice trembling with fear.

"Open the fucking door, Scarlet," he snarls from the other side. His palm slams against the door with a deafening thud that reverberates through my head, amplifying the relentless throbbing pain in my face.

"Fuck you, Scarlet. You know why I fucked Tasha? It's because she doesn't act like she's so goddamn superior. That's why I went to her—to get the fuck away from you."

With trembling hands, I grab my phone, desperately trying to block out the relentless pounding on the door and Beck's cruel taunts. I start to dial 911 but freeze abruptly. If the press gets wind of this, my brother might make headlines for all the wrong reasons, simply because I'm his sister. I can't do that to Nate—he shouldn't be dragged through the mud for something beyond his control.

But if calling the cops isn't an option, how the fuck do I get Beck to leave my apartment?

"I'm calling the cops, Beck!" I scream, my voice trembling against the thunderous pounding on the door.

The banging abruptly stops.

"I'm calling the cops right now, Beck," I repeat, my desperation seeping through as I clutch the phone tightly, praying that this threat will finally make him back off.

"You won't fucking do that. You know the shitstorm it'll bring," he sneers from the other side of the door.

He knows I've always avoided doing anything that might attract media attention and put my brother in the spotlight.

Ignoring his taunts, I press on, pretending to have already made the call and speaking loudly for him to hear through the door.

"Yes, I need to report a break-in at my apartment," I say, striving to keep my voice steady despite the fear gnawing at me. "There's a man trying to force his way in and threatening me."

"Fuck you, Scarlet, you bitch," he spits back.

Ignoring his rage, I keep speaking, using everything I've picked up from reality TV to sound convincing.

"Yes, my name is Scarlet Reynolds, and Beck Wilder, my ex-boyfriend, won't leave my apartment," I say, hoping the urgency in my voice is enough.

Through the closed door, I hear the jarring sounds of objects being hurled and shattered—vases crashing, furniture scraping against the floor. The noise crescendos into a chaotic racket before abruptly cutting off with the sharp slam of the front door.

With my heart still pounding, I approach the door cautiously, straining to catch any hint of Beck's presence. The silence is unnervingly eerie, amplifying the throbbing pain on the side of my face where he struck me. I press my ear against the door, careful not to make any noise that might provoke him further.

I wait in the tense silence, each second stretching into an eternity.

My mind is on high alert, searching for any sign of movement or sound that might indicate Beck is still lurking nearby.

The wait is excruciating. I wrestle with the urge to open the door and peek outside, but a cold dread holds me back—what if he's still out there waiting for me to expose myself?

I clutch my phone tightly, my finger trembling above the call button with 911 still displayed on the screen. If Beck is

lingering nearby, ready to strike again, I know I'll have to call emergency services, even if it means risking my brother's privacy and dealing with unwanted media attention.

The click of the lock on the bathroom door echoes through the silence, sending a shiver down my spine. I cautiously turn the doorknob and step back, bracing for the possibility that Beck might burst in. My head still throbs from his earlier blow, and I'm acutely aware that another hit could knock me out, leaving me helpless and unable to reach for the call button if I need it.

When nothing happens, I slowly inch the door open, peering through the crack.

The sight that meets me is chaotic: my belongings are strewn across the floor—couch cushions, notebooks, my laptop, and various trinkets—tossed and scattered in disarray. But in this moment, none of that matters. What matters is that Beck isn't lurking somewhere, giving me a sense of false hope.

With caution, I ease open the bathroom door, creating a wide enough opening to slip through, all while maintaining a fixed gaze on the apartment's front door. The chain lock dangles loose, and a quiet sigh of relief escapes me as I remember securing it earlier when I got home. Even though Beck appears to be gone, there's still unsettling suspicion gnawing at me. What if this is just a ploy to lure me out? I hold my breath, ears straining for any hint of noise, while my eyes dart around the apartment, scanning for any sign of movement.

Minutes stretch out unbearably slow as I force myself to take a few cautious steps forward. My heart pounds like a war drum in my chest, reverberating through every inch of my body. With every nerve on edge, I scan the room for any sign of danger.

Reaching the front door, I fumble with the deadbolt, locking it with a shaky hand, and then secure the chain lock. Each motion is tinged with dread, as though the very act of securing the door might be my downfall.

Turning to survey the wreckage, I wait in the quiet as a wave of crushing sadness washes over me. I collapse against the door, sliding down it until I'm sitting on the cold, hard floor. My head falls into my hands as I sob, with the realization that I can't stay here any longer. Not after what he did. Not after the violation of my space and safety. I don't want to think about what would have happened if I never made it into the bathroom. Plus, I don't even know how the fuck he managed to get into my apartment in the first place.

# CHAPTER 2

## Ace

I know I have to come clean and tell Nate what happened, but I've got no fucking clue where to even start. The second he finds out I fucked his sister the night of Poppy's foundation party—it's all going to blow the fuck up, and probably tear the band apart. I'm not proud of it. I was ready to bury that shit, take it to the grave. But ever since Xander walked in and caught us in the act, he's been giving me this fucking guilt trip about betraying my friend.

Despite Xander warning me to stay the fuck away from her, I couldn't help myself. The night of Xander and Poppy's surprise wedding, we found ourselves entangled once more. I made every effort to keep my distance, but the irresistible pull of the beautiful blonde with the sexy tattoos was too strong to resist. And now, because of what I've done, my conscience is tearing me apart. I know I've fucked up in the worst way possible, and every time I see Nate, the guilt just rips me to shreds all over again.

While Nate is a superstar, his sister is a whole universe of her own—happy and so full of light—while I'm more like a black hole.

The memory of those two nights we shared lingers in my mind. The sensation of holding her close and fulfilling her deepest desires. And what's weird as fuck is that she's constantly on my mind. It's been over five months since I last got any action, and maybe that's why. Perhaps when the band hits the road again and the groupies throw themselves at me, she'll become just another name on the long list of chicks I've fucked. Maybe I'll even forget the way her gentle touch sent shivers down my spine and how hungry she was for my cock.

It's been five months of inner turmoil, contemplating whether to tell Nate what happened. Every time I go to come clean, Xander steps in and tells me to keep quiet. He insists on keeping it a secret, believing it's in my best interest if Nate, the overly protective brother, doesn't find out.

Xander's convinced it'll end up like last time, when I messed around with a guy's sister back in high school and got my ass handed to me. I expect Nate will do the same, but at this point, I'm ready to face the fallout. I'd rather face the consequences head-on than let this guilt consume me completely.

Nate's never been one to lose his cool; violence isn't his style. He's always been the serious, focused type. But there have been times when his temper flared, especially when rumors swirled about the old label wanting to replace Xander. The idea of him finding out I've been fucking his sister. Well, that's something I can't even start to wrap my head around. I don't want to imagine the pain it will cause him, and on top of that, it will shatter the trust. That alone is fucking unbearable.

I suppose you could say I've matured.

In the old days, I didn't give a shit about hurting anyone's feelings, except for Xander's. He's the only one who really gets me, who knows the real me. Even my father and sister couldn't wait to ditch me. And as for my mother? She was too caught up in her own shit—always chasing the next high and dragging home some asshole to fuck.

Xander, Poppy, and Alex—they're more than just friends, they are my real family. Nate and Theo, too. They accept me for the fucked-up, person I am. That's why ripping Nate's trust to shreds like this is tearing me apart. I know he's gonna lose his shit when I tell him, but eventually, he'll come around. Isn't that what families do? They fight, they yell, they let all that shit out, and then they forgive and move on.

I attempt to wash off the guilt in the shower, but it clings to me like an invisible weight. With a heavy heart, I make my way over to Nate and Theo's place, ready to come clean.

It's been only two hours since we wrapped up recording the last track for our new album. I know if I dive into the studio to edit, I'll miss my chance to confess. Getting lost in the music is like tumbling down a never-ending rabbit hole of pure bliss. Xander's songs are hitting hard; our classic sound is back, and I'm confident the fans will eat it up.

This album is our big fuck you to Victory Records, and that we can succeed without their support. With all the bullshit they've thrown our way, we're determined to make this a success.

Stepping out of my house, I immediately notice Xander standing in front of his place, his gaze fixated on Alex zooming down the driveway on his bike. The pure fucking joy on Xander's face is something else, and I can't help but admire how Poppy and Alex have transformed him. It's amazing how he changes when he's around them—his true self emerges, full of happiness and devoid of any bullshit.

It makes me wonder what it's like to have everything you've ever wanted: to love without fear, to feel completely accepted for who you truly are. Xander's found that courage, embracing his vulnerabilities in ways I've always struggled with. Witnessing the way Poppy loves him, and all of us, without any conditions, is a clear indication of the strong bond that has formed within our family since they joined us.

The sound of my footsteps catches Xander's attention, and he spins around, flashing that grin that's become a permanent fixture on his face.

"Hey, man," he greets me, before turning back to watch Alex, making sure he's safe as he moves further down the long driveway.

"Hey," I reply, stopping beside him.

We stand in silence, mesmerized by the sight of Alex confidently making his way towards one of the many ramps Xander has assembled. Alex pedals hard, soaring over the first three ramps with effortless ease.

"He's really getting the hang of that," I say, as Alex nails each jump.

"Yeah," Xander replies, his voice filled with pride and his grin stretching from ear to ear. "He's already asking me to build higher ramps, but Poppy's not exactly thrilled about it," he adds with a chuckle.

As I look at my brother, a rush of admiration and nostalgia washes over me.

He's come a long way, transforming into a devoted family man, always ready to go above and beyond to ensure Poppy and Alex's happiness.

"What's with that look, asshole?" Xander says, his smile faltering as he catches me staring.

"Nothing," I reply, wishing I felt as content with my life as he does. I turn my focus back to Alex, who's already cleared the rest of the jumps and is now heading back toward us. "I'm going to talk to Nate about Scarlet."

Xander's head whips around towards me, his previous relaxed expression now replaced with a serious one.

"For fuck sake, Ace, don't go there. You know how Nate loses it over Scarlet."

"Yeah, I know," I admit, my words laced with a hint of defeat. "But I've got to. This guilt is eating me alive. I can't even look at the guy without feeling like shit."

"It was one fucking night, Ace. It didn't mean shit, so why bring it up now?" Xander says, his voice laced with concern, sounding strained.

I take a deep breath, knowing this is going to hit hard.

"It wasn't just a one-time thing. We hooked up again the next night, on the same night as your wedding," I admit, feeling the heaviness of my confession.

"Are you fucking kidding me?" Xander's voice erupts with disbelief, his tone now void of any previous cheerfulness. "After you promised me that morning you'd stay the fuck away from her, and you even admitted it was a mistake…" He trails off abruptly as Alex rolls up to us, interrupting the conversation.

"Hey, Uncle Ace," Alex says, his innocent voice slicing through the tension.

With a nod towards the ramps, I comment, "You're really improving," purposely avoiding eye contact with Xander's piercing stare.

"Yeah, I want the jumps to be higher, but Mom's worried I'll break my arm again," Alex replies.

"Well, just keep at it," I comment, taking a few steps toward Nate and Theo's place. "Moms always freak out about everything." Honestly, I don't know if all moms are like that since mine never gave a shit about me.

Xander's voice booms behind me, calling out my name, "Ace." I can practically feel the heat of his stare. If it weren't for Alex, Xander would be in my face, warning me about the shitstorm coming my way if I proceed with this. But I'm determined to come clean anyway. If Nate beats the shit out of me for this screw-up, then so be it. I crossed a line, and I'll own up to it.

When I get to Nate and Theo's place, I skip the knock and just push the door open.

As soon as I step inside, the blaring noise from the TV overwhelms my senses. Alex has been kicking all our asses at Mario Kart for months now, and the familiar sounds emanating from the TV confirms Theo is once again determined to dethrone him. He's always bitching about how it's total bullshit that a six-year-old consistently beats us.

As I step into the next room, the sight of Theo sprawled on the couch catches my eye.

His bare chest proudly displays the intricate tattooed angel wings. His dark, shoulder-length hair is wet, as if he's just stepped out of the shower, and he's dressed in nothing but gray sweatpants.

As I approach, I can see the sheer focus on his face, his eyes fixated on the screen.

"Where's Nate?" I ask, dropping onto the couch next to him, my eyes glued to the TV.

"Shower, I think," Theo mutters, not even glancing away from the screen.

Both of us fall silent, completely absorbed in his character's electrifying performance on the track. It's not until he finally crosses the finish line that his gaze turns to me.

"You good, bro?" he asks with a furrowed brow.

"Yeah," I lie, as I brace myself to face Nate and come clean.

Theo locks eyes with me, his gaze lingering for an extra beat, his keen perception sensing the tension in the air. Despite his talent for teasing and getting under my skin, Theo is aware of when to give me space. I've witnessed him do it with both Nate and Xander. Instead of prying, he casually grabs the spare controller and tosses it onto the couch next to me, making a soft thud.

Without saying a word, Theo exits the game and returns to the home screen, switching the game to multiplayer.

"Fuck, I need to get laid," Theo blurts out. "It's like the goddamn fucking Sahara Desert down there. I was so desperate, I almost asked Nate for a hand job this morning, but I knew he'd fucking deck me."

A smile tugs at my lips, a sense of relief washing over me as the conversation shifts, and I reach for the remote.

"But isn't that what you guys do when you share chicks?" I ask, raising an eyebrow.

"Nah, we don't touch each other's dicks," Theo says with a casual shrug. "Our dicks might bump into each other during a threesome or whatever, but that's about it. I don't think Nate's into that."

"But you are?" I press, genuinely curious.

"Hell yeah, why not?" Theo grins. "The day Nate Reynolds actually kneels down and sucks my dick, I'll be the fucking happiest guy alive."

I smirk, appreciating Theo's blunt honesty. It's one of the things I genuinely respect about him. "Why not just lay it all out there? Speak your mind."

He falls silent, his eyes glued to the game.

Just when I think the conversation's done, he speaks up.

"Because it could fuck everything up between us," Theo says quietly, his gaze fixed on the screen. "Nate's been my rock since I was nine, always there when the shit in my head gets too much. He's the only one who can pull me out of that darkness. I can't risk losing that. He already knows how much he means to me, and I can't jeopardize the one solid thing I've got."

As Theo lays it all out, I realize the depth of their bond, like an unbreakable thread connecting them. I've always sensed something unique between them, but never really dug into it. I had a hunch that their connection went beyond friendship, like there was an underlying tension simmering between them. Hearing that they've never crossed that line takes me by surprise—I'd always assumed their relationship was more than platonic.

We fall into silence, eyes locked on the game. My heart races as Nate's voice grows louder, causing my nerves to kick into overdrive.

Nate bursts into the room, his phone clutched tightly to his ear, his voice oozing with anger. "I'll fucking kill the bastard, Scar," he growls, his anger crackling in the air.

Theo hits pause on the game, his laid-back demeanor instantly replaced by genuine concern as he turns to face Nate, who paces anxiously behind us.

Shit, did Scarlet just rat me out? I wonder, tossing the remote onto the couch and bracing myself for Nate's explosion.

"Do you want me to come out there?" Nate barks into the phone.

Rising to his feet, Theo takes a step forward, effectively obstructing Nate's path and forcing him to halt.

"So how the hell did that asshole get in?" Nate growls.

I let out a deep breath, relieved that Nate's conversation with Scarlet isn't about me. Still, the solemn expression on his face tells me that something grave has happened.

"You need to stay here," Nate says firmly, his tone leaving no room for debate. "Crash in our spare room, Scar. If that asshole touches you again, I swear I'll find him and make him regret it. I'll hop on a plane right now and deal with him." His voice is hard, but then it softens. "Scar don't cry. It's not your fault."

Hearing Scarlet, usually so full of cheer, crying on the phone to Nate throws me off, and I can't shake this weird urge to protect her. Apart from those two nights, her life remains a mystery to me.

"Alright, Scar, here's the deal," Nate says, his voice steady. "Pack a few things and come stay with me and Theo. You need to get away from that asshole. What did the cops say?"

Theo, sensing the gravity of the situation, grabs Nate's arm, his face tense. "What the hell's going on?" he demands.

Nate quickly covers the phone with his hand and lowers his voice. "Beck broke into Scarlet's place. He attacked her. It's a fucking mess."

"Is she okay?" Theo asks, his voice filled with concern.

"Yeah, she got away," Nate replies, pulling his hand back and returning his focus to Scarlet. "I don't give a shit about the media, Scar. Ignoring this won't stop him. Just come stay with us. I'll get you on the next flight. You'll be here in a couple of hours." Nate takes a deep breath, the stress evident on his face.

"Who's Beck?" I ask, even though I know I'm probably overstepping. I've already crossed a line with Nate, but I need to understand who this asshole is.

"Beck is Scarlet's ex," Theo explains. "They broke up ages ago, but he just won't stay out of her life. He keeps showing up and making her life hell."

Nate steps forward and takes a seat on one of the stools at the kitchen counter. "Alright, I'll book the flight right now. Pack your stuff, and I'll send you the details," he says, his voice steady. "Theo and I will pick you up from the airport. We'll be there as soon as you land."

Theo retrieves a tub of yogurt from the fridge, effortlessly tossing one to me while grabbing another for himself. He pulls out two spoons from the drawer and hands one to me.

Choosing the second stool away from Nate, I sit down and open the yogurt container.

"Alright, Scar, I'll see you soon. Love you," Nate says, ending the call. With a careless motion, he drops his phone on the counter; the sound reverberating in the quiet room. He runs his hands through his hair, his frustration evident. "If I ever see that fucker, I'm gonna make him pay," he says.

"What the hell happened?" Theo demands.

Nate looks up, his face etched with anger. "Beck broke into her apartment. He fucking hit her. She managed to get away, but she's not doing well. She's a fucking mess."

"What the hell?" Theo says, clearly stunned.

Nate's jaw clenches, his eyes burning with rage. "She came home from an audition, and Beck was already in her apartment," he says, his voice rising with anger. "The bastard wouldn't leave. When she tried to kick him out, he grabbed her by the throat. Then he kissed her, and when she fought back, the fuckhead hit her."

In a fit of rage, Theo forcefully slams his yogurt container onto the counter, his face contorted with anger. "That fucking piece of shit," he growls. "What the hell are we going to do about this?"

"First things first, we're getting her out of there," Nate says firmly. "She's coming to stay with us until we figure out the next move. Then I'll fucking deal with him."

Just the thought of someone laying a hand on a woman makes my blood boil. "Is she okay?" I ask, trying to keep my voice steady.

Nate and Theo exchange a glance, and I can see the anger and concern etched deeply in Nate's eyes. "She said she's okay," Nate replies, his voice tight with emotion. "But she's scared, and that's what really gets to me."

Theo's fists are clenched, his knuckles white. "We need to make sure that asshole never gets near her again," he growls.

I keep my voice steady, even though I can feel the anger rising inside me. "What about the cops?"

"She didn't want to get them involved," Nate explains. "She didn't want the media sniffing around, especially with her being my sister."

"The media can fuck off," Theo snaps.

"Exactly what I told her," Nate says, as he pushes himself off the stool.

"Where are you going?" Theo asks.

"I'm getting my laptop to book her flight," Nate replies. "She's coming here until I can sort that fucking asshole out." He slips out into the hall, retracing his steps from just minutes before.

Theo finishes his yogurt and gives me a look of disgust. "Beck's a real piece of shit," he says. "I've hated that cockhead since day one." He walks over to the sink, drops his spoon in with a loud clatter, and then glances at my half-eaten yogurt. "You gonna finish that?" he asks.

"Nah," I reply, pushing the tub toward him.

He snatches it up and digs in with my spoon, a cheeky grin spreading across his face.

"I'll leave you and Nate to sort things out for Scarlet," I say, turning toward the front door. "Catch you later, man."

Stepping outside, I immediately realize that Alex's bike is no longer there. Xander sits on the front steps of his house, fixated on his phone, oblivious to the world around him.

He's probably been on edge ever since I brought up the idea of speaking with Nate.

As soon as he hears my footsteps, he quickly glances up, jumps to his feet, and swiftly tucks his phone away in his pocket.

With determination in his eyes, he strides over to me.

"Don't sweat it, I kept my mouth shut," I tell him before he even has a chance to ask.

"Good," Xander replies. "We don't need this crap blowing up before the tour. What's going on with you, man? You've never cared about who you've hooked up with before."

"Yeah, but this isn't just any hookup," I say. "It's Nate's fucking little sister. It's messing with my head, knowing I've broken the bro code."

"I get it, Ace," Xander says, his frustration clear. "You're feeling like shit because of who it is, and if you need to come clean, can you at least wait until after the tour? We don't need any of this drama right now, especially with us being under our own label. That kind of shit could seriously screw things up for us."

"But what if Scarlet spills the beans before I get the chance?" I counter. "It'll look even worse if Nate hears it from her."

"I doubt she'd run straight to her brother to tell him who she's been fucking," Xander says.

"Yeah, you're probably right," I reply. "I just didn't want Nate to hear it from someone else before I had a chance to come clean. I figured telling him now would be easier, but with everything going on with Scarlet, I couldn't bring myself to drop that bomb today."

Seeing the concern in Xander's eyes, I add, "She's crashing at Theo and Nate's for now. She's catching a flight later today. Her asshole ex broke into her apartment and hit her."

"Fuck, is she okay?" Xander asks.

"Yeah, I think so," I reply. "That's why Nate wants her with him. To keep her safe and away from that bastard."

He turns his head, and locks eyes with me, his gaze piercing. "Don't fucking go there again, Ace. For fuck sake, keep your distance this time. He might let the last screw-up slide, but he sure as hell won't if you keep fucking her."

"Yeah, I get it. I won't go there again. You have my word."

"Alright," he says, giving me a shove with his shoulder. "You up for a beer?"

"Fuck yeah," I agree, knowing that hanging out with Xander, Poppy, and Alex will help drown out the guilt gnawing at me.

# Chapter 3

## Scarlet

As soon as my phone buzzes, I instinctively reach into my back pocket and inspect the screen.

**Nate:** Flight's booked, 4 pm.

I feel an overwhelming wave of relief wash over me. My fingers dance across the keyboard as I quickly type back.

**Scarlet:** Thanks. See you soon. Love you!

As I wait for his reply, I gaze at the screen, my eyes watching the appearance of the message bubbles.

**Nate:** Love you too, Scar. Stay safe.

His words wrap around me like a warm, comforting embrace, soothing my frayed nerves. I quickly open the Uber app and book a ride, doing my best to shake off the lingering tension that still trembles through my body.

With my bag packed, I rush into the bathroom, the sound of my footsteps echoing off the tiled walls. As I come face to face with my reflection, I feel an overwhelming urge to look away. My eyes are red and swollen, evidence of the countless tears that have streamed down my face. The bruises on my face tell the painful story of Beck's violent outburst, a constant reminder of the brutality I've suffered. I know makeup can only do so much — it can't hide the swelling or all the visible marks of damage. Still, I reach for my compact and try to hide the painful bruises, knowing that it's probably a losing battle but refusing to give up.

Ever since my phone call with my brother, I've been seething with anger at myself. I should have been more alert and aware of my surroundings.

The apartment was littered with signs, like breadcrumbs, leading to the truth of his intrusion.

The faint smell of smoke lingering in the air, the subtle disarray of kitchen items, and the telltale wrinkles on the bed—each one a haunting reminder that he might have already invaded my space before.

As I pack up my makeup bag, I catch a final glimpse of myself in the mirror. It's not perfect, but it'll have to do.

The dark bruises on my neck catch my attention. I swiftly make my way to my room, where I find a light scarf. I wrap it snugly around my neck, effectively camouflaging the evidence.

After making sure that the marks are completely concealed, I pick up my suitcase and head towards the door. Swinging it open, I'm ready to escape this hellhole.

Stepping into the hall, my nerves are in chaos, swirling like a tornado, while every echoing sound sends shivers down my spine. I can feel my heart pounding forcefully against my ribcage, as if it's trying to break free, as I brace myself, half-expecting Beck to reappear at any moment. The tension in the air is palpable, and every creak or distant noise sends shivers down my spine, intensifying my anxiety.

Each step I take feels like a relentless battle against the fear that clings to me.

With trembling hands, I turn the key in the lock of my apartment door. I rush to the elevator; the seconds ticking by agonizingly slow as a sense of impending doom tightens in my gut.

The abrupt ding of the elevator startles me, causing me to flinch. With a sense of relief, I hurriedly step inside, eager to escape from this place. The possibility of Beck returning keeps me on edge, fueling my determination to escape as quickly as possible.

After the doors close, I let out a shaky breath of relief, but it quickly dissipates, leaving me on edge.

Two floors down, the elevator comes to a sudden stop, and my heart races. This suffocating fear that consumes me now is unlike anything I've ever felt before.

The doors slowly inch open, and with each passing second, my anticipation builds, preparing myself for whatever lies on the other side.

When the elevator doors creak open, I'm met with the sight of an elderly woman, her frail figure wrapped in a floral dress and a worn cardigan, her house slippers scuffing the floor as she steps inside. For a moment, my pulse steadies, finding a fleeting sense of normalcy in her presence.

But as the doors close again, my anxiety ramps up. The elevator jolts into motion, and every second feels like an eternity. My stomach twists with fear, wondering if Beck might be waiting for me on the ground floor.

The thought of running into him there sends a fresh wave of panic, making each descending floor feel like a countdown to something terrifying.

When the elevator reaches the ground floor, I watch intently as the elderly lady shuffles out, my eyes darting around, desperately searching for any sign of Beck. The moment I confirm he's not there, I quickly move toward the front doors but stop just before stepping outside.

I open the app on my phone. My heart skips a beat when I spot my ride approaching the street, and I can't help but let out a sigh of relief.

As I step outside, I make a beeline for the waiting car. The driver pops the trunk for my suitcase, and I slide into the back seat with a sense of urgency. Every second counts as I try to put as much distance as possible between myself and the chaos I'm leaving behind.

As we merge into the flow of traffic, the cityscape blurs into a swirl of lights and colors. I sink back into the seat, allowing the steady hum of the car and the rhythm of the city to soothe my frayed nerves. The thought of soon being with my brother and Theo feels like a comforting balm, easing my anxiety.

But my mind drifts to Ace Roberts, knowing I'll soon be back in his world. He made it clear that what we had was just a casual hookup, nothing more. I shouldn't be tempted to get involved with him again, but damn, the way he made my body come alive. No man has ever touched me like that, igniting a fire inside me that I can't ignore. Not even Beck, he was always too busy chasing his own pleasure. Sex with Ace was raw and intense, something that left me feeling both exhilarated and vulnerable. Just thinking about it now sends a shiver down my spine, a reminder of how deeply he's imprinted on me.

I know we can't go there again.

Ace has made it crystal clear that I'm off-limits, and he told me that with my brother in the mix, there's no way it could ever happen again. Even though the pull is strong and the temptation is there, I need to keep my distance. The intensity of what we shared still lingers. I've replayed it in my mind over these last five months. The way he made me scream, the way he made me come. As much as I want to feel those things again, I have to focus on what's important right now: and that's getting my life back on track.

I'm jolted out of my thoughts as the car pulls up to the airport. The driver slows to a stop at the curb, and I step out, grateful for the shift in focus.

I head straight to the check-in counter, where the attendant's voice cuts through my haze. I drop off my suitcase, watch it get tagged, and then make my way to the cafeteria before my flight.

I'm in dire need of caffeine and something to eat. With forty minutes to kill before my flight, I grab a seat in the airport cafeteria, pull out the gossip magazine I bought for distraction, and try to keep myself composed as I wait to board the plane.

An hour later, I'm airborne, thanks to my brother's generous upgrade to first class. I'm thankful for the luxury, as I rarely get to travel this way. Finally, I can relax a bit, away from the prying eyes and the constant scrutiny of the bruises on my face.

I know I should call my parents to let them know I'll be staying at Nate's for a while, but the idea of having to explain everything makes me hesitate. They're incredibly protective. I can already imagine them trying to convince me to come home and stay with them. But I need to handle this on my own. Besides, if my dad found out what Beck did, he'd be just as furious as Nate, and I shudder to think of the consequences that might follow.

After the plane finally lands, retrieving my bag from the carousel feels never-ending. I do my best to keep a low profile, trying to avoid drawing attention to the bruises on my face.

The airport, usually teeming with activity, appears even more chaotic as I weave my way through the bustling crowd.

I make my way toward the front door area, where I know Nate and Theo will be waiting for me, just like the last time they picked me up. But this time, everything feels different. My nerves are on edge. I'm preparing myself for their reaction, fully aware that they'll be livid once they catch a glimpse of my face.

Scanning the crowd, I strain my eyes, desperately hoping to spot Nate or Theo.

But they remain elusive in the sea of unfamiliar faces.

Just like in New York, the traffic in LA is notorious, so they're most likely trapped in the gridlock. I grab my phone, hoping to find a message from them. Instead, I notice a missed call from an unfamiliar number and a new voicemail waiting for me. I wonder if it's connected to the audition I did earlier today.

I tap a few buttons on my phone and bring it to my ear.

"Hey Scarlet, it's Ace."

The sound of his voice has an electrifying effect on me, and the way he utters my name makes my heart skip a beat. Despite the flood of emotions, I push them aside and give my full attention to his message. I can't help but feel confused as to why he's reaching out to me after such a long time.

"Something's come up, so I'll be picking you up from the airport. I'm running a bit behind, so just hang tight for a bit, and I'll fill you in when I get there."

I'm puzzled how Ace managed to get my number without us ever exchanging it, and what's even more perplexing is why he's picking me up instead of Nate and Theo.

Swallowing hard, I brace myself to face him. He'll definitely notice the bruises on my face, their dark hues stark against my pale skin. The last thing I want is to be seen like this, especially by him. But here we are.

I shove my phone back into my bag and glance around. As people bustle past me, I can't help but keep a watchful eye on the doors, eagerly waiting for his arrival.

Twenty minutes later, my heart leaps as I catch sight of him confidently striding through the large automatic doors. As his eyes scan the crowd, I check him out. Damn, he's hot as fuck. I can't help but be captivated by the sight of his muscular arms, adorned with elaborate tattoos that trace a path all the way up to his neck. His dark, intense brown eyes, chiseled jawline, and tousled hair only add to his rugged appeal. He radiates sex appeal, embodying every girl's fantasy.

When his eyes finally meet mine, a rush of butterflies fills my stomach. With a casual greeting, I lift my hand, though my nerves are jittering beneath the surface.

As he closes the distance between us, I can feel his intense gaze roaming over every inch of my body, igniting a rush of excitement within me. Then his eyes fixate on my face, specifically on the bruised right cheek, as if studying the marks. His jaw tightens ever so slightly, and I catch a flicker of concern crossing his face.

As he looks away, I sense something is off, a tightrope of tension threading between us. Despite the unsettling feeling in my gut, I maintain a steady gaze, closely monitoring his approach.

When he stops in front of me, he shoves his hands into his jean pockets, his brows furrowing as he scrutinizes the bruises on my face as if dissecting them.

I bow my head, trying to shield myself from his penetrating stare.

"What's going on? I thought Nate and Theo were picking me up," I ask, looking back up to meet his intense brown eyes, searching for some kind of explanation.

He shifts his weight uneasily, his tongue darting out over his bottom lip before swallowing. I can tell something is seriously wrong. His voice tightens as he reveals, "Nate and Theo were in a car accident."

I inhale sharply, the shocking news hitting me like a ton of bricks. Tears well up in my eyes, and my heart starts to race. I keep my eyes locked on Ace's face, desperately seeking more information since I am too stunned to utter a word.

"They're alright," Ace says, his tone steady but carrying an edge of concern. "They're at the hospital. I don't know much yet, but Xander's heading there. He'll keep me posted."

As I nod, a solitary tear rolls down my cheek, betraying my struggle to maintain composure. The very notion of my brother and Theo getting hurt fills me with an overwhelming sense of unease. After everything I've faced today, the thought of losing them is unbearable.

"From what we've gathered, Theo was driving when some asshole ran a red light," Ace says.

The tension in my body builds to an unbearable level, and I can no longer hold back the flood of emotions. A sob escapes my throat, shattering the mask of strength I've carefully crafted in front of Ace. Tears soak my cheeks, and I struggle to regain control of my overwhelming emotions. All I can do now is hold on tightly to the hope that Nate and Theo will be okay.

"Hey," Ace murmurs softly, his hand lightly touching my shoulder, giving it an awkward pat.

It's clear that he's struggling to find the right way to comfort me.

# Chapter 4

## Ace

Fuck. What the hell do I do now? I'm completely out of my depth here. My lame-ass attempt at patting her shoulder feels useless, like applying a bandaid on a bullet wound.

Damn, I've never been in a situation with a crying girl before—usually it's just a casual fuck, no emotional baggage involved. Maybe I should call Poppy and see if she can tell me what the fuck I'm supposed to do. Or do I just grab her suitcase and head to the car? But when she looks up at me with those broken eyes, something inside me shifts. It hits me hard, and I have no clue how to handle it.

Awkwardly, I keep patting her shoulder, my touch becoming clumsier and more foolish with each attempt.

She leans into me, her cheek resting against my chest, leaving me at a loss for what to do next. Slowly, I wrap my arms around her, feeling her warmth against me. Damn, her scent brings back vivid memories, and I'm praying my dick doesn't get any ideas—now is definitely not the right moment. Besides, Xander would tear me apart if I fucked this up.

Despite the uncomfortable vibe, I set aside any distracting thoughts and concentrate on the present moment. Right now, all she wants is to be wrapped in someone's embrace, and I'm trying like hell to be that person.

Just minutes ago, I was ready to lose my shit when I saw those fucking bruises on her face. The thought of someone laying a hand on her—Scarlet, the one who's always been a bright ray of sunshine—makes my blood boil. It pisses me off beyond words.

One thing's for sure: if I ever get the chance to come face-to-face with that bastard, he's going to fucking pay for what he did.

As people move around us, a few recognize me, their curious glances making my skin crawl.

Sometimes, flying under the radar has its perks. I'm not as front-and-center as Xander—his face is the one plastered across headlines, especially after the shitstorm with our old label. But when some guy walks by and casually lifts his phone to snap a photo, I feel the urge to tell him to fuck off. I can't, though—not with Scarlet sobbing against my chest. I grit my teeth and swallow my anger, letting it slide for now.

Suddenly, Scarlet pulls back, wiping her eyes, like she's just realized what she was doing.

There's a shift in the air between us, an unspoken line we've never crossed before. Every time we've been together, it's always been nothing more than a casual hook-up. No emotions, no strings—just raw need and release. But now? This feels different.

"Sorry," she mutters, avoiding my gaze as she rummages through her bag. She pulls out a tissue and delicately dabs her eyes, followed by a gentle blow of her nose.

"You good?" I ask, though I already know the answer.

I have never been skilled at providing comfort to others. My only desire is to reach the hospital, hoping that Poppy will be there to take over. I know I'm completely fucking this up, and it would be best if someone who actually knows what they're doing takes over soon.

"Yeah," she answers, her voice shaky as she tries to give me a smile. It's strained, and I can't help but glance at the bruises again.

"Let's get out of here," I say, grabbing the handle of her suitcase.

Just as we start moving, some guy steps into my path. "Hey Ace, can I grab a quick photo?" he asks, holding up his phone like it's no big deal.

"Sorry, man, I'm on a tight schedule," I mutter, hastily dismissing him. The last thing I want is for a picture to start circulating at this moment, bringing even more attention. My only focus is getting Scarlet out of here and to the hospital.

Without giving him a chance to reply, I brush past him and head straight for the exit. I move fast, barely checking if Scarlet's keeping up, though I can hear her quiet sniffles. Each one messing with my head, stirring up emotions I'd rather avoid.

The touch we shared earlier, one meant for comfort, now lingers in my mind, stirring up filthy thoughts I shouldn't entertain about her—especially not now, with Nate and Theo's situation weighing over us.

I'm aware I need to keep my distance, but the temptation to fuck her again is nagging at me. Those two nights we spent together still fucking haunt me.

The way she moaned as I buried my cock deep inside her, how she surrendered to the pleasure, screaming my name. Fuck, it was insane. But I need to push those memories aside. She's Nate's little sister, and no matter how badly I want her, I can't let myself cross that line again.

As we reach the car, my phone buzzes in my pocket. It's most likely a text from Xander, but I resist the urge to check it right away. If it's more bad news, I can't let Scarlet see my reaction.

I open the passenger door for her, and as she slides inside, I catch a whiff of her perfume and it fucks with my head. I make my way to the back, opening the trunk, and tossing her suitcase inside. With the trunk lid acting as a barrier, I retrieve my phone. Unlocking the screen, I feel my gut tighten, preparing for the unknown message that awaits.

**Xander:** It's fucking bad, Ace. Theo's okay, but he's a mess. Nate's in rough shape. Have you picked up Scarlet yet?

I swiftly tap away at the keys, typing out my response.

**Ace:** Yeah, just picked her up and told her about the accident. What should I say about Nate?

As I wait, the tight knot in my stomach intensifies with each passing second.

**Xander:** Tell her they're preparing him for surgery. It's serious.

**Ace:** How serious are we talking?

**Xander:** His right arm and shoulder are broken, along with a few ribs.

**Ace:** Shit. We're on our way.

After shoving my phone back into my pocket, I close the trunk and slide into the driver's seat.

Scarlet casts a worried glance in my direction, her eyes filled with concern. "Ace, give it to me straight. How bad is it?"

Taking a deep breath, I glance over at her, my heart racing as I try to find the right words to break the news.

"Just tell me what's going on, Ace. They're my brothers, for fuck sake," Scarlet demands, her voice trembling with fear.

"Xander says Theo's a mess but he's okay for now," I tell her. "Nate's in pretty bad shape— broken arm, busted shoulder, and a few cracked ribs. They're getting him ready for surgery as we speak. It's serious, but we'll have a better idea of what's going on once the doctors have had a chance to work on him."

Scarlet's face pales, her expression mirroring the weight of the news that just hit her. Her tears start up again, and I'm hit with that all-too-familiar feeling of being utterly useless. Feeling like a complete asshole, I avert my eyes, twist the key, and purposefully avoid making eye contact with her as the engine roars to life. There's nothing I can do to fix this or even make her feel better, and I've got no clue how to handle this kind of pain. It's like second nature for me to comprehend a woman's desires in bed, but when faced with tears and heartbreak, I'm at a fucking loss.

The sense of inadequacy gnaws at me as we leave the airport behind. I can hear Scarlet's soft sniffles, barely audible but enough to make my heart ache, as I grip the steering wheel tightly, my knuckles turning white. I keep my eyes fixed on the road, desperately resisting the urge to reach out and do something, anything, to make this easier for her. But I keep reminding myself that if Poppy is at the hospital, or Theo, who is like a big brother to Scarlet, they will handle this situation better than I ever could. They're the ones who can offer real comfort and support to her—they're the ones who know how to deal with this kind of shit.

The silence in the car is thick and oppressive, punctuated only by the sound of Scarlet's occasional sniffles. Out of the corner of my eye, I notice her grabbing her phone, her fingers tapping away rapidly as she frantically messages someone. For a moment, I wonder who she's reaching out to, but I swiftly dismiss the thought. It's not my place to worry about who she texts—her business is her own.

With an intense gaze, she stares at her phone screen, as though she's using her sheer willpower to summon a message. Frustrated by the lack of a response, she lets out an annoyed huff and shifts her gaze towards the window, seeking solace in the outside world.

With her attention fixed on the view outside, my gaze drifts to the tattoo gracefully trailing down her arm. The intricate vines and flowers that intertwine to form a lion's face just above her elbow is sexy as hell. I can't help but wonder what significance that lion holds for her—there's something about it, something I can't quite grasp, that pulls me in and makes me curious as hell.

As she checks her phone, I concentrate on the road, determined to clear my mind and refrain from eyefucking her at every opportunity. It's probably just my mind playing tricks—after five long months without any groupies to scratch that itch, my head's a jumbled mess. Once we hit the road for the tour in a month, I'll have plenty of chances to let loose, drowning out any thoughts of her.

"Ace," she says.

I glance over and catch her biting her bottom lip. Fuck me. My cock twitches. I shift my focus back to the road, desperately trying to banish those thoughts.

"Yeah?" I reply, my voice sounding rougher than I intended.

"I texted Theo, but he's not responding."

Keeping quiet, my foot hovers over the brake pedal as we approach a red light. As we come to a stop, the sudden sound of a piercing ringtone reverberates throughout the car, pulling me from my thoughts. I glance at the dashboard and see Xander's name flash across the screen. Grateful for the distraction, I press the button on the steering wheel to answer. "Hey."

"Are you guys almost here?" Xander's voice crackles through the speaker.

"We're still in the car, but we're close," I inform him.

"Nate's heading into surgery now."

"Got it," I reply, but before I can say anything else, Scarlet's voice cuts in.

"How bad is he, Xander?" she asks, her voice trembling.

"Hey, Scarlet," Xander replies gently. "The doc said Nate's shoulder is pretty messed up and they need to operate. I don't have any more details yet. Theo asked me to call your parents—they're on their way."

Scarlet desperately wipes at her tears, but they continue to stream down her cheeks.

"Scarlet's been trying to get in touch with Theo. Is he around?" I ask Xander.

"Yeah, he's here," Xander replies. "His phone got messed up in the crash. Hang on, I'll get him for you."

In the background, I hear Xander's voice calling out to Theo. Relief washes over me, knowing that Theo— the guy who can drive me up the wall sometimes—is at least okay. Despite all the crap he pulls, he's still a brother to me, and I genuinely give a damn about him.

"Scar?" Theo's voice comes through the car speakers, rough but familiar.

"Theo," Scarlet's voice quivers with raw emotion, and I can sense the weight of unshed tears in her voice. It twists something deep inside me, a feeling I'm not familiar with, like a knot tightening in my chest.

"I fucked up, Scar," Theo's voice trembles with unfiltered remorse. "Nate's in really bad shape. I can't even describe how messed up it is. I was an idiot. He wanted to drive, but I raced him to the driver's seat for some stupid fucking reason. I should've let him take the wheel. None of this would've happened if I'd just let him."

"You don't know that, Theo. You can't blame yourself," Scarlet responds softly, her voice steady and comforting.

Hearing her give Theo that kind of support hits me hard, reminding me of my own inadequacy in providing the same. If she desired an orgasm, yep, sign me up. But this emotional crap? Fuck, I'm way out of my league.

Making a right turn, the massive hospital emerges before us, its imposing structure serving as a solemn reminder of the gravity of the situation.

"We're almost there," Scarlet says. "The hospital is just up ahead."

"Alright, I'll see you soon," Theo replies.

After hitting the button to end the call, the lingering silence fills the car. With a sense of desperation, I steer the car into the crowded parking lot, hoping to spot an empty space.

By the time I find one and park, Scarlet's already out of the car, moving towards the main entrance with a fierce urgency. Oblivious to the media circus unfolding outside, her sole focus remains on reaching Nate.

I can't help but think they're here for Nate. Whenever Xander made headlines, it was chaos—a feeding frenzy of camera crews swarming around, hungry for their next shot. It wouldn't surprise me if they're already camped out, hoping for some kind of scoop on Nate's condition.

"Scarlet, wait up!" I shout, racing to catch up with her. "There's a shitload of media outside the hospital."

"Yeah, so what? They won't bother me. They don't know who I am," she snaps back, dismissing my warning.

"Will you just fucking listen to me for a second?" I growl, grabbing her arm to make her stop. "The media's a pain in the ass, and I don't want you getting caught up in their bullshit."

"No, Ace. My brothers are in there," she says, pulling her arm free. "You deal with the media. I can't give a shit about that right now."

I reluctantly let her walk ahead, even though every instinct tells me it's a mistake. My eyes check out her ass, and despite everything—Nate's unfortunate situation, the fucking accident—I'm unable to resist. I can't help but picture grabbing her from behind, shoving my cock into her tight pussy, and fucking her like I did at Xander's and Poppy's wedding. I tear my gaze away, muttering under my breath, "Get a grip, you sick bastard. That's Nate's sister, the guy who could have fucking died."

As Scarlet walks past the media, I watch them, some giving her a nonchalant glance while others openly check her out. The way their eyes move up and down her body makes my blood boil.

As she disappears through the double doors, I brace myself for the media shitshow that's about to kick off. As soon as I get close, the camera-hungry vultures and their microphones come forward, desperate for any tidbit of information about Nate.

"Hey Ace, is it true? Theo and Nate were in a car accident and Nate's hurt."

The asshole suddenly blocks my path by shoving his microphone directly in front of me, leaving me no choice but to come to a stop. They close in, their microphones thrust forward like vultures closing in on a carcass.

Frustrated, I snap, "I don't have any information yet," as I forcefully make my way through the crowd. Their relentless bullshit has my blood boiling, my fists clenching as I try to hold back the fury building up inside me. Another jerk intentionally tries to block my path, but I step around him. Then they all run beside me, bombarding me with questions and shoving their microphones at me, each one desperate for the latest scoop.

As the reporters push through the big double doors, they are met with the stern gazes of two towering security guards, who promptly force the unruly pack of assholes back outside.

Ignoring the curious stares coming my way from the people in the foyer, I spot Scarlet at the front of a queue, eagerly waiting to speak to the lady behind the glass shield.

With a quick motion, I pull out my phone and dial Xander's number. He picks up on the second ring, providing me with exactly what I need, as I move towards Scarlet.

"No, I can't give out that information," snaps the middle-aged lady behind the desk, her annoyance evident in her voice.

"But I'm his sister," Scarlet snaps back, clearly pissed.

"Look, you fans will go to any lengths. You have no idea how many times I've heard that already today," the lady shoots back.

I step up next to Scarlet and grab her arm, ignoring the annoyed glare she throws my way. "Come on, the room is this way," I tell her.

A flicker of defiance crosses Scarlet's face as she gives the woman a dismissive glance, before following me. Releasing her arm, I set off in the direction Xander told me, trusting that Scarlet will be close behind.

As the elevator doors slide open on the floor Xander mentioned, Scarlet is the first to step out. I find it difficult to divert my gaze from her tight little body and that ass in those jeans. I know I shouldn't be checking her out with everything that's happening, but goddamn, it's hard not to.

Leaning against the wall across the hall, Xander's furrowed brows mirror the same sense of unease twisting in my stomach. The person I saw this morning, grinning with Alex in the driveway, seems completely different from who I encounter now.

With his head in his hands and his leg bouncing like a jackhammer, Theo sits slumped in one of the chairs, appearing on the verge of losing control. Stress has never been his strong suit, and it's painfully evident in his posture.

As soon as Xander spots us, he pushes off the wall, his face contorting with worry.

As Xander moves, Theo lifts his head, and I can't help but notice the cut on his head, hastily mended with those fucking butterfly clips. Scarlet hurries over to him, and I see Theo's gaze tighten when he takes in her bruised skin - the marks seem to have worsened since I picked her up at the airport.

Theo stands up, his arms wrapping tightly around Scarlet, as if he's afraid to let go. It's impossible to overlook the profound connection between them as Theo effortlessly embodies the role of a protective older brother.

The family dynamic between Nate's household and Theo, who practically lived there, has always fascinated me. I've always admired how seamlessly they welcomed him into their home. I only had my sister, Daisy, but when things got tough, she bailed, leaving me to deal with all the messed-up shit on my own.

"Is she okay?" Xander asks, stepping up beside me. I can't tell if he's talking about how Scarlet's handling the news or the bruises fucking up her face. Either way, it's a goddamn mess.

"Yeah, she seems okay," I reply, keeping my voice low as I glance over at Xander. "Any updates?"

"Yeah," says Xander, his gaze drifting to Scarlet and Theo, sitting together. "He went into surgery a little while ago. His shoulder is pretty fucked up. The doc didn't give me a solid recovery time yet, but it's gonna be a few months at least before Nate's back on his feet."

The news hits me hard. Nate, the heartbeat of our band, is about to have some difficult days ahead.

"Fuck, that's rough," I mutter, feeling the weight of it all. The thought of the upcoming tour next month consumes my mind, especially remembering how excited Nate was to perform on stage again. But the only priority at this moment is his recovery.

"Theo said some old guy ran a red light," Xander says, crossing his arms. "Theo was a wreck when I got here." He glances over at Theo, who looks a bit more composed now, thanks to Scarlet. "Theo's convinced it's his fault that the old bastard ran the light."

"Yeah, I heard him feeding that same bullshit to Scarlet. If he keeps this up, it's gonna fuck with his head."

"Yeah, that's exactly what I was thinking."

As Xander's phone rings, he reaches into his pocket and retrieves it, briefly glancing at the screen to see who's calling. It's Poppy. He answers the call, his voice fading as he steps away from us. "Hey, Princess," he says, his voice dropping to a softer, almost tender tone.

I move further into the room, keeping a sharp eye on Theo and Scarlet. I plop down in the seat across from them and catch snippets of their conversation, hearing fragments of their words as I try to decipher the situation.

"Is anything broken, Scar?" Theo asks, reaching out to touch her cheek. She flinches at his touch.

"I don't think so," she replies.

"What did the doctor say?" Theo presses.

"I don't know," Scarlet admits. "I didn't get it checked out."

"What the hell, Scar? You didn't get it looked at?" Theo's voice rises.

"No, I'll be okay. I'm just worried about Mom and Dad seeing me like this. You know how Dad loses it," Scarlet says, her voice shaky.

"Yeah, he'll probably want to hunt down that asshole, and so do I, and so will Nate the minute he sees what that bastard did to you," Theo replies, his voice edged with anger.

Yeah, get in fucking line. You all can have a crack at that bastard once I'm done with him.

Theo finally pulls his gaze away from Scarlet's bruised face and turns his attention to me.

"You good?" I ask, trying to offer a bit of support.

I can see the strain in his eyes, the effort it's taking him to stay calm.

"Yeah, just trying to keep my shit together," he replies. It's clear he's trying to put up a strong front.

"Nate's tough. He'll pull through," I say, trying to sound reassuring. "And you're not alone in this. Your brothers are here for you." I'm relieved I can offer some support; it's a hell of a lot better than the awkwardness I felt earlier with Scarlet, where I couldn't give her what she needed.

Out of the corner of my eye, I catch Scarlet's gaze, but I purposely avoid making eye contact, fearing that Theo will pick up on the awkwardness between us. As Xander comes back and takes a seat next to me, I feel a slight release of tension.

"That was Poppy," Xander says, glancing at his phone. "She's checking if there's any update on Nate. Apparently, it's all over the headlines."

"Yeah, those assholes were all over me outside, shoving microphones in my face and grilling me for whatever info I had about Nate," I snap, still pissed off.

"And Walter called," Xander adds, his frustration clear. "It's even on the headlines in Australia. He wanted to know if the tour's still going ahead."

"Fuck," I mutter, taken aback. It's insane how fast shit spreads.

Behind us, the sound of footsteps reverberates, causing all of us to abruptly turn. Stepping into view, a young nurse, fresh out of graduation, anxiously clutches her clipboard.

Xander is the first to rise and make his way over to her.

As soon as the nurse spots Xander, her eyes go wide. True to fucking form, she blushes and fumbles with her words, just like all the other women who come into contact with Xander Williams.

"I'm... um..." She licks her lips nervously, glancing between her clipboard and Xander. Her face turns an even deeper shade of red. "The doctor wanted me to give an update," she finally stammers, swallowing like it's the hardest thing she's ever had to do.

I swear, Xander's always had that effect on women. Even back in school, they'd lose their shit over him. One look, and they were practically melting. Nothing's changed—he's still got that same power over them.

The nurse glances down at her clipboard again, desperately trying to regain her composure, but her trembling hands give away her inner turmoil. Her eyes dart between the clipboard and Xander, and it's starting to piss me off. I'm here to get a fucking update on Nate, not to watch Xander play the charming romantic lead. Xander just stands there, his presence adding to her growing fluster. At this rate, we're not getting any news if this chick keeps melting down over him.

Fed up, I get up from my seat and march over to Xander, grabbing him by the arm and yanking him away. "Go, sit the fuck down," I snap, stepping in front of the nurse to get her full attention.

With Xander out of the way and me taking charge, the nurse finally regains her composure. The starry-eyed, dazed chick who was stumbling over her words a moment ago is long gone.

Regaining her professional composure, she starts to speak. "The doctor asked me to update you. Mr. Reynolds is still in surgery. They're currently pinning the bone in his shoulder," she reads from her notes. "It was a clean break, so it's a relatively straightforward procedure."

Glancing down at the clipboard, her eyes move swiftly as they scan over her notes. I wait for her to keep going, but her eyes remain fixed on the paper, and not a single word escapes her lips.

"How long until that shit's done?" I snap, my tone harsh with impatience. I couldn't care less if I come off as intimidating—I need more fucking details on what's happening. What's the point of her coming out here to give us an update if she's not going to tell us anything?

She stares at me, swallowing hard, clearly rattled by my sharp tone.

I feel a hand on my arm and, even though I don't like how my body reacts, I know exactly who it is. I shrug her off, stepping aside and pulling my arm away from her touch. Scarlet steps forward, and her intoxicating scent fills the air around me, overwhelming my senses. However, I forcefully push those thoughts out of my mind. Fuck, I need to get laid.

"Hi, I'm Nate's sister, Scarlet," she says, stepping in front of me. "I think what Ace is trying to say is if there's anything else you can tell us."

I pivot, putting some distance between me and Scarlet, and head over to Xander. I glance up to see his reaction, hoping he hasn't picked up on the effect Scarlet's having on me. Thank fuck, he's too focused on the nurse to notice.

"Yes, his vitals are stable. The head scans came back clear, which is a relief," she says, giving Scarlet a reassuring smile. "We're focused on his shoulder right now. It shouldn't take too long. I don't have the exact details of the procedure—the doctor didn't specify—but the x-rays confirmed it's a clean break. I'll update you as soon as I know more, or the doctor will come out when he's done."

"Okay, thanks," Scarlet says.

The nurse shoots me a sharp look, her eyes filled with irritation before she turns and strides away. It's obvious that she's still seething with anger over my sudden interruption.

# Chapter 5

## Scarlet

As I sit and wait for more updates on my brother's condition, my mind races with worries beyond just Nate's well-being, like my parents seeing my face. Just the thought of them seeing me like this, broken and bruised, makes my stomach churn with anxiety. Nate and Theo get it—they understand the hell Beck has put me through, the suffocating possessiveness and the constant control he exerted over me. They know all the shit I've endured with him over the years. That's the thing with my brother and Theo, I don't hold back; I tell them everything.

Well, almost everything.

I haven't told them about those two wild nights I spent with Mr tall, dark and brooding sitting across from me. He's been avoiding eye contact with me ever since we arrived.

Theo sits beside me, his grip on my hand so tight that it feels like my circulation is being cut off. With anxious energy, his leg bounces uncontrollably, and I reach out and rest my palm on his thigh, hoping to offer some solace. His gaze immediately shifts upwards when he feels my touch, his attention drawn to the bruises adorning my face. I make a mental note to fix them up with more concealer in the bathroom before Mom and Dad arrive.

"You alright?" I ask Theo.

"Yeah, Scar," he replies, his smile appearing forced and not reaching his eyes.

Over the years, I've learned to read Theo's every little quirk, just like I can with my brother. Even though he's putting up a brave front, I can see through the facade and sense the underlying struggle he's going through.

"Don't worry," I reassure him, attempting to lighten the mood, "he's tough. Remember that time he fell out of the tree and broke his ankle? It took several days before he finally broke the news to Mom that he might need to go to the hospital. If he could handle that, he can handle this."

Finally, a genuine smile spreads across Theo's face, accompanied by a light-hearted chuckle.

"Yeah, I kept telling the idiot something was broken, but he wouldn't listen. It's like he thought he was invincible or something."

"I know," I laugh, reminiscing about the countless attempts Theo made to get Nate to admit that something was wrong. I can vividly picture Theo's unmistakable handwriting, with its large, bold letters etched onto Nate's cast, mocking him: "I told you, dickhead, it was broken."

He watches me, a small laugh escaping his lips as he gives my hand a gentle squeeze, almost as if he's savoring the memory. It's a soothing moment, offering a brief escape from the whirlwind of anxiety that has consumed me since Ace broke the news.

As I wipe a stray tear from under my eye, I steal a glance at Ace and Xander. They sit across from us, their faces filled with seriousness as they quietly observe our interaction.

"I'll be right back," I murmur, giving Theo's hand a final reassuring squeeze before getting up and walking towards the bathroom.

As I step into the bathroom and catch a glimpse of myself in the mirror, I'm struck by the sight. The bruise on my face has turned a nasty shade of purple, looking even worse in the dim light.

I move closer, setting my bag down on the counter with a thud. I turn on the faucet, and the sound of rushing water fills the room as I let the cool liquid flow into my cupped hands. I splash the water onto my face, hoping that the sensation will help me forget the overwhelming events of the day.

As I turn off the water, I rest my palms against the countertop, taking deep breaths to calm myself. The facade I've been maintaining is showing signs of wear and tear, revealing the deep-seated insecurities that constantly plague me. As I stare into the mirror, I can't help but imagine the shock on my parent's faces when they see the deep purple bruise on my face. I've always been the one who feels like a leaf caught in the wind, lacking a clear purpose or sense of stability. My life feels like a never-ending mess: no steady job, no reliable income, no safe place to call home. The longest job I ever held was with the band, where coincidentally my ex, Beck, was the lead singer. Relationships? They're as unstable as my career prospects. If I were to join another band, I'd have to navigate through a sea of sleazy dickheads and entitled male groupies who make unwarranted advances. But music is my lifeline, it flows in my blood.

With all their success and fame, I bet it's a whole different world for my brother's band. I know how groupies practically throw themselves at musicians, hungry for a taste of the excitement. Resisting that kind of temptation is a challenge for most guys. My two brothers seem to revel in it; sometimes, it feels like their way of numbing the pain from losing Bianca all those years ago. And Ace? It's clear that he enjoys it as well, his vibe gives it away.

I can't help but wonder if he gives all those groupies the same mind-blowing pleasure he gave me, which was the most incredible thing I've ever experienced. Even though Ace made it clear it was just a one-night thing, he made sure to satisfy me in ways I didn't even know were possible. In that moment, overwhelmed by an insatiable hunger, lost in a whirlwind of desire, I screamed his name. That kind of surrender was completely new to me. Maybe that's why I am filled with a deep longing to feel his touch once more.

Based on what I know about Xander, I don't think he would be into the groupie scene at all. Maybe back in the day, before Poppy and Alex came into the picture, but from what Nate's told me, Xander's been head over heels for Poppy since high school. Their love is something else—stronger than anything I've seen. It's real, deep, and unwavering. That's exactly the thing I desire. I want someone to love me with the same unwavering devotion that Xander loves Poppy. Rather than being seen as just a quick fuck or a pretty face, I strive for a genuine connection with someone who sees me for who I really am, not just the surface.

After reapplying concealer to my face and masking the purple tinge on my cheek, I feel a slight sense of relief, despite the faintly lingering discoloration. With a resigned sigh, I grab my bag, take a deep breath, and head toward the door.

As I crack open the bathroom door, my heart skips a beat when I hear my parents' voices. Peering out, I see them clearly.

With her arm around his waist, Mom stands beside Theo—a constant source of comfort she has provided throughout his troubled upbringing. Mom and Dad have always been there for Theo, encouraging him in everything he does and believing in his potential.

I shift my gaze to Dad, taking in the sight of his tattooed arms crossed over his chest as he engages in conversation with Ace and Xander. He's always had a soft spot for those two, admiring their talent and how seamlessly they integrated with Nate and Theo. From the moment he met them, he could tell they were genuine guys.

I take another deep breath, feeling the air fill my lungs as I prepare myself to face them. I square my shoulders and emerge from the bathroom.

As soon as I step out, I can feel my dad's gaze fixed on me. His eyes narrow, focusing on the attempt I made to conceal the bruises, leaving no doubt that he has connected the dots.

My pulse spikes. I should've known there's no hiding anything from him. I see it in his face—the furrowed brows and determined set of his jaw—as his protective instinct kicks in.

Ace and Xander, sensing his change in demeanor, turn their heads to see what has caught his attention.

"Scar, what the fuck happened to you?" His voice carries a sharpness that demands immediate obedience, and loaded with that heavy authority only a father can wield.

My mother and Theo both cast worried glances in my direction.

With a quick glance at Ace and Xander, I turn my focus back to my dad, forcing a weak smile to appear on my face.

"Oh, you know me," I shrug, trying to play it off, "always tripping over my own two feet."

Yes, I admit that I can be clumsy at times, but deep down, I know that if my dad ever found out what truly happened, he'd be ready to tear Beck apart for hurting his little girl. But for now, this isn't about me—it's about Nate. Right now, he's the one who needs our focus and support.

My mom lets go of Theo and hurries over to me, providing a much-needed distraction. I'm aware my dad isn't buying my flimsy excuse, and I can almost hear his voice demanding more details in the back of my mind. Her arms wrap around me, pulling me into a warm and comforting embrace, providing a much-needed respite. It's mentally draining to conceal my true self, a person who feels lost and lacks a clear purpose in life. As Nate's dream of becoming a famous drummer came true, my own dreams remained trapped in a frustrating loop, forever out of reach.

"Hey, baby," Mom whispers, her warm breath tickling my ear. "How are you holding up?" She pulls back slightly, her smile carrying a touch of sadness. She's perceptive enough to detect that there's more going on than meets the eye. I can't help but wonder if Theo let something slip—his nervousness always gives him away, especially when Mom starts pressing him. He's always been quick to crack under pressure, like that time she grilled him about whether Nate and I were drinking at parties and he immediately spilled the beans.

"I'm just worried about Nate," I say, trying to divert the conversation from any serious talk, especially with my father and the guys present.

"I'm worried too, sweetie, but he'll be okay. We both know your brother and how resilient he is." She smiles warmly and gives me a reassuring squeeze before taking my hand and guiding me back toward the group.

As I lift my gaze, I meet my dad's eyes and then walk over to hug him. I feel his muscular arms enveloping me, creating a sense of safety and comfort. I've always been a daddy's girl, spending countless hours in the garage with him, surrounded by the scent of motor oil working on one of his many motorcycles. He's never treated me differently just because I'm a girl, and I appreciate that he's always given me the same opportunities as Nate and Theo.

As he holds me, I can feel his unwavering support, unspoken yet palpable. "If that asshole hurt you, Scar, you need to tell me," he says, his voice filled with a mix of anger and protectiveness.

"I would, Dad," I say, attempting to brush it off, "but it was just me being clumsy."

Despite knowing I should tell him the truth, I find myself too embarrassed and emotionally drained to confront the situation right now.

The room falls silent as the doctor enters. Hand in hand, my mother and father stand before the middle-aged physician, their expressions filled with both hope and concern.

Stepping closer, Theo's hand finds mine, and I can feel the tension coursing through him as we anxiously await an update on Nate. Ace and Xander take a step back, creating distance as the doctor bombards us with incomprehensible medical jargon that makes my head spin.

When I glance at my dad, I can tell from his puzzled look that he is just as confused as I am. After a few seconds, he raises his hand, signaling for the doctor to stop.

"Hey, Doc, I'm lost here. Can you break this down into simpler terms? I just need to know if my son will be okay."

A sigh escapes the doctor's lips, followed by a slow, solemn nod. "Yes," the doctor says, "your son will be just fine. The surgery went well, and his vital signs are stable. He'll need ample rest and a significant amount of time for his shoulder to recover, but apart from that, he's doing fine. It's going to be a long recovery, but the operation was a success."

I feel Theo's grip on my hand tighten as a visible wave of relief washes over him. My usually composed dad releases my mom's hand and takes a step forward, surprising everyone by pulling the doctor in for a hug. Witnessing my father's tattooed arms embrace the small doctor is a surprising and heartwarming sight, leaving the doctor momentarily caught off guard. With a warm pat on the doctor's back, my dad expresses his gratitude, saying, "Thanks a lot, Doc. You don't know how much this means to us."

"Can we see him?" my mother asks, stepping forward.

"Yes, he's awake, though still a bit groggy. I'll have a nurse come in to escort you to his room."

With that, the doctor exits the room, leaving us in anticipation as we wait for the nurse. Observing my father, I notice how he exhales deeply, his body relaxing as the burden of worry about Nate seems to vanish. I know him well enough to recognize that he'd have concealed his anxiety, always putting on a brave face for my mom's sake, a dependable pillar in times of crisis.

Just then, the petite nurse returns—the same one from earlier, her cheeks still flushed with a touch of embarrassment from her encounter with Xander. Before uttering a word, she glances at Xander, then redirects her focus to my mother and father.

"Follow me," she says. "Your son's room is this way." She spins around without waiting for a reply, leading the way to Nate's room. With brisk, purposeful strides, she heads down a long corridor, her focus fixed on leading us to Nate's room, barely pausing to check if we're keeping up.

Finally reaching the room, she moves aside to allow my parents to enter. Her eyes linger on Theo standing beside me before shifting to Ace and Xander trailing behind.

I've seen this kind of shit way too often, especially with my brother and Theo. Instead of being seen as ordinary guys pursuing their passions, they are treated like celebrities. But Xander's level of attention is on a whole different scale. It's mind-boggling how he manages it. Even a simple task like getting an update on my brother turns into the nurse, stumbling over herself in Xander's presence. I get it; Xander's a big deal. But no wonder Ace had to intervene and speed things up—otherwise, we would have wasted the entire day, waiting for the nurse to break free from her fixation on Xander.

The sight of Nate lying in the bed prompts Theo to tighten his grip on my hand, clearly taken aback by what he sees. Nate looks so frail, his arm and shoulder encased in a stiff, bound cast. His chest grabs my attention, displaying a tattoo that proudly states "Bianca" over his heart—a constant symbol of his unwavering devotion to her, a love that endures with unwavering intensity.

As Theo releases my hand and moves toward the bed, I stand frozen, unable to tear my gaze away from Nate lying there in that damn bed. A whirlwind of emotions crashes over me, and I can't help but wonder what if things had turned out differently? What if I had lost him today? Would he ever know just how much he means to me? Life's fragility hits hard, especially for Theo, Nate, and me. The pain of losing Bianca hit us like a punch to the gut, a stark reminder of life's unpredictable nature.

Xander navigates around me, making his way to the end of the bed, while I can sense Ace's quiet presence behind me. Even though I can't see him, I feel a comforting warmth as his hand rests on my lower back, guiding me gently forward. His touch sends a tingling sensation coursing through my body.

"Come on, Scarlet. Nate needs you," he says softly, nudging me forward.

With my mother and father on the right side of the bed and Xander stationed at the foot, I make my way around to the other side and stand beside Theo. Holding Nate's hand, Theo clenches it with such force that his knuckles whiten. A dense silence engulfs the room, bearing down on us as we quietly observe Nate sleeping, each of us wrapped up in our own thoughts.

Ace moves closer, positioning himself beside me. Without even touching me, his presence alone sends my heart racing, like an electric surge. It's a reaction that I don't experience with anyone else, perhaps because of the profound connection we had a few months ago - those two nights where he pushed my boundaries and awakened sensations I had never felt before. Even though he explicitly stated that our encounter was nothing more than a casual fling—his words, not mine—the impact he has left on me is undeniable.

I lift my head and scan the people standing around the bed, taking in the sight of my parents, their eyes fixated on Nate. My gaze then shifts to Xander, whose eyes remain locked on Ace, their intensity making me feel as if he's accusing him of something. I can't help but wonder if Xander knows the truth of what happened between us. The intensity of Xander's stare makes me suspect that Ace might have let something slip.

In a split second, I divert my eyes, praying that my brother never finds out about this news. I know how fiercely protective he is, just like Theo. High school was a nightmare whenever I tried dating—thanks to Nate and Theo, my reputation as unapproachable spread like wildfire.

But this is something entirely different. Ace is one of them, and I know that if my brother or Theo ever found out, it would destroy the strong connection these guys have. I know them well enough to realize they'd never forgive Ace for crossing that line.

Witnessing the profound connection between these guys, I can't help but yearn for a similar experience, something that has eluded me my whole life. It's incredibly frustrating how my appearance overshadows any chance for genuine relationships, leaving me pursued by men who see me as nothing more than a conquest. This shallow perception has strained my friendships with other women. People wrongly assume I'm promiscuous, making it nearly impossible to build meaningful connections. Now, I feel more alone than ever.

My brief fling with Ace—just a one-night stand, or you could say a two-night affair—only reinforces the painful reality that guys often see me as just someone to get down and dirty with for a night. Despite that, I still crave to be valued for who I am beyond my physical appearance. Since those nights with Ace, I've been left wondering if I'm destined to always be just another conquest, with men treating me as a temporary pleasure and discarding me like I'm nothing more than a passing thrill.

Nate's eyes slowly flutter open, and as he begins to stir, I instinctively reach out, intertwining my fingers with Ace's, seeking solace in our touch.

To my surprise, Ace doesn't pull away; his hand remains steady and comforting, offering a small refuge amidst all the tension in the room. Despite the warmth of our joined hands, my gaze stays locked on Nate, unable to shift away from his fragile state.

"Theo," Nate mumbles, his voice heavy with sleep as he slowly opens his eyes, still adjusting to the brightness.

"Hey, Nate," Theo replies, his voice filled with a gentle yet unmistakable sense of relief. "It's so fucking good to see you, man."

Nate scans the room, his eyes darting around until they finally settle on Mom and Dad. A slow smile spreads across his face. "I told you, Mom, I'd see you before we head out on tour," he murmurs.

"Yeah, you did," she replies, her eyes filled with love and tenderness as she leans in to plant a soft kiss on his forehead.

My brother was over the moon about the band finally going out on their own—selling out stadiums in thirty minutes and adding new dates due to the overwhelming demand. He was so proud that they were managing everything themselves, from the album to the tour. But now, all of that's gone to hell because of this accident. It's going to take months for Nate to get his arm back in shape, let alone play for hours on stage. I can already see the headlines: Broken Oasis forced to cancel their sold-out shows, leaving fans disappointed and speculating about the future.

As Mom pulls away, Nate's eyes meet mine, then drift to my cheek, noticing the marks. I hold my breath, silently pleading that he won't mention Beck's violent outburst in front of Mom and Dad. It's bad enough that everyone here knows what I've been through—Nate bringing it up would only make things more uncomfortable, especially with Dad in the room.

# CHAPTER 6

## Ace

It's late afternoon when Xander and I finally step out of Nate's room, giving the family some much-needed space. Xander's pissed at me, and it's obvious. His body language says it all: hands shoved deep in his jean pockets, eyes avoiding mine like I've got the plague. I know him well enough to read him, especially when I'm pushing his buttons. I saw the way his gaze snapped to my hand when Scarlet grabbed it. What was I supposed to do? Tell her to fuck off and leave me alone? Sure, we're all relieved Nate's going to make a full recovery, but he's got a long, tough road ahead before he's back to where he was.

Xander stops in front of the elevator, his frustration clear as he repeatedly jabs the button, each press harder than the last.

"Yeah, I think you've got it," I say, essentially letting the idiot know that pressing the button doesn't do anything except annoy the hell out of me.

He shoots me a glare and clamps his mouth shut. I know the second we're in that elevator, he's going to explode. That's how we are—always calling each other out on our shit. So bring it on. If he thinks I'm going to take his shit over something I had no control over with Scarlet in that room, he's got another thing coming.

He knows I've told him I'll keep my distance from her, and he gets the guilt eating at me for fucking up with Nate. But I can't shake off her touch—how her fingers felt when she grabbed mine. That's not a conversation that's going to happen, though. There's no way he's finding out about any of that when we start tearing into each other in the elevator.

I spot the starry-eyed nurse from earlier rounding the corner, looking like she's about to lose it. The moment she sees Xander, she hesitates, takes a deep breath, and makes her way over.

This is going to be a shitshow; I almost wish I had some popcorn to enjoy the spectacle. Watching her try to pull herself together in front of Xander—especially with the mood he's in—is bound to be entertaining. The Xander I know might just tell her to fuck off if she stumbles again.

I shove my hands into my pockets, intrigued to see how this will play out. She pulls a pen from her chest pocket, swallows nervously, and steps forward, still clutching that damn clipboard like it's her lifeline.

Xander's eyes remain fixated on the red floor numbers, oblivious to her presence.

Well, he can handle this enthusiastic fangirl on his own. Normally, I'd give him a heads-up about this kind of shit, but screw him—given his attitude toward me, he can fucking deal with it himself.

"Um... Mr. Williams, could I please have your autograph?" she asks in a shaky voice, holding out the pen toward him.

Xander keeps his eyes fixed on the numbers, totally ignoring her. He fucking hates being called that name and despises these moments, forcing himself to wear a fake smile for fans even when he's in such a foul mood.

Despite the hint, the nurse continues on, undeterred.

With her pen and clipboard extended, she stands there patiently, waiting for him to play along. I can't help but get a kick out of watching him ignore her, acting like she's invisible.

She shoots a quick glance in my direction, clearly seeking some backup.

My lips curl into a smirk as I playfully tap Xander on the shoulder. I know exactly what's coming - the intense glare and the expression that screams "fuck off."

"Your little fan over there wants an autograph," I say, deliberately pushing his buttons.

His gaze, once fixed on me, abruptly shifts to her, intense and unyielding. With a sharp tone, he snaps, "I'm not signing autographs today. Fuck off and do your job." With that, he shifts his focus back to the glowing numbers above the elevator.

I've always admired his bluntness and no-bullshit attitude—never giving a fuck about anyone's opinion, except Poppy and Alex, of course. Around them, his softer side always comes through.

The nurse glances at me, as if silently pleading for me to intervene, but all I can do is shrug. Xander sees these moments as nothing more than an opportunity for her to boast to her friends about how she scored his autograph.

Defeated, she scurries off, the sound of her hurried footsteps echoing down the hall.

As Xander turns his head, his eyes lock onto mine, shooting me a menacing glare. With a sharp tone, he snaps, "You're a fucking asshole."

I smirk, meeting his intense gaze head-on, unflinching.

With a familiar chime, the elevator doors slide open, inviting us inside. I brace myself for the usual rant about Scarlet, but instead, he surprises me with something completely different.

"What the fuck are we going to do about the tour, Ace? We've been talking all this big game about going solo, and now this shit happens."

"We can't do shit about any of it. We have to cancel. There's no other way. Nate's gonna be out of action for at least six months," I say.

"Cancel forty-three fucking shows? We just announced six more yesterday. Shit! I can already picture that asshole Lionel sitting there all smug in his office, knowing we couldn't do shit without him," Xander says, running a hand through his hair, frustration evident in his stance.

"Yeah, well fuck Lionel," I say, even though the thought of canceling the tour is fucking heartbreaking. "Even if we were still with the old label, we'd have to cancel anyway. That's just how it goes, Xander. It's gonna suck, and you know the media will blow it up."

"Yeah, I know those fuckers will," Xander agrees. "Those assholes will do anything to stir up shit for headlines." He lets out a heavy sigh, then shifts his gaze from the floor to me. "You need to stay the fuck away from her, Ace."

"I'm trying, asshole."

"Well, damn it, try harder. I don't want any more problems just because you keep thinking with your dick."

Before I even have a chance to respond, the elevator doors slide open to reveal the bustling ground floor. As usual, those waiting there widen their eyes at the sight of Xander. He lets out a sigh of frustration before striding out, and I trail closely behind, matching his pace.

As heads turn our way, memories flood back to the days when Xander and I would hang out at my place in our teenage years. We'd sit around, passing a blunt, and envision what it would be like to be famous. We fantasized about the highs—playing to packed venues, the roar of the crowd reverberating through our bones, groupies ready to do anything for us. But back then, I never imagined every fucking detail of my life would be under a microscope. Now, we are completely exposed to the public eye, our lives laid bare for everyone to scrutinize, always craving the next juicy detail.

When we reach the glass doors to exit the hospital, we see the relentless media, cameras ready, eager to capture every moment.

"Poppy said they're already speculating about Nate's injury," Xander mutters with a clenched jaw, his frustration clear. "But it sounds like they don't have a fucking clue how bad it really is."

"So we keep it simple—his shoulder's fucked up, that's all," I say, taking charge, since Xander usually dodges this shit like the plague. "Let's clear it up and get the hell out of here."

Without waiting for his response, I turn and head straight for the doors, ready to handle these assholes.

As soon as the doors slide open, they swarm like vultures, shoving microphones in our faces while the cameramen scramble to keep up.

"How's Nate?" one of them shouts, pushing in closer.

"Can you update us on the situation?" another one yells, barely giving us room to breathe.

With Xander by my side, we're submerged by a wave of at least twenty microphones and a barrage of questions that pummel us like a storm. I throw up my hands in frustration, desperate to silence them before it turns into a complete shitshow.

Once they finally back off, I take control. "Earlier today, Nate and Theo were involved in a car accident, in case you haven't heard. Aside from a cut on his forehead, Theo's fine. Nate, however, wasn't so lucky. He had shoulder surgery, which went well, and he's recovering now. We'd appreciate it if you could give him some space to heal."

As soon as I finish, Xander and I make our way toward my car, but the assholes aren't done yet. They rush alongside, bombarding us with a flurry of questions and shoving their microphones back in our faces as if we hadn't already given them what they wanted.

"Xander, got any comment on the situation?" one reporter shouts, stepping right into our path.

"No," Xander grunts, brushing past the guy with a swift sidestep, barely acknowledging his presence. Normally, Xander plays nice when the questions are about our music or the crazy-packed shows, but after years of dealing with all the bullshit—the media always painting him as some womanizing rockstar—he's learned the hard way to keep his mouth shut about anything that could get twisted. No point in giving them any more fuel for their fire.

"How's this gonna affect your upcoming tour?" some asshole yells.

"No comment," I snap.

"Xander, are you guys canceling the tour?" another dick shoves a mic right in his face.

I press the keypad, and the car lights flash like a damn beacon, signaling our ticket to freedom. We're almost out of this mess. Just a few more steps.

As the questions keep coming, Xander remains silent, slipping into the passenger seat while I settle in behind the wheel.

With a sudden motion, I forcefully insert the key into the ignition, shift it into gear, and smoothly start rolling. Out of nowhere, a dumbass paparazzi leaps in front of the car, forcing me to slam on the brakes and screech to a halt, narrowly avoiding a collision with the fuckhead.

"Fucking hell, man," I growl, my anger barely contained.

"Just be cool, Ace," Xander says, trying to keep his calm. But it's hard when these assholes act like they've got a death wish.

I roll down the window and stick my head out, shouting at the jerk, "Get the fuck out of the way, asshole!"

But he just keeps snapping photos, completely ignoring me.

"Calm the fuck down," Xander says from the passenger seat, but I'm too pissed off to give a shit.

I shove the door open, and exit the car, not bothering to close it behind me.

Oblivious to the chaos he's causing, the paparazzi prick continues to click away, capturing every moment without a care.

"Move, asshole! There are cars and I can't see!" I say, my voice dripping with anger.

The weight of all the stress I've been carrying suddenly erupts. The guilt of betraying Nate, the sight of him confined to a hospital bed, and the thought of canceling the tour—it's all crashing down on me. As if to add insult to injury, there's Lionel, from our old label, probably laughing and taking jabs in the media that we're fucking helpless without his support.

"Get the fuck out of my way!" I bark again.

Every flash from that prick's camera intensifies my anger, causing a surge of red to fill my vision. I charge ahead, closing the distance until I'm standing right in front of the fucker's face.

In a single, swift motion, I snatch the camera from his grasp and slam it down onto the unforgiving concrete. I watch as it shatters into countless fragments, sending debris scattering across the ground.

Ignoring the stillness that hangs in the air, I make my way back to the car and get in, slamming the door.

"You fucking idiot," Xander says, as I press my foot hard on the pedal, peeling away from the hospital.

# CHAPTER 7

## Ace

"**W**hy the hell did you do that, Ace?" Xander snaps, his voice sharp enough to cut. "You better fucking hope that paparazzi guy doesn't sue us."

It's been a day since my meltdown with that asshole and his camera. I'm still fuming at myself for losing my shit like that. It feels like forever since I last lost it, and that was when that biker wannabe had me by the neck at my mom's place. I'm not fucking proud of it. It's all over the news, a constant reminder of my fuck up, blaring every time I turn the TV on.

This entire situation is an absolute fucking mess. Right now, I should be in the studio, putting the finishing touches on our album before its release next week, right before we hit the road for our tour. Instead, I'm stuck dealing with this bullshit—bullshit I caused. I am completely in the dark about what will come next.

"I already fucking told you, I just snapped," I say, my voice filled with anger, as I grab another beer from the fridge without bothering to offer one to the guys. As I twist off the lid and flick the cap onto the counter, I feel their intense stares burning into me. "Fuck that paparazzi idiot and his damn camera. I called Anita and asked her to reach out and offer a replacement. We've got way bigger problems than that. After making such a big deal about ditching the label, we're going to look like complete fucking idiots. Lionel's probably loving this shit. I can already picture his smug face, grinning about how we had to cancel the tour. He'll be out there, boasting that his label is the only reason for our success, and without his support, we'll fade into obscurity like countless other bands." I take a swig, feeling the cool liquid slide down my throat, downing half the bottle. The stress is eating away at me, and the booze takes the edge off a little.

Theo jumps in, "We can still pull it off. We just gotta find another drummer for the tour. It's not like other bands haven't done it before."

Xander and I exchange a look, both of us ready to tear into him.

Theo always seems to come up with these half-assed ideas that just push our buttons.

Xander's the first to bite. "The tour's in two weeks. Asking someone to learn our entire set in that time, that's a total joke, Theo, and you know it."

"Like I said, other bands have pulled it off. Why can't we?" Theo responds, still off in fantasy land.

My eyes narrow as I shoot him a disapproving look. "Maybe if we had more time, but two weeks? No way in hell anyone's learning our entire set that fast. Those other bands probably had months to get their new drummer up to speed."

Theo's gaze flickers back and forth between Xander and me. "Well," he insists, "I think it might work."

Alright, I'll play along with this idiot.

"Maybe," I reply, not buying any of the shit coming out of his mouth, but willing to entertain the idea instead of announcing the cancellation of the tour. Not to forget that we couldn't pull off one fucking show on our own.

Xander shoots me a look like I've lost my fucking mind. I make my way towards the table and settle down into a seat. "Maybe it could work," I say. "I have no fucking idea if it will or not, but one thing I do know is that when we first started out, I'd have jumped at the chance to play to sold-out crowds. I would've practiced my ass off twenty-four-seven just to snag a spot playing with the hottest band on the planet. That opportunity would've been a no-brainer for me."

"Seriously, you'd have ditched us just like that?" Theo asks, raising an eyebrow.

"Hell yeah, I'd have done it without a second thought," I snap back, not even hesitating.

Theo smirks. "Well, I would've convinced the guys to get rid of our shitty guitarist, anyway."

I casually shrug off his attempts to provoke a reaction from me. "Listen, it could work if we find someone who's willing to work their ass off and is dedicated enough to fill in for Nate on the tour. That's all there is to it."

"It's not happening," Xander declares, his head shaking in disbelief. "There's no way someone can learn our set that fast. We're just delaying the inevitable. We gotta call off the tour."

Theo's eyebrows furrow as he responds, "Why?"

Xander gives him that look, the kind that says, "Are you really this fucking dumb?"

"Seriously?" he says. "Who on earth do we know that can step up and learn our set in just two weeks? Even if someone can cover for Nate, how the hell do we know our songs will keep that same vibe? Each drummer has their own unique style. We just got our old sound back, and now you wanna mess with it? Plus, who the fuck would even be available at such short notice?"

"Scarlet can handle it," Theo says confidently, finishing his beer and leaning back in his chair.

Xander and I exchange a look, and it's clear we're both thinking the same thing. No fucking way she's coming on tour after all the shit that's happened between me and her.

"No," Xander says flatly, his tone leaving no room for argument.

Theo gets up from the chair. "What about you, Ace?"

"No way," I reply firmly, my voice resolute. I've heard her scream my name more times than I can count, watched her come undone orgasm after orgasm, and there's no way in hell I'm reliving that every time I see her on tour. But I'm not about to share any of that with these guys.

Theo heads over to the fridge and yanks it open. "Back in the day, Scar and Nate would go head-to-head in these little beat battles. The whole point of the game was to see who could make the sickest beat." He snatches two beers and slams the door shut before returning to the table. "Nate's pretty damn good, but sometimes Scar would beat him. Think about it, man. She plays just like Nate, and she's just as fucking good. If Nate can't make it, who better to step in than someone who learned from him and can actually beat him?"

"Here you go, Xander," Theo says, handing Xander a cold beer, then shifting his focus towards me. "See, asshole, this is what being polite looks like." He pops the cap off his beer, sending it flying in my direction. "So, what do you guys think?"

I grab my beer from the table and take a long swig, purposely avoiding Xander's gaze so Theo doesn't pick up on anything. I know how he operates—if he puts two and two together, Nate will hear about it before the day's over.

"No fucking way," Xander says, and I can practically see the gears turning in his head. He's worried it'll lead to trouble, that I won't be able to keep it in my pants. But he doesn't need to stress. I'm not going down that road again. Once we're on tour, there'll be groupies lined up, and I'll be damned if I let anything complicate that.

"Ace," Theo says, his voice snapping me back to reality.

"I'm with Xander on this. I don't think she's a good fit," I reply, but Theo continues talking as if my words hold no weight.

"Seriously, who else can we find last minute? Scarlet's here, with nothing better to do, and she's got the time. What other options do we have, for fuck sake? It's either Scarlet or we let Lionel, and the media make us look like we can't handle shit ourselves. It's a fucking no-brainer. Why can't you dickheads see that?" He leans back, glaring at Xander and me. "I'm telling you, she's fucking amazing, just like Nate. I wouldn't say it if she couldn't handle it, you know?"

Frustration etched on his face, Xander runs a hand through his disheveled hair. "I get it, but there's more to it than just filling the spot. We're talking about chemistry and the vibe we've put so much work into."

"Exactly! And if Scarlet can keep that vibe, we should at least give her a shot," Theo says, standing his ground.

Xander's gaze lingers on his untouched beer, and I can almost sense the wheels turning in his head. He was so excited to give Walter his big break on tour, and now this whole mess has thrown a wrench in the plans. Finally, he looks up at me, studying my face briefly before turning his attention back to Theo.

"Where the hell is Scarlet, anyway?" Xander asks.

"She's at the hospital with her parents. She'll be back soon. Guys, trust me, she's the only one who can pull this off. And hey, she knows all of us. She's like our little sister."

Theo's words hit hard, making it tough to swallow. I take another swig of my beer, desperate to silence the thoughts swirling in my mind.

"If we do this," Xander starts, and I immediately shoot him a glare that could cut through steel.

Are you fucking kidding me? After all the shit he's thrown my way, he's actually considering it? I sit there, dumbfounded, listening to Xander weigh the pros and cons.

"We need someone who can handle the pressure. If she's got what it takes, it might work," he says, and my heart starts racing for some reason. "I'm not saying we are, but how do you think she'll handle the media? You know what those fuckers are like?"

"She can totally handle it," Theo says. "Even if you bring up replacing Nate, the media won't give two shits after what Grumpy Pants did yesterday." I can't help but feel even more pissed off as his eyes meet mine, his smirk mocking me. "That's gonna be the only thing anyone talks about for weeks. They wanted a scoop. And you gave them one hell of a fucking scoop."

As he laughs, I can feel the irritation building, knowing that he is thoroughly enjoying getting under my skin.

I stand up, feeling the frustration coursing through my veins. "Fuck you, asshole," I respond sharply.

"Hey, come on, man, I was just fucking with you," he calls out, his voice still laced with laughter.

I storm out of Theo's house, cursing under my breath as his laughter fills the air, intensifying my irritation.

I'm on the verge of going back in there and punching Theo in the face to make him shut the fuck up. Instead, I flop down on the front steps and bury my face in my hands. What the hell are we even doing? Everything's going to shit. Maybe we're not cut out for this. Perhaps Lionel was onto something. We'll fucking crumble without him.

I can't even get my head straight to finish editing the album. How on earth am I supposed to get in the zone with all this shit weighing me down? The pressure is suffocating, and the thought of letting Nate down continues to eat at me. We've come too far to let it all slip away now. I take a deep breath, trying to calm the storm inside, but it feels impossible.

When I hear the metal gates at the end of the driveway creak open, I instinctively lift my head. Scarlet walks in, her head down as she digs through her handbag. She catches my attention right away—her tight top showing off every curve, those tattooed arms on full display, and her short denim skirt that highlights her slender legs. The same legs that were wrapped around me while I was eating her out.

My cock twitches just thinking about it, remembering how she grabbed my hair and rode me hard. I can't stop staring as she heads my way. The memory of her letting go lingers in my mind, unable to be forgotten. All I want is to plunge back in and hear her scream, just like before. But I know I need to cut this shit out. She's Nate's sister, and this kind of thinking is exactly what got me into this mess.

I try to clear my head, focusing on anything—anything but her. If she steps in as Nate's replacement, I don't know how I'll be able to control these overwhelming thoughts. How the fuck am I supposed to avoid her? I'm used to having a handful of groupies eager to please, but none of them gets me going the way she does.

As she continues up the driveway, all I can think about is having her naked and spread out on my bed again. The way she squirmed beneath me, the symphony of her pleasure-filled cries—it's all too much to handle right now. I shift uncomfortably, forcing my gaze to the ground, trying to will my mind to shut the hell up.

But every step she takes draws me deeper into that dangerous territory.

My eyes, despite my best efforts, lift to watch her. When her gaze finally meets mine, she hesitates for a moment, and I can sense the tension in the air. My gaze shamelessly roams over her body as she walks over, taking in every detail.

I catch her swallowing hard, and it brings a mischievous smirk to my face. Good, I'm getting to her, just like she's getting to me. It's a dangerous game we're playing, and with every step she takes closer, the allure becomes harder to resist. She might be Nate's sister, but right now, all I can think about is how badly I want to fuck her again.

"You're really making a name for yourself, superstar," she says playfully. "Remind me not to leave any cameras around."

"You too," I groan, the irritation in my tone hard to miss.

Scarlet stops right in front of me, her eyes locking onto mine. "Why? What do you mean?"

Taking a seat beside me, I find my gaze drawn to her elegantly long legs. The butterfly tattoo on the inside of her left ankle catches my eye—damn, I never noticed that before. *How could you dickhead when you were too busy fucking her to give a shit about the details?*

I try to divert my gaze, but it's like resisting a magnet that pulls me closer.

"That dickhead, Theo, just ripped into me," I mutter, tearing my eyes away from her legs. My gaze rests on my house. I should be in the studio, immersed in the music, fine-tuning our damn album, not sitting here, distracted by the girl next to me.

"That's just how Theo is," she says, dropping her bag beside her, before turning to face me. "Can I ask why you did it?"

I turn my head toward her, and at that moment, our eyes meet. Her intense green eyes captivate me, drawing my attention to the little things I've missed before—the tiny freckles on her nose, the subtle crease in her forehead, and those lips that still make me think about the time I felt them wrapped around my cock. But then my gaze lands on the bruises she's desperately attempting to conceal, and I have to avert my eyes, consumed with anger at the thought that someone could cause her this much harm.

"No idea. I just lost it. I'm fucked up, Scarlet."

"No, you're not, Ace."

"I am, Scarlet. You don't even know how fucked up I am."

"So what if you lost your shit in front of the cameras? It doesn't mean you're fucked up. Stupid, sure, for blowing up in front of the media when cameras are recording your every move," she says, her voice light but serious. I glance at her, noticing the mischievous smirk playing on her lips before she leans in, playfully nudging my shoulder. "Nobody's saying you're fucked up, Ace. It's just how you see yourself."

"You have no idea," I mutter, leaning back on the step. "My life's been fucked up since I was a little kid."

Her eyes narrow and she gives me a skeptical look, as if she doesn't believe a word I'm saying. "I don't think that's true."

"Oh, it is. My sister and my old man were just itching to walk out the door and never bothered looking back. My mother, well, she couldn't give two shits about them or me. Didn't give a shit who was putting their hands on me. It was like I was invisible to her, just another problem she didn't want to deal with. I learned early on that I had to protect myself because no one else was going to do it for me."

Pausing, I feel the weight of my words settle heavily on my chest. I've never shared this kind of shit with anyone, because it stings. It's stings that even my own family couldn't wait to get away from me. That I didn't matter to anyone. Back in my old town, growing up, people threw their stones at me, branding me as fucked up and worthless. Those labels have clung to me, and I carry them like a goddamn badge of shame.

Scarlet's words cut through my thoughts. "That doesn't mean you're fucked up, Ace. You were raised by messed-up people. That isn't a reflection on you; it's on them. I've watched Theo deal with the same thing all these years—how much it's hurt him and how he grapples with his self-worth. His smart-ass attitude is just his way of coping." Her hand reaches out and gently intertwines her fingers with mine. "But how you were raised is on them, not you. You couldn't control that shit. They're just selfish assholes who don't give a damn about anyone but themselves. You're better than that. You know it. Look at who you've become and what you've achieved, despite everything."

Our eyes meet, and I can feel the sexual tension simmering between us, like a live wire ready to ignite. Her touch electrifies me, causing my eyes to wander over her lips, envisioning the sensation of them against mine. The air becomes heavy, carrying with it unspoken desires and lingering memories. The fire in her eyes reveals the same hunger, the battle to maintain composure.

"Scarlet…" I start, but the words catch in my throat as she leans in.

She bites her lip, but then swiftly retrieves her bag and stands up from the step. "I should go," she says, her voice trembling slightly. She's clearly needing to leave before things escalate even further.

"How's Nate?" I ask, just as she is about to reach the door. The media frenzy has been relentless, making it impossible for me to find a moment to check on him today.

She turns to face me. "He's doing better. He knows it'll take a while to recover, but he's handling it. His biggest concern is letting down the fans, just like I'm sure all of you are," she says, opening the door and walking inside.

I sit there, absorbing Scarlet's words as they settle deep within me. Yeah, it's not on me that my family is fucked up, but she doesn't get how hard it is for me to let my guard down. People only see the version of me that's locked down tight—walls up, no heart. I keep everyone at arm's length because if anyone's gonna bail, it's gonna be me making the call. No way am I getting left behind again.

I push myself off the step, feeling the rough texture of the concrete beneath my hands, and head back inside.

As I step into the kitchen, the talk revolves around Nate. Scarlet pours herself a glass of juice while Xander and Theo sit at the table, surrounded by empty beer bottles.

As I move toward my seat, I avoid making eye contact with Scarlet, fully aware of Xander's watchful eyes.

"Yeah, I'm about to go see him," Theo says, shooting a quick look at Xander as I take my seat at the table.

Xander gives him a nod.

"Hey Scar, can you come over here for a sec? There's something we need to discuss."

With my back turned to Scarlet, I take a seat and direct my attention towards the empty beer bottle.

The sound of her heels clicking on the tiled floor fills the room, followed by the distinct sound of the fridge door opening and closing. Making her way to the table, she chooses the chair on the other side, positioning herself directly across from me. When I glance up, our eyes meet and linger for a brief moment before she averts her gaze towards Theo.

"What's up?" she asks, taking a sip of her juice.

My gaze traces the graceful arc of her neck, captivated by its subtle movements as she takes a sip. If they actually bring her on tour, I'm totally fucked.

As soon as Xander speaks, she averts her gaze from Theo.

"Scarlet, we've been discussing the tour, and you understand how important this is. We're doing this on our own now, no more label supporting us, and the new album is about to drop."

"Yeah, Nate and Theo have kept me in on everything."

"Well, now that Nate's out of commission, we need someone to fill his spot. And we"—Xander glances at me, and Scarlet catches my eye briefly before turning back to him—"we'd like you to step in for Nate."

Scarlet's eyes pause for a moment on each of us, before finally lingering on me for an extra beat.

"Listen, guys, I really do appreciate the offer, but I'm going to have to decline," she firmly replies.

"Huh?" Theo's voice rises. "What the fuck, Scar? This is what you've always dreamed of—playing in a band, in front of packed stadiums."

"It is," Scarlet replies, reaching out to grab Theo's hand. "It's always been my dream to play in a band and rock sold-out stadiums, and I'm stoked you're considering me for this gig. My whole life, I've been in Nate's shadow. In every audition, it's always about if I can ride on Nate's fame to make their band popular. My last audition went great, but all they cared about was if I could get Nate to help them score an opening slot. It's like they can't see me for my own talent, and it's exhausting. I really love my brother and I'm super proud of him and you guys, but if I take this gig, it'll just prove that I'm only valued because of who I'm related to, not for my own skills."

Damn, I never thought about how much of a shitshow that must be—constantly living in someone else's shadow, never getting a fair shot, just being seen as a fucking footnote because of who your brother is.

"But hey, Scar, it could be an opportunity," Theo chimes in, always looking for the bright side.

When Scarlet releases Theo's hand, she looks at Xander briefly before turning her attention to me. "Look, I really appreciate you considering me to fill Nate's spot, but to be honest, I don't think I can do it. I hope you can understand why," she says, offering a warm smile that doesn't quite reach her eyes. Standing up, she grabs her glass of juice and walks past Theo, giving his shoulder a reassuring squeeze before heading into the next room.

"Shit," Theo mutters, taken aback by the unexpected turn of events.

"Yeah, it's gotta suck being trapped in your brother's shadow, never getting noticed for your own talent," I remark, shaking my head at the injustice she faces.

"You'd know all about that, asshole—always stuck in my fucking shadow," Theo smirks.

"That's why you're stuck playing bass. Can't handle a real guitar, huh?" I shoot back, my grin mirroring his own.

He smirks, knowing he's lost, then shifts gears. "I didn't know Scarlet has been struggling all these years. She didn't say shit about what she was going through. That's rough."

"Yeah," Xander says, pushing his chair back and standing up.

"Hey, where the hell are you off to?" Theo asks, eyeing Xander as he heads for the door.

"Home first, then I'm going to see Nate," Xander replies, not looking back.

"Well, I'm coming too," Theo announces, shoving his chair back and getting up.

I keep my mouth shut, knowing I need to steer clear of the media shitstorm. I stand up from the table, realizing that hanging around Scarlet and these damn thoughts about her will just pull me back into old habits. Time to keep my distance and get the hell out of here.

# CHAPTER 8

## Scarlet

Stepping into Nate's hospital room, my eyes immediately land on a young nurse diligently checking his vitals. She looks at him with dreamy eyes, but Nate is too absorbed in the TV to even notice.

Not that he'd give a shit, anyway—my brother's locked up his heart tight. It will always belong to the girl he lost all those years ago.

From my vantage point, I observe as Ace exits his car, marches towards the paparazzi, and forcefully hurls the camera to the ground. I smirk at the sight—he usually keeps his emotions buried deep, closed off, unlike Theo, whose nervous twitches always spill the beans. I don't think I've ever seen Ace this mad. But then again, I've never really had the chance to truly get to know him, so what do I know?

As the nurse wraps up and exits, I step into the room. Nate's eyes remained fixed on the TV screen, refusing to look away. Some reporter is outside the hospital where everything happened yesterday, speculating that the tour is definitely going to be canceled now that Nate is stuck in here with a broken shoulder.

"Has the band made a public statement yet, Richard?" The news anchor's voice reverberates loudly from the television.

As soon as Nate notices me approaching, he turns his head. "Can you believe this shit?" he says, before shifting his attention back to the TV.

Standing by his bed, we watch the footage of Ace playing on repeat, the reporter's voice speculating about the future of the tour. "What the fuck was Ace thinking?" Nate says, grabbing the remote and turning off the television.

"He wasn't thinking at all," I reply with a smirk.

"It's not funny, Scar. He's a fucking idiot for losing his shit like that, especially with the media recording his every move."

"Go easy on him. Theo's already been giving him a hard time."

"Good," Nate replies. "That dickhead deserves every bit of it. If it were Theo who'd fucked up, Ace would've ripped him a new one for that."

"From what I saw yesterday, I think he's already punishing himself enough over it."

I reach into my bag and pull out a large bag of chips—Nate's favorite swiped from the cafeteria. I make my way to the other side of the bed, where his functioning arm rests, and tuck them into his top drawer for easy access.

"Have Mom and Dad been in today?" I ask, walking over to the window to admire the breathtaking view. Looking out from Nate's room, the city sprawls out below, complete with the constant buzz of traffic on the highway and the silhouette of distant hills.

"Yeah, they left about an hour ago," Nate replies. A heavy silence settles between us, filled with unspoken thoughts that hang in the air.

I settle back into the chair beside Nate's bed.

Finally, he breaks the silence, his voice shattering the stillness. "I'll rip that asshole apart when I lay eyes on him, Scar."

As I lift my eyes to meet Nate's gaze, I can sense his scrutiny directed towards the marks that are still visible on my face. The swelling's gone, but the bruises are still visible, no matter how hard I tried to conceal them today.

"Just drop it, Nate," I urge, trying to diffuse his growing anger.

"Fuck, Scarlet, you expect me to just forget that asshole laid a hand on you?"

"Nate, I just want to leave it in the past," I say, hoping to calm him down.

"Yeah, but I can't just pretend it didn't happen. Did you get a restraining order or press charges against him?"

"No."

"Why the fuck not, Scarlet?" I can see the frustration written all over his face, as he tries to make sense of why I haven't acted yet.

"Because Nate. What happens when the media gets wind of that? You'll be all over the front page, and it's got nothing to do with you."

"So what? This has everything to do with me, goddamn it. You're my little sis, Scar. Some asshole hurt you. That's way more important than any shit that the media pulls." He reaches out and grabs my hand, his grip firm and protective.

"I don't know," I say, staring down at our joined hands. "I suppose I just didn't want the media to grab hold of it and broadcast it all over the news. It's already embarrassing as it is. I don't need the whole world knowing about what happened."

"It's not about being embarrassed, Scar. You did nothing wrong, so you've got nothing to be ashamed of. This is on that dickhead, not you." The soft pressure of Nate's thumb running over the back of my hand sends a wave of comfort through me, but his words make my chest tighten. When he falls silent, my curiosity gets the better of me, and I finally look up at him. "Last night, when the guys came in, Theo mentioned that you declined the opportunity to take my spot in the band."

I shift my eyes away from him and fix my gaze on the expansive view outside the large window as I speak. "Did he explain my reasons for refusing?"

"Yeah, he did. You know Theo—he can't help but blurt things out. But I want to hear it from you."

I shift my gaze back to Nate. Our sibling bond has always been strong and close-knit. He's been my protector, always there to shield me from harm. I know Theo would've painted a vivid picture of my conversation at that table yesterday; that's just how those two operate.

"Why didn't you ever let me in on that shit, Scar?"

"Because it's my problem, Nate. You didn't need to know, plain and simple."

He falls silent for a moment, and when I glance up, I can see the frustration in his eyes—he's itching to dig deeper but holds back, wary of me shutting him down. I hesitate, unsure if I should dive into this conversation. It's not his fault that his talent shines brighter than mine, but I feel this irresistible urge to explain myself. With Theo, you never really know what might have slipped out.

"I said nothing, Nate, because I didn't want you to see how your fame screws with my career."

"Tell me, Scar. I need to understand what's been happening," he presses.

I take a deep breath, letting it out slowly. He deserves to know, but I can already imagine the heavy burden this will place on him. I know my brother well enough to anticipate his reaction—his face will contort with guilt, as he worries that his success might be hindering mine.

"The day I came home and found Beck in my apartment, I had just finished an audition. I honestly thought I nailed it."

"And I'm sure you did, Scar."

"Thanks, Nate," I say, managing a smile. That's the thing about my brother—he's always been my biggest supporter. "Everything seemed to be going well. It came down to me and another guy. From where they had me sitting, I could hear the questions they asked him about his past successes, so I knew it was down to just the two of us. But when they finished with him and called me over, they didn't ask me anything like that."

"Why? What did they ask?" Nate inquires, his curiosity piqued.

"Well, the first question they hit me with was about you," I respond.

"What did they say?"

"They asked if I was related to you. When I said yes, the three guys exchanged looks, and I could feel it in my gut. This same thing has happened before."

"I'm sorry, Scar," Nate says softly, the sincerity in his voice evident.

"It's okay; it's not your fault. After I answered that question, I thought they'd shift their focus back to my audition, like they did with the guy before me. You know, asking about my music. But they didn't. Instead, they asked if I was in their band, if I could get them on the opening list for your tour." I choose not to mention the uncomfortable moment when one of the guys stared at my chest, giving me an uneasy feeling. But I suppose that's just how things are in the music scene. Even male groupies can be way too forward with female musicians. In my previous band, I lost track of how many times I had to shut them down. "So I just got up and left. It felt like all those other times where they're more interested in my connections than my talent."

"I still don't get why you turned down Theo's offer."

"But that's exactly why I turned it down. It's simple, Nate. I'm always being compared to you. If I joined, I'd just be setting myself up for even more comparisons."

"I think you're making a mistake. Fuck those assholes for treating you like that, but our fans would love to have you on board. Scar, we play exactly the same. Who better to join Broken Oasis than the drummer's little sister?"

"Yeah, but that's the problem, Nate. Everyone will think I only got the gig for that reason."

"No fucking way they'll think that Scar. You're overthinking it. The fans will love that my sister's stepping in for me. Once they hear you play, it'll prove you're the best for the job. The guys wouldn't have offered it if they didn't think you were good enough."

"But they haven't even heard me play."

"No, but Theo and I have told Xander and Ace how badass you are. They know you personally, which is a huge plus. If they brought in someone else, what if Xander or Ace doesn't vibe with them? Xander won't tolerate anyone's bullshit, and Ace—well, you saw how he was with that paparazzi guy. He's got his own demons, just like Theo. If anyone pisses him off, he'll lash out and do something even more messed up. Trust me, we don't need more of that kind of chaos on our hands."

Despite his grumpy outburst, I can't help but smirk at the memory of Ace hurling that camera.

Nate's words continue to echo in my thoughts. He's right—Xander and Ace know me, and I know them. I get the dynamics of the band. The way Xander's influence shapes everything, and Ace's strategic mind that drives it all. Nate and Theo hold these guys in high regard, evident from the mutual respect and admiration they share.

"I think you should go for it, Scar," Nate insists. "Even if it's a big 'fuck you' to all those assholes who never saw your talent and only saw you as a stepping stone for their connections."

Lost in thought, I absentmindedly chew on my bottom lip. Could I actually make this happen? Step into Nate's shoes and learn their entire set list in just two weeks? The thought sends a rush of excitement and fear coursing through my veins.

"This is a fantastic opportunity, Scar," Nate says, his enthusiasm infectious. "And who knows what doors this could open after those sixty days on tour?"

"So you really think I should go for it?" I ask, second-guessing myself again.

"I do. Theo feels the same way. Those assholes don't see your talent, no matter who you audition for. This is your chance to prove them wrong. Show them just how damn talented you really are. Take this opportunity to make a name for yourself. Let them see that it's your skills they should be recognizing, not just using you as a connection to exploit."

I sit there, letting his words sink in as I contemplate the idea of making a name for myself. Can this opportunity truly be the turning point where I break free from my brother's shadow? I've always thrived on challenges, and the rhythmic beat of the drums has captivated me since the day Nate got his first drum set. Learning every song on the band's playlist and putting in the hard work wouldn't be an issue. Right now, the most important thing is finding the strength within myself to seize this chance and prove to everyone, myself included, that I am a gifted musician in my own regard and not just a way to form connections.

"Okay," I say to Nate. "I'll do it."

# CHAPTER 9

## Ace

We're all gathered in the studio at my place. Scarlet's test run on Nate's drum kit is nothing short of explosive, as she plays with an intensity that leaves us in awe.

With his bass guitar draped over his shoulder, Theo's beside me, as if we belong to some exclusive guitar club. Xander's out by the soundboard, adjusting knobs and observing us through the large glass panel.

So far, we have mentioned nothing to the press about the concerts. While Theo and Nate are completely on board with Scarlet stepping in, Xander and I need to be damn sure she's the right fit. We haven't even seen her play yet, and this decision can't be half-assed just because she's Nate's sister.

In the midst of editing the new album, Theo delivered the news: Scarlet would be stepping in for Nate.

At first, it felt like a weight off my shoulders—like maybe we could actually pull this off without the constant scrutiny of the press. But if I'm being real, I'm worried as hell. Expecting someone to learn our entire set list and perfect it within two weeks—that's a fucking big demand. Xander and I are on edge—not because we doubt her talent, but because the tight deadline and the level of commitment required have us questioning everything. Does she possess the determination to make this a reality?

While Theo instructs Scarlet on a few additional beats of one of our latest songs, I set my guitar down and reach for a refreshing bottle of water before making my way towards Xander. Just as I'm about to close the door, I catch a sequence of beats that, if I didn't know any better, could've come straight from Nate.

I shut the door, silencing the noise, and settle into the seat beside Xander, who's closely observing through the glass window.

"What's your take on it?" I ask, twisting off the bottle cap and taking a swig.

"She's pretty solid. There are definitely some similarities between her and Nate. I get what Theo was on about."

"Yeah, I was thinking the same," I reply, unable to tear my eyes away from Scarlet as she loses herself in her drumming.

Seeing her like this, fully immersed in her element, strikes a chord deep within me. I notice the intensity on her face, the tight grip she has on the drumsticks, and her long blonde hair twisted messily into a knot on top of her head. Shifting effortlessly from drum to drum, she finds her rhythm and syncs up with Theo. Her tattooed arms are a blur of motion, perfectly synchronizing with the rhythm of our music. It's clear that she's giving her all to it.

Xander leans forward, his hand moving as he slides a switch to amplify the sound. Right away, it's clear she's nailing it with Theo's guidance.

"Do you think this could actually work?" I ask, as they come to a stop. Theo eagerly shows her the next part of the music.

"She's got fucking talent, I'll give her that," Xander replies, nodding.

"But you're still not fully convinced," I add, my eyes fixed on her and Theo.

"Not quite there yet," he replies, his eyes still fixed on the scene unfolding outside the window. The tension hangs in the air, a silent reminder of the weight of this decision.

As Scarlet and Theo run through the beat again, I push off my seat and make my way back, grabbing my guitar to join in.

By the third run-through, as she finishes learning the song, a smile spreads across her face.

With a rush of excitement, Theo wraps her in a warm, big brother hug, his face glowing with pride. She catches my eye, and I nod approvingly, letting her know she absolutely nailed it.

Just then, Xander enters the room. "Ready to try it with vocals?" he asks Scarlet.

"Yeah," she replies, nodding as she sets the drumsticks aside. She wipes her hands on her shirt, leaving streaks of sweat. I can see the nerves bubbling under the surface. It's completely understandable - she has a lot to prove to her brother's bandmates, and that's no small feat.

As Xander steps up to the mic, I catch Scarlet taking a few deep breaths, gripping her drumsticks tight. She shoots me a glance, and I count us in. As Xander's voice fills the room, she hammers out our beat with precision, her energy electric. Theo and I exchange an impressed look, amazed as she flawlessly hits every beat. If I closed my eyes, I'd swear Nate was right here. If Xander still isn't convinced after this, I'll be right there with Theo, fully supporting Scarlet to step in for Nate.

Maybe Xander's worried about her joining the tour because I've fucked her. He doesn't need to stress over that shit; I can just lose myself in groupies when the urge hits. No problem there.

I ignore those thoughts and focus intently on nailing the chords. It's time to get my head in the game. The next few weeks are going to be a chaotic whirlwind of activity. I've got the album to finish editing—it's due out in just over a week, so I need to get my shit together. Plus, there are extra practice sessions with Scarlet to really fine-tune everything for the tour. The last thing I need right now is a fucking distraction.

As the song reaches its conclusion, I turn around to face Xander. I can tell he's impressed by the way his smirk stretches across his face.

"Told ya she'd fucking nail it," Theo states, a proud grin spreading across his face.

"Yeah, she fucking did," Xander remarks, shooting a quick glance my way before turning his attention back to Scarlet. "You killed it, Scarlet." He then looks over at Theo, who's standing there with a big-ass grin. "You were fucking right. She sounds just like Nate."

Scarlet exhales deeply, feeling the tension release from her shoulders as a smile slowly brightens her face.

Xander reaches for his phone, his fingers unlocking the screen. "Let's do it one more time, and then I gotta go. Poppy and Alex are flying out today to see an old friend who looked after Alex when he was younger, and I want to hang out with them before I drop them off at the airport."

With a quick nod from him, I start counting us in to kick off the song again.

With the final beats coming to an end, we stand there, genuinely impressed. With only a few hours of practice, Scarlet has managed to perform one of our new songs flawlessly, exceeding all expectations.

The sheer joy on her face, that infectious smile—it's clear music runs deep in her veins, woven into her DNA, just like it is for all of us. It gives our lives meaning. I can't help but wonder how she's dealt with the crap of missing out on so much of her own music career, always overshadowed by Nate's success. Fuck, I don't think I could handle that kind of bullshit.

"Nice work, Scarlet," Xander says, clearly impressed. He shoots me a look. "In the coming days, we'll have to release a statement confirming that the tour is still going ahead. I'll have Kit work on it and ask her to set something up."

"Might be best if I just stay away," I mutter, slipping the guitar strap over my head.

"Why?" Theo smirks. "Worried you'll toss another camera?" He laughs. His smart-ass attitude is seriously getting on my fucking nerves. "Seeing the grumpy dickhead make a fool of himself on TV is pure fucking comedy. I love seeing the paparazzi's reaction when you smashed their camera. It's fucking priceless. It's saved on my phone if you wanna see it."

I swear, if that fucker keeps mocking me about the stupid shit I did, he's gonna feel my fury in the form of a fist. I shoot him a glare, but the asshole's grin just gets wider. Yeah, keep smiling, dickhead. Next time you flash that grin, you'll be missing a few teeth.

"Ace," Xander says, pulling my attention away from Theo's antics.

I turn back to him. "You can't dodge the press forever, Ace. You've got to face them eventually."

"Watch me," I say, taking a swig from my water bottle.

"Don't start with that shit. You're going." Xander's eyes bore into me, making it clear I've pissed him off. "I'm out of here."

With a scowl, I watch him make his way toward the door, my eyes locked on him until he vanishes from sight. I can't tell if he's mad because I refuse to talk to the media or if it's a silent warning to stay the fuck away from Scarlet.

"Are you ready to learn another song, Scar?" Theo asks, breaking the tension.

"Yeah," Scarlet eagerly replies.

With headphones on, I'm in the studio, fully immersed in the music as I fine-tune our new album at the soundboard. Nearly an hour ago, Theo left to visit Nate at the hospital, leaving me alone with Scarlet. She's still here, completely immersed in her practice, determined to master the next song, soaking up everything Theo and I have taught her.

As I watch through the glass, I can see her frustration building each time she misses a beat. The fiery determination in her eyes makes it clear that she expects nothing short of perfection.

I drop my head, determined to finish editing this album, knowing I need to stay focused. With meticulous care, I manipulate the buttons, adjusting the sound to achieve flawlessness, eliminating any imperfections, and seamlessly blending Xander's voice with the music. I've got a feeling this album is going to be a hit with the fans—I just need to focus and finish it, blocking out the distraction of Scarlet in the next room. But every time I glance through the glass, watching her work, it's harder to ignore that fire she's got. She's relentless, and it's infectious.

For the next hour, I lose myself in the rhythm of the work—sliding buttons, cutting, and replacing tracks. The process is hypnotic, pulling me in deeper as I block out everything else. Time slips away as I fine-tune each detail, making sure every note hits just right and every lyric syncs perfectly.

I feel a dull ache in my neck and I stretch it out, just in time to see Scarlet hurling her drumsticks across the room, the sound of them crashing against the wall echoing through the air. Just like me, she's been at it for hours, and the weariness is starting to show.

As I rub my eyes and stretch, I can feel the fatigue of the day settling into my shoulders.

Scarlet's frustration seeps into the room, pulling my attention away from the work.

I push myself away from the soundboard, the chair gliding over the smooth tiles as I rise. Without a second thought, I move to enter the other room, ready to deal with whatever's got her so riled up.

Pushing the door open, I find Scarlet sitting there with her head in her hands; her face etched with a mixture of frustration and exhaustion. Her drumsticks lie scattered on the floor. It's clear she's been pushing herself hard.

"Hey," I say, moving further into the room. "You're doing great, you know. We can grab a drink or go over it again if you want."

With a frustrated sigh, she brushes aside the stray strands of hair that have escaped from her messy bun. "Yeah, I could use a break," she says.

Nodding, I turn around and make my way towards the door. Her footsteps echo as she follows closely behind me.

Stepping out into the hallway, I steal a quick glance at her.

"Don't stress too much. You'll figure it out," I say, trying to keep my tone casual, though the words barely mask the undercurrent of tension. "Just take a break and clear your mind."

I move into the kitchen, feeling Scarlet's presence close behind me, the air between us charged with something we're both avoiding.

As I reach into the fridge and pull out a couple of beers, her proximity is almost intoxicating. I turn to face her, our eyes locking in a gaze that lingers a moment too long.

"Here?" I say, my voice coming out rougher than I meant.

As I hand her the bottle, our fingers brush lightly, and I feel a surge of electricity shoot through my body. Her eyes spark with a fire I can't ignore, and for a moment, we just stand there, our gazes locked.

Like a shock of cold water, Xander's warning snaps me out of the heat of the moment. I can't go down that path. I take a step back, creating some distance, and with a twist, I remove the cap from my beer.

"So, umm," I start, trying to ease the tension. My brain desperately searches for words, but comes up empty. Aside from Kit, I'm not used to just sitting down and talking with a woman. Normally, it's a quick fuck and then I'm out of there. "So, what was your old band like?" I ask, hoping to find some common ground and dial down the electric charge between us.

The question lingers in the air, and I instantly regret asking it. The marks still on her face serve as a painful reminder of the abuse she endured from her ex. I see the flicker of pain in her eyes, and I curse myself for bringing it up.

"Good," Scarlet replies, her voice tense. "I loved being in a band, but things got messy when my ex, Beck, started screwing the other girl in the band—and all the groupies."

Awkwardness hangs in the air, making it feel heavy and stifling. Her eyes flicker down to her drink, and she absentmindedly runs her fingers along the cool, smooth surface of the bottle. The tension between us intensifies, causing my grip on my beer to tighten.

"Sounds like you're better off without that dickhead," I say, trying to lighten the mood, though the weight of her past still hangs in the air.

Scarlet's eyes meet mine. "And what about you, Ace? You guys get to live your dream every day. Did you ever expect that to happen?"

She steps closer, her movements slow and deliberate, and I can't help but check her out—her toned legs in those cutoff shorts, the curve of her hips, and the way her tank top clings to her spectacular tits.

When I lift my gaze, I catch her eyes locked onto mine, intense and unwavering. Shit, she caught me checking her out. I quickly avert my gaze, pretending to be engrossed in the fine print on my beer bottle label. A rush of heat travels up my neck and ignites a fiery sensation in my cock, but I force myself to stay cool.

"Honestly? It was a wild ride I never thought I'd get on," I say, trying to regain my composure. "But there is a bunch of bullshit that comes with it." I take another drink of my beer, hoping the bitterness will ground me. "You learn to handle the highs and lows, you know? But it's been a dream of mine and

Xander's ever since we were kids." Despite feeling uneasy, my voice maintains a steady tone, emphasizing the need for a professional dynamic between us, especially now that she's part of the band and Nate's sister.

Leaning against the counter, Scarlet keeps her eyes locked on me. "I can relate. I've had that dream my whole life too," she says. "It's just hard watching it slip away. Sometimes I wonder if I'll ever break through and show them what I'm really capable of."

Her honesty hits me hard, and I can see the weight of her past lingering in her eyes. "But your dream isn't slipping away now, right?" I say, trying to keep it light while holding the boundary I need. "You're stepping into something new, and you've got the talent to back it up." My pulse quickens as I fight the urge to close the gap between us. Clearing my throat, I force myself to focus. "But right now, we need to stay locked on the music."

She smiles, looking down at her beer. "Yeah. The music."

As I take another sip of my beer, I feel my resolve slowly crumbling, my mind overwhelmed with forbidden thoughts. My eyes slowly drift back to Scarlet, captivated by the curve of her lips and the glistening sweat on her skin from drumming. She's standing so damn close, and the scent of her—something light and sweet—hits me, making my pulse quicken.

I'm fully aware that I shouldn't, but I simply can't resist. I take a step closer, feeling the magnetic pull of her. My hand reaches out, almost of its own accord, and brushes a stray lock of hair behind her ear.

She inhales sharply, and I catch the desire mirrored in her eyes, making it impossible to ignore.

"Scarlet..." I start, my voice thick with restraint, and all I can hear in my head is Xander's stern warning. "As much as I want to... God, you have no fucking idea how bad I want you right now... but we can't..."

She bites her lower lip, looking up at me through those long lashes.

Fuck, she knows exactly what she's doing, and it drives me wild. That innocent look mixed with the raw, dirty energy she gives off—it's messing with my head, pushing every button I've got.

"Why not, Ace?" she challenges, her voice laced with defiance, as if daring me to make a move. "We're both adults."

Her words hit me like a spark, igniting a fire within me. My body aches to surrender to her—to kiss her, fuck her, and get lost in all the filthy things I've been thinking about since I first saw her at the airport. Her tight body drives me wild, and I can't believe I'm still craving her, even after having her twice already. That never happens.

My breath is ragged as I step back, desperately trying to regain control over myself. I pivot my body and place my beer on the countertop, seeking a distraction from the heat between us. "We should concentrate on the music," I say mostly to myself. "Let's not complicate things."

She nods, but the intensity in her gaze reveals that she too feels the same irresistible pull, and I know it will be a challenge to keep my distance.

Scarlet turns, mirroring my movements as she sets her beer down beside mine. Closing the distance, her lips collide with mine in a forceful kiss. The moment our lips crash together in a dirty, desperate kiss, I feel it everywhere—a rush of heat to my cock, a surge of electricity that makes my head spin. It's a raw, intoxicating sensation that satisfies everything I've been craving.

As her hands glide up my chest, I pull her even closer. Everything around us fades, leaving only the feel of her hot body against mine and the intoxicating taste of her lips. I'm losing myself in her, drowning in the heat of the moment, and I don't know how the fuck to stop. Every instinct screams at me to push deeper, to take what I want, but the reality of our situation still flickers at the edges of my mind.

My hand threads through her hair, gripping her tight, holding her face in place as my tongue collides with hers. The soft whimper she emits ignites a frenzy within me, driving me to the brink of madness. Every touch, and every sound drives me closer to the edge. I know I'm crossing a line, but right now, I don't give a fuck. I need this—I need her. The hunger to feel her beneath me, to claim her, to have my cock buried deep inside her, burns hotter than anything, consuming me like an addiction I can't shake.

With a surge of urgency, I lift her off the ground, her legs wrapping tightly around my waist as our kiss deepens, messy and hungry. Every breath between us is charged, our mouths moving in sync as if we're both desperate to consume every inch of each other. Her fingers grip the back of my neck, pulling me closer as our kiss deepens, raw and urgent. That alone propels me towards the stairs. Every step feels like a fucking challenge with the way she grinds against me.

"Fuck, you're driving me insane," I growl against her lips as we reach the top of the staircase. I stumble into my room, kicking the door shut behind us, my cock throbbing, desperate for release. "This is just a quick fuck, Scar, you know that, right. Nothing more."

I can't get enough of her taste, the way her body feels pressed against mine, igniting every nerve in my body. My hands grip her thighs, pulling her even closer until there's no room for even a breath of air between us. Each kiss is filthy and raw—like I'm claiming her, marking her as mine.

I'm as hard as a steel pipe, fuck I'm ready to explode if I don't get inside her wet hole any second now. Clothes. Too many fucking clothes. I'm desperate to strip her bare, to feel her skin against mine, the warmth of her body driving me wild. I can't take it anymore—the hunger, the need, the raw urge to claim her. There's no holding back now—it's like a fire that's been building for too long, and I'm ready to let it burn.

With urgency, I put her down on her feet and yank her shirt over her head, tossing it aside. My breath catches when I see her perfect tits in that black lace bra, and I can't help but let out a groan. My hands are on her in seconds, fingers grazing the soft heat of her skin. I lean in, kissing her collarbone, savoring the taste of her, the warmth of her body against mine. Every touch, every breath she takes against me fuels the fire building in my gut.

Just as I guide her backward toward the bed, my fingers teasing at the copper button of her cut-off shorts, she suddenly grabs my hand, freezing me in place.

What the hell? She was just as desperate as I was a second ago. Is she having second thoughts? Fuck, I hope not. If she pulls back now, it's going to take a month for my cock to calm down, and those blue balls of mine are already a fucking nightmare. I hold my breath, waiting for her to speak, for something—anything—that'll either put my mind at ease or send me spiraling into frustration.

"Take that off and lay down," she tells me, tugging at my shirt.

I stare at her, caught off guard. It's always been me taking control, but this shift in power is kind of exciting. There's a spark in her eyes, daring me to fall in line, and despite the adrenaline rushing through my veins, I feel a thrill at the idea of letting go, even for a second. I lift my arm and tug my shirt over my head. Her gaze darkens as she devours the sight of me.

With a grin, I drop onto the bed, my heart pounding, as I keep my eyes locked on her. Every muscle tenses, ready for whatever she has planned, knowing full well I'm at her mercy—and I'm more than ready for it.

Her tongue glides over her bottom lip, and the mere thought of what she could do with that mouth has me fucking harder than I thought possible. Every teasing glance she throws my way makes my pulse race. I can already picture the filthy things she's about to do, and just that alone has my blood boiling, my body aching for her touch.

I watch as she sinks to her knees, her hand reaching for my belt. She unbuckles it, her fingers brushing against me as she undoes the button on my jeans. The slow, agonizing pull of the zipper makes my cock throb, and all I can think about is how much I need to feel her hands on me—or better yet, the heat of her mouth.

"Lift," she commands, her voice firm and unwavering.

Without hesitation, I do as she says, lifting my hips as she pulls my jeans and underwear down in one swift motion. My cock springs free, hard and aching, and I can't tear my eyes away from her as she stares at it with hunger. Her tongue flicks out, wetting her bottom lip, and I bite back a groan, barely holding it together. When she peels my jeans off, I expect her to toss them aside, but instead, she quickly pulls my belt from the waistband, and I feel a rush of excitement spike through me.

"Move up," she orders, gesturing towards the top of the bed.

I smirk, turned on by how she's taking control. This dirty, commanding Scarlet is a whole new side of her—one we've never explored before—and fuck, it's driving me wild.

She walks around the side of the bed with the belt in her hand, a wicked gleam in her eyes. "Put your hands up," she says, kneeling beside me. "Cross them."

I comply without hesitation, watching as she wraps the thick leather belt around my crossed wrists, binding them together with expert precision. She threads it through the metal bar in the bed frame, pulling hard until I'm completely bound, locked in place.

My eyes trace over her tits as she works, and all I can think about is ripping off that bra and sucking on those perfect, hard nipples.

I lean forward as much as my restraints allow, my nose brushing along the soft curve of her ribcage, closing my eyes as I get lost in her familiar scent. It drives me fucking crazy how good she smells. My body aches to touch her, but I'm stuck, helpless beneath her control, and fuck, it's hotter than I ever imagined.

After yanking the belt tight, she steps away, and the loss of her touch sends a wave of frustration through me. But then I see her eyes—they're dark, filled with heat, roaming over my body like she fucking owns it. The way she's looking at me, like she's about to devour me, makes my cock pulse with need. Whatever she's planning, I'm all for it.

"Take off that bra," I growl, voice rough and desperate. "And those shorts. I need to see your hot, sexy body, Scar. I need to see those perky tits, your bare pussy... all of you."

She glances down at me, amusement sparking in her eyes as a wicked smile curves her lips. Leaning in close, just out of my reach, she smirks. "You're not in charge here. I am." Her tone is steady, dripping with authority as she straightens up, letting me see the power she holds over me. "Now, be quiet," she orders, eyes narrowing in warning.

The words send a jolt straight through me, and fuck, if that doesn't make me want her even more. I'm loving every second of this—the way she's taking control, flipping the script on me. My body is buzzing and she hasn't even laid a finger on me yet. How the fuck does she do that? Make me this wild for her, without even touching me?

My eyes follow her every move as she slowly makes her way to the foot of the bed. I lift my head, my pulse quickening as she pauses, just standing there, staring at me with a smug look like she's savoring every second of her control. Then, with deliberate intent, she crawls onto the bed, her gaze fixed on my cock, and I feel it twitch in response to her attention.

Her fingers barely graze the spot where my piercing is, sending a jolt through my entire body. The sensation is immediate, raw, and primal, making me gasp. I hiss as her fingers slowly trail down the underside of my cock, teasing and driving me fucking insane.

Then she leans in, pressing a soft kiss to the tip, and it's a shot of pure pleasure. My entire body tightens, and all I want to do is grab her head and ram my cock down her throat. That's how much I need her right now—need to lose myself in her, lose control, and lose my fucking mind.

The second she drags her tongue along my shaft, I try to pull my hands down, but the belt keeps me locked in place. The slow, deliberate torture of pleasure is fucking unbearable, and I know if she doesn't take me into her mouth right now, I'm not going to survive this sweet torment. Every inch of me is on fire, and her teasing is driving me insane.

"Fuck," I growl, watching her grin at me, my cock standing tall as she circles her tongue around the tip. My hips buck forward, desperate to find her mouth, desperate for more. "Fucking open your mouth, Scar. You're driving me insane."

She just smirks, and I know I'm exactly where she wants me—her in control, dragging this out to make me lose my damn mind. And fuck, I think my mind and my cock are about to explode. Every second feels like an eternity, and the way she's playing me has me teetering right on the edge of oblivion.

She gets up onto her knees, that seductive smirk never leaving her face as she reaches behind to undo her bra, letting it fall to the side. The second her tits are free, all I can think about is coming on them, marking her, claiming her in the most primal way possible. The thought of seeing her painted by me, glistening with my release, makes my cock throb painfully with need. Every inch of me burns with the urgency to own this moment, to have her beneath me, writhing in pleasure as I push her to the edge. I want to drown in her, to lose myself in her curves and softness, making her mine in the filthiest way imaginable.

Then she slips off the bed, my eyes glued to her as she sways her hips, peeling down her shorts and panties, with a seductive grace. When she kicks them off, she climbs back onto the bed, kneeling before me, that look in her eyes dripping with pure filth and lust. My heart races, as she leans closer. And then, finally, I feel it as she wraps her warm, wet mouth around my cock, taking me deep.

"Fucking hell, Scar," I groan, my hands clenching into fists as I fight the overwhelming urge to thrust into her mouth. A loud moan escapes me when she holds my cock deep in the back of her throat. I almost lose my mind and I can feel my control slipping further away. Each soft suck and teasing lick pushes me closer to the edge, and all I can think about is how badly I need to come, to explode inside her sweet mouth.

She stares up at me with those gorgeous eyes, and the sight of my cock stretching her lips does something primal to me. I want to tell her just how fucking beautiful she looks right now with my cock in her mouth, how perfect she feels, but all I can manage is a hoarse, "Fucking hell, Scar!"

The words barely leave my lips before another wave of pleasure washes over me, making it hard to focus on anything but the intoxicating way she's working me.

She slides back down my shaft, savoring every inch, and then glides back up, dragging out the pleasure until I'm a trembling mess beneath her. It's not the quick pace I crave; no, this is pure fucking torture—exquisite, drawn-out torment designed to drive me wild. I thrust my hips forward, desperation clawing at me, and the sound of her gagging around my length sends a rush of pleasure coursing through my body.

"Yeah, choke on my cock like a good girl," I growl, my voice thick with lust.

# Chapter 10

## Scarlet

I can see Ace coming undone, just like I wanted. As I slide my mouth down his shaft, his cock pulses on my tongue, and when he hits the back of my throat, I stay there, relishing the raw, sexy sounds I'm pulling from him. I love the way he watches me with those dark brown eyes, like I'm the most beautiful thing he's ever seen. My mouth moves back up his shaft, slow and deliberate, and the second I hear him hiss, I know I've got him.

"Fucking hell, Scar," he groans, and I just purr, loving the way my name sounds on his lips.

I suck the tip of his cock, my cheeks hollowing out, teasing him before sliding my mouth down over him. But the torment I'm giving him isn't enough—he wants more. He thrusts his hips, driving his cock deeper into my mouth. So, I stay there, letting him take control, letting him fuck my mouth the way he needs. Our eyes lock in that heated moment, his gaze burning into mine as he takes what he wants, and I give in completely, loving every second of it.

He groans, his head falling back as the overwhelming sensation overtakes him, but then his eyes snap open, locking onto me with that fiery, wild heat. I can feel how close he is, the way his cock swells and pulses, desperate for release, chasing that final rush.

But I'm not letting him have it. Not yet. I want him to crave me more, to burn with so much need that I'm the only thing on his mind, the only thing he'll ever want.

I smirk as I lift my head, pulling his cock from my mouth slowly, watching the frustration twist his face. The groan that escapes him is deep, thick with desperation, and I can feel the tension radiating from his body as he fights the urge to take control. If his hands weren't tied, he'd have me exactly where he wants me—fingers tangled in my hair, guiding me until he's buried deep in my throat, using my mouth like every other time we've been together. But now, the power is mine, and I can see just how much it's driving him wild. His eyes burn with hunger, screaming how badly he wants to fuck me, but I'll make him wait, savoring every second of his torment.

If anyone's doing the fucking, it's me. Not him. Not like last time when he had me coming undone with every move, owning my body in a way no one ever has. This time, it's my turn. My turn to take control, to make him unravel until there's nothing left but raw, primal need. I want to see him lose every ounce of restraint, to fall apart beneath me, completely at my mercy. I'm going to make him beg for it, crave it, and then I'll take exactly what I need.

I drag my tongue up his body, savoring every inch of his warm skin, tracing each hard line of his abs, feeling the way his muscles tense beneath my touch. His breath quickens, and I smirk as I slide my leg over, so I am straddling him. His cock presses hard against my pussy, and I can't help but grind against him, letting that delicious friction ignite a fire between us. My lips move over his chest, moving over the ink on his skin, trailing up his neck until I finally reach his mouth. He kisses me with a hunger that makes me breathless. I slide my soaked pussy along his shaft, teasing him while the tension builds with every slow, deliberate movement of my hips.

Ace groans, so I grind harder against him, feeling every inch of his cock running through my folds. His body reacts to mine, his hips lifting, desperate for more friction, for the sweet release I'm teasing him with. Sitting up, I let my hands run slowly over his chiseled chest, tracing the inked lines of his tattoos, his breath coming in ragged gasps.

He's a mess of raw desire beneath me, and it only heightens my own need. I lean down, letting my tits brush against his skin, and whisper, "I'm going to fuck you, Ace. And you're going to beg for it."

His eyes burn with a mix of lust and surrender, and I feel his cock twitch beneath me, throbbing with need. His jaw clenches, muscles straining as he fights for control, but I can tell it's slipping, and fuck, I love every second of it. My body hums knowing I have this power over him, knowing he's right where I want him—ready, desperate, and waiting for me to make him lose every ounce of control he's barely holding onto.

"I want you to ride me until I can't think straight, Scar," he growls, his voice deep and desperate. "I want you to squeeze every fucking drop out of me with that tight pussy."

I turn my attention to his cock, lifting my hips slightly, wrapping my fingers around it, guiding it carefully into position, ready to slide down onto him. As I hold him ready, I pause for a moment, glancing back at him, catching the smoldering intensity in his eyes as he watches his cock, as if waiting for the exact moment when our bodies finally connect. Slowly, I lower myself onto his thick shaft, savoring every inch as I take my time, feeling it slip through my wet opening, my pussy stretching around him. I bite down on my bottom lip, loving the delicious sensation of him filling me, inch by inch. He watches as I take him deeper and deeper. I let out a moan and close my eyes at the divine feeling as he fills me completely.

When I finally open my eyes, I find him watching my face, and I take a moment to savor the sensation of having him buried deep inside me. When our eyes meet, I feel that strong pull—the primal need to give each other what we are craving. I move slowly, twisting my hips just right, coaxing those delicious sounds from him. I can see his body respond, muscles tightening as he pulls against the restraints, yanking at the belt above his head, desperate to escape so he can take control of how we fuck.

I know exactly what he wants.

He wants to flip me over, put my ass in the air, and drive his cock deep into my pussy, claiming me from behind with that raw, primal intensity he's so good at.

I can picture his fingers tangling in my hair, pulling my head back as he fucks me hard, owning every inch of me. But right now, I want his eyes locked on mine.

I keep my movements deliberate, slow, allowing him to feel every inch of me as I ride him, making this moment ours—something more than just another mindless fuck. I want him to understand that this is about more than just pleasure; it's about the connection we share, and the way our bodies fit together like they were made for this.

Sliding down his shaft, I ramp up the pace, and I watch as his eyes flutter shut, a deep groan spilling from his lips. "Fucking hell, Scar," he breathes, his voice thick with need. His eyes suddenly snap open, and as I fuck him, my hands glide down my body, teasingly trailing over my breasts, pinching my nipples while I savor the way his gaze hungrily follows my every movement.

"Rub that fucking clit," he orders, his voice a husky growl as his eyes drop to where my hand is. The moment I slide my finger over my throbbing clit, he lets out a guttural moan. "Fuck yeah. That's so fucking hot."

The way I'm turning him on only fuels my desire. I pick up the pace, grinding down on him, riding him harder and deeper, feeling his urgent need mix with mine. Every thrust, every teasing brush of my finger against my swollen clit tightens the coil of pleasure inside me, driving me closer to the edge. It's like we're caught in a whirlwind of raw desire, feeding off each other's lust, both of us desperate for more, pushing for that explosive release that feels so close yet just out of reach.

I'm getting more turned on watching the way he watches me ride him, his eyes locked onto my fingers as they tease my clit. I drop my head back, surrendering to the sensation, focusing on how fucking good it feels to have him buried deep inside me. The rhythmic pulse of my clit throbs in time with my touch, building the heat between us, pushing me closer to the edge.

"Undo my wrists, Scar," he growls, his voice thick with desire, laced with urgency. I drop my head and open my eyes, locking onto the raw want, the desperate need, the lust radiating from him.

"No," I reply, my voice steady and firm, dripping with defiance. "I said I was fucking you, and that's exactly what I'm doing."

He groans, and I can see the effect I'm having on him. My movements become frantic when his cock finds that sweet spot. A loud moan escapes my lips, the urge to explode building with every pulse, every thrust. The pleasure rolls through me, intensifying, making my body tremble as I teeter on the edge. When the first wave crashes over me, I cry out, unable to hold back, and just as he thrusts his hips hard, driving deeper into my pussy, I surrender to the moment, letting him take over and lead us both into oblivion.

With two more powerful thrusts, everything shatters. I scream, the intensity overwhelming as my body tightens around him. I come hard on his cock, lost in the bliss of it all, needing him to pull every ounce of pleasure from me.

"Fucking hell, Ace," I scream, just like I have so many times before when he draws a shattering orgasm from me—something no one else has ever come close to doing. But fuck me, this man right here, with his incredible cock, is something else entirely.

As I come down from my high, I watch him, his hips thrusting back and forth, relentless. His face is taut with determination, breaths ragged as he chases his own release. The deep grunts he makes and the way his expression twists with pleasure is fucking mesmerizing.

It's like watching a masterpiece in motion, each thrust bringing him closer to that explosive climax, and I can't look away.

Then, I see it—the moment he comes. I feel his hot release fill me, our connection igniting into something primal I can't quite explain. His eyes lock onto mine, and the raw intensity radiates between us as he rides out the last waves of his orgasm, flooding me completely. I grip him tight, my nails digging into his skin as the aftershocks of my own climax leave me trembling, hungry for more of him, craving every inch of his body.

Leaning forward, I crash my lips against his, his hips still rocking, driving his thick cock deeper as he groans into my mouth. It's the hottest fucking thing, knowing I've completely undone Ace—the man who always keeps everyone at arm's length, who's never experienced anything beyond a quick, emotionless fuck. But now? He's mine, unraveled and desperate, connected to me in a way that shatters everything he's ever known.

His kiss is fierce and demanding, a raw mix of need and lust. When his hips finally slow, I pull back, sitting up to catch the glint of his eyes as they ravenously travel over my body. His gaze lingers on my breasts, and I catch him licking his lips, the hunger in his expression making me ache all over. It pulls at something deep within me, a wild craving that I know I shouldn't indulge. I remind myself that, for him, I'm just a good time—a quick fuck, just like he said.

As our breathing steadies, I plaster on my mask, pretending this was just another casual encounter. I can't let him see that it means more to me. Sliding off him, I get up onto my feet and stand at the side of the bed. His eyes track my every movement, burning into me, but he doesn't say a word. Not even when I leave him lying there - hands bound above his head - as I make my way into the bathroom.

I close the door behind me, leaning against it for a second, trying to steady my breath. The intensity of what just happened—how deeply it affected me—is something I need to lock away, burying it deep down where he'll never find it.

After I've cleaned myself up, I head back into the bedroom. Ace's eyes immediately fixate on me as I enter, the intensity of his gaze makes my heart race. I can feel the weight of his stare as I move over to the bed. Leaning over him to free his wrists, the heat radiating off his body is almost palpable, yet neither of us breaks the silence.

As I free him, a flutter of worry creeps in. What if he didn't like it? What if he only wants to fuck someone who fits his own expectations? I step back from the bed, my heart racing as I search for my clothes. I slip on my bra, shirt, panties, and shorts as quickly as I can, all while trying to avoid looking back at him.

But when I finally glance up, I catch him watching me, and embarrassment floods my system, heat creeping up my neck. I quickly make my way to the door, pulling it open with shaky hands. Just before I slip out, I take one last look back, only to find those intense eyes still locked on me.

Fuck. What the hell have I done?

# CHAPTER 11

## Ace

Fuck me. I can't stop thinking about yesterday. It was fucking insane. No girl has ever gotten to me the way Scarlet did. I'm always the one in control, but the way she rode my cock and reveled in it—God, I've replayed it in my head a hundred times, sometimes with my cock in my hand. Who would've thought that shy, sexy little blonde could make me lose my shit like that? Well, fuck, that's a new one.

I've been with plenty of women, sometimes even more than one at a time, and none of them ever made me feel the way she did. All the filthy things they've done, the stuff I've seen—it doesn't compare to how she blew my fucking mind yesterday.

When it was over, I didn't know what the fuck to say because I didn't know how to handle what I was feeling. And yeah, I know I broke the bro code again. But that hot-as-fuck moment with her—I wouldn't trade it for anything. Still, there was this awkward tension between us after, and for the life of me, I can't figure out why.

I snap out of my haze when I hear my phone ping. Moving over to the countertop where I left it, I flip it over to see a message from Xander.

**Xander:** You need to come over here.

Fuck. Has he found out I was with Scarlet again? My heart kicks up a notch, and I quickly type back.

**Ace:** Why?

As my fingers hover over the screen, I feel the weight of yesterday's events crashing back into me. There's no way he could possibly know. Right? I grip my phone, heart pounding, praying like fuck that Xander hasn't found out about what went down with Scarlet. No, if he knew, there'd be no texts—he'd show up here, ready to knock me on my ass.

I exhale the breath I didn't even realize I was holding and stare at the screen. The bubbles flicker for a moment before his message pops up.

**Xander:** Band meeting about the press conference today.

I slump against the counter, relief flooding through me, but my pulse is still racing. I inwardly groan. I've been riding high on the afterglow of yesterday's wild session with Scarlet, and now Xander's dragging me back to reality with this paparazzi bullshit. Just my fucking luck.

Slipping my phone into my pocket, I head for the door, already thinking of some bullshit excuse to dodge the press.

After that mess with the asshole photographer, there's no way I'm dealing with the media right now. Xander can handle it—he's been through enough of this crap, especially after the scandal with the underage girl that Reg, that piece of shit, set up during our Australian tour.

I walk down my front steps and stroll towards Xander's place.

Up ahead, I spot Theo stepping out of his house. Pausing on the front steps, he glances back toward the door. Scarlet appears, enjoying a slice of toast, her tousled hair falling around her shoulders as if she had just got out of bed. She looks stunning, as usual. As I watch her take a bite of toast, memories of what her mouth did to me yesterday flood my mind, and I feel my cock twitch.

Fuck. I quickly turn my head, forcing the thoughts out of my mind.

Now's definitely not the time to be thinking about that, especially with the guys around. They know me too damn well—they'd figure out something's up in no time.

When I reach Xander's house, I take the front steps, two at a time and swing open the door without bothering to announce my arrival. I cut through the front room and head straight for the kitchen. Scattered music sheets on the grand piano tell me that Poppy's been messing around with her favorite songs again. The floor is littered with Alex's LEGO pieces. Now, the place feels more like a home, filled with a welcoming atmosphere that is worlds away from the cold empty vibe when Xander was living here alone.

I walk into the kitchen and spot Xander hunched over the counter, focused on a pile of papers with his half-eaten breakfast beside him.

"Whatever the fuck you're thinking, I'm not doing it," I say, cutting right to the chase.

Xander straightens up, hits me with that look—the one that says, "You're fucking doing it." He doesn't even need to say a word, just raises an eyebrow like he's completely unimpressed. He takes a slow sip of his coffee, his eyes locked on me with that mix of annoyance.

I scowl, crossing my arms. "I'm not in the fucking mood to deal with this media shit. I've got more important things to do, like finishing our damn album." Behind me, I hear voices growing louder—Theo and Scarlet are on their way in. But I keep my eyes locked on Xander, letting him see exactly how pissed I am.

As Xander sets his coffee cup down with a resounding clink, Theo and Scarlet enter.

The atmosphere shifts with their arrival. Theo flashes me that cocky smirk of his, his eyes gleaming with confidence, while Scarlet's restless gaze darts between me and Xander, like she's waiting for someone to snap.

"Quick, take a seat, Scar," Theo says with that annoying grin. "It's pretty entertaining watching these two fuckers go at it."

I shoot him a glare, but his smug grin just makes it worse.

"No one's going at it," Xander snaps, clearly fed up with Theo's bullshit. He grabs his coffee and the stack of papers, then strides over to the table where Theo and Scarlet are already sitting.

When Xander sits down and notices I'm still standing there, he nudges a chair out with his foot, a silent order for me to join him. Then he lowers his head, shuffling through the papers like it's the most important thing in the world.

"Kit has scheduled a press conference today at twelve," Xander announces, lifting his gaze to lock onto mine. "We're all required to be there to make a statement about the upcoming tour and to introduce Scarlet."

I let out a frustrated sigh and head over to the table. I can already picture the storm of questions and scrutiny headed my way.

"You know this is just going to turn into a shitstorm about what happened three days ago," I say, pulling out a chair, all while avoiding eye contact with Scarlet, who's sitting across from me.

"Ace, I fucking get it," Xander snaps, his frustration palpable. "Trust me, I know how those assholes operate. I've dealt with their bullshit firsthand. But this is about our label now. If we want to prove to the world and that prick Lionel that we can stand on our own, you need to get your head out of your ass and face this. Every media outlet is gonna run with the story that we can't make it without Victory Records," he says, leaning forward on his elbows, glaring at me like I'm a damn idiot. "This is our chance to show them and our fans that the tour is still on and to officially introduce Scarlet as Nate's replacement. You need to be there and put all that bullshit aside."

"You know they won't let it go. They'll just keep pushing," I say, frustration creeping into my voice.

I glance over and see Scarlet and Theo watching us as we keep firing questions at each other.

"I know," Xander replies, his tone clipped. "But you can deflect. Just keep steering the conversation back to the tour. We've been doing that for years, so it shouldn't be that hard."

Theo rests a hand on my shoulder, that stupid grin of his making me want to punch him right now.

"You'll be fine, man. Just don't pull any of that dumbass shit you're famous for. If you go full "Ace" on them, I'll make sure to distract them with my epic dance moves." He laughs.

I can't help but grin at the asshole; he always knows how to lighten the mood. Scarlet bursts out laughing at his comment, and I glance over at her, a smile forming on my lips. Her eyes lock with mine as she laughs, and I can't tear my gaze away while the laughter around the table slowly fades.

Then Xander's voice cuts in, pulling Scarlet's attention away from me. "Scarlet, did you ever do a press conference with your old band?"

"No," she replies, a smile dancing on her lips. "If we had, no one would've shown up or given a damn."

Her smile is infectious, and I can't seem to tear my eyes away from her. I know I should play it cool because if I don't snap out of it soon, Theo will catch on to what's been brewing between us, and Xander will definitely know I've gone there again with her.

"Bit of a heads-up, Scarlet," Xander says, taking another sip of his coffee before setting the mug back on the table. "These guys can be real assholes. If they latch onto something, they'll run with it, so we need this press conference to go smoothly. Usually, Ace handles the talking for the band, but with everything that's gone down, I'll do most of it this time. I'll start with a statement about the tour and introduce you as Nate's replacement for the two-month run. After that, they'll get a chance to ask you questions."

Scarlet glances around the group, a flicker of anxiety flashing in her eyes. "What kind of questions?"

"Probably the usual stuff," Theo says, flashing a reassuring smile. "Questions about your music, how you're feeling about joining the band. Just standard shit, you know. You'll be fine, Scar, trust me." He reaches out, wrapping his hand around hers and giving it a comforting squeeze. "You'll nail it."

Scarlet's eyes soften, and she nods, her nervousness easing a bit. It's clear that with Theo's support, she can handle the pressure of the tour. I've always seen Theo as the class clown, the fucking idiot, the guy who's always up for a laugh, but with Scarlet, there's a different side to him. He's not just the comic relief. He's her rock. Always there to reassure her and back her up. And I can't help but feel a twinge of jealousy, wishing I could be that for her too.

"Scarlet, I really hate to bring this shit up," Xander says, his tone shifting to something more serious.

Scarlet turns to him, her brows knitting together in concern, while Theo and I exchange glances, both of us wondering where this is going.

Xander takes a deep breath, clearly choosing his words carefully. "I see your bruises are healing," he says, motioning to his own cheek to indicate where Scarlet's marks have faded. "But you need to keep them covered. If the media catches a glimpse, they'll start digging into shit we don't want to deal with. We can't afford that kind of distraction right now."

"I promise you they won't see them," Scarlet replies, her voice a little softer as she drops her head, clearly feeling a bit embarrassed.

I catch Theo giving her hand another reassuring squeeze, silently backing her up.

Theo chimes in. "Nate will be watching the press conference from the hospital," he says, his tone filled with warmth. "He's proud of you, Scar. So am I. And so are Mom and Dad," he adds, and I can see how much those words mean to her, like a lifeline pulling her back up.

There are those words again.

Mom and Dad.

It hit me earlier, back in the waiting room, when I saw Wes and Rose, Nate and Scarlet's parents, walk into the hospital. Theo called them Mom and Dad like it was the most natural thing in the world. I've never been close enough to Theo to dig into his past, but from what he's let slip, I know he had a rough upbringing. Still, I have no fucking clue how he ended up with Nate's family or how he managed to fit into their lives so seamlessly that they see him as one of their own.

As soon as Wes walked into the room, striding straight to Theo giving him a fatherly pat on the back, and Rose wrapped him in a warm hug, speaking to him like she'd been his mom his whole life, a sharp stab of envy pierced through me. I just stood there, staring, trying to make sense of it all. How do they love him like that? Like he's really theirs, as if he was born into their family? It doesn't make any sense to me, especially when my own mother couldn't give two flying fucks about me, and I'm her own flesh and blood. The contrast hits hard, twisting something deep inside me, making me question why I've never had that kind of connection, that unconditional love, from anyone.

"Kit has arranged a car to pick us up at eleven-thirty, so be ready," Xander says, downing the last of his coffee.

"Is that it?" I ask, glancing at him to see if there's any more bullshit he wants to throw my way.

"Yeah," he replies, and I can sense that if Scarlet wasn't sitting here at this moment, he'd be telling me to pull my fucking head in.

I push back from the table, my mind spinning with all the shit I've got to handle—like the new album that's just sitting there, waiting for me to dive into it. That's where my focus should be, not on this fucking press conference. But I get it. If I don't show up to introduce Scarlet and confirm the tour's still on, those assholes will twist it into something ugly, making it look like I don't want her there or that the band's falling apart. I can't let that happen.

Before we go out to greet the media, Kit takes us to one of the back rooms and explains our assigned seating arrangements at the table. I can already hear the soft murmur of voices and the excited buzz of anticipation coming from the other room.

"Now, Ace," Kit says, placing herself in front of me.  My gaze falls upon the tiny woman who has successfully intimidated grown men on countless tours over the years. Despite her small stature, she's got an undeniable presence that demands respect. "No doubt those assholes out there will bring up the camera incident, so when they do, just redirect the conversation back to the tour. And don't let them get under your skin."

"So, in other words," Theo adds with a sly smile, "don't go full Ace on them."

I shoot him a glare, my gaze piercing through his soul. I hate to admit it, but he's not wrong. My reputation for going off-script isn't exactly a secret, and if I'm not careful, this press conference could devolve into a shitshow. I can already see the headline, "Rockstar's latest meltdown becomes media sensation." I just need to keep my cool and not let those fuckheads bait me into saying something stupid.

Taking a deep breath, I force myself to stay calm, though I'm already bracing for the inevitable. If Theo keeps pushing my buttons, it's only a matter of time before I snap and end up thumping him before the day's over. Since we got into that town car to come here, he hasn't stopped with his annoying shit.

The guy gets even more annoying when he's nervous, like he believes cracking jokes will keep his anxiety in check. But if the dickhead keeps it up, he's gonna have a lot more to worry about than just a press conference.

"Relax, man," Xander says, his hand squeezing my shoulder in a half-assed attempt to comfort me. It's meant to be reassuring, but all I feel is the weight of his expectations pressing down on me. "You've been through worse. Stick to the plan, and we'll be outta here in no time."

Yeah, right.

As if I can just zone out while a bunch of vultures pick at our bones.

I nod, but inside, I'm a whirlwind of emotions. It's not just about introducing Scarlet; we're also trying to salvage our reputation, and prove we're more than the drama that constantly follows us. The tension is creeping back, and I can feel it building up inside me. I need a release, and punching Theo is starting to sound like a decent option to blow off some steam.

It's funny. I finally understand why Xander always seemed like he wanted to rip someone's head off when I pushed him into doing these press conferences every time he made headlines. The difference is, Xander never actually messed up like I did.

"Now, Scarlet," Kit says, her tone all business-like and firm, "if they ask you anything uncomfortable out there-"

Scarlet swallows nervously, her anxiety starting to show. "What kind of things will they ask?"

"Any fucked-up thing they can dream up," I reply.

The room goes dead quiet.

All eyes, including Scarlet's, fixate on me—I've definitely made things worse. Scarlet's anxiety is off the charts now.

Theo's sharp look makes it clear that I've made a mistake and should keep my fucking mouth shut. He turns back to Scarlet, his face softening as he tries to reassure her, his voice gentle and comforting. Xander and Kit stay quiet, their expressions speaking volumes—silent messages that cut deeper than anything they could've said aloud.

Theo tries to ease the tension. "It'll be mostly about the music, Scar. You'll see. Plus, you probably won't get hit with too many questions since Xander's doing most of the talking today—especially now that Ace has royally screwed up." He throws me a sharp glare, making it obvious just how pissed he is with me.

Already fed up with being here, I let out a slow exhale, trying to chill the fuck out and keep it together.

"Relax," Kit says to me, her voice soothing, like she's trying to tame a wild animal. "You've done this a hundred times. Today's just another day." She then turns to face everyone, her confidence radiating. "Alright, you ready?" With that, Kit strides toward the door, and I can feel the tension crackling in the air, primed to explode as we brace ourselves for the chaos waiting outside.

Xander leads the way, with me bringing up the rear, while Scarlet and Theo stay close together like they're in some kind of protective bubble.

When Xander gives the nod, Kit swings the door open, and we step through. The flash of cameras greets us like a sudden storm as we make our way toward the table, the noise in the room fading to an inaudible murmur. Kit follows us through the doorway and takes her place to the side, her gaze steady as she observes us settling into our seats.

I grab the bottle of water on the table, trying to quell the anxiety gnawing at my insides. Fuck, I've never felt this off at one of these events before. Usually, I'm the one steering the ship, radiating confidence and control, but today feels different. The air is thick and stifling. I scan the room, taking in the sea of reporters, their eyes glinting with eagerness, all waiting for one of us to slip up so they can spin it into a headline. The pressure builds, and I can feel their expectations weighing down on me, making it hard to breathe.

As the sound of papers rustling reaches my ears, I instinctively look down the table to find Xander preparing to begin. He glances up and flashes that polished media smile—the kind that's all rehearsed and perfect, a stark contrast to the real Xander. It's a far cry from the guy who's been my anchor through everything. I'm thankful to be part of that inner circle; without him, the guys, Poppy, and Alex, I'd feel lost. They're my family too, the ones who truly matter in my life.

Cameras flash, and reporters adjust their microphones, their eyes fixed on us, eager for the drama about to unfold. My heart pounds in my chest, each beat a reminder of the stakes at play. This isn't just about us; it's about everything we've built together and how quickly it could all unravel under the world's scrutiny.

Xander clears his throat, signaling the start of the press conference. "Good afternoon, everyone. Thank you for being here today. We have some important updates to share. As many of you are aware, our talented drummer, Nate Reynolds, was recently involved in a car accident. The good news is that he's expected to make a full recovery, but he'll need some time off to focus on healing. In the meantime, we're thrilled to announce that Scarlet will be stepping in as our drummer for the tour."

I notice that Xander deliberately omitted Scarlet's surname, likely to dodge the comparisons she was worried about. The room zeroes in on him, hanging on every word as he spins the story Kit's carefully crafted, shaping the narrative the way only he can.

The usual murmurs of the reporters fade into the background, and I scan the crowd, trying to read the energy, gauging how they might react to Scarlet stepping up. Will they accept her? Or will this only fuel the media's hunger for more drama?

"Scarlet brings a tremendous level of talent and energy to the band," Xander continues, his voice steady and commanding. "We've been blown away by her during rehearsals, and we're confident she'll keep delivering the high-energy performances our fans expect. I want to assure everyone that the tour is going ahead as scheduled. We're thrilled to hit the road with Scarlet and can't wait to see all our fans at the shows."

As he speaks, I can see the shift in the room. The reporters are scribbling notes, their interest piqued. If only they can see what we see in Scarlet, maybe this could mark the beginning of something great for her.

When Xander finishes his statement, the room goes dead silent for a moment, like everyone is holding their breath. Then, just as the media realizes the briefing is over, the silence explodes into a barrage of questions from all directions.

"Can you give us more details about Nate's condition?"

"How long will Nate be out of action?"

"Why was Scarlet chosen as Nate's replacement?

"What makes Scarlet the right fit for the band?"

"Scarlet, how do you feel about stepping into Nate's role?"

"What do you think makes you the right choice for the band?"

"Scarlet, can you tell us more about your background?"

The intensity of their inquiries crashes over us like a tidal wave.

Scarlet's face reveals her nerves as she steals a glance at Theo, who responds with a comforting nod. Xander, ever the pro, raises his hands to quiet the room, commanding attention with a practiced ease.

"One question at a time, alright? Raise your hands, and we'll call on you in order."

Hands shoot up everywhere, reporters desperate to get their questions answered.

Xander scans the room, his eyes fixating on a reporter in the front row, their pen poised over a notepad.

"You in the front row," Xander says.

"Xander, can you give us more details about Nate's condition and how long he'll be out?" the guy asks, practically bouncing in his seat.

Xander takes a moment to gather himself, then responds, "Nate's dealing with a few broken bones that require a significant amount of time to heal. It's going to take a few months, but trust me, he's determined to return as soon as he can, no matter what." He flashes a confident smile, then moves on, pointing to another reporter. "Next question."

"Why was Scarlet picked as the replacement? What makes her the right fit for the band?"

I can feel the tension in the air—everyone's hanging on Xander's every word, ready to catch whatever drama unfolds. It's like watching a pack of sharks circling, just waiting for a drop of blood. And here we are, right in the middle of it all, exposed and vulnerable.

Xander glances at Scarlet before responding. "Scarlet is seriously talented and knows our band inside and out. She has extensive drumming experience and has truly impressed us. We're confident she's the perfect fit to keep the tour rolling smoothly and deliver the high-energy performances our fans expect," he explains, his voice steady and authoritative.

His assurance is like a lifeline thrown to Scarlet, and I can see her visibly relax a bit. The way he champions her only reinforces what we've all seen in rehearsals—the passion and skill she brings. It's a calculated move, positioning her not just as a replacement but as an integral part of our journey forward.

He then nods to another reporter, signaling for the next question.

A middle-aged reporter turns his gaze toward Scarlet, and I watch her shift awkwardly in her seat, clearly feeling the weight of the moment.

"This one's for you, Scarlet," he says, the anticipation in the room palpable. "Stepping in for a drummer who has such a major impact on the band, how do you plan to maintain his style and energy while you're only here for the tour?"

The question hangs in the air, a heavy challenge aimed right at her, and I see the flicker of nerves cross her face. She hesitates for a moment, her eyes scanning the room as if searching for the right words. I can practically feel her nerves radiating off her, but I know she's stronger than she appears. She'll get through this. Leaning forward, she speaks into the microphone.

"I have plenty of experience with his style," Scarlet responds, her voice growing steadier as she gains confidence. "My goal is to maintain the band's sound and energy throughout the tour. I understand there will be comparisons, and I'm ready for that, but my focus is on delivering the best performance possible for the fans."

Before she can settle back into her seat, another reporter jumps in.

"You mentioned your experience with his style. Can you elaborate on your background and how you're connected to him?"

Scarlet hesitates for a moment, her brow furrowing as she carefully considers her response. She finally chooses to be upfront. "Actually, he's my brother," she admits, a hint of pride creeping into her voice. "I've learned a lot from him over the years."

A buzz of disbelief fills the room, and another reporter exclaims, "Wait a minute, you're saying you're Nate's sister?"

"Let me jump in here," Xander interjects. "Yes, Scarlet is Nate's sister. She possesses the talent and style that align perfectly with the band. We're confident she's the right choice. Now, who has the next question?"

I can see Scarlet relax slightly at Xander's reassurance, and it's a reminder of how much this team has her back.

"Ace, have you taken any steps to address the situation with the paparazzi after the camera incident?"

My stomach clenches with unease as the question lingers in the air. "No comment," I reply, shifting uncomfortably in my chair. I had a feeling this shit would come up sooner or later, and it's just as awkward as I expected.

"Next," Xander jumps in, cutting off any further questions on that topic and pointing to another reporter.

"Xander, with the new album dropping soon, what can fans expect in terms of sound and direction compared to your previous work?"

Xander leans forward in his chair, speaking into the mic. "With the new album dropping soon, fans can expect us to return to our original sound while incorporating some new elements. Now that we're under our own label, we've really focused on recapturing what made our music special from the start. It's going to be a great mix of familiar vibes and new energy." He gestures toward the back of the room, signaling for another question.

"Ace, following that incident where you smashed the camera, how are you dealing with the aftermath, and have you reached out to apologize?"

I shoot a glare at the asshole, my patience fraying.

All these idiots care about is stirring up gossip.

Leaning forward, I rest my elbows on the table.

"Listen, we're here to talk about the new album and our new drummer, so let's focus on that."

I lean back in my chair, crossing my arms over my chest, frustration simmering just beneath the surface. Xander gestures for another question, clearly eager to steer us away from this bullshit.

"Scarlet, is it because you're Nate's sister that you got this role?"

I glance over and catch the hurt flicker across Scarlet's face. No wonder she hates this shit; they don't see her talent; they only see her as Nate's sister.

"What kind of fucking question is that?" I snap, my tone biting and unforgiving as I glare at the jerk who dared to ask her that.

Everyone turns to look at me, including the three band members beside me, and a murmur ripples through the crowd. The atmosphere shifts, thick with tension.

"This conference is over," Xander declares, his tone leaving no room for argument as he stands and collects his papers from the table. He shoots me a pointed, disapproving glare, clearly signaling that I've completely fucked up.

Pushing their chairs back, Scarlet and Theo follow closely behind Xander as he heads out of the room. I get up and fall in line behind them, feeling the intensity rise as the assholes in the crowd shout questions, their desperation evident in their attempts to provoke me. I ignore every single one of them, my eyes locked on the door, just wanting to escape this chaos.

Kit slams the door shut, ending the onslaught of blinding flashes and deafening shouts.

Xander swiftly turns towards me, his eyes filled with a fiery frustration. "What the fuck, Ace?" he snaps, stepping in close, his anger unmistakable.

"What? It was a fucked-up question, and you know it," I shoot back,.

"They always have fucked-up questions." Xander's gaze narrows, piercing through me as if he's trying to read my mind. "Back when we were with the old label, you'd do anything to make sure we stayed out of the headlines. Now that we're out on our own, it's like you're just constantly fucking up. What the hell is going on with you, man?"

# CHAPTER 12

## Scarlet

It's been a week since that press conference, and every damn day, that asshole's question keeps replaying in my head like a broken record, making me question why I even agreed to do this. The moment the question left his mouth, a surge of anger hit me, and I had no clue how to even begin to respond. I wanted to lash out, and tell him to go to hell for treating me the way everyone else does when they learn who I am. But I couldn't. That's just not me.

Despite all the shit he's dealing with, I'm glad Ace had the guts to call out that idiot, and his stupid question. I wish I could speak my mind like that, without constantly needing to wear a mask in front of others. That's what I really admire about Ace. He never holds back. No sugarcoating, no bullshit. He just tells it like it is, and maybe that's something I need to learn.

Every day since then, I've been grinding away, immersing myself in the music, and committing to memory each song and its place in the setlist. The guys, especially Theo, have been remarkably patient and supportive. He's always been there for me, supporting me through thick and thin. But no matter how hard I practice, that journalist's words keep echoing in my head. What if I'm not good enough? What if they only gave me the gig because I'm Nate's sister?

No, that can't be it. They wouldn't jeopardize everything by putting me in a position that could potentially ruin their shows. With a burning desire to prove my critics wrong, I push myself to the limit, practicing relentlessly until I reach my breaking point. I have to nail this—there's no room for error, especially since the guys are relying on me.

On top of everything, I'm pissed that Ace is straight-up avoiding me. Every time the band gets together to run through the songs, he turns his back like I don't even exist. When I ask questions, he doesn't even bother to acknowledge me. It's always Theo and Xander who step up and help. At first, I told myself he was just stressed, needing to focus on getting the album out. But it's been four days since the album dropped, and nothing's changed. He's still ignoring me, acting like I'm invisible. What the hell is his problem?

On a brighter note, the album hit number one the day it dropped, and the guys were over the moon. That night, they headed to the hospital to celebrate with Nate. I wasn't too keen on tagging along, thinking I'd let them enjoy their milestone without me. But Theo wasn't having any of it and practically dragged me along. Even though Ace didn't say a word to me all night, I could still feel his eyes on me. Every damn time I glanced in his direction, he'd quickly look away, like he hadn't just been staring at me a second ago.

What the fuck is up with that? This hot-and-cold bullshit is driving me nuts. I know he sees me as nothing more than a casual fling, and yeah, it was awkward as hell after we hooked up, but come on. He can't even manage two words now. Seriously, what the hell is that about?

Sitting here in my brother's house, I can't help but feel an overwhelming sense of loneliness, as if the walls themselves are closing in on me. Theo's off visiting Nate, and once again, I didn't want to tag along and feel like a third wheel. I slump back on the couch, feeling the weight of the oppressive silence. Letting out a deep sigh, I yearn for someone to confide in, a girlfriend, anyone to talk to about the man who constantly consumes my thoughts, the man who's been avoiding me like I don't exist.

Last night, we had a big family dinner to say goodbye to Dad. Now that Nate is recovering, he's going back to run his business, leaving Mom behind to assist Nate once he's discharged from the hospital. As I sat across the table from Xander and Poppy, waiting for my meal, something hit me hard. Observing the way Xander's gaze lingers on Poppy, and the way she is his entire world, it made me yearn for the same—someone who supports me unconditionally, loving me for exactly who I am.

That envy sparked something deep inside me—a newfound determination. I'm done with Ace. No matter how much I crave him or how badly I want to feel his touch, I won't allow myself to be treated like a casual fling anymore. I deserve better than that, and I'm not settling for being his plaything. Not anymore.

After dinner, we all went to visit Nate at the hospital, and that's when I found out he'd gone behind my back and hired a mover to pack up all my stuff and put it in storage. He organized everything with my landlord, and the whole thing was done without me even knowing. As much as I love Nate, sometimes it feels like I have zero control over my life. When he told me, all I wanted to do was scream at him, but instead, I forced a smile to keep the peace. However, I did manage to tell him that it should've been my choice, not his.

The truth is, even though I'm pissed, part of me is relieved. The idea of going back to that place, and having to deal with Beck again...Well, it scares the shit out of me.

With everything weighing me down—the pressure of the tour and the uncertainty of the future—I ended up sleeping in this morning. I just couldn't bring myself to get out of bed. I could feel myself spiraling back into that dark place, and there was no way I was going to visit Nate like this.

When Theo walked into my room and flopped down beside me, I knew he could sense that something was off. He's always been able to read my moods like a book. When he asked what was wrong, I tried to hide my emotions with a forced smile, but he could tell I was faking it. He pulled me in for a hug, the kind he always gives when he knows I'm struggling.

With Mom checking out of her hotel and moving into this house tonight, it's time for me to get my shit together. Otherwise, she'll start asking questions I'm not ready to answer. Mom has this uncanny ability to see right through me, and the last thing I want is for her to worry or pry into the depths of my thoughts. I just need to pull myself together and put on a brave face—at least for her sake. I can't let her see just how much I'm struggling right now. It's like I have to wear this mask of strength, even when I feel completely broken inside.

Once I finish showering and have a quick bite to eat, I make my way to the recording studio to hone my skills. With the tour kicking off in just three days, I need to go through the entire playlist, running every song through my head.

Making my way up the front steps of Ace's magnificent home, I take a deep breath. I push open the door, my heart racing as I imagine the sight of him. But when I notice he's not there, a wave of relief washes over me, and I let out a sigh. With everything I'm dealing with, I'm just not in the mood to face him today. I just want to immerse myself in the music.

Making my way toward the drums, I grab the folded paper with the entire setlist from my pocket. I put it down beside the drum kit, knowing it'll be a handy backup if I need a quick reference, though I'm confident I can pull it off without looking at it. As I hold the drumsticks in my hands, I take a moment to center myself and let their familiar weight soothe my nerves. This is exactly where I belong, and I'm determined as ever to prove it.

With a deep breath, I dive into the first song, letting the rhythm take over and pushing all my doubts aside. Each beat feels like a step closer to showing I'm a drummer in my own right—someone who deserves to be here, not just because of my brother, but because I've got the talent and determination to back it up.

As I lose myself in the music, I transition smoothly from one song to the next. Each track builds my confidence, and I can feel myself hitting every beat exactly as it should be. By the time I reach the last song on the playlist, "Creep"—a cover the guys always perform—I allow myself to finally relax. I savor the soft, slow beat, taking a moment to catch my breath and appreciate the progress I've made.

As I take a deep breath and look up, my rhythm stumbles the moment I spot Ace standing in the doorway, casually leaning against the frame with his arms crossed over his chest. His eyes, intense and burning with an almost predatory gaze, send a shiver down my spine. The air crackles with an undeniable charge between us, that makes it nearly impossible for me to maintain a steady rhythm.

Despite the distraction, I push through, but his piercing gaze makes it difficult to concentrate. Every beat I play feels scrutinized, and I exert all my focus to resist the magnetic pull he exudes. Determined not to let him affect my performance, I lower my head, attempting to shield myself from the intensity of his gaze, which seems to trace my every movement.

But even with my eyes down, I can sense him moving closer, the subtle shift in the air signaling his approach. My heart pounds, the rhythm of the drums syncing with the rapid thumping in my chest. I can't let this moment break me; I refuse to be distracted by the chaos he brings into my head.

When the song ends, I sit there, sweaty and breathless, reluctant to look up. After taking a few deep breaths, I finally lift my head. Ace strides over to the far wall, grabs two bottles of water, and starts making his way back toward me. His eyes move over me and the desire to feel his hands on my body is overwhelming.

"You're really getting it now," he says, handing me a bottle.

I take the bottle from him, remaining silent, still pissed about the way he's been totally avoiding me.

Ace sits down on the nearby step, unscrews the lid, and takes a long drink. As he tilts his head back, I can't help but watch the way his throat moves as he swallows. Just as he lowers his head, I avert my gaze and focus on opening my own bottle.

"You should have said you were coming," Ace says. "I would have jammed with you."

After taking a quick sip from the bottle, I replace the lid, trying my best to maintain my composure. "I just wanted to make sure I had it right," I reply, leaning forward to set the bottle down near my feet.

"Theo mentioned Nate's coming home tomorrow," Ace continues, catching me off guard. It's unusual for him to engage in small talk, especially considering his recent behavior.

"Yeah," I respond, confused as to why he's talking to me now after avoiding me for so long.

"Listen, Scarlet," Ace says, his tone suddenly serious. When I lift my head to meet his gaze, our eyes lock for a brief moment before he looks away. "When we get out on tour, the press can be real assholes. You saw how they were the other day. That comment they made was fucked up."

I look away, fumbling with the drumsticks in my hands. "It's cool, Ace. It's no different from the crap people usually say. I'm used to it."

Even though I'm not facing him, I can feel the weight of his gaze, penetrating and intense. "I just want you to know," he continues, his voice steady and unwavering, "that no matter what they write or say, Xander and I wouldn't have brought you into the band if you weren't up to the standard. This is a big deal for us—the first tour under our new label. So it wasn't handed to you just because of Nate. I want you to remember that, no matter how much those fuckers keep spouting their bullshit. They'll twist things to make headlines, and half of it isn't even true."

Nodding, I feel a slight release of tension, like a burden lifted. "Thanks, Ace. It means a lot to hear that."

He nods in acknowledgment, then his eyes sweep across the room. After a moment, he stands and makes his way towards his guitar. "You want to go over some songs together?" he suggests, his tone more relaxed.

"Before we do that, can I ask you something?" I say, trying to keep my voice steady. I'm not usually this straightforward, but it feels important to bring it up.

"Yeah," he replies, his eyes locked on the guitar as he slips the strap over his head and adjusts it on his shoulder. When I remain silent, his attention shifts back to me.

"Can I ask why you've been avoiding me?" I ask.

I catch a flicker of surprise on his face, and I see him swallow hard. His gaze drops to his guitar as he fiddles with the neck. "It's just easier that way, Scar," he says.

"Easier, how?" I press.

He lets out a deep breath, clearly reluctant to answer my question. "It just is, that's all," he says, his tone abrupt as he shifts the topic. "Now, are you ready to go through the set?" His gaze remains fixed on his guitar, avoiding mine, as if the instrument provides a shield against the conversation.

Ace's fingers effortlessly pluck a few strings on his guitar, the sharp and crisp sound instantly snapping me back to reality. As he counts us in, I shift my focus to the task at hand, ready to dive into the work. With each beat, I remind myself to push aside the confusion and channel my energy into the music.

Like everyone else, I am excited to finally have my brother home. Theo and I hang up colorful balloons, filling the room with a festive atmosphere, while Poppy expertly bakes a mouthwatering welcome home cake. Ace and Xander take charge of the beers and have a ton of pizzas delivered. However, it's difficult to overlook the peculiar feeling of seeing my brother in such a broken state. I can see it in his eyes; he absolutely hates being like this. He'd give anything to be a part of the tour, doing what he loves—being on stage in front of thousands of fans, feeling their energy.

As we sit around the table, surrounded by leftover pizza and cake, I can feel Ace's gaze on me. Each time I catch him looking, he quickly shifts his eyes away, as if it's an instinctive reaction, which leaves me feeling both frustrated and confused. What the hell is going on with him? Why the hell won't he make eye contact? It's getting harder and harder to overlook the mounting tension between us, and it's driving me insane. I want to bridge whatever gap has formed between us, but it feels like I'm stuck in a game I don't understand, with rules that constantly elude me.

At the table, everyone's eyes are fixed on Alex. He sits on Xander's lap, leaning forward, his elbows on the table as he enthusiastically shares his recent adventures with a woman he lovingly refers to as GG.

Glancing around the table, I can feel the love and warmth emanating from everyone towards this little boy. It's truly a beautiful sight. I catch Theo's radiant smile and Nate's joyful grin, both of them wearing expressions of pure contentment. Despite everything Theo has been through, there is a genuine happiness that radiates from him. Seeing him and Nate like this fills me with a profound sense of peace.

With my eyes back on Alex, Nate's hand reaches out to take mine, giving it a comforting squeeze. It's a gesture he's done countless times over the years. I give him a smile, attempting to conceal the whirlwind of anxiety brewing within me. Worries about making mistakes, becoming a headline for the wrong reasons, and confirming others' doubts plague my thoughts.

Nate doesn't let go of my hand. Instead, he turns his attention back to Alex, who is animatedly recounting a trip to an animal sanctuary. Nate's thumb glides softly over the back of my hand, offering a comforting touch that calms my anxiety and anchors me in the moment. As the conversation shifts to the upcoming tour, I see a spark of excitement illuminate Ace and Xander's expressions. They eagerly talk about the sold-out stadiums and the thrill of performing live.

Meanwhile, I try to zone out, pushing away the nerves about stepping into the spotlight. The sound of my name brings me back to reality in an instant. As my eyes lift, I feel the weight of everyone's attention focused solely on me.

"You ready to show me, Scar?" Nate asks, glancing sideways at me.

I nod, forcing a smile. "Yeah, sure."

Poppy and my mom stand up, their hands full of plates as they encourage everyone else to do the same. The room buzzes with activity as plates clink together and chairs screech against the floor.

"She's so good, Nate, we might just let her stay in and let you take a permanent vacation. Better watch out!" Theo teases, with a wide, playful grin. I can see how much more at ease he is now that Nate is back home; his relaxed demeanor is a stark contrast to the tension he's been grappling with.

Theo's attention shifts as Alex comes bounding up to him, his eyes sparkling with excitement. "Do you want to see the animals I got from the sanctuary, Uncle Theo?" Alex asks eagerly, practically bouncing on his feet.

Theo's face lights up with a wide grin. "I thought you'd never ask," he replies. "But I've got to make it quick—I need to show Uncle Nate how Aunt Scarlet's stealing the spotlight in the band!"

Nate and I watch in silence, both of us smiling as Theo gets up and follows Alex toward the front door.

"You okay?" Nate asks, noticing my quiet demeanor. "You seem a bit off."

I glance over at him, feeling a pang of vulnerability. "Just a little worried about messing everything up, I guess."

Nate gives my hand a reassuring squeeze. "You'll be fine, Scar. I've seen you handle way worse, and I know you've got this."

His confidence in me eases some of the tension I'm feeling. "Thanks, Nate. I just hope I can live up to everyone's expectations."

"You don't need to worry about that. Everyone here has your back, Scar, and we all believe in you. I know I do."

I nod, taking in the nearly empty room. The kitchen is alive with the rhythmic clatter of dishes and the steady hum of running water as Poppy and Mom chat, their voices blending with the sounds as they finish up the last of the plates and stack them in the dishwasher.

"You're gonna have a blast, Scar," Nate says. "Just remember to enjoy every moment." He slowly rises from his seat, moving cautiously due to the stiff cast and the immobilization of his arm. Looking down at me, he asks, "Ready to head over to the studio?"

"Yeah." I push myself up and walk alongside Nate as we leave the house.

Stepping outside into the soft twilight, heading toward Ace's place, Nate's mood undergoes a noticeable change. "You know," he mutters, his voice filled with intensity, "this shit with Beck isn't over. If I ever cross paths with him again, I'll kick his ass."

I turn to him, shaking my head. "Nate, drop it. I don't want to think about Beck or any of that right now. I've got enough on my plate without adding that mess to the mix."

As we approach Xander's place and are just about to walk past it, the front door swings open. Theo and Alex step out, and Alex's excitement is infectious. "You should have seen it, Uncle Theo! It was like they were in the wild—so different from the zoo. Sometimes, it was even hard to spot them!"

Theo chuckles, ruffling Alex's hair. "Sounds like a trip me and Uncle Nate need to experience too. Maybe we'll all go together one day."

"Really? You'd take me with you?" Alex asks eagerly, his eyes lighting up as he bounces down the front steps.

"If your mom and dad say it's okay, you can definitely come," Theo replies with a warm smile.

As soon as they reach the bottom of the front steps, Theo falls into step beside Nate, while Alex dashes around to squeeze between Nate and me. I watch as Alex slips his small hand into Nate's. "I'm glad you are home, Uncle Nate," he says.

"Me too, Alex," Nate replies, his smile widening as he looks down at the little boy. The warmth in his gaze reflects the deep bond he now shares with his nephew.

"Where's Dad?" Alex asks, his eyes scanning the area.

"I think he's at the studio," Nate says. Before we can say anything more, Alex releases Nate's hand and sprints down the driveway towards Ace's house.

The three of us watch Alex's excited sprint, his tiny legs propelling him swiftly as he races up the front steps and disappears into the house.

"I want one of those," Theo says. "Never been interested in having a kid before, Alex."

"Me too," Nate agrees with a chuckle.

"Well, you two have to stop sleeping with those groupies first and find someone to settle down with," I reply. As soon as the words escape my mouth, I realize my mistake. As Nate and Theo exchange a glance, a heavy silence settles, the weight of my comment about Bianca hanging between us.

"Sorry, guys," I say, with remorse. "I didn't mean to bring that up."

"It's cool, Scar," Nate says, his voice steady yet tinged with sadness. "You know how much we loved her and why it's something we can't revisit."

I reach out and take his hand in mine, offering the same comfort and support he's always extended to me. I find myself in a rare position of being the source of reassurance for him, attempting to repair the damage that my words had unknowingly created.

After entering Ace's house, we make our way towards the studio. The air is alive with anticipation as Theo and Ace casually throw their guitar straps over their shoulders. Xander confidently stands before the microphone. Meanwhile, I settle in behind the drum set, trying to find a comfortable position.

Nestled in the corner, Nate and Alex sit comfortably in the cozy chairs. Nate's intense gaze never wavers, as he closely follows my every move with unwavering concentration. As we gear up ready to play, I can feel the rush of adrenaline pulsating within me.

As Ace counts us in, the vibrant rhythm envelops us, and we dive headfirst into the music. Nate's unwavering stare throws me off balance, causing me to stumble slightly, missing a beat. I try to recover quickly, aware that the guys have noticed my slip-up. Determined not to let it distract me, I push through, focusing intently on every note and blocking everything else out to get it right.

As we reach the third song on the playlist, I glance up and catch Nate's smile, his eyes sparkling with joy. It's a proud, genuine grin—the kind he used to flash whenever I outplayed him in our childhood competitions. Seeing that familiar look again feels like a warm embrace, a silent affirmation from someone who's always had faith in me. It's as if he's telling me, without words, that I'm doing just fine, and that assurance fuels my performance.

# Chapter 13

## Ace

After our flight and checking into the hotel, it feels like I've barely had a moment to breathe before we're rushing off to sound check. One fuck-up tonight, and we'll be making headlines for all the wrong reasons. We've already had enough negative buzz lately, and I'm hell-bent on making sure this tour is a goddamn triumph, just like our album that shot to number one worldwide.

Inside the town car, it's just Theo, Scarlet, and me. Xander took off earlier to catch up with Walter and his band. They should be into their sound check by the time we arrive.

Theo's next to me, with Scarlet on his other side. It's hard not to notice her restlessness, as her fingers tap anxiously against her leg and she shifts in her seat. Her anxiety is palpable, even though there is no apparent reason for her to feel nervous. She's insanely talented, and I'm confident the fans will fall for her just like the rest of us have.

As the car rolls up to the stadium, we spot Neil, our burly security guy, standing by the entrance. Despite his imposing stature, a warm, friendly grin spreads across his face. He swings the door open, and I step out, Theo following closely behind.

Theo glances at Neil's wide grin and quips, "Watch it, Neil—keep smiling like that, and you'll end up as the friendly giant at a kids' birthday party!"

Neil lets out a hearty laugh, and I can't help but think about how much he's changed since we first met. Back then, he was all about business—never cracked a smile. Now, he's practically one of us, joking around and helping to cut the tension before a big show.

Scarlet steps out of the car, and my eyes can't help but linger on her long, sexy legs, the mini skirt showing off every curve. A surge of desire hits me hard, setting my whole body on fire. I quickly tear my gaze away, forcing myself to get a grip, reminding myself that I can't let my thoughts go there—not again.

I turn away, shoving my hands into my pockets, trying to focus on the massive stadium ahead. But the moment she steps up beside me, her scent—pure fucking temptation—slams into me, igniting a fierce throb in my groin. Every damn time, she manages to get under my skin.  Fuck, I need to keep my shit together. Tonight, I'll deal with this the only way I know how—by drowning these cravings in groupies. A double dose of groupies, that's the plan. Drag them back to my room, lose myself in the chaos, and forget all about her—for a little while, at least.

Neil leads us through the front doors, and I make a point to keep my distance from Scarlet. As we walk, the sound of Disturbed and Twisted, Walter's band, echoes through the stadium. I have to give credit where it's due—Xander nailed it with this choice. Unlike the garbage our old label used to push on us—bands that didn't fit our vibe, just trying to use us to pump up their weak-ass sales—Walter's band hits the mark. They're the perfect match for our sound, raw and powerful.

As we navigate through the narrow back corridors, I can sense Scarlet's presence lingering closely behind me. No matter where I go, she's always there, lingering like an ever-present shadow.

Neil leads us into the green room and sticks close to the door as the rest of us file in. As usual, a shit load of food lines the far wall—Kit always nails it with the setup. Without missing a beat, I head straight for the table, grabbing a handful of peanut M&Ms. They're my ultimate fucking weakness, and after the tension of the day, I need something to take the edge off.

I turn around and spot Theo already slumped on the couch, head back, eyes closed. He pulls this shit every time. I used to give him hell for it when we first started out, but now I understand. It's his way of grounding himself, and with Nate out of the picture right now, he probably needs it more than ever.

But my attention shifts to the sexy blonde pacing the room. She's moving back and forth, taking deep breaths and letting them out slowly. I watch her shake her hands, opening and closing them like she's trying to squeeze the stress away. I should probably say something to calm her down, but emotional shit isn't exactly my strong suit. If it were one of the guys, I'd have already told them to sit the fuck down because they're driving me up the wall. But she's not one of the guys. She's the girl who's been living in my head like a fucking parasite that just won't leave.

The door swings open, causing every head in the room to turn towards Xander as he enters. Scarlet resumes her restless pacing, Theo shuts his eyes, and

I continue to munch on my M&M's, my eyes locked on Xander as he closes the door and approaches.

"Walter's band sounds solid," I comment just as he reaches for something behind me on the table—probably the fucking M&M's. We used to live off this shit in my old garage, pulling all-nighters to perfect our music, using the sugar rush to stay awake and fight off the exhaustion.

"Yeah, as soon as I heard his demo, I knew he was a perfect fit," he replies, turning with the bowl of M&Ms in hand and leaning against the table. He pops a few into his mouth, then glances over at Scarlet. "What's going on with her?"

"Not sure," I respond, grabbing another handful of M&Ms. "Maybe it's just her pre-performance routine or something." I'm not keen on digging deeper, especially with Xander around. I need to maintain some distance and make it seem like I'm genuinely trying to steer clear of her. I toss a few more M&Ms into my mouth, my eyes still lingering on Scarlet.

"Scarlet," Xander says, handing me the bowl and pushing himself off the table.

The moment she hears his voice, she stops pacing and turns to face him. I can see the nerves etched all over her face.

"Are you okay?" Xander asks, his brow furrowing with concern.

I continue shoving M&Ms into my mouth as Xander walks over to Scarlet. Theo gets up from the couch and trails behind him, leaving me sitting here, mindlessly stuffing my face with candy, unsure of what else to do. Comforting people isn't my thing, and I'm not about to draw attention to it with both guys already over there. Besides, I've been told to keep my distance, and that's exactly what I intend to do.

She nods, letting out a deep breath that makes her shoulders sag like she's carrying a shitload of stress. "Yeah, I'm just nervous, that's all."

"You'll be fine, Scarlet," Xander reassures her. "It's just sound check. Nothing to stress over. Just treat it like you've been doing back home, and you'll nail it." He places a reassuring hand on her shoulder, and I can't help but watch, trying to figure out how the fuck he makes it look so effortless. I attempted the same thing the other day at the airport, and it felt awkward as shit. I guess having Poppy and Alex around has turned him into a pro at this comforting stuff.

She smiles, but it's not the real deal. It pales in comparison to the genuine joy I saw when Xander and Poppy tied the knot. I've witnessed her flash that forced smile too many times, like she's trying to convince everyone that everything's okay. But I see right through it—she's putting up a facade, attempting to make it seem like everything's fine when it's clearly not.

"You good, Scar?" Theo asks, grabbing her hand. He's not buying that fake-ass smile either.

"Yeah," she says, "I'm fine."

Xander strides back over, grabs a bottle of water from the table, and shoots me a look as I crunch down on another M&M.

"We should probably get out there," he says. "She needs to be around music, not cooped up in here stressing herself out."

I stay silent, continuing to munch as I watch him head over to Theo and Scarlet.

Setting the bowl back on the table, I grab a bottle of water and trail behind them into the hall.

As Neil leads us toward the stage, I quickly gulp down my water, feeling refreshed and ready. Shouting to be heard over the music, Theo's up ahead, trying to talk to Scarlet. Once I finish the bottle, I toss it to the side of the aisle. Yeah, I know Kit's gonna be fucking furious about that—some recycling rule or something—but I'm not carrying that empty bottle around all night just to find a fucking bin.

We stop at the side of the stage, captivated by the electrifying performance of Disturbed and Twisted—three guys and a chick on bass. She's got this hot, raw vibe, dark hair, and a canvas of tattoos that run all over her arms and legs. She's definitely my type, the kind I'd love to get down and dirty with for the night. But that's never gonna happen. Not just because I'd have to see her every day on this tour, but from what I remember when Walter and his band had drinks with us one night after a show in Australia. I noticed there's some messy love triangle happening between her, Walter, and the drummer.

Walter is absolutely nailing it as the frontman, and I'm left wondering how this band hasn't blown up already. If Xander hadn't wandered into that burger joint, they might still be struggling to get by. It's pretty damn awesome that we can help make their dreams a reality now that we've achieved our own success. I glance over at Xander and catch that big, proud grin on his face. He's clearly thrilled to give someone else the opportunity to chase their dreams.

When Xander played me that demo from Walter, I thought they sounded solid, but seeing them live is an entirely different experience. They're absolutely impressive. I'm itching to elevate our label—to give other bands a genuine shot at their dreams. Walter's band could be the next big thing we sign, and that would seriously bolster our label with some real talent.

Once they finish up, we step onto the stage. Xander makes a beeline for Walter, tossing him a bottle of water he snagged from the shelf by the entrance.

Walter's face lights up with a massive grin—he's clearly stoked. They share a few words, and Theo and I drift over, with Scarlet sandwiched between us.

The rest of the band grabs their water bottles by the drum kit. I scan the group, struggling to recall their names but drawing a blank. My gaze lands on the girl first—no surprise, she's eyeing Xander with keen interest. Then I shift my focus to the lead guitarist; he nods at Theo, then at me, before finally acknowledging Scarlet.

But it's the prick with the drumsticks who really gets under my skin. The way he's eyeing Scarlet, his tongue flicking out to wet his lips, sends my blood boiling. I know exactly what's going through his mind—I've been there myself, imagining all the filthy shit he could pull, and how easily he could turn those thoughts into reality. Back in high school, I played those games to get my kicks, but now that I've got fame on my side, I can pick and choose who I'm interested in. This guy, though, is clearly plotting how to make Scarlet his next conquest, turning her into just another notch on his bedpost, and I don't fucking like it.

I'm keeping my cool for now—there's no need to blow up in front of Scarlet and the rest of the guys. I'll handle this asshole later, out of earshot. The way he's holding out his drumsticks towards Scarlet, looking like he's got some sleazy agenda, is really starting to test my patience.

"Do you need these?" he asks, his eyes glued to Scarlet's tits like a total prick.

I'm ready to step in and set this prick straight, but Theo's already on it. He slides in front of Scarlet, cutting off the guy's view, his posture making it clear that he's not here to play around. "She's got her own asshole. They're in her fucking hands, dickhead," Theo snaps.

I can't help but grin at that.

Theo's usually the jokester, always the wisecracking asshole, but seeing him like this—protective and dead serious—is a rare sight.

Xander and Walter both turn to assess the situation. Walter wastes no time—he strides over, his eyes scanning the group as he senses the rising tension. "What's going on?" he demands, shifting his gaze from one person to the next, finally zeroing in on his drummer. "Jack, what the hell's your issue?"

So that's the dickhead's name—Jack. If he keeps pulling this crap, I'd be shocked if he's still around by the end of the tour.

He smirks, glancing between Theo and Walter. "Just a little misunderstanding, man. The accent might've confused them. You know how it is, Walt," he adds, shooting a brief look at Theo.

I'm not buying his bullshit for a second. The smug prick thinks he can just brush off what he just pulled, and I don't fucking like it.

"Just head to the green room," Walter says, gesturing to the rest of the band. "I'll join you in a minute. I need to have a quick word with these guys."

The girl and the guitarist exchange quick nods with Walter, offering us a smile before slipping past. Jack hesitates for a moment, his eyes flicking between us as if he's weighing his options, but he eventually trails after the rest of the band.

Walter watches them leave, his gaze steady as they disappear down the corridor. Once they're out of sight, he finally breaks the silence.

"Look, I'm really sorry if anything went down back there," Walter says, his tone genuine. "We truly appreciate the opportunity you're giving us."

"Just keep your drummer away from Scar, and we won't have any issues," I say, the words slipping out before I can think twice. Shit. I realize too late that I just used that name—the one I only use when I'm balls deep inside her. Scarlet's head whips around, her expression fierce. I scramble to recover, trying to salvage the moment. "What I meant was, all female band members are off-limits. There are plenty of groupies to go around."

"Yeah, I'll make sure they get the memo," Walter replies. He glances over at Scarlet, his expression softening slightly. "I'm really sorry if Jack made you feel uncomfortable. He can be a real dick sometimes."

"It's not a problem," Scarlet responds, with a forced smile.

Yeah, fucking hell, it definitely is.

Xander steps in, trying to ease the tension before it gets any more awkward. "So, are you sticking around to watch the show?"

"Yeah, I'd love to, but I need to handle this shit with Jack first," Walter says, looking annoyed.

"No problem," Xander replies with a nod, his gaze locked on Walter as he strides off the stage.

Once Walter's out of sight, Xander turns to us, his brow furrowing. "What the fuck just happened?"

Theo doesn't miss a beat, shaking his head in disbelief. "That dumbass was hitting on Scarlet."

Eager to shake off all the bullshit, Scarlet strides through the group toward the drum set. I follow her, making my way to the side of the stage where Kit keeps my guitar. But in the back of my mind, I'm already plotting. Once I get that prick alone, I'm going to lay it all out—make it crystal fucking clear what'll happen if he pulls that crap with Scarlet again. It's going to be a long conversation, and I guarantee he won't enjoy a single damn second of it.

I open my guitar case, the familiar velvet lining brushing against my fingers as I lift out my instrument.

"Alright, watch and learn how a real guitarist plays, old man," Theo quips, flashing his signature cocky grin as he grabs his bass.

"Old man? I'm only three months older than you, dickhead," I shoot back, slipping the strap over my shoulder.

"Whatever, Grandpa. Let's see if you can still play without breaking a hip," Theo teases, plucking a string on his guitar with a smirk.

"Ha," I chuckle, shaking my head. "Keep dreaming, kid. I'll show you how it's really done. But don't worry, I'll try not to embarrass you too much," I say, flashing him a smirk as I strum a few notes to warm up.

"You two dickheads finished with your bullshit?" Xander says, effectively ending our conversation.

Theo and I glance over at Xander standing at the mic, while Scarlet sits behind the drums, her drumsticks raised and ready. I catch the same nervous energy lingering around her that I noticed back in the green room—like she's still fighting to steady herself.

The sound crew waits, clearly eager to get things rolling as Theo and I rush to our spots, plugging in our guitars. I give the signal, counting us in. But it doesn't take long for me to notice Scarlet stumbling over a few drumbeats. Even though she's clearly focused, the pressure is getting to her. As she misses another beat, I see Theo and Xander share worried glances. She's not the same relaxed pro she was in the studio yesterday, where she nailed every track without a hitch. Today, tension's eating at her, and if she doesn't pull it together, tonight's performance could be a disaster for all of us.

As the first song wraps up, Theo raises his hand. "Hold on for a sec," he calls, walking over to Scarlet. Xander and I share a knowing glance—we both know what's at stake if she can't pull it together. The media will jump on her like vultures, turning the narrative from Nate's talented sister to someone who just can't perform on stage. And that's bullshit, because I know how damn good she is. I watch Theo give her a quick, supportive hug—like a big brother reassuring her—before heading back to his spot. He shoots me a nod, signaling that he's ready to dive into the next song.

The next two songs go off without a hitch, the band finding their groove.

Meanwhile, I catch Walter's band lingering on the sidelines, observing us play. They're casually leaning against the stage wall. But Jack? He's got his eyes glued to Scarlet, practically salivating like a fucking creep. I grit my teeth, stealing a quick glance at her, wondering if she has noticed my discomfort, but her attention remains fixated on the music, locked into her performance like a pro. I shift my gaze to Theo, and as soon as we make eye contact, he gives me a subtle nod, silently acknowledging that the dickhead is still hovering, biding his time.

By the time we finish playing, Scarlet seems to have chilled out after that shaky start. Xander strolls over to her with a grin. "Nice job, Scarlet," he says, his tone softer than usual. "It was a bit rough at first, but you pulled through. Just make sure that shit doesn't happen tonight, alright?"

Then he turns to Theo and me with a smirk. "Good job, assholes," he adds. "I think we're good to go." He shifts back to Scarlet, who's gulping down her water. "Unless there's something you want to go over, Scarlet?"

"No, I'm good," she replies, a bit of relief creeping into her voice. "I'm sorry about the first track. I just need to get these damn nerves under control, that's all."

After I've stowed my guitar back in its case, I spot Xander lingering nearby, clearly waiting for me. Theo and Scarlet have already made their way off the stage, heading toward the green room. Walter's band must've headed down there too because they're nowhere to be seen.

Xander gives me a sidelong glance. "You think it'll go alright tonight? You know what's at stake, Ace."

"Yeah, I know. It'll be fine," I reply, trying to sound more confident than I feel. I'm sweating bullets inside, worried it might all go to shit. "She'll get it. It's just the pressure messing with her head. When the time comes, she'll nail it."

I'm saying it more for Xander than for myself, trying to ease his worry. I've always been the one to help him keep his cool, just like I did back when his old man was causing all that chaos.

He nods, and as we turn to the side of the stage, we catch sight of Kit. She greets us with a warm smile as we approach.

"If you guys want to grab a drink with Walter's band before you head out, there's some cold beer in the green room," she says.

"Thanks, Kit," I reply, nodding at her.

A cold beer sounds perfect right now. I continue toward the green room, while Kit starts chatting with Xander about Alex. I head off on my own, eager to grab that beer and check in with Scarlet. She needs to shake off whatever's messing with her head. We need her focused tonight—the pressure is on, and this performance has to be flawless.

As soon as I step into the green room, I spot Scarlet sitting with a cold beer in hand, chatting with the other girl from Walter's band.

Theo is off to the side, engrossed in conversation with the other guy from their band.

My focus narrows in on the prick who was hitting on Scarlet earlier—he's sprawled on the couch, deep in discussion with Walter. They look way too relaxed, casually passing the time, just like Xander and I usually do.

With a cold beer in hand, I reach for the last of the M&M's from the bowl before settling onto an empty couch. I plop down, my eyes scanning the scene while I attempt to rid myself of the tension that's been gnawing at me.

Jack glances my way. "Hey, man, sorry about earlier," he says, his voice low as the room falls silent. Then, shifting his gaze to Scarlet, he adds, "I'm really sorry for what happened out there. It won't happen again, I swear."

He gets up from the couch and walks over to Theo, extending his hand for a shake. Theo takes it, giving Jack a firm grip that clearly says he's not taking any bullshit. When Jack moves over to me, I grab his hand with a solid squeeze, making it crystal fucking clear that if he tries anything with Scarlet again, there'll be serious consequences.

After a brief pause, I release my grip, and Jack makes his way towards Scarlet. This time, as he shakes her hand, his eyes remain fixed on her face, not daring to glance downwards. Once he's done, he returns to his spot next to Walter, the room's tension slightly easing, but not enough to make me lower my guard.

"I just want to thank you guys for this opportunity," Jack says. "I was out of line, and I want to apologize."

Xander strolls in, grabs a cold beer from the cooler, and plops down next to me on the couch. We dive into a conversation about how Walt's band is settling in, adapting to life in a foreign country, and gearing up for the upcoming shows. Xander's relaxed demeanor helps dissolve the last remnants of tension in the room, allowing me to let my guard down a bit and soak in the positive vibes before we take the stage for tonight's performance.

Scarlet comes over and sits down beside me, her presence hitting me like a jolt of electricity. The warmth radiating from her sends a rush through me, making it hard to focus on anything else. My heart kicks into overdrive, but I do my best to keep my cool. What the hell is going on? How does she have this effect on me? I've already been with her—three times, in fact—and yet there's something about her that makes me crave her even more. Usually, my motto is "no strings attached," which makes it easier because I'm the one who gets to walk away. But for some reason, Scarlet is making it damn near impossible.

My eyes stay locked on Jack, making sure he's true to his word about not hitting on her again. He never once looks in her direction, and I can't help but smirk as I finish my beer. At least that's one less asshole I don't have to worry about.

My cock's been pulsing with need since I first saw her tonight, rocking that fucking get-up. Tight black ripped jeans, a top that clings to her body, showing off those perfect tits. Long tattooed arms on full display, tousled long blonde hair, thick eyeliner making those gorgeous eyes pop. The second she walked into the hotel lobby, waiting for the town car, I couldn't stop staring. She's every man's fucking dream, every fantasy, and I want to go there over and over again. I didn't give a fuck if anyone saw me eye-fucking her tonight. I couldn't tear my eyes away from her, and honestly, I didn't give a shit if Xander was watching.

I know every fucking guy at the show tonight is going to be checking her out, thinking the same filthy thoughts I had the moment I laid eyes on her. And if any of those asshole groupies think they can get close, they'll have to go through me first. Hell, I'm sure Theo won't let anyone near her either. We're both on the same page about this—no one's messing with Scarlet while we're around.

Ever since we got back to the hotel, I've been stressing over tonight's show. I wanted to swing by Scarlet's room earlier, maybe walk her through the last-minute details, hoping it would calm her nerves. But there's no way I trust myself to be alone with her right now—not after what went down at my place.

The only way to stop myself from crossing that line again is to avoid her altogether. But tonight, when I'm fucking those groupies, I know Scarlet's going to be the only thing on my mind. It's like she's branded into my brain, a fantasy I can't shake no matter how hard I try. She's always there, pulling me back in, and I have no fucking idea why.

Even now, as we wait for Walter's band to finish up, she's all I can think about. Every dirty thought I've had since we hooked up is running wild through my head, and I know I need to shove them aside and focus on why the hell I'm here. This show is too important for me to be distracted, but with Scarlet so close, it's a losing battle. The more I try to push her out of my mind, the harder it is to forget what we've done—and what I want to do again.

Scarlet anxiously paces back and forth, just like she did earlier today. Theo's lounging on the couch, his eyes shut tight, lost in whatever mental zone he's in. Xander's sitting between us, his eyes darting back and forth as he follows Scarlet. Judging by his expression, it's clear that he's more worked up about this than I am.

The silence is abruptly broken by the sound of Scarlet's phone ringing, halting her pacing. She makes her way over to her bag and fishes it out. Xander and I share a quick glance, but stay quiet as she answers the call. Almost immediately, her expression softens, and I catch a glimpse of a genuine smile—the kind I haven't seen all day.

"Hey, Nate," she says, her voice lighter, turning her back to us as she sinks into the conversation.

"How do you think she'll handle tonight?" Xander asks, keeping his gaze fixed on Scarlet. "She's just as nervous now as she was earlier today."

"I'm hoping she can pull it together," I reply. "But those nerves might mess with her head. We knew it was a big ask going in."

"Yeah, I'm still torn about whether we should've just canceled the tour. This could be the end for us, Ace," Xander says, his voice heavy with worry.

"She'll be fine," Theo chimes in, turning his head to look at both of us. "Trust me. I've got every bit of faith in Scar. And you should too."

Xander and I exchange glances before turning our heads back to Scarlet as she hangs up the call.

"That was Nate wishing me luck," Scarlet says, her voice a bit steadier.

The door swings open, and Kit steps in. "Walter's just wrapping up. You guys are on in ten minutes."

"How's Walter's band doing out there?" Xander asks before she can shut the door.

"They're killing it out there," Kit replies, giving us a quick smile before closing the door behind her.

Xander sits next to me, grinning like he's just hit the jackpot. It's obvious how much he loves giving people a hand, and I've got to admit, it's pretty damn cool. Watching him now—my old buddy, my partner in crime, the guy who's come so far from being that broken kid with an asshole for a father—it's hard not to feel a sense of appreciation. Seeing how much he's grown, how much he's changed, is something that hits me in ways I never expect.

We've both been through hell—me with my screwed-up life, watching my mother bring home whatever cruel asshole she wanted, always chasing the next high, and Xander dealing with his own demons. We were just two kids drowning in the chaos, trying to survive in a world that saw us as worthless. And now, look at us—actually making a difference, helping people, carving out our own place in this crazy world. It's a far cry from where we began, and despite all the shit we had to wade through, every second of it feels worth it.

I can't help but laugh out loud, thinking about those two young dickheads we used to be—dreaming big in my garage, and now here we are, living it, just like we'd always imagined. Xander shoots me a glance, and Theo does the same. Then I catch Scarlet's eye, when she looks right at me. It's rare for me to laugh like this—I'm usually buried in my own fucked-up headspace, dragged down by all the baggage I carry around. But damn, who could've scripted this? I glance back at Xander with a grin, feeling the weight lift, even if it's just for a moment.

"I was just thinking about those two dickheads that used to sprout all that bullshit back in my garage." I watch as a smile creeps onto Xander's face, and he leans forward in his seat. "If we told them this was their life now—"

"They'd call us out on our bullshit," he says, his eyes meeting mine briefly, a silent exchange of memories and hardships passing between us. He lifts his hand, giving my shoulder a soft squeeze.

He rises from the couch and makes his way to the side wall, eagerly grabbing a bottle of water and gulping it down—a pre-show ritual he always follows before we hit the stage. I scan the room and spot Theo talking to Scarlet. She seems to have loosened up a bit. But something still feels off—Nate's absence leaves a noticeable void, like a piece of the puzzle is missing. Ever since our Australian tour, we've dreamed of making it on our own, and now that we're on the brink of something huge, it feels fucking incomplete without him here. I pull out my phone from my back pocket and fire off a quick text to him.

**Ace:** Miss you, man. Wish you were here with us.

I rise from the couch, pocket my phone, and stretch out my shoulders, cracking my neck to shake off the tension and get into the zone. Just as I do, the door swings open, and Walter's band spills into the room, still riding high from their performance. They're sweaty and elated, faces lit up with huge grins. Two of them head straight over to Xander, grabbing bottles of water from the table before flopping onto the couch, utterly exhausted. They've clearly left everything out there for the fans, and the buzz of their excitement fills the room.

"How was it?" I ask, turning to face the group.

"It was fucking unbelievable," Jack replies, lifting his bottle and chugging down half of it.

"Yeah, it's what I always dreamed it would be," Walter adds, a wide grin on his face. "But seeing that many people out there... well, fuck, I don't think anything will ever compare to that in my life." He extends his hand to Xander. "Thanks, man. You have no idea what you did." Then he turns to me and Theo. "What you guys did."

"Well, you guys have got forty-two more concerts like that," Xander says, glancing at the guys sprawled on the couch.

"Fuck yeah," Jack replies, a grin spreading across his face.

I chuckle, thinking back to how earlier I was all set to take this guy down for eyeing Scarlet. But now, seeing this wild, crazy side of Jack, I've got to admit, the guy's kind of growing on me. He's been a whole rollercoaster of personalities today—the cocky prick, the apologetic guy who owned up to his mistakes, and now this wild party animal. I can't lie; he'd probably be a blast to hang out with on the party scene. I bet Walter's got some insane stories about the two of them growing up, probably just as crazy as the shit Xander and I used to get into back in the day.

The door creaks open, and Neil pokes his head in, his eyes scanning the room until they land on me. "Kit's gonna have my head if you guys aren't out there in the next few minutes," he says, his voice all business.

As we head toward the door, the guys behind us shout their goodbyes, throwing out last-minute wishes of good luck. Arms crossed, Neil waits for us with a mischievous smirk, like he's plotting something. As we finally step out and the door clicks shut behind us, he turns to face us, his smirk stretching into a wide, toothy grin.

"Got a message from Nate for all of you," he says, his tone dropping just enough to grab everyone's attention. "And just so we're clear, this is straight from him—not me. He said if you screw this up, he's gonna kick all your asses." His eyes shift over to Scarlet, and his grin softens. "And for you, he wants you to know that you've got this."

"Yeah, I'd like to see him try and kick my ass," Theo says with a smirk. "That idiot's talking out his ass. I'd probably trip over my own feet and end up taking the fucker down. The guy's a pussy—couldn't throw a punch to save his fucking life."

I chuckle, feeling relieved to hear that. When I finally come clean about what happened between Scarlet and me, at least I know Nate won't be using his fists.

"You're forgetting about Nick Johnson," Scarlet says.

"Yeah, but Nick was a complete asshole who deserved that shit," Theo says, shaking his head.

Alright, scratch that. Looks like Nate can throw a punch after all.

Neil heads toward the stage, and we trail behind him. I see that Scarlet's gone quiet, her hands fidgeting. When Neil leaves us at the wing of the stage, she lifts her head and locks eyes with me. I give her a nod, silently telling her that she's got this.

"Alright, let's fucking do this," Xander says, his voice cutting through the tension as he tries to fire us up.

We're nearing the end of the show, and Scarlet's absolutely fucking killing it on the drums. Every beat, every rhythm, she's nailing it.

From where I'm standing, I can see Xander watching her, and he's clearly impressed. That tough guy act he always pulls is nowhere to be seen.

As for me? I can't take my eyes off her. Watching her lose herself in the music. It's a hell of a sight, and it's hard as shit to look away. And that smile on her face? Shit, it's hot as fuck.

Theo's got the biggest smile on his face. It's clear he's proud as hell, and I know he'd probably lose that grin if he knew what was going on in my head right now.

The crowd erupts, and Scarlet's drumming only intensifies the frenzy. As we prepare for our signature closer, "Creep," the energy shifts. The wild cheers fade, replaced by an electric anticipation that's almost palpable, like the entire audience is holding its breath, waiting for the moment the song kicks in. Right on cue, the sea of phones lights up, illuminating the stadium like a sea of tiny stars.

I take it all in, and it hits me: this is it.

This exact moment is what I live for. Up here, I'm not the fucked-up mess I feel like most of the time. I'm alive and fully myself. This is who the fuck I am, and I wouldn't trade it for anything. Not the past, not the bullshit, none of it. This is where it all makes sense, where it's all worth it.

As the song reaches its conclusion, Xander turns to me with that familiar shit-eating grin, and it's obvious—we crushed it. All the doubts we had about branching out on our own. Gone. We fucking nailed it. I scan the crowd, taking in the sea of faces, the deafening roar of their cheers, and it hits me hard. Our first night, our first concert under this new label? It's been a goddamn triumph.

Xander raises his hands, signaling for silence, and in an instant, the crowd falls into an eager hush, hanging on his every move. It's like he's got this magnetic pull, controlling thousands of people with just a gesture. The stadium is alive, crackling with an energy that pulses through every corner, and you can feel it—everyone is waiting, breath held, like he's some kind of world leader.

Then, right on cue, some chick yells, "Fuck me, Xander!" And that's when I catch that signature grin of his—the one that spreads like wildfire across his face whenever someone screams shit like that. It's classic Xander, all charm and zero interest. That playful, I'm flattered smile. Totally for the crowd, part of the act. He's got this way of making them feel like they're the center of his universe.

Xander leans into the mic, completely brushing off the comment. "As you all know, one of us couldn't be here tonight" The crowd instantly erupts at the mention of Nate. "The media's been running their mouths, saying the person filling in for Nate tonight only got the gig because she's his sister." He glances over at Scarlet. I flick my eyes over to her, spotting that quick flash of uncertainty—like she's wondering what the hell Xander's about to drop. "Come out here, Scarlet," he says.

Scarlet hesitates for a moment, glancing between us and the crowd, her expression a mix of nerves. Then, with a deep breath, she stands and walks towards the front of the stage, drumsticks still in hand.

The cheers grow louder. It's her moment, and I see the flicker of doubt on her face as she steps into the spotlight.

The crowd lets out a few whistles, and I know every dude out there is probably imagining all kinds of filthy shit they'd like to do to her. It pisses me off, but I can't blame them—she's hot as hell. Some idiot gives an obnoxious whistle, and I watch her drop her head, blushing, her long blonde hair sliding forward to hide her face.

Xander grins and continues speaking. "This is Scarlet, and yeah, she's Nate's sister. So fucking what? She just showed you all how badass she is up here." The crowd cheers, and I spot Theo beaming a huge smile. Xander's not done, though. "To all those media fuckheads making a big deal out of it—fuck you. You don't know shit about talent. So shut the fuck up and let the pros handle it."

The crowd roars in approval, their energy surging even higher, as if they're rallying behind Xander's words. Xander's eating it all up, milking every second of the chaos. Scarlet stands there, her cheeks flushed, caught between disbelief and pride. It's like Xander just gave her the ultimate vote of confidence, and I can see her nerves beginning to melt away under the crowd's adoration.

Xander raises his hand again, attempting to calm the crowd, signaling for them to quiet down. "I just want to say thanks for making tonight absolutely epic," he yells into the mic. "Without you all, we wouldn't get to do what we love every night—this is our life, and it's all because of you. And we're just getting started."

Amid the thunderous applause and cheers, Xander gives Theo and me a nod. We put our guitars aside and join him and Scarlet at the front of the stage. We throw our hands up, giving the crowd one last wave, letting their wild energy wash over us like a tidal wave. It's pure adrenaline, a powerful reminder of why we live for this moment.

As we trail behind Xander across the stage, the crowd's deafening roar echoes in our ears. Once we reach the wings, Xander spins around, a wild grin plastered on his face. "We did it, man! We fucking did it!" he shouts, extending his hand toward me.

I grab it, pulling him into a hug, feeling that surge of victory slam into me, then he steps back and does the same with Theo.

Then Xander turns his attention to Scarlet, his grin softening while still shining with pride. "Don't ever let anyone put you in Nate's shadow. Those assholes don't know anything. You absolutely owned it out there, Scarlet. You fucking nailed it."

"See? I told you assholes she was just as fucking good," Theo chimes in, pulling Scarlet into a hug.

Xander slaps me on the back, all proud and shit, but I barely register it. My attention is glued to Scarlet, her chin resting on Theo's shoulder, a genuine smile illuminating her face as if she's just conquered the world. When our eyes lock, I nod at her, silently conveying that she absolutely crushed it, all while keeping it low-key in front of the others. This moment is hers, and I'm here to support her.

Xander grips my shoulder, and the energy of the night still pulses through my veins. All I want right now is a drink and to get completely wasted, relishing this huge accomplishment we only dreamed about months ago. Ever since I smashed that damn camera, I've felt a weight on my shoulders. But now that we've pulled it off, I'm itching to dive into some groupie action and ride this adrenaline wave for as long as possible. Tonight belongs to us, and I plan to celebrate it hard.

# Chapter 14

## Scarlet

I'm so glad that's over. What a wild rush! Despite Nate's advice that I should take it all in, I just couldn't. I couldn't afford to let my guard down; knowing how important this night was for the guys, I deliberately kept my eyes away from Ace. Just one look at him thriving on stage would've derailed my concentration and turned everything upside down.

Ace does that to me. When Nate got Mom, Dad, and me tickets to watch their first concert from the wings, I couldn't take my eyes off Ace. That was before I joined my old band and hooked up with Beck. I don't know what it was about Ace that day, but even then, he had this irresistible pull. The way he lost himself in his music, the intense concentration on his face, even though he barely smiled—the few times he did, I couldn't look away. He made me so damn nervous back then, and every time he glanced my way, I got butterflies, just like I still do today.

Theo wraps his arm around my shoulder, pulling me into a warm embrace. Tonight was a big deal for him too, not only because of the label and the guys, but also because he's the one who fought to get me here—I know he's proud. That's the thing about Theo; he's always there, pushing what's best for me.

"You killed it out there," Theo says, as he pulls me in tighter and plants a kiss on my head.

I let out a deep breath, feeling the stress finally melt away. I can finally relax now, relishing in the sweet taste of victory after successfully completing the first concert. With only forty-two more to go, I'm determined not to fuck a single one up. Too much is riding on this.

My attention turns to Ace and Xander, who are walking ahead of me, their excitement evident in their animated conversation. I can't help but let my gaze linger on Ace, tracing the intricate tattoos that adorn his arms and admiring the way those black jeans cling to his sculpted physique. I can't help but check out his ass—dude's in fucking shape. A part of me wonders if he'll end up with a few groupies tonight. I hope not, but I know I have no control over that. He's clarified that we are nothing serious, so he'll probably sleep with whoever's willing. I let out a deep breath, the high of the night fading as I contemplate the possibility of Ace being with someone else.

As we step into the green room, I catch Kit laying down the law for Walter's band. Jack is practically salivating at the chance of getting some action. I get why Theo went off on him; he's done the same thing to every guy who's ever shown an interest in me. It's been his thing since high school—making any guy who even glanced my way his next target. Back then, it was my nightmare; every time a guy showed interest, I knew Theo and my brother would make things hell for them.

But I don't get why Ace stepped in like he did. I could see the anger in him, the way he stared Jack down with that intense glare. Was it just some alpha male pissing contest? Who the hell knows? But if Ace is going to act like that every time a guy shows interest, it's going to get real old, real fast. Don't these idiots realize I can handle myself? I have a voice, and I'm perfectly capable of telling someone I'm not interested. I've said as much to Theo and my brother countless times over the years, but they never seem to get it through their thick heads.

I drift over to the far wall, trailing behind Ace and Xander as they head to the table with the drinks. They each grab a beer from the ice bucket, already celebrating, while I choose a bottle of water. Kit's voice rings out behind us, outlining the rules and expectations for the night, detailing what's required from Disturbed and Twisted, who are already partying on the couch.

I glance over and see Sabrina, the only girl in the other band, looking my way with a warm smile. She's been really kind, and earlier we talked about how challenging it can be to be surrounded by so much masculine energy. She mentioned that she's grown up with these guys and would be lost without them. I feel that pang again, the one that reminds me of how alone I feel sometimes.

As Kit wraps up her briefing, she turns to Ace and Xander. "We might have Broken Oasis head out first to sign some stuff for the fans. After that, we'll all come back here to the green room and bring in the rest of the backstage party guests."

This whole scene is new to me. Even though I've played a few gigs with my old band, it was never on this scale. I know that once we head out to where Kit is taking us, it'll feel like a completely different experience—one I'm not entirely accustomed to.

Ace, Xander, and Theo down their beers, setting the empty bottles on the table before following Kit out of the green room. As Xander and Kit take the lead, I can't help but notice Ace's unwavering gaze directed at me. My heart skips a beat as he quickly averts his gaze and catches up with Xander and Kit down the lengthy corridor, his usual no-bullshit vibe radiating from him.

Theo comes up beside me, grabbing my hand as we trail behind. Despite my efforts to stay focused, my eyes are drawn to Ace. I watch him run a hand through his hair, noticing how his muscles flex with every movement. I know I shouldn't crave him as much as I do, especially knowing that in the end, it'll only hurt.

As the door swings open and Xander steps into view, the fans erupt into an explosive chorus of high-pitched screams. The noise is deafening. Ace follows, and the uproar doesn't let up; if anything, it grows louder. Theo and I step in next, but the crowd's frenzy remains unyielding. It's clear—these guys are gods in the eyes of these people, worshiped and revered in every possible way.

Kit hands out black Sharpies to all of us, and as I scan the area, I realize there are no tables set up. We line up in a straight row, side by side, and I watch as the girls at the front step forward, eager to get close to their idols. Some of them completely miss me, their attention solely on the guys. The moment they stand in front of them, they lift their shirts, flashing their tits for signatures.

It hits me—each of these guys could have any groupie they want. The adoring, wide-eyed looks on their faces, as they smile and gaze at the guys make it clear why they thrive in this environment. They live for the thrill of being chosen as the ones they want to fuck, the ones they want to spend the night with. I roll my eyes as Theo uses his usual pickup line, his cocky grin shining as he charms the girls, soaking up every ounce of attention. The urge to elbow him and express how repulsive his words are is hard to resist. Sure, charm is one thing, but this goes beyond what's acceptable.

A swarm of guys rushes forward, closing in, and I spot one in baggy jeans holding a Broken Oasis cap. Their predatory gazes lock onto me, and it's the same old shit I've seen a million times—they view me as nothing more than a trophy to conquer or a plaything, never as a human being. Male groupies are the worst. Back with my old band, I dealt with a few who thought it was okay to make crude comments or touch me like they owned me.

I know Theo will flip out if one of them steps out of line. His protective instincts kick in whenever I'm around idiots like this.

"Hey, beautiful," one of them says, flashing a cocky grin like it's some kind of magic spell.

Yeah, real original—like I haven't heard that a million times.

The guy in the middle inches closer, his gaze sliding down to my tits. It's clear he's putting on a show for his buddies. There's always one asshole who thinks he's the exception, that alpha ego-driven idiot who believes he can charm me into spreading my legs like I'm some easy fuck.

He throws me a wink, and I brace myself for the inevitable shitty pickup line. He glances around at his friends, and I can tell they've probably already swapped all their filthy stories about what they want to do to me.

He turns back to me, grinning, and lifts his shirt, pointing to the spot just above his baggy jeans where his boxers peek out. I don't even bother looking down—that's exactly what this asshole wants: for me to check out his junk. But he keeps grinning like he just pulled off some slick move.

"Can you sign here, or are you game enough to sign my dick?"

The idiot beams like he just scored the winning touchdown, throwing a smug wink at his buddies as if he's accomplished some epic stunt. It pisses me off.

I glance over to see if Theo's caught wind of this moron's request, but he's too busy signing whatever fans shove at him.

"Sure," I say to the dickhead, playing along with his creepy game. "But I doubt your dick's big enough for my name anyway."

His buddies around him stifle their laughs, and I watch that cocky grin start to fade from this dickhead's face. Just as I lean forward to sign the jerk's stomach, I feel a hand on my arm, and I know exactly who it is by how my body reacts.

"Put your fucking shirt down. She ain't signing that shit."

I glance up at Ace, noticing the intense glare he shoots towards the idiot, like he's ready to tear him apart. Theo stops what he's doing, his eyes fixated on the scene unfolding before him. Don't these two morons realize I can handle this douchebag on my own? I've been doing it for years.

"You heard him," Theo says, positioning himself next to Ace. "If she signs that shit, then so do I, and so does he," he adds, nodding toward Ace, who still has a firm grip on my arm. "And trust me, you don't want the big guy here signing that shit."

The guy instantly drops his shirt, the smug look wiped clean off his face. I glare at Ace, feeling a mix of embarrassment and irritation as he moves me back like I'm some fragile flower.

Kit appears, her eyes scanning the scene. "Everything okay here?" she asks, clearly trying to figure out why the line has come to a halt. I lean forward, catching sight of Xander at the front, surrounded by eager fans, effortlessly signing body parts, posters, and a bunch of random crap while posing for photos like it's just another day at the office.

Despite my attempts to break free from Ace's grip, he responds by tightening his hold, pulling me closer. He positions me securely between him and Theo in the line.

"What are you doing?" I ask, just as he finally lets go of my arm.

He ignores me, diving back into signing autographs and posing for photos.

"Asshole," I mutter, not caring if he hears—because, well, he is. I catch the annoyed look on his face as he forces a smile, one that looks more like he's just bitten into something sour.

"You were awesome tonight," a young fan says, pulling me out of my irritation. I push the frustration aside and smile at her, letting it go as I sign the poster, even though it's just featuring the four guys.

With everything signed and Kit ushering people out, I turn to Ace.

"What the fuck was that?" I say, not giving a damn that my raised voice has drawn everyone's attention. I notice Ace's eyes dart sideways towards Xander, who's watching us with a concerned expression.

Ace shrugs like it's no big deal. "You know what they wanted," he says.

"Yes, and I can handle assholes like that. I have for years. Do you honestly think that every guy who comes my way is just going to get to fuck me? I'm not some easy lay, Ace, no matter what you might believe." I turn sharply and walk back across the room, throwing Theo a pointed glare on my way out. As I do, I realize I might have just hinted to Theo that there's more going on between Ace and me than he realizes.

# Chapter 15

## Ace

By the time we arrive in the green room, the afterparty is already in full swing. The hungry looks from the groupies are impossible to miss, each one eager for the chance to satisfy us. Their shrill screams pierce through the noise, and I have to bite my tongue to stop myself from telling them to shut the fuck up. Instead, I make my way to the back of the room, with Xander following closely behind. I brace myself, anticipating his question about what the hell happened with Scarlet back there. I've been scrambling for some bullshit excuse, but the truth is, I do not know what the fuck came over me. All I saw was that prick lifting his shirt, while his buddies laughed and egged him on, and that's when I snapped. Seeing them treat Scarlet like she was just some quick score pissed me off in ways I can't even explain.

A few of the groupies make their way toward us. I grab a couple of ice-cold beers from the bucket, placing one into Xander's hand as I casually lean against the table. Xander mirrors my posture, and the girls flock toward us, their shrill giggles getting on my nerves as they press in closer.

Even though everyone knows Xander's married—thanks to the headlines that hit a few days after the wedding—that doesn't stop these girls from crowding around him. I glance over and see the irritation flicker across Xander's face as one girl moves in, her tits practically spilling out as she presses up against him.

"I want to fuck you, Xander," she purrs, as she sensually traces her finger along his chest. "Let us show you a good time." The other two girls around him nod enthusiastically, their eyes gleaming with excitement, showing they're up for anything.

I'm doing my best to ignore the two chicks, their hands eagerly exploring my body. If it means I can lose myself in this bullshit for the night, I'll let them touch. But right now, all I really want to see is Xander completely lose his shit over these no-boundaries groupies.

"And I want you all to back the fuck off before I kick your skanky asses out of here," Xander growls, slapping her hand away. "Touch me again, and I'll break your fucking fingers."

The girls instantly step back at his harsh tone, and I can't help but laugh, lifting my bottle in a mock toast. Xander's head snaps around to glare at me.

"Careful, you're starting to sound like me," I say, wrapping my arm around the one groupie who didn't bolt when Xander went off. I hold her close; she's the one I'm planning to have tonight —already staking my claim.

"Never," Xander replies with a smirk, taking a swig of his beer. But then his face goes serious. "What the hell happened earlier between you and Scarlet?"

Fuck. I take a long sip of my beer, stalling while I try to come up with some sort of answer. "Some dickheads were hitting on her, making her the punchline or some shit." I avoid making eye contact with him, knowing he'll see right through my bullshit.

"So? Groupies always hit on us, you know that. You can't expect it to be any different for her."

"Yeah, but we've never had a female member before. I just didn't want her to feel uncomfortable," I say, downing the rest of my beer. I glance over at Theo, who's now surrounded by eight groupies, basking in their attention like the attention-seeking asshole he is.

Off to one side, I see Scarlet talking to three guys. Neil stands beside her, sticking to my orders to throw out anyone who tries anything with her tonight.

"Well, I'll leave you to it, man," Xander says, patting my shoulder, his eyes flicking down to the groupie under my arm.

He pushes off the table and makes his way across the room.

I wonder what he'll do now to pass the time.

Back in the day, Xander would've jumped right into this scene, picking out any girl in the room to help him drown out all the shit in his head. But now, as a happily married family man, he doesn't even glance at anyone. His whole world is Poppy and Alex.

I never thought Xander would ever be the relationship type, but he's turned into a mellow version of himself when he's at home. He's content with the life he's built, and I know he'd give up everything he's worked for in a heartbeat for his family. It's something I'll never understand. I'd never give this shit up for anyone. Especially when I can get a meaningless fuck any time I want.

I watch him walk over to Kit and strike up a conversation. Now that Xander's gone, a few girls come my way. Some of them are the same ones he told to fuck off earlier, so it's no surprise they're making their rounds from band member to band member. With only Theo and me left, they know they have to work hard to stand out.

The girl with the big mouth and even bigger tits catches my eye, and I give her a nod to come over. When she steps in front of me, her starry eyes light up, clearly thrilled to be chosen. I know I can ask her to indulge in any of my wild fantasies tonight. As she moves closer, I set my empty beer on the table. I don't bother with names—this is just a one-night thing.

"You wanna have a good time?" I ask, keeping my tone relaxed. She grins and nods eagerly. I glance back at the girl under my arm, but something across the room catches my attention.

Scarlet's eyes lock with mine, and a sharp jolt hits me right in the chest. Her gaze shifts to the groupie under my arm, and I catch a fleeting glimpse of hurt that passes over her face. When our eyes meet again, it stings like hell.

I push those thoughts aside, feeling the weight of guilt settle in my chest. That's what I do—I'm fucked up, and I hurt people. Ignoring the sharp ache in my chest, I make my way across the room, the girls still clinging to me. I need to escape, to find solace away from Scarlet's piercing stare.

In the back seat on the way to the hotel, with a girl on each side of me. One leans in to suck on my neck while the other rubs my cock through my jeans, eager to get me going. Normally, this would be all I need, but tonight something's off. I close my eyes, trying to lose myself in the moment, but even as I get hard, all I can think about is the hurt in Scarlet's eyes. That look. The way it cut deep, hangs heavy. It's impossible to shake the fact that I made her feel that way.

My mother's voice echoes in my head, just like it always does when I'm on the edge of losing my shit. Her words—how the world would be better off without me, how fucked up and worthless I am—play on a relentless loop. The memory of her wishing I'd fucking died instead of taking my first breath still stings. It's hard to shake off the weight of all the shit she used to say; even though they're just words, they feel like they've seeped into my skin. Maybe that's why everyone ends up leaving. I'm no good for anyone, just a burden dragging people down. Every dark thought gets amplified by her cruel taunts, as if she's inside my head, pulling me back into the darkness she's always excelled at creating.

As we pull up to the back of the hotel—a spot hidden from the media's prying eyes—I unbuckle my seatbelt and lean forward.

"Get the girls back to the stadium or drop them off at home," I say, not even glancing at either of them as I shove past to get out.

"Wait... What the hell?" one of them pipes up as I step out of the car.

"Are you fucking serious?" the one with the big tits yells.

I continue walking, not giving a damn that I ruined their night. Whatever. They only want me for who I am. They do not know how hard it is to breathe sometimes. So fuck them and fuck the entire world that puts me on a pedestal. No way I can let them see the fucked-up version I am.

Despite the chill of the night air, my mind remains cluttered and chaotic.

I hit the elevator button, watching the illuminated numbers slowly count down. When the doors finally slide open, relief washes over me as I step inside, grateful that no one else is around at this hour. I'm too fucked up to fake a smile or pretend everything's fine. The elevator dings as it reaches the top floor, and I step out, desperate to reach my room. All that matters right now is raiding the mini-bar, lighting up a joint, and drowning out the chaos in my head. It's strange how just an hour ago, I was riding high—on top of the world with our new label, the tour, and fans going wild. Now, though, I'm spiraling downward, demons from my childhood rushing back, threatening to drown me in their darkness.

After wiping out the mini-bar and stumbling out of my room, the late hour feels suffocating. The bar downstairs is supposed to stay open all night—at least that's what the damn sign said. I've already finished a joint and ten tiny bottles of alcohol, but it's still not enough to drown out the chaos in my head. When these dark thoughts take hold, sleep feels impossible. Jabbing the elevator button, I stand, head down, waiting for it to drag its ass up here. Thank fuck it doesn't take too long.

Stepping back into the elevator, I slump against the back wall, closing my eyes to try to block everything out. When the chime signals I've hit the lobby, I head straight to the bar to find it mostly empty—just a few lost souls nursing their own troubles. I slide onto a stool and signal the bartender, who nods and starts pouring. As the first few shots hit the counter, my phone buzzes in my back pocket. Pulling it out, I see Xander's name flash on the screen. I wonder what the hell he wants at this hour.

"Hey man," I say, trying to keep it casual.

"Hey, what are you doing?" Xander asks.

"Just grabbing a drink. What about you?"

"Monsters fucking up your head again," he says, and I can hear the sympathy in his voice.

I crack a smile. No one gets me like Xander does. "Yeah, you could say that."

"Turn around."

Spinning in my seat, I spot him in a booth along the back wall. A bottle of whiskey sits on the table, with a half-full glass beside it.

I hang up the phone, and down four of the five shots in quick succession, relishing the familiar burn in my throat before grabbing the last one. With the shot in hand, I make my way over to Xander.

He watches me as I approach, and I can't help but wonder what the hell he's doing here at this hour. Setting my shot glass down on the table, I slide into the seat across from him.

"What triggered it this time?" he asks. He knows better than anyone how easily I can get pulled back into the shit from my past.

"I don't know," I say, downing my shot, not wanting to admit it was because of how I hurt Scarlet. Someone so shiny and bright, getting fucked over by someone like me. One minute, I was ready to dive into some pussy, and the next, the look on her face—the pain I caused—sent me spiraling back down like a wave pulling me under. "What are you doing here?"

"Can't sleep," Xander says, lifting his glass and taking a long sip. "I talked to Poppy not too long ago, then figured I'd swing by here for a drink."

"It's different now on tour for you, I guess," I say.

"Yeah, it is," he replies, a small smile tugging at his lips. "But I wouldn't change it. I'd never survive if I lost them."

"How the hell did you do it, man? How'd you let someone in?" I grab Xander's bottle and pour myself another shot, glancing up at him with a mix of curiosity and envy before setting the bottle back down on the table.

"You mean letting Poppy in?" he asks, raising an eyebrow.

"Yeah," I reply, eager to avoid diving into the details too much.

"I don't know. It just kind of happened," he replies, shrugging it off. "It snuck up on me, I guess you could say. Why?"

I don't answer. While I respect his honesty, it's a far cry from the old what-if bullshit we used to ramble on about as kids. But now it's different between us; now Xander lays bare his heart on the table, and it feels like a whole new level of realness.

"Hey, I thought you'd left earlier with two groupies," he says, giving me a look. He knows I usually get out of my head by fucking my feelings away.

"Yeah, I did. Just didn't feel like it once we got here."

Xander smirks, raising an eyebrow. "Guess even your cock's got standards now. Never thought I'd see the day."

I chuckle and down the shot. "Yeah, well, I guess it turns out even my cock's got a conscience. Who knew?" I grin at Xander, appreciating the rare light moment, feeling grateful to have my best friend sitting with me. "Glad you're here, man. This shit's easier to handle with you around."

There's a relentless pounding at the door, or maybe it's just the thumping in my head from a late night with Xander.

The knocking comes again, louder this time.

I roll over in bed and shout, "Whoever the hell that is, better fuck off!"

But the knocking continues, each thud amplifying my headache and fueling my irritation.

If it's Theo, he's really going to get it.

I push the covers aside and, with my head pounding and eyes still half-closed from barely a few hours of sleep, drag myself to the door.

"For fuck sake, stop the damn pounding!" I yell, yanking the door open. "What the fuck do you want?" Through my half-closed eyes, I see Kit standing there. She just brushes past me, not giving a shit that I'm fuming.

"Don't you ever check your phone?" she snaps.

I turn slightly, keeping the door open as I watch her step further into the room. With a resigned sigh, I close the door, realizing she isn't planning on leaving anytime soon.

She grabs my scrunched-up jeans from the floor, and tosses them at me, hitting me square in the chest.

"Put these on. As manly as you are, I'm not having a serious conversation with your dick out."

I bend over, shove a leg through, and almost lose my balance. Fuck, if I had to guess, I'm still hungover as hell. Xander and I finished that whisky bottle and didn't drag our sorry asses out of the bar until around four this morning. When I finally manage to get dressed, I look up and see Kit in the kitchen, making coffee.

"What time is it?" I ask, scanning the room for a clock. Not spotting one, I make a beeline for my phone.

"Eight," she says, just before I grab it.

"What the fuck, Kit?" I growl, stumbling over to the couch and flopping down, my palms rubbing at my sleepy eyes. "What's so fucking important that you had to drag me out of bed at this hour?" I check my phone and see eight missed calls, all from Kit. She comes back with a cup of coffee and hands it to me. The fact she's bringing me coffee tells me something is seriously wrong. I take the cup from her as she sits down on the couch beside me.

Taking a sip, I keep my eyes on her. This isn't the usual Kit. She's usually a no-bullshit, take-no-prisoners type, but the look on her face and the fact she's been bombarding me with calls this morning has me on edge.

"Just fucking say it, Kit," I tell her. "If it's about those girls from last night, nothing fucking happened, no matter what they say."

"It's not about that, Ace."

"Then just fucking tell me."

"How's your relationship with your mother?" she asks, her gaze steady. No one but Xander knows about the shit that went down with my mother—I've kept that locked up tight all these years, buried deep where no one can reach it.

"Why the fuck are you asking?" I snap. I fight to keep my anger in check, every muscle in my body tensing. It takes all my willpower not to hurl the coffee cup across the room, but my mind's racing, trying to figure out why she's digging into this now, after all this time. What the hell has happened to make her think this is okay?

"There's never been a relationship with her. She's not someone I fucking talk about." I push off the couch, shoving the coffee cup back into her hands. No way in hell am I having a therapy session with Kit about this shit.

As I move across the room, I can feel her eyes drilling into me, and it's fucking infuriating. It's like she's peeling back my layers, exposing the little kid inside who was never loved—the little boy who used to cry when one of his mother's asshole boyfriends thought it was fun to put out a cigarette on his arm. If she keeps looking at me like that and pushing this shit, I'm about to fucking snap.

"Ace," she says, her voice cutting through the tension like a knife.

"No, Kit, I don't want to fucking talk about it, alright?" I snap, grabbing a shirt from the floor and yanking it over my head. When I turn around, she's not on the couch anymore—now she's standing at the end of the bed, giving me that intense look that makes my skin crawl.

"You might not have a choice about that," she says, her tone steady. "The press has been digging around ever since that incident with the paparazzi, and my sources just told me that your mother and her husband are doing a sit-down interview with Jerry Goldman."

Just hearing Goldman's name sends a chill down my spine. The guy's known for his brutal interviews, cutting right to the heart of the matter and exposing everything. He's a fucking master at pulling in ratings, and now my past is about to be dragged out for everyone to see, like dirty laundry hung out for the world to scrutinize.

She pulls out her phone and turns it toward me. "Do you know this man?"

The photo on the screen displays a guy I know all too well—the wannabe biker who almost took my head off back in the day, but he's slightly older. He had me pinned against the wall, swinging at me, barely missing my face.

"Judging by your expression, I take it you do," she says.

The fury in my eyes must say it all.

"What's she saying?" I ask, dropping onto the edge of the bed, struggling to make sense of this mess.

I haven't seen her in years, and the last thing I need is for her to stir up shit now. Kit takes a seat beside me, her expression serious.

"She's painting you as a ticking time bomb," Kit replies. "She claims you've always acted out, that your temper's completely out of control. According to her, you attacked her husband in a violent rage, and he had to throw you out to protect her."

I lift my head, locking eyes with Kit, my heart racing. "That's bullshit. The fucker attacked me. I was just a seventeen-year-old kid trying to defend myself. Xander was there—he'll back me up."

"Xander's not on the call sheet for today's interview, and you should know this topic might come up," she says, her expression grave. "He won't be there to back you up if they bring it up."

Shit. Xander mentioned last night that I have an interview with Scarlet scheduled for today.

I stand up from the bed, restless, and begin pacing back and forth, running my hands through my hair. The thought of unearthing the past, the memories I've fought so hard to suppress, is messing with my head.

Kit rises from the bed, her eyes fixed on me. "If they bring up Goldman or anything about your mother, just redirect the conversation back to the tour and Scarlet. That's why she's with you—to squash all those rumors about her landing the gig just because she's Nate's sister. After she killed it last night, we need to make her the main focus." She steps closer, placing a hand on my shoulder. "You've got this, Ace. You're the spokesperson for the band. This is what you do."

Her words hang in the air, but they don't do much to calm the storm raging inside me. I nod, fully aware of how relentless the media can be, always on the hunt for a story to boost their ratings. Why didn't I listen to Xander in that damn car? What the fuck made me throw that camera?

"If you need me, Ace, just give me a call," Kit says, making her way to the door.

I don't respond, still lost in my thoughts. It isn't until I hear the door click shut behind Kit that I snap back to reality. Grabbing my phone, I dial Anita's number, praying like hell she has some legal bullshit that might be able to shut down this interview with my mother before it even starts.

Sitting in the car next to Scarlet, for once my thoughts are not filled with the usual fantasies I have about her. I'm still fuming over what Kit dropped on me this morning, and the anger only grew when Anita told me there's nothing she can do to stop that damn interview. No matter how deep the media digs, they won't uncover the full extent of my messed-up past because I'm not bringing that into the light. It's better left buried where it belongs.

So lost in my thoughts I don't notice we've stopped at the studio until the door swings open for me to get out. I climb out of the car, and as Scarlet slides across the seat, I instinctively reach out to help her. She looks up and smiles, and I can see the tension from last night melting away between us. Once the car door slams shut behind us, we start moving forward, but Scarlet doesn't let go of my hand, and for some damn reason, neither do I. In this moment, her touch feels like a lifeline, grounding me and pulling me out of my head.

As we're led into the studio by a young guy with a clipboard and an earbud, we navigate a long, bright hallway. Scarlet's thumb gently brushes the back of my hand, and when I turn to look at her, I find her gaze already fixed on mine.

"Are you okay?" she asks, sensing something is off. "Kit didn't say much about what's going on, but she mentioned that if anything comes up, just steer it back to the tour. I'm guessing that's what's got you down."

"Yeah. You could say that," I reply, not really in the mood to spill the details.

She takes the hint and redirects her attention to the guy leading us, who's taking us through a maze of doors. He eventually stops and swings one open, gesturing for us to step inside.

"Someone will be in soon to set up your mics," he says before walking out and leaving us alone.

The moment he departs, Scarlet swiftly releases my hand and strides towards a nearby table. She snatches a paper cup and fills it with water. I watch her for a moment; her calm presence feels like an anchor right now.

The door swings open, and in walks a guy with big front teeth and a man bun, holding two portable mic packs. He sets them on the small counter to the side, then turns to us, grinning wide. "Hey, great concert last night," he says, his gaze fixed on Scarlet. "You really rocked it out there."

"Thanks," she replies, tossing her empty paper cup into the trash.

"Now, you'll both be seated at the far right end of the set. The interview will last about eight minutes," he says, pulling out one of the microphone packs and heading over to Scarlet first. "There will be three people asking you questions." He hands her the pack. "I'll let you clip this onto the waistband of your jeans." I can't help but appreciate how he shows her respect by letting her handle it herself. Most guys would be itching to touch her, but he keeps it professional.

Once Scarlet's all set up, he moves over to help with my mic.

"Do you mind if I get a photo with you guys? I'm a huge fan," he asks as he finishes setting up my mic.

"Yeah, sure," I reply.

He pulls his phone from his back pocket and holds it out, grinning like a kid on Christmas. Scarlet and I lean in, our faces lining up behind him for the shot.

After he snaps the photo, he turns to us, still beaming. "Thanks for that! My wife is gonna flip when she sees this. I'm definitely framing it and rubbing it in. She's just as big a fan as I am."

He heads toward the door but stops right before he leaves. "Someone will come get you in a few minutes," he says, with a quick nod. "Nice meeting you both." And just like that, he's out the door, leaving us alone again.

Scarlet lets out a deep breath, her fingers twisting nervously like they did before we hit the stage yesterday. I can see she's on edge, and honestly, I am too, but it's not the usual pre-show jitters. I've been through this a thousand times. It's the thought of what might come up about my mother that's really messing with my head.

I sink into the chair as I nervously wipe my sweaty palms on my jeans. A few seconds later, the door swings open, and a middle-aged lady enters, smiling as she tells us to follow her. After we make our way down the corridor, we pause off to the side while they cut to a commercial break. When they wave us on, we step out onto the set. Scarlet takes the seat at the end, and I settle into the chair between her and one of the hosts.

We exchange quick hellos, but their words barely register. My mind's else-where, as I struggle to steady my breathing. As someone starts the countdown for the show to go live again, I block out all distractions and channel my focus solely on the task at hand.

The primary host next to me looks straight into the camera and introduces us.

I catch Scarlet fidgeting out of the corner of my eye, her nervousness still evident despite her attempts to hide it.

The host flashes a smile, then turns slightly in his chair to address us, ready to dive into whatever questions they've got lined up.

"Well, let me kick things off by saying your fans are absolutely buzzing online about the show you put on last night," the host says, his tone dripping with that polished enthusiasm that comes with the territory.

I flash a tight smile, just enough to look genuine without going overboard. I know how I can look when I push it too far, and the last thing I need is to come off like a deranged clown auditioning for a horror film.

"Yeah, it was a great night," I reply, keeping it brief.

Then he pivots to Scarlet. "You're the hot topic on social media, stepping in for your brother. Fans are saying it felt like Nate was right there on stage."

Scarlet smiles, keeping it cool like she's been in the spotlight forever.

"Oh really?" she laughs, the sound light and effortless. "Wow, that's a compliment in itself."

The guy in the middle leans in, directing his question at me. "Your album has hit the number one spot worldwide," he says, a glint in his eyes. "That must be a relief after everything that's happened."

I flash a tight, controlled smile, already sensing the ulterior motive behind this idiot's words.

Despite a powerful urge to tell him to fuck off, I keep my answer smooth and casual.

"Yeah, the album's something we're really proud of. We've all worked hard to get back our original sound. Going out on our own, handling our music the way we want, and doing tours on our terms—I think the fans have shown they like where this is headed."

"How has the camera incident impacted the tour?" he asks, that eager glint in his eye making it obvious he's just itching for some drama to chew on for his ratings.

My jaw tightens for a second, but I don't let it show. "The tour's been going great. Fans are showing up in droves, and that's what really matters. We're focused on the music and making sure our fans get the best damn show possible every night."

"Now that you're in one of the biggest bands on the planet, how does your family feel about that?" He stares at me, smirking like he's just unearthed a juicy secret.

I shoot a glance at Scarlet, then back at this jackass, my patience barely holding. "What are we doing here? This is about the band, the tour, and how Scarlet stepped up for Nate, giving the fans exactly what they wanted."

He leans in, his smirk widening. "Yes, but those fans also want to know if there's any truth to the rumors and accusations made by your mother."

Is this fucking asshole serious? I shift in my chair, fighting to keep my cool. "As I said, this is about the band and the tour. We're here to talk music, not about the past."

He leans in closer, the smugness practically radiating off him. "So, you don't deny the accusations, then."

I bite back the urge to punch the fucker in the face. "I'm not here to say anything about that. Let's focus on the music and the tour—what the fans actually care about."

"They say..." He glances down at his notes, and all I want to do is jump up, rip them out of his hands, and shove them down his fucking throat. How dare he treat my pain like it's some spectacle for the masses? "I think your mother called you a ticking bomb. Said she was scared to live with you. It was her husband who had to throw you out—fearing for her life."

My blood boils as he crosses that line, digging up shit that has nothing to do with why we're here. The rage bubbling inside me threatens to spill over, but I force myself to breathe, gripping the edges of my chair to stop me from losing it. I'm ten seconds away from walking out of this fucking circus.

"These are serious allegations. Don't you think your fans deserve to hear your side of the story?"

I've had enough. I push my chair back and stand up. "You know what? I'm done with this bullshit. I came here to talk about the band, not to relive my personal hell to boost your ratings." I tear off my microphone and fling it onto the chair.

As I storm off the set, I can hear the host stumbling over his words, desperately trying to salvage the wreck of an interview. But I couldn't give a shit. As I push through the door and step into the corridor, a sudden realization hits me—I just left Scarlet in there all alone. Great fucking move, Ace.

Leaning against the wall, I can feel the anger boiling inside me as I berate myself for bailing. That prick's insistence on dragging up the past was eating me alive. I tilt my head back and close my eyes, trying to keep the demons from clawing their way back to the surface.

What the fuck is wrong with me? I can feel the weight of the world pressing down, and it takes everything I have not to lash out at the walls around me.

As I try to zone out, I feel a hand on my arm—her touch unmistakable. I snap my eyes open and meet the worry in her gaze. My eyes roam over her face, taking in every detail before settling on her lips. Without a second thought, I grab her face and pull her in, slamming my lips against hers. The kiss is raw, desperate, and intense. She meets my urgency with equal fire, and I feel it burning through me.

I've never felt this intense desire for anyone before, and at this moment, I crave her more than ever. Amid the chaos in my head, I long for her to calm me and help me find my breath. I don't care about it being right or wrong. I just need her light to push back the darkness threatening to consume me.

"I fucking want you," I whisper against her lips. "I fucking need you."

She nods, and then gently intertwines her fingers with mine. Without a word, she guides me down the hall. We head straight out of the studio and towards the town car parked in the lot. Everything's a blur, but I'm focused on one thing and one thing only—her.

# CHAPTER 16

## Scarlet

As I lead Ace to my hotel room, I can't get over what just happened during the interview. After years of navigating Theo's demons, I've learned to recognize when someone's hiding more than they're willing to show. I saw it in Ace today—the raw pain in his eyes, the way he flinched at those prying questions. Those wounds run deep, and for that jerk to drag them out just for the sake of ratings felt beyond cruel.

I feel for Ace deeply, and with each passing day, I know I'm falling more in love with him. All I want is to take away his pain. But I can see he doesn't need sex to fix things, even if he thinks it's the answer. What he really needs is something more meaningful—something he might not even realize yet. It's the same with Theo, who always thinks that the solution is sex when, in reality, it's anything but.

As soon as I open my hotel room door, I grab his hand and pull him inside.

He looks broken—a stark contrast to the lively Ace I know, the one who'd chase after anything on two legs just to get his fix. It's like something inside him has shut down, leaving behind a shell of the man he usually is. The spark that once lit up his eyes has faded, and that confident swagger, the armor he's built around himself, is completely gone.

I toss my bag aside and lead him over to the bed. He releases my hand and pulls his shirt over his head. My breath catches as I take in the stunning ink that stretches across his chest and abs. He's beautiful in every sense of the word. It takes everything in me to not reach out and touch him. But I remind myself of the promise I made—not to let myself be his plaything again. Besides, after tonight, things will probably go back to how they were—just another person to fuck and forget.

When he goes to unbutton his jeans, I stop him before things escalate any further. "Ace," I say, my voice firm. "We're not having sex."

He looks up at me, his face a mix of confusion and disbelief. I make my way to the bed, kneel on it and extend my arm towards him. "Come lay with me," I beckon gently.

As he steps closer, I shift to the middle of the bed, maintaining steady eye contact. If I could read his mind right now, I'm sure he would be wondering what the hell I'm doing. "Lay down," I say gently.

"Why would I lay down if we're not gonna fuck? Jesus, Scar, why the hell did you bring me in here?" His voice is desperate, like he's clinging to the only way he knows to keep the demons at bay, to feel some semblance of control.

"Just humor me, Ace," I say, my tone gentle but firm.

He shoots me a glare before sitting on the edge of the bed, elbows on his knees, fingers threading through his hair. The tension in his expression is unmistakable—the battle raging inside him, torn between staying and bolting out the door.

I lean forward, pressing my chest against his back and wrapping my arms around his shoulders. I place a soft kiss on his shoulder, and I feel him tense beneath my touch. His head turns, eyes searching mine. "Just lay down with me, Ace. Please."

He lets out a long sigh and kicks off his shoes.

I move back across the bed, as he lies on his back, staring up at the ceiling as if trying to figure out why he's here. I lay down beside him, turning my back to him before reaching for his hand. With a gentle touch, I guide it around my waist, adjusting his position so that he's spooning me.

His body is tense, uncertain, and clearly not used to this kind of closeness.

I press myself against him, feeling the warmth of his chest against my back. Despite the tension between us, it's comforting. I can sense his mind racing, but I hold on to the hope that this simple act of intimacy might offer him a moment of peace, a brief escape from the chaos swirling in his head.

I push aside the distraction of his bare chest and concentrate on what I can give him—something real: a gentle touch, warmth, and comfort.

Fucking away his feelings won't help him escape his pain; he needs to feel human, grounded, and safe, even if it's just for a little while.

After what feels like an eternity, doubt starts to creep in. But then, I notice it—his breathing shifts, slowing down, becoming more even. His arm tightens around my waist, and I feel the faint brush of his face against my neck.

Slowly, his body begins to relax, the tension melting away bit by bit. I've seen Theo find this kind of solace with Nate countless times before, and I can only hope Ace is finding that same peace now, drawing comfort from our closeness in a way that words or actions couldn't offer.

Once he's finally calm and relaxed, I ask the question that's been eating at me since the interview.

"That thing Kit mentioned this morning—it was about your mother, wasn't it?" I ask softly.

His body tenses up and I brace myself, expecting him to snap or shut down, to tell me to mind my own fucking business. Instead, he takes a deep breath and lets it out slowly.

"Yeah," he murmurs, his voice barely above a whisper. I wait, hoping he'll open up, but he stays silent, his grip on me tightening just a little, like he's holding on to me and his secrets at the same time.

"Did something happen, Ace? You can tell me, you know," I say gently, trying to ease him into sharing more.

"Scar, I don't want to talk about it," he murmurs against my neck, his breath warm on my skin. He presses a soft kiss there, and a shiver runs through me, but I stay still, resisting the pull to respond. "This shit has fucked me up my whole life. You don't need to know about it."

Before I can say anything else, his phone rings, cutting through the stillness. He doesn't even flinch. Rather than reaching for his phone, he leans in, seeking solace in the quiet comfort we've built, as if this moment with me holds more significance than anything waiting on the other end of that call.

I let it go, deciding not to question him any further. If he's not ready to confront the wounds of his past, I won't force him. Instead, I stay close, wrapped in his embrace, my heart quietly aching for what he's going through. With each steady breath, the tension in his muscles melts away. Soon, his breath deepens into a soft, steady rhythm, and I know he's finally drifted off to sleep, finding peace at last.

This man has no idea how deeply I care for him, how much it hurts to see him like this. But for now, my only goal is to give him what he needs—comfort, closeness, a safe place to fall apart if that's what he needs. And as I lie here, cradled in his arms, I'm just grateful for the chance to be here for him, to be someone he can lean on, even if he doesn't realize it yet.

Glancing at the clock on the wall, I notice that two hours have passed without him moving. His arm remains tightly wrapped around my waist, while his face stays nestled close to my neck. His phone has buzzed twice, and I can't help but wonder if it's Kit trying to reach him, likely checking in after what happened during the interview.

A gentle knock shatters the stillness of the room. I glance at Ace, who remains undisturbed, his breathing steady and deep, his arm warm and heavy around my waist. Carefully, I slide his arm to the side and shift my body, gently returning his arm to its place on the bed. He stirs slightly but doesn't wake. There is a second knock, this time more insistent.

Quietly, I tiptoe across the room, feeling the plush carpet under my feet, as I reach for the door. As I open it, Theo stands there, his face etched with concern. With a finger pressed against my lips, I gesture for him to be quiet, then take a step back, letting him in.

Closing the door behind me, I turn around to find Theo standing there, his eyes locked on Ace. The look on his face tells me he senses something is going on between us.

Gently, I reach out and place my palm on his chest, hoping to grab his attention. His dark eyes lock onto mine, searching for answers.

"Theo," I say softly, "it's not what you think. Just let me explain."

"Did he fuck you?" Theo demands, his jaw tight and his gaze hard.

"No," I reply firmly, "he didn't. We never had sex. Something happened today during the interview and he was spiraling. He got lost in his head, just like you do sometimes. I was just trying to help him calm down, like how Nate helps you."

He nods, letting out a breath, and his expression visibly relaxes. "Is he okay," he asks, glancing back at Ace.

"For now, yes," I whisper. "The interview didn't go well. They started asking Ace some really personal questions, and it turned into a mess."

Theo's brows furrow in concern. "What kind of questions?"

I take a deep breath, weighing how much to share. But knowing these guys, they probably have some sense of Ace's struggles. "They dug into his past. It mostly revolved around his relationship with his mother."

Theo's jaw tightens. "Fucking assholes."

It's clear how much Theo cares for Ace, despite how often they get under each other's skin. Beneath all their bickering and tough exteriors, there's a bond that runs deep.

He glances at me, then wraps his arm around my shoulder, pulling me into a protective hug. "Just look after him," he says softly. "But Scar, if he crosses a line or tries anything, I won't hesitate to knock the asshole out cold."

I give him a small smile, knowing full well that if he or Nate ever found out what's already gone down between Ace and me, they'd lose it. The last thing I want is to get caught in the middle of their brotherhood. But the way I feel about Ace—how deeply I care—it scares me more than anything.

"I'll check in later," Theo whispers. With barely a sound, he slips out of the room, closing the door behind him, and leaving me alone in the silence.

My gaze drifts back to Ace. He's still out to it, the tension from earlier nowhere to be found. It's rare to see him like this—so peaceful, almost vulnerable. His light brown hair falls over his forehead, tousled, and I watch his chest rise and fall gently with each breath. I wonder what he's dreaming about. Has he finally found a moment of peace, or are those demons still haunting him, even in his sleep?

I pull my eyes away and walk over to the chair by the window, sinking into it slowly. Sunlight filters through the curtains, casting the room in a warm glow. I reach for my phone and begin scrolling through my feed. Yet, I find my gaze drifting back to Ace every now and then. Even in sleep, he still manages to hold a part of me captive.

# CHAPTER 17

## Ace

Another day, another city. We've left San Francisco behind, the first leg of the tour wrapped up, and now we're all crammed onto the bus, heading toward Salt Lake City.

I haven't said a word to Scarlet about what happened the other day. I have no idea how to bring it up because I never wanted her to see me for the broken asshole I really am. When I woke up, I just lay there for a moment, watching her, taking in her beautiful face. But as soon as she sensed my eyes on her and looked over, I just had to get out of there. I've never let my guard down like that with anyone before, but somehow, lying next to her on that bed calmed me, and pulled me out of my head. And for the first time, it felt like I could finally breathe.

Xander and Kit ripped me a new one when they found out I bailed in the middle of that interview, leaving Scarlet to fend for herself. But from what I've heard, she handled it like a fucking pro. Especially when that prick threw a question at her about my past, asking if she knew whether the rumors were true.

Xander and Kit agreed that it's best if I avoid the media and just focus on the tour. Honestly, I'm relieved. Xander knows how relentless the media can be once they sink their teeth into something, and he knows how this shit messes with my head. I can't go back there. I'm not opening up to anyone, and I sure as hell won't let the world see that side of me. But still, I can't help but wonder what bullshit story they'll spin.

While the rest of the band is asleep in the back of the bus, it's just me and a bottle of whiskey holding down the fort. I take a long swig from the bottle, letting the burn settle in my throat—a reminder that I can still feel something, even if it's just the sting. Setting the bottle aside, my fingers dance over the strings of my guitar as I work through a few riffs. There's something here, a sound that might be the perfect fit for what Xander's been working on, but I keep pushing it, chasing after the right note.

After the third attempt at tweaking the tune, goosebumps rise on my skin. I don't need to turn around to know she's there; I can feel her presence like a shift in the air. It happens every time she's near, this strange, electric current that surges through me. A feeling I've never experienced before, and it's fucking with my head. Maybe it's because she's the one girl who's completely off-limits—the one I should never have touched in the first place. Back in the day, if someone told me I couldn't have or do something, I'd prove them wrong. Maybe that's why I'm like this around her—it's that defiant part of me, always craving what I can't have.

I keep my head down, strumming a few strings, trying to focus, as she makes her way towards the kitchen area at the front of the bus. I steal a quick glance at her as she stands before the fridge, staring into it like she's not sure what she wants. She bites her bottom lip, and it drives me fucking wild. My eyes trace over her — that tight t-shirt revealing the bare curve of her hips and lower back, those damn dimples on either side of her spine, and those tight sleep shorts that hug her ass just right.

A surge of desire hits me like a tidal wave, my body reacting, cock throbbing with need. All I can think about is being back inside her, feeling her squirm beneath me, hearing those sexy noises she makes, and getting lost in the smell of her skin. What is it with her? Guys like me don't get attached. We get our dicks wet, and then we move on. But with her, it's different. It's like every time I touch her, I'm hooked deeper. I crave more than just the physical, more than just a quick fuck.

Holding a bottle of water and a tub of yogurt, she closes the fridge. As she turns around, I force my eyes back to the guitar, determined to focus on the music. Being trapped on this bus, with her mere inches away at all times, is pure torture. Her perfume lingers in the air, its sweet and addictive fragrance impossible to ignore. It's as if every part of her is designed to fuck with my head. My fingers stumble over a few strings, and I have to bite back a curse.

I fight the urge to glance at her, trying to keep my shit together, even though all I want is to turn around, grab her, and take what I know I shouldn't want.

The silence between us is thick, suffocating. It presses down on me, making it damn near impossible to focus on anything but the raw need clawing under my skin. My fingers strum aimlessly at the strings, but my mind's a million miles away from the music. I'm trapped in this tug-of-war, torn between the urge to break the silence, to say something—anything—that might cut through this unbearable tension, and the fear that if I do, I'll just fuck it all up. So I stay quiet, letting the silence stretch on, even though it's slowly killing me.

Then she says my name—soft but clear—and it cuts through the noise in my head like a damn knife.

"Ace."

The way she says it sends a jolt through me, making my heart race.

My fingers falter on the strings, and I close my eyes for a moment, trying to gather my thoughts. But before I can stop myself, I'm looking up, my eyes locking with hers. The lump in my throat tightens, and I know I should say something, but the words refuse to form. Instead, I drop my head back down, staring at the guitar as if it's the only thing holding me together.

She sits down across from me on the small couch, her gaze unwavering, almost daring me to make a move.

That jittery feeling rushes through me again, my body on edge like it's ready for something. I'm trying to play it cool, but the heat of her presence makes it impossible. Every inch of me is wound tight, stuck between wanting her more than anything and fighting like hell to keep it in check. It's like a battle I can't win, no matter how hard I try.

"Ace," she says. "Why have you been avoiding me since that day we did the interview?"

I try to brush it off. "I haven't," I say, but the lie hangs heavy between us, and she can see right through it.

"Please, just look at me," she insists.

I hesitate, gathering the nerve to meet her gaze. When I finally do, the genuine concern in her eyes catches me off guard.

"It wasn't anything to be embarrassed about, if that's what's bothering you," she says softly.

"It's not," I say, though deep down, a part of me is screaming that it absolutely is. I can't stomach the idea of going down that road with her, letting her see all the broken pieces I've tried to hide for so long. She pulled me back from the edge that day, out of my own fucked-up head in a way no one ever has. She deserves better than the way I've been treating her, better than all the bullshit I keep putting her through.

I take my time, setting the guitar aside on the couch. I know I owe her at least some kind of explanation.

I grab the whiskey bottle from the table, hoping it'll give me the courage to say something—anything—that might explain why the fuck I am the way I am. As I unscrew the cap and take a long swig, the burn in my throat grounds me, preparing me for whatever's next, though I have no idea how to even start.

I'm not about to spill all my baggage—not to her.

"Sometimes... things from my past creep up on me. Stuff I thought I buried a long time ago." The words scrape out of my mouth, rough and jagged, like I'm pulling them from a place that's been locked up tight for too long. "Things from my childhood that still mess with me. They just... trigger something inside, and I lose control."

I steal a glance at her but quickly look away, avoiding the pity I expect to find in her eyes.

"I don't wanna get into it—not because I don't trust you, but..." My voice trails off as I stare at the bottle in my hand, wishing I could just down the rest to avoid this conversation. She doesn't need to know all my demons. Scarlet has this light to her, this brightness I don't want to dim with my shit. I can feel her gaze still on me, and I finally raise my head to meet it. "I don't want to drag you down with me. You're better than that, Scar—better than all of this."

She stands up and comes forward.  The moment she sits down beside me, my heat races, and my mind zeroes in on the urge to touch her. But I push those thoughts aside as she turns her head and speaks.

"Ace, whatever it is, I can handle it. I want to be there for you, no matter how dark it gets." She reaches out, her hand brushing against my arm, and that simple touch ignites something inside me—feelings I've been trying to shove aside.

Strange feelings that confuse the hell out of me.

"I've seen how things get with Theo," she continues, her voice steady. "I know it's heavy, but I still want to be there for you, no matter what."

Footsteps echo behind us, and Scarlet quickly jerks her hand away just before Theo stumbles out, half-asleep. His hair's a mess, like he's been through a rough night. He stands there in nothing but his boxers, his bare chest on full display—and, of course, a waking boner.

Scarlet immediately averts her gaze, her cheeks flushing.

Theo shuffles over and flops down on the couch, staring straight at me while rubbing his crotch. Why the hell is he touching his junk while looking at me? Is he still half-asleep, or is this some weird sleepwalking shit? With this guy, anything's possible.

His eyes shift downwards to the bottle in my hand, while he continues to scratch his junk. "Gonna share that shit?" he asks.

"If you stop looking at me while you touch your cock," I snap, shooting him a glare.

He smirks, that shit-eating grin spreading across his face. "What's wrong, Ace? Afraid I'm thinking about you while I'm doing it? You should be flattered."

"Fuck off," I growl back. "Save your fucking fantasies for someone else."

Theo just smirks and winks. "Maybe I'm just practicing for your next big show."

"Alright, you two," Scarlet interjects, her voice cutting through the banter. "Theo, see that couch cushion over there?"

Theo turns, looking genuinely confused. "Yeah?"

"Grab it and put it in your lap," she orders. "Nobody wants to see you sitting there in your underwear, especially not me."

Theo snatches the cushion and hurls it at me, then drags another one over his lap.

"Happy now?" he grumbles at Scarlet before turning his attention back to me. "So, are you gonna share that drink or what?"

I can't help but smirk as I lean forward to pass him the bottle, taking note of the firm, no-nonsense tone Scarlet used with Theo. It's impressive how she manages to get him to listen, especially given how often he brushes everyone else off. But with her, he actually pays attention.

I'm sprawled out on the bed in my hotel room, trying to figure out how to kill time. I could hit up Xander, but he's out with Neil, heading to the airport to pick up Poppy and Alex. They're flying in to be with him tonight.

A knock at the door breaks my boredom.

I swing it open to find Theo standing there, decked out in shorts and a t-shirt, a towel draped around his neck.

"Put your dick away," he says, barging into the room and forcing me to step back. "Want to go for a swim?"

I shut the door, feeling relieved for the distraction. A swim sounds like just what I need. I head over to grab my swim shorts.

"Scarlet's meeting us there," Theo adds, flopping down on the couch like he's got all the time in the world, waiting for me to get ready.

I pause, turning to face Theo, my mind racing. There's no way I can go now. I need to keep my distance. Seeing Scarlet in a bikini is a fucking disaster waiting to happen. I can already picture it: me in the water, pressed against the wall, trying to hide the boner that's bound to spring up the moment she walks in. The temptation of seeing her like that, knowing I can't touch her, will be way too much to handle.

"You know what? I think I might just crash here," I say, trying to sound casual. "Got a headache from staying up most of the night talking shit with you."

"Nah, come on, fuck that. We never do anything together," Theo insists.

I keep my cool, shrugging it off.

"Nah, I'm tired. You go ahead. I might go later if I feel like it."

He gives me a look that says he can see right through my bullshit, but then he just shrugs and gets up from the couch. "Okay," he says, heading for the door. "Catch ya later, asshole," he yells over his shoulder just before stepping out.

With Theo gone, the silence in the room wraps around me like a heavy blanket, and boredom creeps in. I grab the remote, flop down onto the bed, and flick the TV on.

Some show Xander likes is playing—some Housewives shit where bitches keep tearing each other down. I've sat through this garbage at his place a few times, and it never fails to piss me off. I start channel surfing, hoping to find something that doesn't involve these bitches.

After flipping through about ten channels, my heart skips a beat. As I hit the back button, my mother's face appears on the screen, sending chills down my spine. The sight hits me like a punch to the gut, dragging me right back to that scared, broken kid with all the scars. Kit never mentioned when the interview would air, and I sure as hell didn't ask—I didn't want to know what kind of shit she might spew. But now, seeing her face up close on the screen, I can't bring myself to change the channel. Something about it keeps me frozen, unable to look away, even though every part of me is screaming to shut it off.

She looks older now, her hair streaked with gray, her face etched with the hard lines of a life wasted on drugs. Those deep creases around her mouth tell stories of every cigarette she's smoked. When I was younger, I thought she was beautiful, but now all I feel is a deep, seething hate. Hate for the woman who could never love me.

As the camera pulls back, it reveals Jerry Goldman, the hard-hitting interviewer, with his usual no-nonsense expression, ready to tackle the tough questions. But it's the asshole next to my mother that really grabs my attention—the wannabe biker still dressed like he's ready for a bar fight. I remember him all too well; the way he pressed his hand against my neck, pinning me to the wall. I can still see Xander clawing at his grip, desperation etched across his face as he fought to pull him off me.

Goldman's voice slices through my thoughts like a razor. "So, can you tell me why you've decided now to come out and set the record straight?" he asks, his tone dripping with curiosity and just the right amount of skepticism.

"With all the attention about the camera incident, I thought it was time that everyone knew the real Ace Roberts," my so-called mother replies, her voice smug and dripping with insincerity.

My grip on the remote tightens, causing my knuckles to turn white as I listen to her words. Each syllable feels like a punch to the gut.

Goldman leans in closer, his voice probing like a predator stalking its prey. "And what is it that everyone should know?" he asks, as if he's ready to pry open every dark corner of my life.

The close-up of my mother on the screen leaves a bitter taste in my mouth. How could she possibly know the real me when she never even bothered to give me a second glance? To her, I was just a nuisance, an obstacle in her life. The cruel, fucked up things her boyfriends did to me didn't matter—she laughed them off like they were some kind of joke, completely oblivious to the pain I endured. From the age of five, they'd beat me mercilessly, shoving me aside as if I were nothing more than a piece of furniture. To her, it was all just a sick form of entertainment.

"Everyone knows Ace Roberts, the rockstar. But nobody knows the person I've feared my whole life. The violent, unpredictable son who—" She takes a breath, relishing the moment before delivering the final blow, "who is capable of anything."

My chest tightens with anger and disbelief. The room feels like it's shrinking, the walls closing in around me, trapping me in this fucking nightmare.

Goldman raises an eyebrow, leaning in even closer. "Anything? That's a serious accusation, Mrs. Fletcher. Can you provide an example of this "anything" you're claiming?"

My mother sighs, sliding right into her victim act like it's second nature. "There was an incident when he was seventeen. His stepfather, Larry," she glances at the scumbag sitting next to her, "tried to protect me, and Ace didn't take it well. There was this moment when he grabbed me and wouldn't let go. That was the day I genuinely feared for my life, truly believing it could be my last. A boy should never lay a hand on his mother like that. I just can't understand where I went wrong, raising a son with so much hatred in his heart. If Larry hadn't been there, I don't know what I would've done."

She's fucking lying. Twisting the truth to put on a show, just like she always does. My pulse pounds in my ears, a relentless beat fueling the anger already building inside me. I can feel it rising, heat creeping up my neck, and the rage clawing at me, begging to be unleashed as I stare at the screen, watching her spin her web of lies.

"So what you're saying is that Ace has always been an abusive person?" Goldman asks, looking straight into the camera.

My mother keeps going, her voice trembling just enough to sell the lie. "I've always been terrified of what he might do to me. His father, and his sister, not being able to cope with Ace's violent outbursts, ended up leaving."

"Really? His father and sister left because of how violent Ace Roberts was?" The camera zooms in on Goldman's face, and I can see the wheels turning in his mind. He smells the blood in the water, ready to expose me as the monster she's making me out to be.

My anger boils over, yet I can't look away from the screen.

Goldman shifts his gaze to that smug bastard, sitting next to my mother.

"Larry," he says, "is it true that Ace Roberts, a well-known member of the most successful band on the planet, is a dangerous man?"

The smirk on Larry's face widens. "You know, Jerry," he starts, leaning in like he's about to drop some juicy gossip. "Ace has always had a temper, even as a kid. He's got a wild streak a mile wide, and fame just made it worse. I've seen him snap, and when he does, it's like a switch flips. I've had to step in more than once to keep him from doing something he'd regret. So yeah, I'd say he's dangerous. You never know what he's capable of when he loses it."

My pulse spikes, anger bubbling up, ready to explode. He's feeding them the exact bullshit they want—painting me as the fucking villain.

I hurl the remote at the wall above the TV, the plastic cracking against the drywall before bouncing off and clattering to the floor. But the impact doesn't do a damn thing to ease the rage boiling inside me; it only fuels it, making me want to lash out even more.

Goldman leans in closer, his eyes narrowing as he ramps up the tension. "So you've witnessed Ace Roberts snap? Can you share what that moment was like and what led up to it?"

"Well, Jerry, it was just before I threw him out of the house for his violent outburst. Lola and I were hanging out in the house one day, and he came in wanting something—"

"What did he want?" Goldman presses, eager for more dirt.

"Well, you know what, Jerry, I can't really remember," the asshole replies, casting a glance at my mother.

"You can't remember, you lying piece of shit, because it never fucking happened!" I scream at the TV.

"Go on, tell us what he did," Goldman presses. He's practically salivating, ready to feast on the drama.

"I caught him stealing money from my wallet," the asshole says, leaning in like he's about to drop a bombshell. "When Lola confronted him about it, he just lost it. He grabbed her by the throat and threw her to the floor. That's when I knew I had to get him out of the house, because if he stayed, I shudder to think of what could've happened next." He glances at my mother, his smirk widening. "I knew I had to do what was right. No man should ever lay a hand on a woman, especially not a son against his mother."

"So, Lola, your son Ace actually physically assaulted you. He grabbed you by the throat and threw you to the ground," Goldman says, pausing to emphasize the moment, as if he's savoring the drama.

"No, I fucking didn't!" I scream at the screen, desperate for my voice to break through the barrier between us and set the record straight.

Something inside me snaps. My vision goes red, and before I can think twice, my hand is reaching for the lamp beside the bed. The anger surges through me like a wild current, and I feel like I might explode.

My mother's face flashes onto the screen, eyes brimming with fake tears. At this moment, I know that anyone watching—especially with Jerry Goldman, the ratings king, leading the charge—will probably believe every word this bitch spews, painting me as the villain in her bullshit story.

"Yes, that's true, Jerry," my mother sniffs, delicately dabbing at the corners of her eyes with a tissue. "Ace Roberts is a violent man."

The rage detonates inside me like a fucking bomb. I snatch the lamp off the bedside table, the cord yanking out of the wall with a violent tug as I hurl it straight at the TV. The lamp crashes into the screen with a sickening crack, glass splintering everywhere as the image distorts and fades to black. But even that destruction fails to calm the storm raging within me—it's not enough. Not even close to the release I need.

I jump off the bed, fists clenched, and grab whatever I can find to unleash my fury. The chair goes flying across the room, crashing against the wall. The coffee table gets flipped over and slammed into the drywall until it splinters into pieces. Next, I target the mirror above the dresser, my fist smashing into the glass, shattering it into a million shards. My breath comes in ragged gasps, my hands raw, but none of that matters. Nothing fucking matters because all I can hear is her voice echoing in my head, branding me as a monster. And maybe that's exactly what I am.

# Chapter 18

## Scarlet

The elevator dings, and I step out into the hotel corridor, cool air sweeping over my skin as I head back from the pool. My damp hair sticks to my shoulders, and I pull the towel tighter around me. It's been a long day, and all I want now is to collapse into bed and sleep.

As I pass Ace's room, a loud crash stops me in my tracks—something heavy slamming against the wall. I freeze, my heart racing as I strain to listen. Another crash follows, accompanied by a string of furious curses. What the hell is going on?

I move closer, every nerve on high alert. The sounds intensify—glass shattering, objects being smashed. My chest tightens, as a sense of worry creeps in.

Taking a deep breath, I press my ear against the door, straining to make sense of the chaos inside. My mind races—Ace isn't usually the type to lose his temper like this. But whatever's happening in there, it's definitely not good.

I hesitate for a moment, then quickly knock three times. The second I do; the room goes dead silent.

"Ace?" I call out. My stomach twists with unease as I wait, the silence hanging heavy in the air.

I knock again, a little harder this time. For a moment, there's nothing but silence, and then I hear heavy footsteps approaching the door.

My heart pounds as the door swings open, revealing Ace standing there, his chest rising and falling like he's just run a marathon. The ink covering his chest draws my gaze for a second, but it's the wild, desperate look in his eyes that makes my breath hitch—like he's barely keeping himself from falling apart.

I glance past him, and my stomach drops. The room is a complete mess—furniture flipped over, shards of glass scattered everywhere, and the TV screen smashed to bits. It's like a hurricane ripped through, leaving nothing but destruction in its wake. Whatever happened, it's bad—really bad.

His jaw clenches, and I can see it—he doesn't want me here. His eyes, dark and intense, are a storm of emotions: anger, but something else too, something raw and vulnerable. He's spiraling, and every instinct screams at me to turn around and leave him to it, but I can't. I love this man, even though he has no idea. Maybe he'll never know, but that doesn't change a damn thing about how I feel. It hurts like hell to see him like this—so fucking angry, so lost.

"Scarlet, just go—" he begins, his voice strained, but I push past him into the room.

His hand grazes my arm, like he's trying to stop me, but I don't let it.

"Ace," I whisper, turning to face him. My voice is shaky, barely holding steady. "I'm not walking away while you're like this."

His eyes lock onto mine, and for a split second, I catch a glimpse of something—raw and real, like he's letting me in. But just as quickly, it vanishes, the walls slamming back up. I watch as he shuts me out again, retreating behind the defenses he's built to protect himself.

He just stands there, staring at me like he's lost, like he doesn't know what the hell to do next. The tension between us is so thick it's hard to breathe, but I refuse to back down. Ace might want to shove everyone away, but I'm not going to let him self-destruct like this. Not if I can help it.

"I'm serious, Scar," he says, his voice rough and low, carrying a warning that makes my heart ache. There's a flicker of vulnerability in his eyes that he's trying to bury, but it's there, just beneath the surface. "You should go," he growls again, but he still doesn't move.

Instead of answering, I take a step closer, closing the distance between us. I can see the battle raging inside him—the push and pull of wanting to let me in and wanting to shove me away. His hands clench at his sides like he's trying to hold himself back, but the desperation in his eyes is impossible to ignore.

"Don't do this to yourself," I murmur, my voice barely above a whisper, but I know he hears me.

I reach out, pressing my palm flat against his chest. His skin is hot under my touch, his heart thudding beneath my fingers.

He grabs my wrist, his grip firm but not painful, and for a moment, I brace myself, thinking he's going to shove me away. But then his eyes soften, just for a heartbeat, and before I can even process it, he pulls me in closer, his lips crashing against mine.

It's desperate, almost frantic, like he's trying to drown out the chaos in his head with the feel of me. His hand moves to the back of my neck, holding me to him as if he's afraid I'll slip away. I can taste the anger, the frustration, the hurt—all of it pouring into this kiss, and I kiss him back with everything I've got, hoping he can feel it, hoping it's enough to reach him.

Every rational thought vanishes, overtaken by the heat of his mouth on mine. I know it's reckless, and that I should pull away, but I can't.

With his firm grip on my waist, he pulls me closer, and I become one with him.

I cling to him, fingers digging into his shoulders as his tongue explores every inch of my mouth. He's all I can think about—his taste, his scent, the feel of his body pressed against mine. I need to put an end to this before it escalates. But I can't. I'm lost in him, caught up in a whirlwind of emotions I can't control.

His hands grip my hips, fingers digging in as he lifts me off the ground, pressing me against the wall with a force that knocks the breath out of me. I gasp, but he doesn't give me a chance to catch it, his mouth crashing back onto mine with a hunger that makes my head spin.

My legs wrap around his waist instinctively, pulling him closer, like I need him to keep me grounded. Everything is a blur—his body pressing into mine, the heat between us scorching, the way his lips move against mine like he's starving for something only I can give him.

I'm drowning in him, in the intensity of this moment, and I know I should be scared, should be telling him to stop, but I don't. Because, for the first time, I'm seeing the real Ace—raw, unguarded, and stripped of all the bullshit. And even though it's chaos, even though it's fucking insane, I don't want it to end. I want to be the one to pull him back from the edge, to hold him together when he feels like he's falling apart.

His lips scorch a path down my collarbone, every kiss igniting a fire that spreads through my veins like wildfire. I can feel the tension in his body, the way he's holding back, as if he's afraid of losing control but can't stop himself. It's like he's teetering on the edge, torn between restraint and the undeniable pull that's drawing us together.

"Ace," I whisper. My fingers tangle in his hair, urging him closer, wanting more of the heat that radiates from him.

He pauses, lifting his head to look at me, his eyes dark with need, a storm brewing behind them. "Scar, I—"

"Just kiss me," I breathe, cutting off his words. There's no more time for hesitation, no more room for doubt. I need him to drown out the chaos, to let us both forget everything but this moment.

Ace carries me to the bed, laying me down on the crumpled sheets. He grinds his arousal against me as his lips skim down my neck, hot and insistent.

"Ace," I gasp, my hands gripping his shoulders, urging him to look at me.

"Let me just fuck you, Scarlet, please," he pleads, his voice raw with desperation.

I nod, lost in a haze of desire that has taken over my senses. Because that's what I want—I want to feel him in the most primal way, to lose myself in the heat and passion between us.

His hands move with an insistent urgency, fingers slipping beneath my towel, teasing my skin and igniting a fire with every touch. I arch into him, my body craving more, desperate for every tantalizing caress. His kiss deepens, fierce and possessive, his tongue exploring with a hunger that leaves me breathless.

His fingers trail slowly up my thigh. When they finally find that sweet spot I've been yearning for, my breath hitches, and a soft gasp escapes my lips. As his tongue claims my mouth, driving deeper and more possessively, he pulls my bikini bottoms aside, his fingers slipping through my folds.

The moment his fingers make contact, I can't help but moan into his mouth. He explores me with a confident rhythm, teasing and tantalizing, and I'm completely lost in the heat of the moment, my body arching instinctively against his touch. Every touch has me begging for more, my need for him intensifying beyond control.

And the second he kisses down my neck, I close my eyes, surrendering to the sensation. Each tender kiss ignites a desperate longing that demands release. The way his fingers tease my clit, circling and pressing just right, sends waves of pleasure crashing through me, making my breath come in short gasps.

His lips trail lower, exploring the soft curves of my body, and I can feel the heat pooling in my core. When he reaches the towel still wrapped around me, he pauses, his gaze locking onto mine with a smoldering intensity. With a slow, deliberate motion, he grips the edge of the fabric and pulls it away.

"Take that off," he commands, nodding toward my bikini top. "I want to see your tits."

I lift slightly, pressing my breasts into his face as I reach behind to undo the strings.

The moment I do, a moan escapes my lips when he hungrily sucks on my nipple through the fabric.

This man drives me wild every time we're lost in each other, consumed by desire.

When I finally untie the string around my neck and toss my bikini top aside, I can't help but notice the way his eyes darken, filled with lust as they roam over my chest. I'm captivated by his gaze, the way it devours me, while his fingers continue to tease my clit.

"Fuck, you're beautiful," he breathes, the raw need in his voice making my heart race. It's an intoxicating sense of power, witnessing his reaction to me.

His fingers continue to work their magic, circling and teasing, and I'm left breathless, teetering on the edge of ecstasy. With every gasp and moan I let slip, I can feel him growing more feral, more desperate.

"Ace," I gasp, urging him on, "please, don't stop."

He gently inserts a finger inside me, and I moan.

"Fuck, you feel amazing," he says, his voice low and filled with need. "I can't wait to get my cock inside you."

The way he says it sends a thrill down my spine, igniting a hunger deep within me. I arch my back, urging him deeper, craving more of him. His movements are slow and deliberate, drawing out every gasp and whimper from my lips, making me feel every inch of what he's doing to me. Then he uses his thumb, going back to teasing my clit in those small, maddening circles. The pressure builds, each stroke sending jolts of pleasure through me. I bite down hard on my bottom lip, trying to keep myself from crying out, knowing I'm so close—so achingly close.

"Fuck, Ace," I pant, my voice barely a whisper, trembling with need. My hips move on their own, pressing into his hand, desperate for more. The intensity of his touch, the way he knows exactly how to drive me wild, it's almost too much to bear.

"I can feel how close you are,' he whispers in the side of my neck. "You're so fucking beautiful like this."

Every movement of his thumb, every tantalizing circle on my clit, while his fingers pump inside me sends waves of pleasure crashing through me, and I arch my back, desperate for more.

"Fucking come for me, Scar," he breathes, his voice a dark, seductive command. "Let me see you fall apart."

And with those words, the coil inside me snaps. Pleasure explodes through me, my entire body shuddering as I come undone beneath his touch. I cry out his name, lost in the ecstasy he's giving me, everything else fading away until there's nothing but him, his hand, his voice, his body pressed against mine.

# Chapter 19

## Ace

My dick aches with an insatiable craving that burns hotter than anything I've ever felt. It consumes me, that raw hunger for her, a desire so intense it leaves me breathless.

There's a part of me that's untouched, a territory I've never dared to explore, and all I want is to please her—to dive deep into the heat of her body.

Her scent hangs in the air, intoxicating, and it drives me wild, making me crave her even more. She's stunning—fucking beautiful—as I watch her ride the waves of pleasure, her face contorting in this mesmerizing dance of ecstasy. The lines around her eyes deepen, telling the story of her orgasm, while the soft moans escaping her lips create a melody that echoes in the room.

It's awe-inspiring, watching her come down from that high, and I can't help but feel a primal thrill knowing I'm the one who brought her there. I'm rock hard, throbbing with need as I slide my fingers back inside her, watching her ride out those final waves of bliss. I fucking love it—knowing she just came all over my hand.

I get off the bed, and she watches me, her gaze never leaving mine as I hook my fingers under the waistband of her bikini bottoms. Slowly, I slide them down, over her thighs, past her knees, until they're finally off her ankles. I toss them aside, my eyes locked on hers, and all I can think about is fucking her. I want to feel her tight walls squeeze around my cock, to lose myself in her the way I have before.

We don't say a word as I strip off my jeans and boxers. My cock springs free, hard and ready, and I catch the way her eyes zero in on it, her tongue darting out to wet her bottom lip. Fuck, that simple move makes me groan. I wrap my hand around my length, giving it a slow, deliberate stroke, watching her reaction.

"Come suck my cock," I command, my voice low and rough, my gaze burning into hers.

She smirks and slides off the bed to stand in front of me. Her eyes never leave mine as she sinks to her knees, a move that sends a jolt of need straight through me. Seeing her like this—waiting, willing—does something that I can't quite put into words. It's like she's got this power over me, and I'm fucking lost in it.

She glances up at me, her eyes dark and full of heat, and I can't resist. My thumb drags over her bottom lip, then I push it into her mouth. The moment I do, she sucks on it, her tongue swirling around the tip, and fuck, I can barely hold back.

"Open your mouth," I growl, my voice thick with need. "Let me fuck it."

She opens her mouth wide, and I step forward, putting my cock to her lips, then sliding it in slowly. I groan at the incredible feeling as I push deeper, holding it in the back of her throat. Fuck me, I can feel my cock pulsating as she sucks, drawing me closer to the edge.

Slipping my hands into her hair, I grip it firmly to hold her in place while her mouth delivers the kind of pleasure I desperately need to escape from my thoughts.

At first, I move slowly, sliding in and out of her mouth, feeling her soft, warm lips wrap around my cock. I close my eyes, immersing myself in the sensation, but only for a moment. The sight of her with my cock in her mouth is the hottest fucking thing I've ever experienced. No other girl has ever made me feel this way—like she truly gets me, like I'm the only one who matters at this moment.

What the hell is going on? Lately, I've been grappling with these strange feelings that keep creeping in, like I wouldn't care if she were the only girl ever to suck my cock. It's a mix of emotions I can't quite pinpoint or understand. Where the fuck is this shit coming from?

I groan as I pick up the pace, thrusting in and out of her mouth, building toward that explosive climax. Just as I'm about to lose it, I pause, holding myself deep in the back of her throat to keep from coming too soon. When she gags, a thrill shoots through me—it's a fucking turn-on, knowing I have complete control over this moment. I possess the power. But a voice in the back of my mind keeps telling me she holds more control over me now than I ever had during this whole fucking thing going on between us.

She groans around my cock, the vibrations sending a jolt of pleasure through me, making me hiss with desire. "Fuck yeah," I growl, sliding in and out of her mouth, my grip on her hair tightening as I fuck her with a frenzy that drives me absolutely wild. The way she responds to me only stokes the fire of my need, pushing me further over the edge.

I let out a moan, more vocal than I've ever been, as I thrust my hips forward, lost in the pleasure. "Damn, Scar. You're gonna make me fucking..." My muscles strain as I come hard, my release spilling down her throat. I continue to move in and out, savoring every last wave of my orgasm. The way she looks up at me from her position to watch me—intense and intimate—drives me wild, a sight that's as sexy as hell.

With my cock still buried in her mouth, I exhale, my fingers gliding along her jaw. I can't tear my gaze away from her stunning face, her long, blonde hair cascading over her tits. This girl holds a power over me that makes me come undone every damn time. She's the only chick I've fucked in the last six months, which is totally out of character for me.

"Ride me," I command, craving the way she made me feel the last time we were in my bedroom. I want her to lose herself in the moment, just like before.

She releases my cock from her mouth with a loud pop and rises to her feet, a wicked smile dancing across her lips. I sit back on the bed, ready to surrender control to her. Gently, I pull her into my lap, feeling her warmth envelop me as she settles against my body. The anticipation builds as I look into her eyes, urging her to take the reins, to let go and ride me like she wants to.

As my hands move toward her breasts, I delicately caress her curves with the tips of my fingers. Her tits never fail to leave me in awe; they're absolutely fucking amazing. The way they fit perfectly in my hands, soft and inviting. I can feel her body respond to my touch. It's more than just physical; it's an undeniable connection that pulls me deeper into this moment with her.

She lifts herself, and I watch, entranced, as she slowly guides me into her pussy. I have no idea why I love seeing my cock disappear inside her, but damn, it does something primal to me. The sensation is fucking incredible as she stretches around me, and I can tell it feels just as good for her. Scarlet closes her eyes, letting out a low moan that deepens with every inch I push in. Each gasp and sound from her only fuels my desire, urging me to explore deeper. Her body molds to mine, and I can't help but think that this is different from the mindless encounters I've had before.

"Now fuck me, Scar," I urge, desperate for her to give me the pleasure I crave.

My entire body tingles as she slides along my shaft, each movement sending electric shocks through me. Leaning forward, I kiss and suck at her neck, not giving a damn if I leave a mark.

But then I pull back, utterly captivated by the mesmerizing sight of her riding me. Her damp hair falls over her tits, and I reach out, grabbing a handful of it, pulling it back to hold her head still.

I lock my gaze with hers, losing myself in the depths of her eyes, both possessive and enthralled by the connection between us.

There's a raw intensity in the air, a blend of pleasure and something deeper that I can't quite place.

As she rides me, I can't help but let out a low growl, fully aware that even though I wanted to just fuck her to get out of my head, this isn't just about lust anymore—it's about something much more dangerous.

"That's it, enjoy my cock, Scar. Fuck it like it's yours," I say, gripping her hair tighter, ensuring she can't shift her gaze from mine. Every girl I've ever fucked, I've always turned their faces away—never wanting to see them, only wanting them on all fours, putting their wet holes on display so I can take what I need. But with her, for some fucking reason, it's different. I need to see her. I need to see the pleasure written all over her face, the way her eyes flutter and her lips part in moans.

As she rides me harder, her expression shifts from concentration to pure fucking ecstasy, and I can't help but groan out loud at the sight. Her hips move with an intoxicating rhythm, each thrust sending shockwaves of pleasure through me. I grab her ass with my spare hand, gripping it tightly, feeling every curve beneath my fingers.

"I'm close," she gasps, her voice almost breathless. I can see the pleasure building within her, that delicious tension ready to explode.

"Come on my cock, Scar. Milk me, baby," I urge, my voice low and rough, desperate for her to completely lose herself in the moment. I shift my hand from her ass, sliding a finger into her mouth. She sucks it eagerly, and I can't help but groan. Damn, this girl is so fucking hot.

I withdraw my finger from her mouth and reach around to her ass, gently inserting the tip inside her. The way she gasps, her eyes fluttering shut as she breathes out a breathy "Fuck," sends a jolt through me. She's lost in ecstasy, riding me hard as I move my finger in and out of her, our bodies syncing in perfect rhythm, pushing us both closer to that edge.

It's like I can taste her ecstasy, and it drives me wild. "Now fuck me harder and don't stop until we both come."

With her hands resting on my chest, she moves in a rhythmic motion on top of me, chasing her pleasure with every thrust. Her breathing grows erratic as she fucks me, and I work my finger deeper into her tight hole. I can feel her body arching, completely consumed by the intensity of the moment, each movement drawing us closer to that electrifying climax.

"Are you almost there? Because I'm about to—" She doesn't even get the chance to finish her sentence. Her mouth drops open, and her face lights up with a breathtaking expression as she comes. A loud moan escapes her lips, and she tightens around me, gripping me firmly as her juices flow down onto my balls.

Once her orgasm fades, she slumps into me, and I grab both of her hips, taking over completely, fucking her like there's no tomorrow. Each thrust is driven by my primal need. A pulsating sensation rushes through my body, causing my abs to tighten and my cock to throb. Scarlet sits up and threads her fingers through my hair, pulling it roughly, just like I did to her earlier. When she pulls my face towards her, our lips meet in a filthy kiss that consumes me.

She slips her tongue into my mouth, and I eagerly reciprocate. Tremors and spasms ripple through my body. My muscles tense, and my body craves more—more of her. I desperately try to hold on. The pressure within me builds as I fuck her. I feel it in my balls as they tighten, feel it in my gut as I come hard, harder than ever before. The pleasure rockets through me as I release inside her, kissing her like I'm fucking possessed. Each wave of bliss sends shivers down my spine, and for a moment, nothing else exists but us—lost in this intoxicating dance of desire.

We're both breathless, gasping for air as I collapse onto the bed. Scarlet still sits on top of me, our sweaty skin sticking together, my cock still buried inside her. She rests her cheek on my chest as we lie in a haze of post-orgasm bliss. When she finally gets up off me and heads over to the bathroom, I can't shake the nagging thought that she might leave like she did before. I lay there catching my breath, the tension of the moment still hanging in the air.

After a few seconds, she comes back into the room, stepping over the shit I've scattered around the floor. She climbs onto the bed beside me, her skin warm against mine as she snuggles close, her breath brushing softly against my neck. I should feel satisfied now, maybe even a little lighter after everything we just shared, but the weight in my chest grows heavier than ever.

She lifts her head to look at me, and I can feel her eyes, searching, questioning. I know what's coming before she even opens her mouth. I brace myself for it, but when her voice finally breaks the silence, it hits me like a fucking punch to the gut.

"Ace... why did you trash the room?"

My eyes stay fixed on the ceiling, my heart pounding in my chest. I don't want to answer. I can't bring myself to tell her about the shit that lives rent free in my head, but her gaze is relentless, like it's reaching into the darkness I've kept buried for years.

"It's nothing," I mutter, praying that she'll drop it.

She shifts beside me, propping herself up on her elbow. "It's not nothing," she says softly. "Please, Ace. Talk to me."

I close my eyes, taking a deep breath. She's the last person I want to talk to about this, not because I don't trust her, but because other than Xander, I've never let anyone in like this before. Especially not someone like her—someone I actually give a damn about.

"I saw my mother on TV," I start, my voice gravelly, as if the words are clawing their way out. "She was doing an interview, spewing all this bullshit about me. About what kind of person I am."

Scarlet doesn't say anything, but I feel the shift in her—the subtle way her body tenses slightly, waiting for me to continue. So I do, even though each word feels like I'm peeling my skin off.

"It just... brought up a lot of shit, that's all" I admit, my voice barely above a whisper. "Stuff I've tried to bury for years. All the shit I went through as a kid. All the times I had to deal with her boyfriends—those fucking assholes who thought they could do whatever they wanted because she never gave a shit."

I try to avoid looking at her, not wanting to see the pity I expect to find in her eyes, but I can't help myself. When I finally meet her gaze, it's not pity I find, but sadness that cuts me in ways I never expected.

"They used to hurt me, Scar," I say, my voice cracking. "One of them... he used to burn me with cigarettes." I lift my arm, exposing the scars I've tried to bury beneath ink. "I couldn't wait to get these covered up," I admit, the shame still raw, "because I was embarrassed for anyone to see them." I glance at the tattoo that now hides the worst of it. "This was my first tattoo," I tell her quietly.

She reaches out, her fingers brushing gently over the ink on my arm. Then she leans in, pressing a soft, lingering kiss to the tattoo, like she's trying to kiss away all the pain and scars that time left behind. The tenderness in her eyes is unbearable; it's like she's feeling every bit of the hurt I've been through, and I can't stand it. It's too much. I pull her closer, my hand sliding to the back of her neck as I crush my lips against hers, desperate to make her forget everything I just said, to erase the sorrow in her eyes and replace it with something else—anything else.

She kisses me back, but it's different this time—she slows me down, softens the pace, making each kiss deeper, more deliberate, just as intense but laced with something I can't put into words. It's like she's telling me without speaking that she's here, that she's not going anywhere, no matter how fucked up I am.

Something's shifting inside me. I'm getting too close, and it scares the shit out of me. I feel it in the way my chest tightens every time she's near, in the way it tears me up inside to see her hurt. I don't know what to do with any of this—these feelings I can't even begin to name—and it's freaking me the fuck out.

When she rests the side of her face against my chest, I hold her like she's the only thing that's keeping me from falling apart. Maybe... just maybe it's okay to let her in. Perhaps she's the one who can help me make sense of all the messed-up crap. And that thought alone terrifies me more than anything else.

I take a deep breath, my fingers gently stroking her hair, trying to push away the fear gnawing at me. "Scarlet, I don't know how to do this."

"Do what?" she asks.

"I've kept all this shit buried for so long. Never talked about it. Never let anyone close enough to see all the damage."

Scarlet's head remains against my chest, her breathing calm and steady. She shifts slightly, her fingers lightly tracing the lines of my chest as if trying to soothe me.

"You don't have to have all the answers, Ace," she says. "You don't have to know how to do this. Just... let me in a little bit at a time."

I lie there, staring up at the ceiling, feeling the warmth of her body pressed against mine. Her fingers gently trace the ink on my chest, sending shivers through me with every touch. I let her comfort me, ignoring the wreck I made of the room. For once, the chaos in my head seems to settle. There's no noise, no anger—just the steady rhythm of her touch. I focus on that, on her, letting her be the one thing that makes sense in all this mess.

"So, how are you planning to explain the mess in your room?" Her voice carries a subtle smirk, like she's trying to lighten the mood. "Or are you just gonna blame it on being a rockstar?"

I can't help but laugh, the ridiculousness of what I did breaking through the heaviness in my chest. "It'll be fine. Money can buy silence. Xander did it once with all the shit they were putting in the headlines about him. It never leaked."

My phone rings. I glance over at the bedside table, but it's not there—neither is the table. It's buried somewhere in the chaos I created. I don't even bother getting up. Whoever it is can wait; I'll deal with them later. Right now, nothing else matters but this moment, with her lying beside me, her warmth grounding me in a way nothing else ever has.

The phone rings again, and before I can ignore it, there is a persistent banging on the door. It is loud and aggressive, as if someone is breaking it down with an axe.

"Open the fucking door, Ace!" Theo yells from the other side, his voice laced with fury.

It's like a sudden splash of cold water, snapping me out of the warmth of the moment with Scarlet. My heart races, not just from his anger but from the sheer unpredictability of it all. I shoot a quick glance at Scarlet, to see her tense.

She sits up in bed, her worried gaze landing on me, amplifying the anxiety clawing at my insides. The nagging thought that he might have uncovered what's happened between us looms. The air feels heavy with tension, and I can sense my grip on reality slipping as I prepare for the fallout that's bound to come.

I let out a heavy sigh as my phone rings for the third time. Cursing under my breath, I drag myself out of bed, hastily grabbing some clothes as I head for the door.

The pounding intensifies, each thud echoing like a countdown.

"I know you're in there, fucker! Now open the fucking door!" Theo says furiously.

I glance back at Scarlet as she slips into her bikini, and a wave of dread washes over me.

Shit, the minute Theo sees her in that, he'll know exactly what's been going down between us. She gives me a worried look, running her fingers through her hair in a futile attempt to smooth it out as the relentless pounding on the door echoes in the room. Wrapping a towel around herself, she moves away from the bed, her unease palpable.

The sudden sound of Scarlet's phone ringing only amplifies my suspicions that Nate and Theo are already aware.

With Theo persistently knocking, my phone blowing up, and now hers ringing, it feels like the walls are closing in. It wouldn't surprise me if Xander is on his way here, ready to lecture me about being a fuck-up. The look of shock and disbelief on Scarlet's face as she clutches her phone tight tells me all I need to know: our secret has been discovered, and there's no escaping the fallout.

"Ready?" I shout over the noise.

"Yeah," she nods, then swipes her finger across the screen to answer the call. "Hello?"

I turn back to the door, taking a deep breath to brace myself for whatever shitstorm is about to hit.

When I yank the door open, Theo bursts through, and the usual jokester I'm used to is nowhere to be seen. Instead, he's transformed into a man full of rage, his expression fierce and unyielding. I've never seen him like this before, and it fucking terrifies me. I can feel my heart racing as I try to gauge how bad the situation really is.

Before I even get a chance to step back, Theo unleashes a punch, his fist slamming into my jaw.

"She's not some fucking groupie, you fucker!"

I stumble back a few steps, my balance wavering, but somehow, I manage to stay on my feet. Pain flares in the side of my face, but I refuse to show it; the idiot actually got me good. Damn, he can throw a punch. I see the fury burning in his eyes, and I don't even try to defend myself.

But then Theo's attention shifts to Scarlet as she moves across the room, carefully navigating through the chaos I've created. The worry etched on her face thickens the tension in the air, making every second stretch painfully long. A second later, Theo turns back to me, his eyes wild with anger, and I brace myself, ready to let him take another shot.

But he hesitates when Scarlet steps in front of him, standing tall and resolute.

I watch as his face, so full of anger, soften just a little when he sees her, but it's only for a fleeting second. It quickly morphs back to pure rage as he zeroes in on me. I can feel the storm brewing within him, and I know I'm about to get my ass handed to me.

"Theo, stop," Scarlet says, her voice firm as she keeps the phone pressed to her ear. I can hear Nate's angry voice cutting through the line, but it's all muffled and I can't make out a damn thing he's saying.

"No, Scar," Theo growls. "Not until I knock some sense into this fucker."

She switches the phone from voice to screen, and my stomach sinks as I see the fury etched across Nate's face. Shit, Xander was right. There's no way Nate is going to forgive me for this, and I can't shake the feeling that Theo won't be far behind in his judgment. Once they discover this isn't just a one-time fling, the fallout is going to be catastrophic.

"You guys need to listen to me now, and not say a word," Scarlet says, her tone leaving no room for argument.

"No way, Scar," Nate snaps. "This fucker had no right to get involved with you like this."

"Oh my god, will you two just stop?" Scarlet says, her voice sharp. But even as she speaks, Theo continues to glare at me with fire in his eyes, as if he's ready to rip me apart. I know that if Scarlet weren't standing between us, the asshole would've unleashed his fury on me already. "I can make my own decisions. I've told you both that a million times, but you never seem to listen."

"No, you don't get it, Scar," Theo spits out, his frustration boiling over. "This fucker uses chicks, and I'm not gonna let him use you."

His words cut deep into my core. Theo's right. They've both witnessed the wild days, the endless groupies, the relentless partying before we hit it big. They know my fucking slogan—the more groupies at once, the better. So, I completely understand why they'd think I'm just using her for a quick fuck. But it's not like that at all. There's something between Scarlet and me—something I can't even begin to put into words, something I don't fully understand myself. And the worst part is, I'm lost on how to explain any of this shit.

I step around Scarlet, bracing myself for Theo's next blow. "It's not like that, man," I say, struggling to keep my voice steady.

"What?" Theo laughs, his voice dripping with sarcasm. "You're telling me I haven't just walked in on you fucking her?"

"Theo," Scarlet snaps, but he's too fired up to even react. The anger blazing in his eyes and the way he's breathing like a bull ready to charge makes it clear he's not interested in any excuses I might have.

"How long, Ace?" Nate says, his tone cold and piercing. "How long have you been fucking my sister?"

I swallow hard, trying to push the lump in my throat down. This is it. Time to come clean.

"Look..." I start, but the words catch in my throat. I need to figure out what this thing with Scarlet is before I can explain it to them. I'm not about to spill my guts to these guys who know me as the asshole who dives into pussy to avoid dealing with my own crap.

"Can I ask... how did you guys find out?" Scarlet's voice comes from behind me.

"It's all over the fucking headlines," Nate snaps through the phone, his voice sharp with anger. "If I was right there right now, I'd kick your fucking ass, Ace." Hearing his voice crack stings like hell. Beneath all that rage, I can sense the deep betrayal I've caused, and it hits me hard.

"What's all over the headlines?" I ask, genuinely dumbfounded by whatever the hell they're talking about. Every time I've been with Scarlet, we've been alone—there's been no one around to see a damn thing.

Theo digs out his phone, tapping away like he's on some kind of mission. Scarlet and I watch, both of us wondering where the hell this is headed. He then turns the phone to us, and my stomach drops when he shows us a grainy photo. It's blurry, but I recognize it immediately. It's us—me and Scarlet, kissing. The image looks like it's straight out of a surveillance camera, and I know exactly when it was taken. It was right after I bailed on that interview, when I was spiraling and kissed her.

I look up at Theo, the words stuck in my throat, because it's all laid bare before us. No one could misinterpret it; with the media buzzing around us, there's no doubt that the entire world thinks we're together. The gravity of that truth presses down on me, constricting my chest.

"Fuck," I mutter, running my hands through my hair, desperately trying to figure out what the hell to say.

"Yeah, fuck is right," Nate snaps through the phone.

"Look, Nate," I start, but the words falter. I'm grasping for something—anything—to calm him down, but I don't even know what the fuck I'm aiming for here. I've never had to justify why I've fucked someone before. I've always just done my thing, no explanations needed. But now? Now, I'm lost as shit, tangled up in my own emotions and the fallout of this mess, with no clue what the fuck to do next.

"It doesn't matter," Scarlet cuts in. "I don't owe you guys any explanations. This isn't fucking high school anymore, so back off. We're adults."

Theo doesn't say a word; he just keeps his eyes locked on me, anger still blazing in them. "We're not letting this go," he says.

"I know that, and I wouldn't expect anything different," I reply, knowing how protective the two of them are.

"Oh my god, will you guys just leave it alone? I'm not a teenager anymore. Get over measuring your dicks for fuck sake," Scarlet snaps, clearly frustrated.

"Scarlet, just go," I say, bracing myself for the inevitable fallout. I know I'm about to take my punishment for breaking the bro code, but right now, I need her to get out of the line of fire.

"What?" Scarlet replies, stepping in front of me defiantly. I shift my eyes down to her, feeling the weight of the situation bearing down on us. She's not backing down, and I can see the resolve in her stance, but I need to protect her from this storm. "I'm not leaving you to face this alone."

"Just go," I say, and I can see the hurt flash in her eyes before it quickly morphs into anger.

"For fuck sake, I'll leave so you all can have your little pissing contest," she snaps, her voice sharp as a knife. She glares at me, then at Theo, her frustration palpable. With a huff, she hangs up on Nate and storms out, slamming the door behind her.

Theo's glare finally breaks when his phone rings. He yanks it out of his pocket and answers the call, his eyes still locked on me.

"Yeah, she's gone. It's just us and the fucker now," he says, his eyes boring into me like they could set me ablaze.

"Put Nate on speaker," I demand, refusing to back down. If we're diving into this shitstorm, I'm not about to waste my breath by repeating myself.

Theo takes the phone away from his ear and switches it to loudspeaker.

"I know I shouldn't have crossed that line," I start, nervously rubbing the back of my neck. "I never meant for it to happen."

"Yeah, right. More like you never meant to get caught," Nate cuts in, his tone dripping with disdain, and I can feel the weight of his judgment.

"Look," I say, trying to find the right words. "It's different with Scarlet. I don't even know what the hell it is, but—" I let out a long breath, stumbling to find the words.

"Look, I don't give a shit about your existential crisis," Theo snaps. "Or whatever the hell you're trying to sell us. Save it, Ace. We're not interested in your bullshit excuses right now."

I take a deep breath, trying to calm the storm inside me, knowing I'm walking a tightrope here. "I get it. I know it's hard to believe, but this thing with Scarlet, it just fucking happened. All I know is that this isn't some groupie bullshit. I just—fuck, I don't know how to put it into words."

Theo's eyes narrow, but he stays quiet, listening as I struggle to put my feelings into words.

Nate's voice comes through, sharp and loaded with anger. "How long has this shit been going on?"

I take a deep breath, steeling myself to come clean. "Since Xander and Poppy's wedding."

The room sinks into a heavy silence, thick enough to cut with a knife. Theo's gaze pierces me, unwavering and brimming with rage, while Nate's voice crackles over the phone, sharp and frosty. "Since the fucking wedding? Are you fucking kidding me?"

Then it's Theo's turn to unleash his anger. "You've been sneaking around and fucking her for that long? Behind our backs?"

"Stay the fuck away from Scarlet," Nate warns, his voice low and menacing. "You've really fucked up this time, Ace. Don't even think about going near her again. You and I have a serious problem, and when I see you again, I'll kick your fucking ass."

Theo steps forward, his anger ready to erupt like a volcano. "Yeah, what Nate said. If you come near her again, you'll fucking regret it."

His eyes bore into mine with a final, seething glare before he lands a solid punch to my jaw that sends me staggering backwards. He doesn't wait for a response—he just storms out of the room, slamming the door with a final, explosive bang.

# Chapter 20

## Scarlet

It's been two days since Theo barged into Ace's room and treated me like some high school girl in need of saving. The whole thing was infuriating. What's even worse is that Ace cast me aside, telling me to get out as if this whole situation didn't involve me. Since then, I've been avoiding them all—dodging their calls and ignoring Theo's relentless texts. I can't help but wonder what they said to Ace, especially considering he's now closed off to me.

But I can still feel his eyes on me. It's maddening. Why can't my brothers get it through their heads that I'm a grown-ass woman, not someone they need to protect all the damn time?

With drumsticks in hand, I'm in my hotel room tapping out a beat on the coffee table, my mind a whirlwind of frustration. Why is this so fucking hard? Why can't they just stay out of my business? I'm dying to know what they said to Ace, to figure out where things stand, but I refuse to be the one to ask. I'm too angry, too hurt. Yet deep down, I know that if he touched me, kissed me, all this frustration would melt away in an instant.

After another killer performance last night, I should be riding high, but this shit just keeps looping in my head. My phone pings, and I glance at the screen to see another text from Theo. I ignore it. I know he'll take my silence as a rejection, and maybe it might sting a little, but I need to make a point. They can't keep doing this to me forever. I need to set some boundaries.

I've never felt this alone, and it's infuriating because Ace and I were finally starting to bond. This time was different—different in the way we connected, in the way he opened up to me about the things I know weigh on him. It didn't feel like just another casual hookup. Thinking back, I realize he didn't give me his usual bullshit line about being nothing more than a quick fuck. And the way he looks at me now—it's not just lust. There's something deeper there, like he sees me in a way no one else ever has, like I'm the most beautiful thing in his world.

I know from what Ace told me the other day that he's never really had love in his life—never had anyone who truly saw him for who he is, flaws and all. And here I am, feeling an undeniable connection between us, but I can't shake the thought that it may never reach that point. I don't even know if he's capable of letting himself fall for someone, especially after everything he's been through.

A knock at the door pulls me from my thoughts, interrupting the rhythm I've been tapping out on the coffee table. I get up off the floor, leaving my sticks behind as I take a deep breath. It's probably just Theo. I remind myself to maintain the distance between us, even though it hurts just as much to keep him at arm's length.

I pull open the door, surprised to find Ace standing there. Hands shoved into his pockets, hair tousled and falling over his forehead, looking sexy as hell. Just seeing him causes my heart to race. His eyes sweep over me slowly, like I'm a goddamn feast, and it's clear I'm affecting him. I see it in the way his tongue darts out over his bottom lip, like he's fighting not to lose control. And honestly, that's exactly what I want—I want him to completely come undone.

"Hey," I say casually, turning away, feeling smug that I'm still wearing my tight sleep shorts and a snug top that barely covers my stomach. I know that if I glance back, his eyes will be on my ass. Instead, I head to the couch and sit down, deliberately avoiding his gaze, though I can still see him out of the corner of my eye. He walks over and sits beside me. That's when it hits —the scent of him, a captivating blend of rich leather and cedarwood. It stirs something deep, making it hard to focus. All I want is to get lost in him, but somehow, I maintain my composure.

Both of us remain silent, waiting for the other to speak, the clock ticking away like a countdown. He runs his hand through his hair, tension radiating off him as he searches for something to say that might ease the silence. But after he told me to leave the room like I was nothing, I refuse to be the one to break the silence. I'm used to my brothers treating me like this, but I never expected Ace to do the same. It stings more than I care to admit, the realization that even someone I care about could dismiss me so easily.

Finally, after what feels like the longest, most awkward silence in history, he speaks. "I'm sorry about the other day, Scar, and I'm sorry I've been keeping my distance." He turns his head, and I can see the truth in his eyes. "I've been an asshole, and I know it."

"Yeah, you have," I reply, not giving him an inch. My whole life, I've been treated like I don't have a brain to make my own decisions, and having the man I love do that too, it hurts like hell.

"I just don't know..." He lets out a sigh, and I can see the struggle written all over his face. He glances around the room before his eyes return to me. "I'm fucked up, Scar. I have no fucking idea what I'm doing or what I'm feeling."

For a moment, the vulnerability in his voice tugs at something deep inside me, a flicker of hope igniting.

"But you're here," I say softly. I can see it in his eyes—the flicker of something more, a hint that maybe he feels as I do. "What happened in the room once I left?"

"Just Theo and Nate letting me know how I fucked up and broke bro code."

The sheer absurdity of it makes me roll my eyes.

"I did, Scar, big time. Theo gave me another punch to bring that point home. The fucker's got a mean right hook, but I'd never tell him that." He rubs his jaw, a smirk playing on his lips.

"It's ridiculous how those two think they can control my life."

"They're just looking out for you, that's all."

"No, they want to control everything I do, and I'm sick to death of it. I can fuck whoever the hell I want, and it's none of their business."

I cross my legs, and catch the way his gaze drops, lingering just a little too long. He shifts in his chair, trying to get comfortable, but I can tell the sight of me in these tight shorts is getting to him. His eyes keep darting over me, and I notice the way his body tenses with every little movement I make. I can't help but smirk, knowing I'm getting under his skin.

To push him further, I let my hand slide slowly up my thigh, brushing against the edge of my shorts. I shift my position, making my shirt rise a little higher to reveal even more skin. His gaze follows my every move, and I notice his clenched jaw as he fights to maintain his composure.

Leaning in slightly, I let my fingers trail teasingly along his leg. Before I even reach the top of his thigh, I can see how rock hard he is beneath the fabric. I glance up at him, catching that raw, unfiltered desire burning in his eyes.

"Scar," he breathes, and even though he knows he shouldn't go there—especially with Nate and Theo aware of us—that heated look in his eyes tells me he's desperate to. Desperate to lose himself in me, and that's exactly what I want.

I close the distance between us, sliding onto his lap and straddling him, my body pressing against his. I drag my nose down the side of his neck, as his hands grip my hips, holding me firmly in place. "I don't care what they say, Ace," I murmur, my lips brushing against his skin. "If I want to fuck you, that's between you and me—not them."

I pull back to search his face, my heart racing as his nostrils flare. His eyes roam every inch of my features, and God, I want to see this man come apart at the seams, to shatter into a million pieces. With that thought spurring me on, I grind against him.

"Scar," he says, and I feel his fingers digging into my skin, more possessive on my hips.

"Do you want to fuck me, Ace?" I ask, my voice steady despite the intensity of the moment. I don't care anymore; I can see the war raging inside him, the way his breathing shifts. Those dark eyes grow heavy with lust. I can feel the tight band of his self-control weakening, so I push him further. "I want you to fuck me, Ace." His jaw tightens, and before I can register what's happening, a surprised squeal escapes me as he grabs me and lifts me effortlessly, getting up from the couch as if I weigh nothing. His grip on me remains unyielding as he strides toward the bed, his intense gaze fixed on mine. As we move, his lips crash against mine with a fierce, urgent need, and I can feel the raw hunger radiating from him. I cling to him, desperate to feel more, as he pulls me closer and lowers me onto the bed. Our breaths mingle, heavy and uneven, every touch and kiss setting my skin on fire.

"Stay fucking still," he says, his voice low and commanding. It's not a request; it's an order—one I'm not stupid enough to disobey. He shifts off me, peeling my tiny shorts away with effortless ease, followed by my shirt. I lay there, breathless, watching as his jaw tightens and his eyes scan my body, taking in every curve and contour, before pausing on my pussy. My chest rises and falls with quick, frantic pants as he spreads my legs wide. I can see the tension in his face, a mix of desire and restraint.

A shiver races down my spine as his fingers trace a slow path along my body, lighting up every nerve. My heart pounds in my chest, his intense gaze never wavering. Each touch pushes me closer to the edge, winding me tighter, drawing soft moans from my lips. The hunger he stirs in me is overwhelming, and the need building inside feels like it's about to break loose, impossible to contain.

His fingers trailing down the sensitive skin of my inner thighs. Up and down, slow and deliberate. When he zeroes in on that one spot that makes me gasp, he lingers there, teasing me just when I least expect it. It's like he's learning my body, mapping out all my pleasure points so he can exploit them in the most deliciously wicked ways.

My breath catches, and I bite down on my lip, trying to stifle the moan threatening to escape. The heat between us is unbearable, and I squirm beneath his touch, my hands gripping the sheets as I struggle to stay still. Every nerve is on fire, and all I can think about is how much I want him to push me over the edge, to lose myself completely in him.

"Ace," I breathe out, feeling his fingertips graze softly over my pussy, igniting a need for him that swells to almost unbearable levels. A whimper of frustration escapes me when he suddenly shifts course, trailing his fingers across my hip bone, deliberately avoiding the spot that's beginning to throb with desire. "Please."

I bite my lip so hard it hurts, and just when I think I might burst, I finally feel his touch where I ache the most. My thighs tremble as he outlines the shape of my pussy, each stroke sending ripples of pleasure through me. The tension builds, and I'm lost in the heat of the moment, craving more of him with every fiber of my being.

Without warning, his movements come to a rapid halt, and he leans in closer, inhaling my scent like he's savoring the moment. The intensity in his eyes speaks volumes, a silent promise that has my heart racing and my body aching for him.

"Ace," I gasp, squirming as he trails his tongue up the length of my slit. His eyes are locked on mine, and the sensation makes an unintelligible sound escape my lips. I grip the top of his head, urging him on as he shifts directions, moving his tongue in slow, torturous circles. It's a delicious blend of pleasure and frustration. I exhale sharply, my body craving more, and when I look down at him, I catch a glimpse of the small smirk spreading across his face. Then, without warning, he blows hot air across my pussy. The sensation is mindblowing.

My entire body ignites when he begins licking and sucking on my clit. I whimper and writhe beneath him, pleasure lighting me up from the inside, building and building until I can barely contain it.

"Oh God," I moan, shamelessly grinding against his face, craving more. His tongue applies just the right amount of pressure, flicking and sucking in all the right ways, changing direction just when I think I know what to expect. Damn it, this guy is about to make me melt from the inside out with the pleasure he's giving me. I know that in about ten seconds, I'll be losing my fucking mind.

I moan loudly, grinding harder and quicker against his face, taking exactly what I need as he pushes me over the edge. My orgasm crashes with such intensity that it takes several moments for me to recover. When I finally come back to my senses, I notice his penetrating gaze. It's predatory, and I see the smirk tugging at the corners of his mouth, radiating arrogance—as if he knows exactly what he's done to me and he's reveling in it.

# CHAPTER 21

## Ace

As she explodes in my mouth, I can't help but revel in the power I have over her—just with my tongue. I stand up, and before she can even catch her breath, I lean forward and slam my lips against hers. I want her to taste herself, to savor just how fucking amazing she is. The moment I slip my tongue past her lips, she melts against me. Goddamn, this girl is quicksand, and I know I'm sinking deeper under her spell.

I pull back, desperate to feel my cock buried deep inside her, craving the sensation of her tight walls wrapping around me, hungry for the sound of her moans. I yank off my shirt, kick off my shoes and socks, and quickly shed my jeans. My hard cock stands at attention, ready for the excitement that's about to unfold. I grab a condom from my pocket and toss my jeans aside. Lifting it to my teeth, I rip the edge of the packet open, and as I slide it on, I can't help but notice Scarlet's eyes glued to my cock, filled with need.

I grab her legs and yank her to the edge of the bed, her thighs spread wide, that glistening pussy on full display. I can't help but moan at the sight of her, ready and waiting for me. Fuck, I need to be in there. Lining up the head of my cock at her entrance, I push in slowly, feeling her stretch around me, the heat and tightness almost overwhelming. "Fuck me, you feel so fucking good," I growl, savoring the sight of my cock disappearing inside her.

When I'm all the way in, I pause, relishing the heat and the way she wraps around me, holding me like a damn vice. It's a rush, knowing I could easily lose control and fuck her senseless like I usually do. But with her, it's a whole different ball game. I know sometimes she craves that rough edge, wanting me to take her hard, but other times, she likes to slow it down, teasing the hell out of me.

My hand slides up around her throat, fingers splayed, gentle but possessive as I start to fuck her. A helpless whimper escapes her lips, and that sound drives me wild.

"Oh God," she moans, her body responding to me like a live wire.

I pinch her nipple, loving the way she reacts, the way she tells me exactly what she's enjoying. The louder she gets, the better. None of that fake-ass shit—she's raw and real, and I can feel every note of pleasure that slips from her lips.

A low growl escapes me as I cup her tits, my tongue swirling over her hardened nipple, loving the way she shudders from my touch. Her breathing quickens as I tease her with a playful bite. My hands slide down to grip her hips, holding her tight as I drive my cock deep inside her, relentlessly, claiming her with every thrust. She clutches the sheets, her knuckles going white as she surrenders completely, her body arching, responding to every grind, every filthy, deep stroke that leaves her trembling under me.

Her gaze locks onto mine, pure pleasure lighting up her face as she bites down on that bottom lip, trying to hold back the screams I want to pull from her. I want to hear every moan, every desperate cry as she loses herself to the way I'm fucking her, pushing her to the edge and driving her insane. I pause, letting her teeter there, so close, holding her just on the brink, her body begging for release.

She meets my eyes with that defiant stare, and I can't help the grin tugging at my lips. I lean down, letting my tongue trace over the soft skin between her tits, teasing her just enough to leave her squirming. "I want to fucking hear you," I growl against her skin, my voice thick, dripping with need. "So be a good girl, or I'm not going to give you what you want."

Then I fuck her, feeding off her moans—just how I like it. My hands tighten on her hips, hard enough to leave her aching, to remind her of this for days. The way I'm fucking her—it's fierce, relentless, like it's the only thing that keeps me grounded, like she's the only thing I need to hold onto. Her sounds, her scent, her body—all of it consumes me, like a drug I can't stop chasing. A drug I've willingly chosen, and fuck, I don't know how to stop or even know if I want to.

"Oh god," she gasps, and I can feel it—the pressure coiling tight inside me, the edge so fucking close. The way she's moaning and writhing beneath me, I know she's right there with me, ready to crash. I pick up the pace, skin slapping together in a wild, desperate rhythm. Leaning forward, I crush my lips into hers, the kiss brutal—tongue and teeth, raw, consuming.

"Fuck," I growl, my hips hammering into hers, each movement a fierce balance of punishment and reward. She digs her nails into my ass, trying to pull me deeper with every savage thrust, her body trembling beneath me. My mouth grazes her throat, and the moan she releases vibrates against my lips, her entire body shuddering in response. I pull out, then slam back into her with everything I've got, driving us both to the edge of oblivion.

Then it hits—hard. A guttural groan tears from deep within me as I shatter, my release filling her. My mouth against hers is desperate and hungry. Heat pulses as I lose myself completely, still grinding into her, riding out the last wild surges of pleasure. We're a mess, bodies slick and spent, but fuck, the need for her still simmers beneath the surface. I want to drown in her, to claim her completely until there's nothing left but us.

Breathless and panting, our bodies still tangled as the aftershocks ripple through us. I lie there, staring at her. Something about the way she looks back at me... fuck, it's messing with my head. There's something in her eyes I don't quite understand. It's not just lust or satisfaction—it's deeper, something more, something I can't put my finger on.

I shake the feeling off, pushing it down before it can get a grip on me. This isn't supposed to mean anything. It can't.

I get up and pull off the condom, tossing it into the trash without a second thought. But as I return to the bed, a weight settles in my chest. It clings to me like a shadow, something I can't quite name—something I don't want to feel. Attachment. No matter how hard I try to brush it off, it lingers, gnawing at the edges of my mind.

Sliding under the sheets, I pull her towards me, my arm draped over her waist. It's a habit now. The need to touch her, to feel her close, and it's starting to feel like something I don't know how to fight. My mind is at war with my body, telling me I should get the fuck out, keep my distance, but instead, I stay right where I am.

Fuck, the whole band's been giving me the silent treatment. Even Xander—he tore into me the second he found out. Said this shit would drive a wedge between us all, and, of course, he was right. I haven't said a word to anyone since. Just kept my distance. We've had bad blowouts before, some brutal ones, but we've always come back from it. This time, though? It feels different. Feels like something's broken beyond repair.

Theo? That bastard hasn't let up. He doesn't even need to say anything, just sits there with that fucking glare like he's waiting for me to screw up again. Like he's counting down to the moment he can rip into me. I don't know if we can come back from this.

What hit me the hardest was the silent treatment from Scarlet, as she ignored my texts and calls. I can't wrap my head around why that hurt so much.

Why the hell is she the only thing occupying my thoughts lately? Last night, not a single groupie caught my eye—I didn't want any of them. All I craved was her. And when she killed it on that stage, damn, I was bursting with pride. She owned that moment, as if she had been born to do that.

We should all be reveling in our success under the new label, riding the high together. But instead, this mess I created is wedged between us, like a wall I can't tear down.

And then, throw my mother into the mix, and it's an even bigger fuck-up. Kit told me yesterday that the media's been hounding her, relentlessly trying to get my side of the story. But there's no way in hell I'm doing that. No way I can relive all that shit. There's no way in hell the world needs to hear all the shit I went through. Meanwhile, she's out there selling her story like it's the damn gospel. And now it's everywhere—every feed I scroll through on my phone, like a constant reminder.

Scarlet shifts beside me, resting her chin on my chest, staring up at me with that smile on her face. And fuck, seeing her like this does something to me. Makes me feel good, like I'm the reason she's smiling like that. I lift my hand and tuck her hair behind her ear, wanting to memorize every detail of this moment.

"You're beautiful, you know," I say, and I can't believe those words came out of my mouth. It's not something I've ever said to anyone before, but with Scarlet, I'm doing shit I never thought I'd do. She has this way of getting in, pulling my dark shit to the surface, and somehow making it okay. It's like with her, I don't need to hide who I am. And that shit fucking terrifies me.

Now that the guys know about Scarlet and me, I couldn't give a shit if they find out what we just did. They don't understand—this feels different from the chicks I've fucked before. With Scarlet, I can actually talk about shit, and she won't judge me for it. She makes me feel safe enough to let my guard down. I want to hold on to this feeling, but part of me is screaming to pull back before I end up revealing too much.

And the sex? Well... Fuck, that's off the charts too, in a way that's hard to put into words. It makes me want to keep coming back for more, which is another thing messing with my head. Normally, I'm the type to bail right after I've fucked a chick—no strings attached. It's always been that way, even back when I was just a horny teenager looking for the next thrill. But lying here beside her, I don't feel that usual itch to get up and disappear. So, I just stare at her, feeling something that's both foreign and fucking weird, but there's this warm, comforting vibe rolling through me.

"What are you thinking about?" she asks.

I can't help but smile at her question. "Just thinking about what happened the last time we were like this," I say.

"Well, didn't that turn into a shitshow," she says, her voice dripping with amusement. "I'm just waiting for Theo to come pounding on the door." She laughs, and that sound hits me in a way I don't expect. I smile.

That's another odd thing I'm doing these days—smiling. My fingers trace the twisting vines on her arm that lead into the lion's head.

"What does this mean?" I ask, as I study the ink on her arm.

She lifts her arm, her gaze lingering on the intricate ink. "The vines symbolize growth and resilience, while the lion's head represents courage—the kind that pushes you to face your fears head-on."

"What fears do you have?" I ask, genuinely curious.

Her eyes flicker with a hint of vulnerability. "I fear never fitting in, never finding the right place where I truly belong. Sometimes it feels like I'm lost, searching for a spot in this world, and I haven't found it yet."

Her words hit me like a ton of bricks, and a heavy feeling settles in my chest. It strikes a chord within me, more than I care to admit. I want to let her know that she's not alone, but I can't find the words. Instead, I just nod, wishing I could take away that fear for her, wishing I could show her she's not as lost as she thinks.

"Do you want to do something today?" I ask, trying to keep it casual, but a part of me is wishing for more than just another round in bed.

"What do you mean?" she replies, her brows knitting together in confusion.

"You know, something other than this," I say, a grin on my face, as I gesture between us. I don't want her to think it's a date or anything serious—because it's definitely not—it's just two people hanging out and having a good time. "Like, go see the sights. It's our only day left here before we get back on the bus. With all the shit that's gone on, I thought we could use a break and maybe go check out a few things."

"Yeah, but what can we do? You're famous. It's not like we can just go for a stroll through the city," she says.

I laugh, thinking back to that time on our New Zealand tour when we used disguises to blend in and see the sights without anyone spotting us. Theo's ridiculous get-up comes to mind, with his seventies porn-stache, and I can't help but grin. It stings a bit, realizing that those days might be over now—of hanging out with the guys.

She raises an eyebrow. "What's so funny?"

"Whenever we would go out somewhere like today, we all would wear disguises," I explain, trying to lighten the mood. "Xander started the whole thing back when he used to sneak off by himself. But you should see Theo's get-up—he rocks these massive sideburns and a mustache that looks straight out of an old porno film."

She bursts out laughing, her eyes sparkling with that infectious energy. "Yeah, that sounds just like him."

But then I notice her smile falter, a hint of sadness creeping in. It stings to realize she's thinking about Theo, and it fucking sucks that I've come between them.

"So, when do you want to head out?" she asks.

"We can head out now if you're up for it," I say. "But first, you might need to hit Kit up for some kind of disguise."

She gets up off the bed and stretches, and damn, it's a sight to behold. "I need to hit the shower first," she says, grabbing her phone.

As she stands there texting Kit, I can't help but let my eyes wander over her tight body, and my cock reacts. It's impossible to ignore how she gets me so worked up. She's fucking beautiful—hot as hell—and those tattoos covering most of her body just make her even hotter.

She drops her phone onto the bed and turns toward the bathroom.

I get up and follow her, driven by the thought of getting in on some steamy shower sex. There's no way I'm fucking missing out on that.

As I wait in the lobby for Scarlet to arrive, looking like some damn blonde surfer dude, all I can think about is what went down in the shower. The moans I pulled from her are etched into my mind, and I know I'll be reliving those moments again, with my hand wrapped around my cock, just like I've been doing these past few days. Every time I think about the filthy things we've done, it's like my body's wired to remember every detail—her skin glistening, her breath hitching, the way she wrapped her legs around me. It's impossible to ignore how much I fucking crave her.

I pull out my phone and check the time. I'd left Scarlet in her room while she waited for Kit to deliver her stuff. We agreed to meet at eleven-thirty, and I've got a few minutes to kill. I sink into one of the seats, fully aware of the stares coming my way. My disguise seems to be drawing more attention than it should. Much like Xander's, but it's the only way I can move around without people recognizing me. Better to be under the radar than out in the open, exposed and vulnerable. I'd rather deal with the awkward glances than have some overzealous fan or a tabloid reporter shove a microphone in my face, trying to catch me off guard.

As Scarlet moves towards me, I catch a few guys checking her out as they pass by. She flashes me that smile, the one that drives me wild, and I know she's totally smirking at my disguise right now.  I get up onto my feet.

"What do you think?" she asks, her voice teasing as she twirls a lock of that black wig between her fingers.

I step closer, lowering my mouth to her ear. "You're gonna leave it on while I'm fucking you tonight." The words spill out, low and rough.

This whole situation is so wrong yet so right, and the way she looks right now only makes it harder to think straight. Just the thought of her in that wig, has me revved up and ready to forget about everything else.

She pulls back just enough to meet my eyes. "But we're on the tour bus tonight," she reminds me.

I let out a low groan. "Well, I guess we'll have to get creative." I take a deep breath, feeling a rush of excitement as I stare at her for a second longer than I should. And then, I do something I've never done before. I reach out and grab her hand. It's not my usual move—holding hands is too damn intimate, too close, like I'm letting someone get under my skin.

She looks up at me, and I catch a spark of surprise in her eyes. She glances down at our joined hands with a smile playing on her lips.

"We've got a cab waiting," I say. "Kit set it up. I thought we could hit the lake, get away from all the bullshit for a while."

We walk out of the hotel, side by side, heading toward the cab. The driver's already waiting, and I help her in—yeah, it feels a bit intimate, but I brush it off. Just something different, I guess. No big deal.

I slide in beside her, and lean back in the seat, trying to chill, but my mind's all over the place. The city noise fades as the door shuts, and I can't help sneaking glances at her instead of looking out the window.

Just as I'm lost in thought, her phone buzzes, breaking the silence. She pulls it out of her handbag, and I catch a glimpse of the screen.

It's a message from Theo.

**Theo:** I'm sorry, Scar.

I watch the screen as she quickly types out a reply, her thumbs moving fast over the screen.

**Scarlet:** I know. I'm sorry too.

**Theo:** Be careful, Scar. That's all I ask.

**Scarlet:** I'm not a little girl anymore, Theo.

**Theo:** I know. I love you.

**Scarlet:** I love you too.

Not wanting her to catch me spying on her messages, I quickly avert my gaze as she slips the phone back into her handbag.

I can't fucking wrap my head around how easily people toss around "I love you." I've heard Xander say it to Poppy and Alex countless times, and Theo and Nate have their brotherly bond, tossing it back and forth without a second thought. It's like they're speaking a foreign language—one I've never learned. Hell, I can't even imagine what it would feel like to say those words.

# Chapter 22

## Scarlet

The energy on stage tonight is off the charts—we're absolutely killing it, and the crowd is buzzing. But there's an undeniable tension between Ace and Theo, and I can only hope the fans aren't picking up on any of it. Though, judging by the crowd's reaction, they seem completely lost in the music, enjoying the show.

Suddenly, a thought strikes with the force of a freight train: what if this is as good as it gets for me? The question gnaws at my mind, a heavy weight settling on my shoulders. This is what I've always dreamed of, but the fear of it slipping away terrifies me. Am I ready to face that reality?

As the song fades out, Xander steps forward, commanding the stage to address the crowd, while Theo and Ace move toward the platform where the drum kit sits. This part of the show is usually a moment for them to take a sip of water and catch their breaths before launching into the next track. But tonight? The tension between them is palpable.

I keep my focus on the crowd, praying that these two idiots don't come to blows. The deafening roar of the fans fades as I catch Theo shooting a sideways glance at Ace. But Ace? He's stone-faced, staring straight at Theo. What the hell is going on between them?

While grabbing the bottle of water from the ground beside me, my gaze accidentally locks with Ace's. There's something in his eyes—a raw desire that sends a thrill of excitement through me. For the first time, it feels like we're finally making progress. He's letting me in, piece by piece, and it's thrilling.

Every day, I'm falling harder for Ace, and I know it's dangerous as hell given his unpredictable nature. Sometimes, it feels like he's on the verge of pushing me away. Yet, there are those surprising moments that catch me off guard—like when he grabbed my hand earlier today in the hotel lobby. He's never done that before. In those rare glimpses when he lets me in, it feels like something real is forming between us, even if Ace would never admit it.

It's a bit ironic, really, because despite all the warnings from Nate and Theo to stay the hell away from Ace—especially after whatever happened in that hotel room—I can't help but laugh at how their antics have somehow pushed us closer. Their attempts to protect me have only tightened the bond Ace and I are building, whether they realize it or not.

Theo gulps down his water, his eyes narrowing into a fierce glare as he turns around to face Ace. He's definitely pissed. The way Ace and I glanced at each other clearly didn't go unnoticed. Theo tosses his now empty bottle to the side. As his gaze meets mine, I see a warning in his eyes before he confidently strides back to the opposite side of the stage, purposefully creating distance between himself and Ace.

This shit needs to end. The tension between Theo and Ace is not only affecting their own dynamic, but I can also feel it spreading into Xander and Ace's. It's only a matter of time before it all goes to hell.

Maybe I should call a band meeting tonight on the bus. I know it's not really my place since I'm just a fill-in, but I can't keep being the reason everyone's walking on eggshells. These guys should be celebrating their success and living the dream they've worked their asses off for, not dealing with this constant tension.

As Xander moves over to grab a drink, Ace plucks a few strings of his guitar, sending the crowd into a frenzy. As soon as Theo joins in, the energy levels soar, making it impossible to overlook the mounting tension between them. This isn't just music anymore; it's turned into a competition. Xander, sipping his water, watches the two of them as they inch closer to the middle of the stage.

Each guy is determined to outplay the other, making it more like a pissing contest than a performance. Theo smirks at Ace, a silent challenge passing between them, and Ace meets his gaze without flinching. He steps in even closer, and suddenly, it's a full-blown guitar showdown.

The crowd eats it up, cheering louder with every note. Theo's fingers fly over the strings, showing off, pushing Ace to step it up. Ace responds without missing a beat, his eyes locked on Theo's, daring him to take it further. The sound of their guitars battling it out echoes across the venue.

I glance across at Xander, still watching, a smile tugging on his lips. He knows this isn't just about the music. It's personal.

Finally, Ace hits a riff so hard and clean that Theo hesitates for a split second. It's enough for Ace to step back, smirk in victory, and let the last note hang in the air. The crowd goes wild, their cheers deafening. Theo shakes his head, backing off with a tight grin. As he steps forward, he gives Ace a pat on the shoulder. It's a small gesture, but it's enough to give me hope that maybe, just maybe, things can get back to the way they were between them.

The whistles and cheers from the crowd make it clear just how much they loved that showdown. I spot the smiles on both Theo and Ace's faces, the tension easing just a bit. Xander grins as he strides back to the mic, soaking up the energy. Within seconds, Ace counts us in, and we're back into the set.

The night's been unforgettable, the adrenaline still coursing through us as we pile onto the tour bus. Theo drops onto the couch, cradling a half-empty bottle of whiskey. He's unusually quiet, and though he doesn't mention it, it's clear that he misses Nate. The two of us haven't really talked since that day in Ace's room, and tonight, I'm determined to change that. I need him to hear me out.

As soon as I sit next to him on the couch, Theo turns his head, offering me a small smile. It's barely there, but enough to bring out his dimples and reveal a flicker of relief. He knows I'm dropping my guard, letting him in, and that little gesture tells me he's ready to listen.

He holds out the whisky bottle, and I take it, letting the burn slide down my throat before passing it back.

"You were killing it out there tonight," Theo says, and despite everything that's happened, his words resonate with me. That's the thing about Theo—no matter how frustrated I might feel, he always manages to lift me up.

"So were you," I reply, a smile creeping onto my face.

"Are we good, Scar?" Theo asks, his gaze steady and searching, like he's looking for some kind of reassurance.

"Yeah, we're good," I reply. "But I wanted to talk to you about some things." I glance over at Ace and Xander by the fridge, grabbing beers, engrossed in their conversation. I don't want them overhearing this, so I redirect my attention to Theo. Later, I plan to give Nate a call to have the same conversation. "I know you don't like what's been going on between me and Ace," I say, treading carefully to avoid pushing too hard.

Theo tenses, his jaw tightening before he takes another swig from the bottle. "That's because I know what he's like, Scar. He's solid with us, no question. But with women? He views them as nothing more than a distraction, a way to escape. Nate and I... we just don't want you to be another notch on his belt. You deserve better than that."

His words hit hard, but I can't deny there's some truth in them.

"I know what I'm doing, Theo," I say, striving to sound confident.

He searches my eyes, a look of concern etched on his face. "Don't fall in love with him, Scar. He'll only break your heart."

I hold his gaze, letting his words sink in, the weight of the situation pressing down on me.

"Please tell me you haven't already gone there, Scar," he says, his voice softening into a near whisper, almost pleading.

I can't bring myself to answer; the silence between us speaks volumes.

I glance down, picking at a loose thread on my ripped jeans, avoiding Theo's intense gaze. He's watching me closely, reading every subtle shift in my body language. I don't know how to tell him it's already too late—that I've fallen hard for Ace—without setting him off. I dread seeing the disappointment or frustration flicker across his face.

"Fuck, Scar," Theo mutters, reaching for my hand. His touch is rough but oddly comforting. "He'll never love you. You know that, right? He's broken, just like me."

The words hit hard, and I swallow, struggling to keep it together. I can't ignore the truth in what he's saying, even if it hurts like hell.

I lift my head, meeting his gaze.

"But you loved Bianca."

"Yeah, I did. Loved her more than life itself," he admits, his voice cracking as tears glisten in his eyes. The pain of that love, of losing her, is etched all over his face, and it hits me hard. Theo loved Bianca with everything he had, and I know that kind of love doesn't just fade away. It scars you, changes you forever.

"I don't want you to get hurt," he continues, his tone heavy with concern. I can feel the weight of his words, and it's crushing. He doesn't want me to endure the same pain he did.

"I don't want that either, Theo. But I can't help who I love," I reply, my voice steady despite the turmoil inside me. He releases my hand and pulls me closer, wrapping his arm around my shoulder.

"I know you can't," he murmurs, planting a gentle kiss on the top of my head. "I just want you to know that when that time comes—when he can't return that love—I'll want to kill the asshole for hurting you. But I'm always here for you, Scar. Always."

I lean into him, grateful for his support, even as I step into something I know I can't fully control.

"Please don't hold a grudge against him. I don't want to come between the two of you," I say.

Theo sighs, resting his cheek against the top of my head. "Don't worry. It's just what we do. We piss each other off, but we always come around. It's just gonna take a little longer for me and Nate this time because... well, he should never have gotten involved with you, Scar. I think it's going to take even longer for Nate to forgive him."

We sit quietly for a while, the adrenaline from the night slowly fading. The bus doors close with a soft hiss, and the engine hums to life.

Xander and Ace wander over and take their seats on the couch across from us. When Ace's eyes meet mine, there's a brief spark of connection, but he quickly looks away.

Theo feels it too; I can sense his body tense beside me, wrestling with the reality of what's going on between Ace and me.

I push myself up from the couch, creating some distance to allow the guys to work things out, hoping they can communicate or at least try to repair their strained relationship.

"Where are you going?" Theo asks.

I turn back to him and flash a light smile, hoping to ease the tension just a little. "I'll leave you guys to talk."

Before I can step away, Theo grabs my hand and pulls me back down onto the couch. "Fuck that, Scar. This is what we do after a great night. We sit and celebrate."

I raise an eyebrow, smirking. "Funny, I thought it was usually you finding a groupie."

He grins, that familiar Theo charm breaking through. "No, not when we're on the bus. Though, that hasn't stopped me from trying to sneak one on, but it just doesn't feel the same without Nate."

Theo turns his head, and I catch the brief moment when his gaze meets Ace's. Ace quickly looks away as soon as Xander's voice breaks the silence.

"That little guitar battle you guys did," Xander says. "You should do that shit again."

I glance over at him and spot a smirk on Xander's lips. "And next time, Ace, how about letting the dickhead win at least once?" he adds, throwing Theo a grin.

"Fuck off," Theo replies, rolling his eyes. "I let the asshole win."

"Yeah, right," Ace shoots back. "The day you win will be the day I fucking let you."

Theo grins. "Keep dreaming, old man. Even a broken guitar can play a decent tune. You're living proof."

"Coming from the guy who thinks three chords make a masterpiece, that's rich."

Theo raises his whisky bottle in a mock toast. "Hey, better three solid chords than six strings of pure bullshit, right?"

With each passing hour of the night, the atmosphere undergoes a gradual transformation, accompanied by the constant hum of the bus as it makes its way to the next city, seven hours away.

When Ace and I made our way down to the lake earlier today, there was one of those rare moments—just the two of us, sitting on a bench with ice creams in our hands. That's when he started opening up about his mom. He said it feels like the walls are caving in with all the bullshit stories she keeps spinning, and how the media won't stop hounding Kit to get his side of things. I understand why he doesn't want to go there. I've watched Theo struggle with memories that send him spiraling. The past has such a tight grip on them both, even when all they want is for it to vanish. But the truth is, it won't vanish—not until they confront it head-on.

Xander left us about an hour ago and made his way to the back of the bus after getting a call from Poppy. So now it's just the three of us. Nursing the last drops of his whisky, Theo remains sprawled out on the couch. It's clear he's lingering, his eyes darting between Ace and me, as if waiting for one of us to retreat to the bunk beds in the back. The last time we found ourselves in this situation, Theo had no problem leaving me alone with Ace. But now that he knows about our secret affair, I'm pretty sure he's sticking around, convinced he's playing the ultimate cock block for Ace.

Theo's had way too much to drink. He's gone quiet, sinking into a brooding silence, clearly stewing over whatever's on his mind. "Why, Scar?" he asks Ace. "Why not just fuck a groupie instead? Why'd you have to go there, man?"

Turning my head to Ace, I hope this conversation won't escalate any further. His gaze locks onto Theo's, and I see him swallow hard before glancing down at the empty bottle in his hand. He fiddles with the label, making me wonder if he's trying to ignore Theo. But then he looks up, meeting Theo's gaze, and I brace myself for what's coming next.

"It's not about just fucking around with groupies, Theo. This is different." Ace's voice is steady but tight.

Theo blinks, clearly trying to wrap his head around Ace's words. "Come on, Ace. I know you better than that. You really expect me to believe that you fucking care for her?"

Ace's gaze hardens. "Yeah, you could say that. And I know you won't remember this shit in the morning."

Theo remains skeptical, his brow furrowing. "You think you're fooling anyone? You're not exactly the poster boy for long-term relationships. So what makes this one different?"

Ace's jaw tightens as he glares at Theo. "Look, I'm not here to convince you of anything. I just know it's not the same as the other shit."

Theo scoffs, clearly not buying it. "Oh really? Since when did you become the expert on feelings?"

I can feel my patience wearing thin, caught in the middle of their escalating argument and the tension that's suffocating the room. "I'm heading to bed," I say, my frustration seeping through. "I can't deal with this right now."

Without waiting for a response, I head towards the back of the bus, needing to escape and find a little space to breathe.

# CHAPTER 23

## Ace

I watch as Scarlet makes her way to the door at the back of the bus. I can't shake the guilt for having this conversation in front of her. Theo's furious and clearly drunk, and I've never seen him like this—brooding and stewing over shit. I wait until the door clicks shut behind her before shifting my focus completely back to Theo.

Theo downs the last drops of whisky, his eyes narrowing into a glare.

"I don't get why this is so hard for you, man," I say, the frustration slipping into my tone. "I've tried to explain—"

"Because it's fucking Scar, dipshit," he interrupts, his voice rising. "Of all the fucking chicks out there, you had to go after her. I've seen your game. I know why you fuck them. So don't feed me some bullshit story to make it sound alright. This will never be okay."

I'm at a loss for words. How do I explain this pull I feel towards her, something I've never experienced with anyone else? It's like trying to explain why gravity keeps my feet on the ground—it's just there.

"Yeah, I know, Theo" I finally admit, feeling the weight of his words settle heavily on my chest. "And I shouldn't have crossed that line, but like I said before, I do care about her."

Theo's eyes flash with anger. "Yeah, right. Until the next chick comes along and wants to suck your fucking cock. You fuck girls to escape the shit in your head, to forget the past. Scar deserves more than that, more than you. And I won't let you treat her like some damn groupie."

I take a deep breath, working to keep my cool. "You think I don't fucking get that? I'm not here to screw around with her feelings, Theo. Sure, I've got a shit track record, but I'm not about to be the asshole who treats her like just another quick fuck. I know she's got a good heart, and I'm not about to mess with that."

Theo's eyes narrow, his gaze sharp. "Then fucking prove it. Scar's had enough guys mess with her, and this isn't just about you and me—it's about what she deserves." His jaw tightens. "I know you're no fucking good for her, Ace, but if you're not gonna keep your distance, then you better fucking deliver. I need to know you're not just another fuck-up in her life." He looks at me, his voice low and deadly. "Because if you do, I swear to god you'll regret it."

Even though every part of me wants to tell the asshole to fuck off, I have to give him credit.

His loyalty, that fire to protect the people he cares about, is something I can't just brush off—no matter how much it's pissing me off.

"I fucking warned you Ace this would happen," Xander says coming towards us.

Theo's eyes snap from me to Xander, betrayal written all over his face. "Wait... you knew about this? You knew what was going on between him and Scarlet?"

I can see it in Theo's eyes—the hurt, the betrayal.

Xander and Theo are close, and Theo looks like he's just been stabbed in the back.

"Yeah, I knew," Xander says, his voice steady despite the tension swirling around us.

Theo stands up from the couch, jaw clenched, and storms to the back of the bus without a word. I knew this was coming, everything Xander said has happened, and now here we are, knee-deep in shit. Dragging Xander into this mess was never part of the plan, and it pisses me off that it's gone this far.

"Well, that's just fucking great," Xander says, shooting me a sharp look. "Now everyone's gotta deal with this shit just because you couldn't keep your cock in your fucking pants."

It's been a few days since the blow-up on the bus, and the guilt's been eating at me nonstop. I can't stand the fact that I've become the wedge driving this tension within the band. Xander's still pissed, but he's been sending the occasional text, checking in like he always does. He knows how quickly my mind can spiral, and even though he's angry, those small gestures tell me that we'll find a way through this. Maybe, given enough time, we'll figure out how to get past it all.

Theo? He's a whole different story. The usual sarcastic asshole has gone dead silent on me—cold shoulder, side-eye, the whole damn package. And honestly, I get it. Sometimes I think he's right. Scar deserves someone better than me, better than the mess I bring. Deep down, I know I'll never be the guy she really needs, the one she deserves.

I can't help but wonder if Xander went through this same shit with Poppy all those years ago. But I doubt it. He knew what love felt like because of his mother, even if it was just for a short time.

Me? I've never had that. Never had anyone show me what love is supposed to feel like. So how the fuck am I supposed to recognize it if it's staring me right in the face? I don't even know if these feelings I've got are love. And if they are, I don't want it. It's screwing with my head, making me do things I wouldn't normally do. It's making me... soft. And I fucking hate it.

I've been holed up in my room for hours, feeling like I'm teetering on a tightrope. One wrong move, and everything could blow up all over again. I'm not ready to face the band, not after all the shit that's happened. But damn, this boredom is starting to gnaw at me, and I don't know how much longer I can take it.

Lying on the bed, I scroll through my phone, and it's the same old shit. Headlines plastered with my mother's face, each one, dragging me back to all the shit she put me through as a kid. Here I am, twenty-five years old, still feeling like that powerless little kid she hurt time and time again. It infuriates me that she still has that hold on me.

I toss my phone aside and stare up at the ceiling, trying to figure out what to do next. Maybe I'll head down to the pool for a swim. Fuck, what if Theo's down there? It already stings that he's giving me the silent treatment. Who would've thought I'd actually miss that annoying dickhead and all his bullshit?

I sit up, frustration boiling over as I swing my legs over the side of the bed, my feet sinking into the plush carpet. Before everything went to shit, Xander gave me a song he was working on. Maybe I should dive into that—at least it'll give me something to focus on, something to help me pass the time.

I get off the bed and grab a joint from my bag, lighting it up, hoping it'll help relax me and clear my head. After I grab my guitar and go to sit down, there's a knock at the door. With guitar in hand, I walk over and glance through the peephole to find Xander standing there.

I open the door and step back to let Xander in. He glances at the instrument in my hand and raises a brow.

"You working on that song I gave you?" he asks, stepping inside.

"Yeah," I reply, wondering why he's here.

If he's come to lecture me about all the shit that's happened, he can turn his ass around and walk right out of here. Hell, I'll even hold the door open for the bastard.

I walk over to the bed, toss my guitar down, and then head over to the couch, sitting beside him. His eyes follow my every move, like he's just waiting for me to break the silence, to say something first.

"What's up?" I ask, feeling the tension thick in the air.

I pass the joint to him, like old times, sharing it the way we used to when we'd just sit around, shoot the shit, and let all the crap in our heads float away.

He grabs the joint, taking a slow, deliberate drag, before handing it back to me. "Just haven't seen much of you these past few days. Thought I'd check in."

"Thought I'd keep my distance," I reply, running my hand across the back of my neck.

"I wanted to see how you're holding up with all the shit still going on with your mother," he says, watching me closely, his gaze piercing through the mask I'm trying to wear.

I take a drag from the joint, exhaling slowly before answering. Despite everything that's happened, even with him pissed at me, Xander still gives a damn about the shit I've been through, the demons I'm stuck fighting. He's always been my bro, and that's one thing I know won't ever change.

"Everywhere I fucking look, she's there, sprouting her shit," I say, glancing at him. "I don't know why she's doing it."

"Do you want to set the record straight?" he asks. "I know it's hard, but it might shut her up."

I look away, staring across the room. "I can't go there, man. I can't relive all that shit again, even if it means she'll finally shut the fuck up."

"Okay," he replies, his expression shifting to something serious. "I need to ask you something, and I want you to be straight with me, Ace. No bullshit."

I glance back at him, curiosity creeping in about where this is going. Our conversations lately have shifted from the usual bullshit to more serious, grown-up topics. Guess that's what happens when you get older—things get deeper. Or maybe it's because Xander's got Poppy and Alex now, letting his guard down a bit. But now I can't shake the feeling that he's about to probe into this thing with Scarlet. Even without him saying a word, that thought has me shifting uncomfortably.

"Scarlet," he says. "Why the hell couldn't you stay away from her when I asked you to, Ace?" He leans over and takes the joint from my fingers.

I direct my gaze to the floor, the weight of his question pressing down on me. How the hell do I explain this magnetic pull I feel whenever she's around? I don't even know where to start, but he asked for the truth, and that's what I'm going to give him.

Finally, I look up and meet his gaze. "I don't know why. Every time I tried, I just couldn't put any distance between us."

He nods, studying me closely. "Seriously, man, do you actually enjoy being around her? Like, beyond just the physical stuff. I mean, can you just chill and talk, or is it all about the sex?"

"Fuck, what is this, twenty questions?" I shoot back, trying to lighten the mood. But honestly, I'm baffled about why the hell he's digging into this. We never talk about shit like this.

"Just humor me, Ace," he replies, passing me the joint.

"Yeah, with her it's more than just fucking around," I admit, running a hand through my hair. "We actually sit and talk about stuff—shit I've never shared with anyone before."

With a smirk on his face, he leans back on the couch, making me feel stupid for laying out all that mushy crap. Shaking his head, he mutters, "Fuck."

"What?" I ask.

"I've been there, Ace," he says, a nostalgic look creeping into his eyes. "Those confusing-as-shit thoughts you're dealing with, wondering why the fuck you can't just walk away from her like you've done with every other chick you've hooked up with. It's as confusing as shit right now, isn't it? And let me tell you, it doesn't go away."

He's right—it's confusing as hell. I don't have a clue where this conversation is going, so I stay quiet and let him keep talking.

"Remember that night we ditched school and crashed at your place, working on those last three songs?" Xander says.

"Yeah." A smile creeps onto my face as the memory hits me, crystal clear. That night, we dreamed about escaping that shit hole of a town—our last taste of freedom, where we were just kids chasing the life we wanted so badly. We even made plans with the cash I'd lifted from my mother's dickhead boyfriends. But after that night, a few days later, Xander was never the same. I take another drag from the joint.

"Those nights I tried to stay away from Poppy, she was all I could think about. Didn't realize it back then, but I was in love with her," he says. "I fought it hard, Ace. I fought it like hell because it didn't sit right with me. To feel like that when I'd never given a shit about anyone else before." He pauses to gauge my reaction. "I spoke with Poppy last night and told her everything that's been going on. She thinks it might be more than what I'm seeing. That your feelings for Scarlet might be genuine, even if you don't know it yet."

I choke on the smoke in my lungs. No way he's thinking this has anything to do with that love bullshit everyone keeps talking about. I cough again, trying to clear my throat. "Forget sharing any of this shit with Poppy—this isn't some love shit." I watch him flash that smug smirk. "And don't you two have better things to talk about than me?"

He laughs out loud, and for the first time since he arrived, it feels like the old Xander—the one who makes everything seem a little less heavy. "Trust me, we've got way better shit to talk about than your ugly ass. I was just venting about what's been bugging me."

Hearing that he shares stuff like that with Poppy doesn't surprise me; I've seen how they are together. She calms Xander down, and he turns into a different person around her. I'm different around Scarlet, too—not at all like I am with the guys. Maybe there's something to what he's saying, but I'm still not buying into this love crap.

"How's Theo been with you lately?" I ask, trying to shift the subject.

"Still quiet. Doesn't say much," Xander replies.

"I'm sorry, man. I never meant to come between you guys."

"He'll come around."

"You know, he used to drive me nuts with his bullshit. And if you tell him this, I'll deny it faster than you can blink—but I actually miss that fucker." I pause, staring off into space as I reflect on the mess I've made. "I've got no fucking clue how to fix things with Nate and Theo," I admit, frustration lacing my words. "How do I make them see that I'd never treat their sister like some fucking groupie?"

"Trust me, I get it," Xander replies. "I could never talk to you about that stuff either. It's tough. All you can do is show up. Stop avoiding them."

My phone buzzes, jolting me out of my relaxed state. I hand the joint to Xander and get up to see what the notification is about. It's a text from Kit.

**Kit:** Hey, where r u?

**Ace:** In my room. Why?

**Kit:** Stay there. I'm on my way.

I stare at the screen, trying to wrap my head around what the hell is going on. Xander, noticing the shift in my expression, puts out the joint.

"What's going on?" he asks, leaning forward on the couch.

"Kit's on her way," I reply.

Just as the words leave my mouth, there's a knock at the door. I move over, open it, and step back to let her in. She walks by, flashing me a tender smile, and then sits down in the chair opposite Xander.

"What the hell has she done now?" I ask, bracing for the worst.

It's got to be about my mother—why else would Kit be here?

I move back to the couch and sit down beside Xander. "Just give it to me straight. No bullshit."

Kit glances at her phone, then back at me. "It's not about your mother—it's your sister, Daisy. She reached out."

Her name hits me like a punch to the gut, a reminder of how she, just like everyone else, bailed when I needed her the most. Fuck, they're all crawling out of the woodwork now. Next, it'll be my father—whoever the fuck he is. I was barely old enough to remember anything about him.

"What did she want? Is she trying to cash in on my fucked-up childhood too?" I ask, feeling the anger simmering beneath the surface.

"She just reached out, Ace," Kit replies, her tone steady. "She wants to connect with you."

"No." I push myself off the couch and start pacing. "She walked away a long time ago. Didn't give a fuck about me then, so why the hell should I care now?"

Kit stands up and walks over to me. "If you change your mind, let me know. She gave me her number." She offers me a soft smile before exiting the room, leaving me and Xander in a silence that feels heavy as hell.

I stand there, feeling the weight of it all.

If I hadn't lost my shit on that fucking camera, none of this would be coming back to haunt me. I glance at Xander, who's sitting there, watching me like he's waiting for me to crack.

I stay quiet for a moment, trying to collect my thoughts. Xander's gaze doesn't waver, and it pisses me off how calm he looks.

"What?" I finally snap, running my hands through my hair and tugging at the roots, as if that'll somehow relieve all this pressure.

He leans back, crossing his arms. "So what's it gonna be, Ace? You gonna let this shit eat you alive, or are you gonna do something about it?"

I scoff and start pacing the room. "Do what? Call her up and act like the last how many fucking years didn't happen? Like she didn't bail on me and leave me to handle all that shit by myself?"

Xander stays silent, letting my words hang in the air, heavy and suffocating.

I stop and turn to him, my chest rising and falling. "You can't talk. Remember what happened when you faced your old man again? This isn't any different."

"But she wasn't the one who did any of that shit to you, Ace."

"No, but she fucking walked out and left me to deal with it alone." I shake my head. "You really think calling her is gonna fix everything? You want me to forgive her? Act like none of it ever happened. Fuck that."

"No one's asking you to forgive her," he replies softly. "But maybe talking to her and asking her why she left could give you some answers."

I walk over and sit back on the couch, slumping against the cushions. "I don't know if I can do it, man."

Xander and I sit in silence for a while. His presence is steady, grounding me. We don't need words; the weight of our shared experiences is enough to know that we're not alone in our struggles.

Eventually, he shifts the conversation to last night's show and how everything we've been working for since leaving the label is finally starting to come together.

It's a hell of a lot easier to focus on that—on the wins, on the music.

He mentions meeting up with Walter later today for a drink and asks if I want to tag along.

I decline. I'm not in the mood to pretend everything's okay and slap on a happy face for the day.

After Xander heads out, I grab my phone and shoot a quick text to Scarlet. Being around her always pulls me out of my head, like she's got this way of cutting through all the noise.

**Ace:** What r u doing?

I stare at the screen, waiting for those damn bubbles to pop up, but they never do.

Impatience gnaws at me, and I start second-guessing myself. I should've just walked over there. Her room's only three doors down.

Fuck it. I shove my phone into my pocket, slip on my shoes, and within seconds, I'm out the door, striding down the hall toward Scarlet's room.

I knock, and she opens it almost immediately.

That smile hits me straight in the chest, the kind that makes everything feel right because I know I'm the reason it's there.

"Hey," I mutter as I step inside.

Without a second thought, I pull her close to me the instant the door clicks shut. No words, just a desperate need to kiss her, to feel her close. As our lips meet, she melts into the kiss.

When I pull back, I take a moment to soak her in—those eyes, that smile, the way she lights up the room just by being here. "What do you want to do today?" I ask, curious about her plans. Yesterday, she and Theo spent time sightseeing together, and I'm relieved that, at least with him, I haven't screwed things up like I have between him and Xander.

"Not much," she replies, crossing the room, before glancing back at me with a grin. "I've got something to show you," she adds, reaching for her phone. "Oh, you texted me," she notices, her eyes lighting up. "I was in the shower."

The thought of her soaping up that hot, naked body causes my cock to twitch. I can't help but wish I'd been there with her—feeling her slick, wet skin under my hands, holding her against the wall, listening to her moan as I pound into her. My mind races with all the things I'd do if I had been there.

But then she's back, focused on her phone, swiping and tapping, yanking me out of my daydream as she moves closer, bringing whatever she's been checking out with her.

"I get what you're saying," she replies, letting out that soft laugh I could listen to for hours. She angles her phone toward me, revealing Theo in all his glory—sporting those ridiculous sideburns and that porn-stache. "I told him he looks like a joke, and he actually seemed to love it. He's such a moron," she adds, shaking her head with a smile.

As I study the photo, an unexpected wave of nostalgia crashes over me. Shit, I miss that idiot way more than I thought I would. His stupid comments and relentless teasing—it's wild to realize how much I crave that banter, but here I am. Not that I'd ever say that to his face, though.

"Want to grab a bite at the restaurant downstairs?" I ask, not really caring what we do as long as we're together. I need to make it clear to Scarlet—and everyone else—that this isn't just about sex, even if the thought of making her come on my cock is always there in the back of my mind. But it's about so much more than that.

Scarlet shoots me that playful look, like she knows exactly what I'm thinking. "Sure, let's go," she says, snatching her jacket off the back of the couch.

As we step out, I take her hand in mine. The silence between us feels easy, comfortable, but it's also the kind of silence that lets my mind wander. I start to think about all the shit still weighing on me—Theo, my mom, and Daisy, my sister.

We stroll down the hall, and as we turn the corner, we nearly crash into Theo. He's just come from the pool, looking like a wet dog with that goofy grin plastered on his face. For a moment, I almost forget the tension between us. His gaze drops to our entwined hands, and I see his jaw tighten with a hint of unease.

"Where are you two headed?" he asks, trying to sound casual, but I can tell he's testing the waters. I'm curious about what went down between him and Scarlet yesterday—usually, he'd be losing his shit by now.

Scarlet glances at me, then back at Theo. "Just grabbing something to eat. You wanna join?"

I hold my breath, waiting to see if Theo's going to blow us off or tag along. "Yeah, why not?" he finally says. "I could use a bite."

As he moves forward, Scarlet and I hang back, waiting for him to disappear into his room. My gaze remains fixed on the door, contemplating whether it might be better to let Theo and Scarlet grab something to eat on their own. But if I want to show Theo that my connection with Scarlet is genuine, and not just fucking like everyone assumes, I need to step up and prove myself to him. Normally, I wouldn't give a damn about Theo's opinion, but with this, I do.

Within a few minutes, Theo's back, wearing jeans and a shirt, his hair still damp from the pool. He shoots me a look, as if daring me to say something. I meet his gaze head-on, a playful smirk on my face, showing him that his attempts to intimidate me won't work. He strides past me, his footsteps echoing down the hall as he makes his way toward the elevator.

I watch him go, the smirk firmly planted on my face. Yeah, bring it on, asshole. Show me what you've got. I'm ready for whatever shit you throw my way.

Scarlet and I fall in line behind Theo as we wait for the elevator. When the bell dings and the doors slide open, he steps inside and moves to the back wall. We enter, our backs turned to him, but I can feel his gaze boring into me, scrutinizing every single move I make.

I start to wonder what this must look like to Theo. He's never seen me like this before. It's always been the same old story—Ace, the guy who chases anything with two legs just to get his dick wet. I know he thinks that's exactly what I'm doing with Scarlet, and I've got no idea how to prove him wrong.

I'm not one for romantic bullshit. Hell, even when Xander started showing affection toward Poppy after they finally worked their shit out, it felt weird seeing my friend like that. I guess it's the same for Theo. He's never seen me like this, and no wonder he's got a fucking problem.

The elevator doors slide open, and Theo brushes past us, stepping out of the lift. I can't help but smirk at the idiot, knowing we've got some shit to settle.

"Theo," I call out. He stops a few steps away, hesitating as if weighing whether to turn around and hear me out or just keep walking.

"What?" Theo snaps, still facing away but ensuring Scarlet and I have to part to get around him. She hesitates at his side for a moment before heading toward the bar, leaving us to sort out this shit. I know this isn't the best place to air our problems for the world to see, but damn it, something's gotta give. I step right in front of him, locking eyes as he does the same with me.

"We need to talk," I say, my tone firm. "About Xander."

Theo doesn't say a word, he just stands there, a wall of silence between us. I need to know if things between him and Xander are okay.

I grasp his arm and guide us into a secluded corridor, away from prying eyes. If this is my only shot to talk to him—since he's been ignoring all my texts and calls—then this is where we're having this conversation.

"Xander's not at fault here," I say firmly. "I am."

"So you're telling me he didn't know you fucked Scar?" Theo's voice is raw, hurt seeping through his tone.

I swallow hard. "Yeah, he knew," I admit, not backing down.

"And that is the problem," Theo snaps.

"Seriously, Theo, what the hell did you expect Xander to say?" I shoot back. "He told me to stay the fuck away from Scarlet. Would you have walked up to him if he had a sister and told him who she was fucking?"

Theo swallows hard.

"Yeah, I thought not," I press on, my voice steady. "Look, I know this shit looks fucked up. I swear to you, that I will never hurt her. I don't want to do that kind of shit."

He stays quiet, and I fucking hate that he's not throwing me his usual bullshit. "Will you just fucking talk to me, asshole?"

"I don't know what you want me to say, Ace. Look, she cares about you way more than you care about her. She made that perfectly clear."

Fuck, this shit's getting way too real. I'd give anything to see Theo back to his usual cocky self instead of this serious, hurt person before me. He needs something solid, something real—and I don't know if I can pull that off. But fuck it, I'm gonna give it a go.

I take a deep breath, bracing myself to lay it all out for him. I'm not even sure what Scarlet's told him, but this is what he needs to hear from me.

"I need you to listen to me without cutting me off. If you interrupt, I won't be able to get through this, and it's hard enough as it is."

He crosses his arms over his chest, giving me that look of his—the one that says he's clueless about where this is going.

"You know what it's like with me and chicks," I say. "I just fuck them and walk away." His jaw tightens, and I realize this isn't the best way to start. "But I swear, it's not like that with Scar." I pause, searching for the right words.

"Go on," Theo says. At least he's willing to listen now. But it's tough to find the right way to say this, especially to someone like Theo, who's been through the same shit and uses sex as a way to forget all the crap life throws at us.

"I don't know how to explain it, but it's just not about the sex with Scarlet." I catch a glimpse of something in Theo's expression—maybe he doesn't want to hear about the sex part since he thinks of her like a sister. But I push on anyway. "I genuinely enjoy hanging out with her. Last week, we just chilled by a lake, talking about random shit. It's not some game or a fling; it's different. I get that you might not believe me, but it's..." I let out a sigh. "I don't fucking know, and I know it sounds fucked up coming from me, but it's not just about a quick fix or getting off. It's about being with her, really talking, and spending time together. I can open up to her about stuff that I can't discuss with anyone else. I'm not asking you to just take my word for it, Theo, but I need you to at least give me a shot to prove it."

He eyes me for a moment, his gaze sharp and unyielding. "You hurt her, Ace, and you're dead to me."

"I wouldn't expect anything less," I reply, appreciating his loyalty.

# Chapter 24

## Scarlet

I'm not sure what happened between Ace and Theo in the corridor earlier today, but lunch was at least somewhat more pleasant, despite a few tense moments. It's been a good day, mostly spent with Ace, who's been surprising me in ways I didn't expect—like showing up at my door this morning. Usually, it's me showing up at his hotel room, wondering what he's doing.

Lately, he's been more relaxed around me, despite all the stress with his mother.

He's opening up more about his problems in a way that feels easier than before. It's good for him. He needs to let it out, and I'm glad he's turning to me.

Every day, I fight the urge to tell him how I feel, holding back because I'm not sure how he'll take it. Something's shifted between us; it's not just a quick hook-up anymore. The last time I heard him say it was just a quick fuck was at his place, and everything has felt different since then.

As I get ready in my room for tonight's show, I can't shake this thrill building up inside me. Stepping onto that stage feels like a jolt of pure energy, waking up a part of me I never knew existed. Back in my old band, playing to packed stadiums was nothing but a dream, and now, I get why the guys live for it. I know Nate misses that feeling—it's obvious every time we talk. Even though I hate that he got hurt, I'm grateful he pushed me to take this gig.

I've had so many opportunities with this, but there's still a nagging worry that once the tour wraps up, everything will go back to how it was—me out of a job, back to auditioning, only to find out they're really just interested in what opportunities my brother can give their band. And, of course, there's a voice whispering that after this Ace might fade into a distant memory.

For now, I'm focused on savoring every second, soaking up the energy of this incredible experience. Being part of something this big fills me with gratitude, and I'm determined to make the most of it while I've got the chance.

I open the door and am instantly caught off guard by the sight of Ace standing in the hallway, waiting for me. His eyes roam over me, as if he's undressing me with his gaze.

Just the thought of him stepping forward, pulling me back into the room, and losing ourselves like we did earlier today is almost overwhelming. There's a fire in his look that sparks something primal—a raw, intense desire I've never felt with anyone else.

He steps closer, and the heat pooling in my pussy flares as he closes the distance and captures my mouth with his. The kiss is intoxicating, making me forget everything—even my own damn name.

"All I want to do right now is fuck you," he growls, his words making me shiver as he grinds against me, feeling the hardness of his cock. It takes every ounce of my self-control not to beg him to take me right here right now. If he did, we'd definitely be late, and the last thing I need is to stir up more trouble with the band. We've already caused enough chaos just by being together, and the thought of them finding out we're fucking around because we're late is a risk I can't take.

"Ace," I whisper, letting my head fall back as he sucks on my neck. I close my eyes, losing myself in the sensation. "We need to go," I murmur, trying to refocus on what really matters.

"In a minute," he growls, his voice dripping with that sexy edge that makes it impossible to think. If I don't step away now, my resolve will shatter.

I grip his chin, pulling his face toward mine. I see it in his eyes—the raw desire, the way he wants me, the way he's desperate to fuck me. It's all laid bare, and it's almost too much to handle.

"You're coming back to my room tonight, and I won't take no for an answer," I say, my voice firm and low.

His lips curl into a cocky grin, the kind that makes him even sexier. "I was coming back to your room anyway," he replies, his tone dripping with confidence.

I slip out of his grip and step into the hallway, Ace close behind. It feels liberating, like he's finally lowered his guard, letting me glimpse the real Ace—the one hidden beneath all his defenses.

As we step out of the elevator, I keep a careful distance from Ace, catching sight of Xander and Theo watching us from across the foyer. Their stances mirror each other, hands shoved into their pockets, a noticeable space between them that speaks louder than words. Whatever happened between them, it's obvious they're not over it. I asked Ace about it earlier, but he brushed it off, not wanting to talk. I just hope they sort it out soon.

Theo flashes me a smile as I approach, wrapping an arm around me in a brotherly hug. "Are you ready for a great night," he asks.

"Yeah," I reply, feeling a surge of excitement. It's great to have him here, sharing this experience with me.

I glance up to find Xander waiting for Ace. Their bond is unmistakable, a camaraderie that speaks volumes. From what Ace has told me, Xander was his rock during the hardest days—his anchor when everything felt like it was slipping away. Ace often says he wouldn't have survived those struggles without Xander by his side.

Theo and I push forward, trailing behind Neil and a couple of security personnel as they guide us through the main entrance and onto the bustling street. Usually, we would discreetly exit through the back to avoid attracting any notice, but unfortunately, the hotel's rear section is currently closed off for the loading of vehicles.

Kit was livid that first time we had to use the main entrance; it drew the attention of the press and the swarm of fans waiting outside. With the news now spreading rapidly, the crowd has grown even larger, buzzing with excitement as fans eagerly await a glimpse of their favorite band member. I can't comprehend how these guys manage it day in and day out—the unrelenting demand from fans to catch a glimpse, reach out, and scream their names.

As soon as we step out the door, the deafening roar fills the air, making it hard to hear anything else. Amid the chaos, I feel Theo's hand tightly gripping mine. The thought that this might ignite further rumors in the press lingers in my mind. Given the media frenzy surrounding those leaked photos of Ace and me kissing after that disastrous interview, it wouldn't be surprising if a story starts circulating about me moving on to Theo.

Theo lifts a hand and waves to the adoring fans. Some hold posters decorated with love hearts, their names, and all the scandalous things they want to do with them. It's a reminder of how these guys can have anyone they desire. The thought of what might happen after this tour, when I'm no longer part of their world, lingers in my mind. Will Ace go back to his groupies? He's never clarified what we are, and I've never shared my true feelings with him. Maybe tonight, when he comes to my room, it's finally time to tell him how I feel.

Just as we're about to hop into the limo, I hear it—and so does Theo.

We both freeze in our tracks.

A handful of fans off to the right are waving signs with Ace's name, but the word "abuser" is scrawled in bold letters across them. The mood changes instantly, a sharp edge slicing through the excitement as the angry chants and boos swell, their voices blending into a harsh, accusing chorus that fills the air.

"Abuser!" a woman with black hair yells, her voice cutting through the chaos. Theo and I share worried glances before turning to Ace. The carefree energy he had just moments ago has evaporated, replaced by a serious, wounded expression. He avoids eye contact as he rushes into the limo, and it stings to see him like this.

Xander steps forward, his voice booming as he faces the crowd's hostility. "Back off!" he shouts, defending Ace against the onslaught of accusations and angry jeers. "You don't know what the fuck you're talking about!" Frustration laces his words as he continues, "He never laid a hand on his mother; it was the other way around!" He's desperately trying to make them see the truth, but it's obvious these people aren't real fans—they're just troublemakers eager to stir up chaos.

As Neil pushes Xander back from the angry crowd towards the limo, Theo grabs my hand and pulls me inside. I glance over at Ace as we settle into the car. He's sitting there with his head bowed, his eyes fixed on the floor. The weight of the accusations and the public outcry is clearly weighing him down, and my heart aches for him.

"You okay, man?" Theo asks softly, his voice tinged with sympathy, clearly shaken by the chaos outside.

Ace doesn't react, his gaze is fixed on the floor, almost as if he's shut himself off from everything around him.

Xander climbs into the car, his expression is fierce as he looks over at Ace. "That's fucked up, man," he snaps. It's clear he's seething at the unfairness of it all.

But Ace remains unmoved, trapped in his own thoughts and weighed down by the accusations. I push off my seat between Xander and Theo, sliding over next to him. I can see him starting to shut down, spiraling into that dark place he usually retreats to when this kind of shit hits hard. He doesn't look at me, so I gently reach out and slip my hand into his. Even though I can feel Theo and Xander watching me closely, my focus is entirely on Ace.

To my surprise, he lets me weave my fingers through his and holds my hand, though his gaze remains fixed downward. I give his hand a gentle squeeze, and that small gesture finally encourages him to turn his head and meet my eyes. "Are you okay?" I ask softly.

He nods, but his eyes quickly drop back to the floor, his thoughts clearly elsewhere. I glance at Theo and Xander, catching their gaze as they silently observe us. I shift my focus between the two of them, attempting to decipher their expressions. Theo offers me a reassuring nod, his eyes conveying support, but I still wish I knew exactly what he is thinking.

The ride to the stadium feels suffocating, as if a heavy fog has settled over us. I can't shake the feeling that the echoes of the crowd's curses and Xander's fiery defense are forever imprinted on camera lenses, ready to be broadcast to the world.

Xander and Theo both wear expressions of concern, their eyes locked onto Ace.

"I think it's time to come out and set the record straight, Ace," Theo says.

Ace lifts his head to meet Theo's gaze.

"As hard as it is to hear," Theo continues, his tone steady but filled with compassion, "I know just how fucking difficult this is, Ace. But you can't be blamed for that shit. You can't be held responsible for having fucked-up parents who are just trying to grab money by any means."

"Maybe you should reach out to Daisy and see what she wants," Xander suggests.

Reflecting on our earlier conversation when Ace mentioned his sister reaching out—despite his desire to keep her at arm's length—I think it might not be such a bad idea for him to reconnect with her, especially now that things have escalated.

The limo finally pulls up, and Xander and Theo are the first to jump out, ready to face whatever awaits us outside.

"Are you sure you're, okay?" I ask, kneeling in front of him to catch his eye before he can step out of the limo.

"Yeah," he responds, but his voice lacks conviction.

"Just focus on the music for now," I say, hoping to guide him toward some relief. Losing himself in the music might be his best escape right now; it's what I do when everything gets too much.

We're in the green room, waiting to hit the stage, and Ace is already deep into the booze. Walter's band is out there, about to wrap up any minute now. I've watched him down three beers, and if he keeps this up, he'll be too far gone to give his best performance tonight. It feels like he's trying to drown out the shit from earlier, but I know that kind of escape won't lead him anywhere good.

I make my way over to Xander, who's got his eyes glued to Ace with a detached intensity. I sit down next to him on the couch.

"I'm worried about him," I say, trying to keep my voice steady.

I brace myself for Xander's typical response—the one where he tells me to fuck off and that it's not my concern. But tonight, he just keeps watching Ace, and the sharp retort I expect never comes.

When Xander still doesn't respond, I begin to think he might just ignore me. But finally, he turns his attention to me. "I'm worried too. I'd go talk to him, but he probably doesn't want to hear what I have to say."

Xander turns his gaze back to Ace, and I can see the weight of the situation pressing heavily on him.

My brows furrow in confusion. "Why? What do you mean?"

Xander's eyes remain locked on Ace as he speaks. "The fucker's been drinking since we got here. If he grabs another bottle, I swear I'm going to throw it against the fucking wall. You need to go talk to him."

I nod and stand up, striding toward Ace, who's resting against the table, draining the last of his third beer.

The moment our eyes lock, I catch that lustful glint in his gaze as it sweeps over my body. Shit, I hope Theo didn't see that—didn't catch the intent behind those eyes.

He turns slightly, tossing the empty bottle into the plastic bin with a loud thud. As he reaches for another, I step forward and grab his hand, halting him mid-motion.

"Ace," I say firmly.

His eyes flicker towards me, a mix of annoyance and something else that I can't quite place. I'm not sure how to get through to him when he's like this, but I know I have to try.

Kit bursts through the doorway, immediately drawing everyone's attention. "On in ten," she announces, her voice cutting through the room. "They're on their last song now."

She glances at Ace, and I can see she's picked up on the tension in the air. As she strides over to him, she gives me a quick, knowing look, a silent acknowledgment that she senses something's off. Turning her full attention to Ace, she asks, "How are you doing?"

Ace meets her gaze but remains silent, his eyes revealing the internal struggle he's facing. Kit takes a deep breath, her expression shifting to one of seriousness. "I was planning to wait until after the show to share this with you, but considering what happened at the hotel, you might as well hear it now."

She pauses, allowing the weight of her words to settle in the air. Ace's brows furrow as if bracing himself for whatever is coming next.

Shit, if she's got more bad news lined up, I can't even imagine how he'll react. Xander and Theo seem to be on the same wavelength because, in no time at all, they're both at Ace's side, ready to offer their support.

"Kit," Xander says, like he's trying to warn her against dropping any more bombs on Ace right now.

But Kit, ignoring Xander's warning, locks eyes with Ace. "Your sister's here tonight. She told me she wants to set the record straight about your mother. If you decide you never want to see her again after that, she'll accept it."

Ace's voice drips with bitterness as he responds, "And why would she want to do that? She didn't give a fuck back then, so why care now?"

"Ace..." Xander interjects, his tone shifting to one of pleading. I can hear the desperation in his voice, a rare crack in his usual tough demeanor.

Ace turns his head to Xander, and for a moment, they lock eyes. There's something unspoken that passes between them.

Ace's jaw tightens, and his eyes narrow. "You really think one conversation with her is going to fix everything? That suddenly the world's just going to believe her over my mother?"

Theo steps forward. "I know how hard this will be for you, Ace. It would fucking terrify me to go back into that world, but if she's willing to set the record straight, you should at least hear her out. She could fix the shit that happened tonight."

My gaze softens as I turn to Theo. Despite everything that's happened between them, he's stepping up, setting aside all the complicated feelings to offer his support. Right now, Ace needs that more than anything. It's clear they have each other's backs, no matter what.

"I can go with you if you want," I offer.

He nods, swallowing hard, and I can see the dread etched across his face at the thought of facing his sister.

"The fans can wait," Kit says firmly. "We need to have this meeting now, rather than let it weigh over you during the show."

Ace's shoulders tense, but he nods anyway. Xander steps closer, lifting his hand to rest on Ace's shoulder, a quiet show of support.

"You can do this, man. I know you can," Xander says, his voice steady and infused with the kind of confidence that's meant to lift Ace up.

"Of course, the dickhead can," Theo chimes in, his tone echoing that same unwavering belief.

Kit pulls out her phone, dials a number, and raises it to her ear, her expression serious as she prepares for the conversation. "Neil, have you got eyes on Daisy?" she asks. Her gaze shifts to Ace, whose grip on my hand tightens as if he's bracing himself for what's about to happen. "Yeah, bring her to the green room, please."

# Chapter 25

## Ace

I have to remind myself to breathe as the reality of facing my sister again after all these years sinks in. I don't have a fucking clue what I'm supposed to say to her, or what she thinks she can say to make any of this shit better. But here we are.

Kit's standing beside me, watching closely, along with Xander and Theo, but the words coming out of their mouths fall on deaf ears. My mind's too fucked up to process what they're talking about. Instead, I zero in on the one thing that's keeping me grounded—the soft touch of Scarlet's hand holding mine.

When Xander gives my shoulder a squeeze, I finally lift my head. He steps aside, Theo close behind, and without saying a word, they both quietly leave the room, giving me the space I need to face this.

A knock on the door sends my heart racing, and Kit moves to open it before I can even brace myself. The door opens and there she is—Daisy. She looks older, sure, but the face is the same. Her smile wavers, and her eyes are already wet, glistening with unshed tears. She still looks like the sister I remember, still as pretty, but all I can feel is the heavy reminder of what she did—leaving me to deal with everything alone when she bailed. That wound. It's still wide open, and letting go feels damn near impossible.

"Ace," she says, her voice wavering as she moves toward me, but she freezes when I push up off the table. She looks unsure, like she doesn't know if she should come any closer. Honestly, I don't know either. Right now, all I can think about is the regret of not having more to drink.

A tear rolls down her cheek, and she hastily wipes it away, her hands trembling. I can see this is tearing her apart, too, but that doesn't make it any easier for me. Standing here after all these years, after everything that's happened. The pain resurfaces, raw and fresh, mixing with anger and confusion, and I can't shake the feeling that nothing can really fix the broken bond between us.

"Why now? Why do you want anything to do with me now?" My voice cracks, the words raw and spilling out like a dam breaking. Every bit of pain and confusion I've buried over the years surges to the surface. "You didn't give a shit back then, so why now?" My voice trembles, heavy with the weight of all those years spent wondering where she was, and why she disappeared. She was everything to me—my big sister, the person I looked up to. And then, out of nowhere, she vanished, leaving me to face hell alone. To deal with the aftermath, to pick up the broken pieces she left behind. Anger flares in me, as sharp as ever, and I feel that familiar sting of betrayal all over again.

She looks down at her hands, cupping them together like she's holding onto something fragile, something precious. "I know I did, Ace, and I'm sorry. It's been the biggest regret of my life." Her voice trembles as she meets my gaze, and I can see the pain etched on her face. The stray tear that trickles down her cheek seems to pull at my heart, as if they're dragging my own emotions to the surface.

I let go of Scarlet's hand and sit down in one of the couches. I have no clue what anyone expects from this meeting.

Maybe they think I'm gonna blow up at Daisy, finally unload all the shit I've been carrying for years. But as I look at her now—broken, vulnerable, carrying her own weight of regrets—it hits me that maybe it wasn't as simple as I'd convinced myself. The anger that's been smoldering inside me all this time. It suddenly feels...hollow, like it doesn't have the fuel I thought it did.

"Come sit down," I say, gesturing to the end of the couch. The words come out rough, but I try to keep my voice steady. It's the least I can do to give her a chance to explain herself.

As she moves over to take a seat next to me on the couch, Kit quietly slips out the door, giving us some much-needed privacy. Across the room, I catch Scarlet's gaze; she tilts her head towards the door, silently asking if I want her to leave too. I give a small shake of my head—she doesn't need to go. I need her support to help me navigate this mess, even if it's just having someone I trust by my side.

"I'm so sorry, Ace," Daisy says, taking a seat on the couch. Her voice is thick with emotion, making it hard for me to listen to. "I never reached out to you because I didn't want you to think it was only because of your fame." She wipes her tears with trembling fingers, and seeing her like this hits me hard. It's painful to watch someone I once put on a pedestal looking so broken.

"Can I ask why you left?" I finally manage to say, struggling to keep the hurt from overtaking me.

Her gaze locks onto mine, brimming with guilt and pain that's impossible to ignore. "The guys she'd bring home," she begins, her voice trembling as she searches for the right words, like she's sifting through a pile of broken glass, "the way they'd look at me... it was like..." She trails off, eyes squeezing shut as if the memory itself is too sharp to handle. I feel the weight of what she's trying to say, the words unspoken yet hitting with brutal clarity.

I reach out and take her hand, hoping to offer some support, something to ease the heaviness in the room. When she opens her eyes at my touch, the vulnerability I see in them makes my chest ache. It's a look I never want to see on her face again.

"I'd lock my room every night," she continues, her voice trembling. "Remember when you used to sleep on the floor beside my bed? I did that because I was scared, Ace. I wanted to protect us from what was happening."

The memories rush back—how she used to look after me, always my protector when I was younger. Hearing her now, revealing the hurt she hid behind that role, hits me in a way I'm not prepared for. It's like the past and present are colliding, old memories woven through the rawness of our pain, stirring up a storm of emotions I can barely hold back.

"When our mother passed out on the couch," she begins, her voice cracking, "one of her boyfriends was in my room when I walked in. I knew right then after what he did to me, I had to get out of that house." She takes a deep breath, and I gently run my thumb over the back of her hand, hoping to offer some comfort. Her confession adds a layer of understanding I hadn't considered before, twisting the knife of guilt deeper into my gut, making me angry that she had to go through that. "There was no way I could take you with me," she continues, her voice unsteady as she fights to maintain her composure. "I had no idea where I was going. I lived on the streets for the first year, Ace. I had every intention of coming back for you, but..." She sniffs, her tears falling freely. "But I never did. I'm so sorry."

I glance over at Scarlet, who's wiping her own tears away, and it hits me hard: all this time, I thought my sister had just abandoned me without a second thought. But now, seeing her like this—broken and raw—I finally understand that she loved me just as much as I loved her.

She's not to blame for any of this. The real blame falls on our mother. The one who put us both through this nightmare. I want to forgive Daisy—for the pain I thought she caused, for the years I felt abandoned.

"It's not your fault, Daisy. It's our mother's," I say, the anger simmering, just beneath the surface, as I think about the wreckage she left behind. She exploited her own bullshit story, making herself the victim while leaving us to deal with the fallout. She left us with scars that run deep, that cut in ways no one else will ever understand.

I shift in the seat, moving closer to hug her—something I never do. But right now, it feels like it's the only thing that makes sense. Like I need to shield her from everything we've been through. It's not just for her, though; it's for me too. A way of silently saying she's not to blame. She never was, no matter how much we've both been broken by all the shit we've carried.

When I finally pull back, Daisy looks up at me, and I see my own eyes reflected in hers. That same haunted look I've seen in the mirror too many times.

"I want to set the record straight, Ace," she says, her voice thick with emotion, sniffling as she wipes away the last of her tears. "I want to tell everyone the truth—that all those stories our mother spins are pure bullshit. She's just trying to profit off your fame. Let me do this for you. I know I walked away, and I never came back to get you. But let me fix it now. Let me make it right."

My eyes linger on her, carefully studying every minuscule change in her expression. It's clear that she needs this as much as I do, maybe even more. This storm has been raging around us for what seems like forever, but standing united against it brings a small sense of calm to the chaos.

"Okay," I finally say, nodding as I meet her eyes, the flicker of courage in them steadying something inside me. "Will you stay? We can talk after the show."

Her small smile hits me with a wave of nostalgia, taking me back to the days when I'd sit beside her, showing off my shitty, crayon-scrawled drawings. That smile of hers always seemed to make everything better, even when the world around us was crumbling. It reminds me of just how much she meant to me—more than a sister.

She was the one who held things together, more of a mother than the woman who claims that title now.

"I'd like that," she says, and for the first time in what feels like forever, I feel something shift—like maybe, just maybe, there's a chance we can move forward.

Standing up, I feel torn between wanting to stay and talk with her, and the realization that I need to haul myself out onto that stage.

The fans are waiting, and I have no fucking idea where Walter's band is—by now, they're usually in here, celebrating another killer night.

Daisy stands up too, I glance over at Scarlet, feeling this surge of gratitude that she's been here with me, helping me get through all of this.

"This is Scarlet," I start, fumbling for the right words. Fuck, what do I even call her? I've never had to introduce someone like her before, and it's way more complicated than it should be. I take a breath, trying to keep it simple, even though nothing about this feels fucking simple at all. "She's a member of the band." It's lame, I know, but it's all I can manage right now. Then I turn to Scarlet. "Scarlet, this is my sister, Daisy."

Scarlet steps forward with a smile, extending her hand to Daisy. They exchange a quick greeting, and I watch the brief connection between them.

"Do you want to watch the show from the wings?" I ask Daisy, feeling awkward as hell. I've never had anyone here like this—someone who genuinely wants to be in my corner.

"Yeah, I'd like that, Ace," she says, with a smile.

Walking over to the door, I pull it open and find Neil standing there, clearly under Kit's orders to keep everyone out. In front of him are the members of Twisted and Disturbed, their faces flushed, and their clothes soaked from pouring their souls out on stage. Letting Scarlet take the lead, I follow behind as we make our way out, with Daisy trailing behind me.

As soon as we exit the room, Neil moves aside, allowing the band to flood into the green room. The energy shifts instantly as they pour in, ready to celebrate the night's success. The buzz of excitement fills the air, a stark contrast to the heaviness of the conversation that had just taken place seconds before. It's like stepping from one world into another.

Scarlet and Daisy head out in front, with Scarlet animatedly pointing out various things and showing Daisy the ropes of what goes on behind the scenes. It's nice to see them connecting.

Neil walks beside me, his expression all business-like. "The guys are waiting near the stage," he says.

As we reach the side of the stage, I spot Kit, Xander, and Theo waiting. The second Xander catches sight of me, he looks over, and Theo and Kit turn to follow his gaze.

When Scarlet reaches the group, she steps aside to give me room to come forward. "Guys, this is my sister, Daisy," I say, trying to keep things casual even though my nerves are buzzing.

Daisy smiles, her gaze landing on Xander. "Yes, I remember Xander from when he was little," she says, and I can't help but grin at the memory.

Back then, whenever she picked me up from school, Xander was always there with us. That was around a year after he lost his mom, and his home life had turned to shit.

I glance at Xander, who's smiling back at her with that easy charm of his. "Good to see you again, Daisy," he replies, with genuine warmth in his voice.

"And this is Theo," I say, gesturing toward him.

Theo flashes my sister a charming smile, his usual flirtatious energy dialed back for the moment. He takes her hand and gives it a firm shake. "Nice to meet you, Daisy."

Fuck, it hits me—I never asked about her life. Not once did I bother to find out if she's married or has kids. There's this entire part of her world I know nothing about, like a stranger's life running parallel to mine.

"Are you watching from the wings?" Kit asks, giving me a quick look to make sure it's alright.

"Yeah, she is," I reply, feeling a flicker of warmth at the thought of her supporting me.

"I'll keep an eye on her," Kit assures me. "Now you guys need to get your asses out there. The crowd's getting restless."

I glance back at Daisy, and she gives me a reassuring smile—a small gesture, but it gives me the boost I need.

I turn toward the stage, noticing the rest of the guys are already out there.

As I make my way to grab my guitar, Theo slips his strap over his head and catches my eye.

"Hey, Ace, you okay?" he asks.

I nod, though I can feel the weight of everything. "Yeah, just... a lot going on." I try to brush it off.

"Just remember, we've got your back, man," he says with a reassuring grin.

I can see how genuinely concerned Theo is, and it's clear he gets just how tough it is for me to revisit one of the most challenging periods of my life. His small gesture of reaching out means a hell of a lot to me. Despite the tension we had earlier in our conversation at the hotel and his skepticism about my relationship with Scarlet, it's reassuring to know Theo's got my back. We might clash, and he might annoy the shit out of me more times than I'd like, but I know through all the bullshit, I can always count on him to stand by my side when it counts.

"You up for the challenge tonight, old man?" Theo asks, a grin spreading across his face as I turn around.

I know exactly what he's getting at—he's itching for another guitar showdown. If he thinks I'm going to go easy on him, he's got another thing coming.

"Don't think I'll go easy on you," I reply, a smirk tugging at the corners of my mouth.

Theo laughs, his eyes sparkling with mischief. "Good. I was worried you might need a nanna nap first."

I laugh, feeling the mood lighten.

As the curtains pull back, the deafening roar of the crowd engulfs us like a tidal wave. As I count us in for the first song, a rush of adrenaline surges through me.

Throughout the night, I sneak quick looks at the side of the stage, catching glimpses of my sister beaming with a heartfelt smile. It's such a relief to realize that she never really left me; it's like a weight has been lifted off my shoulders. I was always in her thoughts, even if it felt otherwise.

She's right, though—if she'd reached out a few years back, I'd have thought it was all about the fame and shut her out. Watching her mouthing the lyrics along with the crowd brings a feeling I can't quite put into words. It's like a missing piece finally falling into place. I never imagined she'd be here, cheering me on, let alone knowing the words to our songs. I give her a smile, and when she smiles back, there's a quiet understanding between us that bridges years of silence and hurt. For the first time, it feels like things might actually be okay.

My attention shifts to Scarlet, completely lost in the music and fucking owning it. Watching her like this is something else. The way she moves, the way she lets the rhythm take control of her body, has me craving her more than I thought possible. I can't wait to get back to that hotel room tonight. The thought of peeling off her clothes, and exploring that gorgeous body, has me craving her more than ever. I'm itching to show her just how much she turns me on, how her every move sends heat pooling low in my stomach, making my cock hard and my breath hitch. The thought of tasting her, feeling her soft skin beneath my fingers, and watching her eyes flutter with pleasure as I take my time sends a thrill through me. I can almost hear her breathy moans in my mind, feel the heat radiating from her skin. Tonight, I'll show her exactly what she does to me, and nothing's going to hold me back.

As we hit the final song of the night, "Creep," I'm still riding high from the adrenaline. Theo poured everything he had into our guitar showdown, strutting around wearing that cocky grin, convinced he could actually take me down. But once again, I owned that stage. He put up one hell of a fight, but he never stood a chance.

While Xander moves to the side to grab his guitar, Theo and I head over for a quick drink. We down our drinks, sharing a quick laugh before moving back into position. As the opening notes of "Creep" echo through the arena, Xander holds out the mic, and the crowd erupts, belting out the lyrics with raw passion. This song means everything to them, especially to Xander. The connection between the band and the audience is electric, palpable in every heartbeat and every cheer. As Theo and I move to the front of the stage, we watch the sea of phone lights swaying back and forth in unison. This is what we live for—the energy, the vibe, the way we touch people's lives.

And then I feel her.

I don't even need to see her to know she's there. My instincts kick in, and I pull her close, wrapping my arm around her shoulder and drawing her into a tight hug. I plant a kiss on the top of her head, and the crowd's roar amplifies at the unexpected display of affection. Then it hits me hard—showing this kind of vulnerability in front of thousands of people is completely out of character for me.

Theo slaps me on the back, grinning wide, and I turn to catch his nod of approval. It's a small gesture, but it means a lot. For the first time in ages, it feels like things are starting to fall back into place between us. I can feel the weight lifting, and it's like we're on the path to better days ahead.

The night has been a success, and for once, I'm actually smiling. Despite the shitstorm of my mother's media circus and the assholes chanting that crap outside the hotel earlier, I'm riding a high. It feels different, lighter somehow, though I can't quite pinpoint why. Maybe it's the adrenaline still pulsing through my veins or the fact that we truly connected with the crowd in a way that felt authentic.

As we wrap up and prepare to say our goodbyes to the crowd, I hang back with Scarlet and Theo, letting Xander take his time leaving the stage first. Once he's gone, the three of us start making our way across. I pause for a moment, waiting for Scarlet, and when she looks up at me, there's a shift deep in my chest. Something's changed between us—I feel it. She's all I can think about. Through all the chaos, she's been right there, steady, never judging me the way I thought she might. She's seen the broken, fucked-up parts of me, and somehow, she still accepts me, flaws and all.

As I reach the side of the stage, where my sister stands waiting, I can't shake the feeling that her presence here has sparked something deep within me. It's like she's illuminated a part of me I didn't even know was dark.

"That was amazing, guys," she says, glancing at us while we grab bottles of water from the table. Her eyes lock onto mine. "I'm so proud of you, Ace."

Her words hit me hard, unfamiliar and raw, making me have to avert my gaze to hold back the tears. It's a feeling I haven't experienced before—pride, acceptance, connection.

Xander comes over and rests his hand on my shoulder, grounding me in the moment. He then turns to Daisy and asks. "Are you coming down to the green room with us?"

Daisy looks between Xander and me, her warm smile still bright on her face. "I'd love to, if that's alright with you guys."

I nod, knowing we still have much to discuss. It's a lot, but I want that. I want to understand her life and all the things she's done. It wasn't until this moment that I fully realize how much I missed her or how much anger I've been carrying, convinced that she was just another person who left me behind. It was never her fault. She did what she had to do to survive that house of horror. While those bastards were cruel to me, they hurt her in ways I can't even imagine.

I am ready to heal, and having her next to me is the first step in that process. I want to be the brother she needs, the support she deserves. This isn't just about me anymore; it's about us, about finding a way to move forward together.

As the rest of the band head towards the green room, Daisy and I follow slowly behind them. "Just a heads-up," I say, walking beside her. "It gets pretty wild in the green room. There's this other band from Australia with us, and then there are the groupies—wild ones who seem to think boundaries are optional."

I give her a reassuring smile, hoping to ease any nerves she might have. I want her to feel comfortable in this environment, even if it's a bit overwhelming. "But don't stress about any of it. Just grab a drink and relax. Once I'm done with everything, I'll come find you, and we can catch up."

Turning to Daisy, I realize there's so much I don't know, things I never bothered to ask. "Hey," I say, my voice softer. "Are you... married? Any kids?" The words feel strange, like I'm talking to someone I just met instead of the sister I've known all my life.

A broad smile spreads across her face, lighting up her features. "Yes, I'm married to a loving man, and I am a proud mother of three beautiful daughters."

"Wow," I say, taking it all in. "Three daughters? That's a lot of girls."

"Yeah," she says, her eyes lighting up with excitement. "And someday, they'd really love to meet their uncle."

The thought of family brings a strange, comforting warmth that settles in my chest. I can almost picture those little girls running around, full of life and energy. "Xander has a son named Alex, so that's four for me now—one nephew and three nieces."

It slowly sinks in: I'm not just her brother anymore. I'm part of something bigger, something worth holding onto, something worth fighting for.

# Chapter 26

## Scarlet

By the time we get back to the hotel, it's late, and the night's been nothing short of incredible. We absolutely killed it on stage, and the crowd was devouring every moment. But the real highlight wasn't the show—it was seeing Ace and Daisy sitting off to the side, talking into the early hours of the morning. None of us wanted to break up their moment. You could feel how much they both needed this, like years of silence and distance were finally beginning to crumble away.

By the time Kit finally kicked out the last groupie—after Theo, of all people, had had enough, which, honestly, still blows my mind—the rest of us just sat back, letting Daisy and Ace have their moment.

I never thought I'd see the day when Theo would tire of groupies, but maybe tonight was different. Watching Ace and Daisy reconnect seemed to settle all of us, like we were all feeling the weight of the moment.

Throughout the night, I glanced over at Ace, noticing the glint of tears in his eyes during the more intense parts of their conversation.

Seeing Ace—the tough, grumpy guy—letting his guard down like that was something I never thought I'd see. His gentle demeanor towards her made me realize the depth of his love for Daisy, a love that has remained strong despite the years and miles that had kept them apart. There's a raw intensity to it, something powerful that reveals just how much he's been carrying all these years.

It's added this whole new layer to him, one I didn't know existed.

What surprised me even more was what he did on stage.

Out of nowhere, he reached out and wrapped his arm around me in front of thousands of people. Ace has never shown that kind of affection before, not publicly anyway.

Hell, even Theo looked shocked, though he didn't say a word to me about it. I could see it in his face. Tonight felt different somehow, like a wall came down between us, even if just for a moment.

As we take the elevator up in silence, the mood feels heavy. Xander is silent, engrossed in his phone, while Theo leans back against the wall with his eyes closed. It hits me how different things are for him without Nate. Those two have always been inseparable. Now, there's a quiet grief in Theo, a shadow that says just how deeply he misses Nate.

Ace stands next to me, his gaze fixed on the floor, completely lost in his head.

The elevator doors slide open, and we all step out. Xander's the first to disappear into his room, barely giving any of us a glance before closing the door behind him. Ace's room is next, but before he can make a move, I grab his hand and pull him toward mine.

Theo watches us, his eyes narrowing as if he's deciding whether he should step in. But I shoot him a look—a warning that tells him not to even think about it. This isn't about him; it's about Ace and me, and whatever happens next. Finally, he seems to get the message and keeps his distance, staying quiet.

Theo doesn't say a word as he disappears into his room, leaving Ace and me alone in the hallway. I slide my key card into the lock, and as soon as the door clicks shut behind us, Ace is on me. He pushes me against the door, his hands firm on my hips, and his lips find mine with a hunger that steals my breath. There's a raw, unrestrained intensity in the way he kisses me, like he's been holding this in for far too long. It's not just a kiss—it's an all-consuming need that leaves me weak at the knees.

His hands slide down to grab my ass, and with a swift, powerful motion, he lifts me up. My legs instinctively wrap around his waist as he carries me, possessive and in control. His hand slides down to grip my ass, while the other tangles in my hair, holding me exactly where he wants. His mouth claims mine, deep and demanding, drawing a moan from me as he guides us toward the bed.

The way he controls every move, every touch, sends my pulse into overdrive.

We stop at the bed, and I brace myself for him to drop me onto it as he has done so many times before, but this time, he just holds me close, kissing me like he can't get enough—like he's devouring me to satisfy some insatiable hunger. When he finally pulls back, his forehead rests against mine, our breaths mingling as we both pant like we've just been through two rounds of fucking already. His eyes drift shut for a moment, like he's drinking in every beat, every breath, savoring this second between us as if it's something sacred.

"I want you naked and sprawled out on this bed," he growls, his voice dripping with that raw dominance that sends a shiver straight down my spine.

It's sexy as hell, this commanding side of Ace, the way he lets me know exactly what he wants. If only he was this clear with his feelings.

He sets me down on my feet at the edge of the bed. I lift my shirt, starting to pull it over my head, but I'm moving too slow for his liking. In one swift, possessive move, he grabs the fabric, yanking it away and tossing it aside like he can't stand to wait a second longer.

His gaze drops hungrily to my tits. His tongue darts out to wet his bottom lip, like he can't wait to taste them. I reach behind to unhook my bra, but before I can even pull it off, he's there, yanking it down my arms in one swift motion. He flings the bra across the room, leaving me exposed and vulnerable. The heat of his desire wraps around me like a blazing fire, igniting every nerve in my body.

As I kick off my shoes, he leans in, taking one of my nipples into his mouth, sucking and teasing it. I moan as I tilt my head back, momentarily losing myself in the overwhelming sensation. The warmth of his mouth pulls me under, and for a moment, I forget I need to be naked for him. But his free hand pinches my other nipple, jolting me back to reality.

"Get undressed," he commands, his voice rough, and then he dives back in, sucking harder. The heat pools between my legs as I fumble to undo the copper button on my jeans. I slide them down, along with my panties, letting the fabric glide down my hips and off my legs until I'm completely bare.

The moment I'm naked, he stands tall, looking down at me with a hunger that is all consuming. "Get on the bed," he orders. "Lay down," he says, then swiftly pulls his shirt off and tosses it aside.

My eyes roam over his chiseled abs and the black ink that captivates me every time. He's fucking beautiful, every inch of him, from his body to the art that adorns it.

I settle back on the bed, still mesmerized as he strips down, yanking his jeans off like they're burning him. My focus sharpens on his hard cock, the piercing catching the light. He reaches down, stroking himself with a casual confidence that sends a thrill through me.

"Spread your legs," he commands, and when I look up at him, I catch the sly grin playing on his lips. He knows exactly how much I love the way he takes control, how much it drives me wild.

I spread my legs, feeling a rush of excitement.

"Wider," he demands, his tone leaving no room for argument.

He's savoring every second, teasing me as he drags his cock slowly along my soaked pussy, drawing out every inch of tension. Just months ago, by now he would have already flipped me over, pushed me on all fours, and taken me without a second thought. But tonight, he's intent on making me wait, making me want it even more.

His gaze stays on my pussy, dark with hunger as he gives himself a stroke.

"As much as I want to taste your pussy," he murmurs, voice laced with raw need, "I need to fuck you even more right now."

His filthy words send a wave of heat coursing through me. He leans down, reaches into his jeans to retrieve a condom, tears it open with his teeth. The sight of his mouth slightly parted as he rolls it onto his hard cock is utterly intoxicating, and I'm unable to look away.

When he looks up, the intensity in his eyes makes my heart race. He moves onto the bed, gripping my knees and spreading them wide. My breath hitches as he aligns his cock with my entrance, his gaze locked onto my pussy. With a deep thrust, he fills me completely, and I can't help but moan at the delicious stretch.

"Fucking hell," he groans, his gaze fixed on my face as he starts to move slowly, savoring every moment as he watches my reactions.

He picks up the pace, each thrust hitting that sweet spot, pleasure shooting through my body. I get lost in the moment, my eyes fluttering shut as I try to savor the feeling.

"Open your eyes," he commands, his voice a deep growl. "When you come, you see who the fuck is getting you off."

I obey, forcing my eyes open as he fucks me harder and harder, each thrust pulling more moans from me. Waves of ecstasy crash over my body, pushing me closer to the brink of something explosive. The need to surrender builds, an irresistible urge to let go completely.

But just when I think I might break, he suddenly slows, as if he wants to draw this moment out, not ready to chase his orgasm just yet. He leans in, pressing his lips to mine in a soft kiss, a stark contrast to the frantic desperation he had only moments ago. This kiss is warm and gentle, igniting a different kind of fire within me.

"God, you feel so fucking good," he groans, his voice thick with lust as he watches me. His face hovers above mine as he fucks me slowly, and I catch a glimpse of something vulnerable in his eyes, something that tells me he's letting me in.

And in this moment, I know I have to lay it all out. I can't hold back any longer. I have to tell him how I feel. "I love you, Ace," I whisper, my voice trembling with the weight of my emotions as my fingers trace his jawline.

I feel his body tense up the moment the words come out. He swallows hard and stops moving. A knot of doubt tightens in my chest as he turns his head away from me. Did I say something wrong? The look he was giving me moments ago has vanished, replaced by an expression I can't quite read as his gaze comes back to me. I see it immediately—he's pulling back, retreating, as if my words are too much for him.

He pulls out of me, and the sudden emptiness hits me hard. Sitting on the edge of the bed, Ace runs his hands through his hair. I move closer, placing a hand on his back as I lean forward to see his face.

"Ace, is everything alright?" I ask.

He remains silent. The conflict on his face and the uncertainty in his eyes are painfully clear, and it cuts me deep.

Theo was right. He'll never love me—not in the way I love him. In a frenzy, he hastily reaches for his jeans and pulls them on while I watch, unable to do anything. I know exactly what's coming next; he's about to bolt, to run away from the words I just uttered—run away from me.

I pull the sheet up over my body, wrapping my arms tightly around my legs, trying to shield myself from the sudden emptiness that has settled in the space between us. The room feels colder now, as if the warmth we shared has vanished with his retreat.

Silence fills the room as he grabs his shirt and shoes, and I don't dare say a word. He pauses at the door, casting one last, lingering glance my way. In his eyes, I catch the turmoil and uncertainty, a battle to understand my feelings. He seems lost, unsure of how to process what I've just said or how to respond to me in this moment.

Then, without uttering a single word, he turns and walks out, leaving me alone in the haunting quiet of the room, the weight of my unreturned love heavy in the air.

As the door clicks shut, a thick, almost suffocating silence wraps around me. I remain frozen, my gaze fixed on the spot where he stood just moments ago, desperately hoping he will come back. But deep down, I know he won't.

I squeeze my eyes shut, but the tears still manage to escape, burning a trail down my cheeks. My chest tightens, and a sob escapes my throat, shaking my entire body. I curl tighter under the sheets, attempting to hold myself together, but it's no use. The dam breaks, and I bury my face in the pillow, allowing the tears to flow freely.

I've never experienced this kind of ache before—this deep, soul-crushing pain that comes from loving someone who can't love me back. And now, I'm alone in this room, surrounded by nothing but the haunting echo of my own heartbreak.

# Chapter 27

## Ace

I haven't slept a damn wink. Scarlet's words, "I love you", are on a relentless loop in my head, refusing to let me rest. This shit just got real, a reality check I wasn't ready for. I feel like the biggest asshole for just walking out, not saying a single word, not even a weak-ass attempt at a thank you. But what the hell do you say when someone lays it all out like that? When they actually tell you they love you. No one's ever said that to me before—no one. And my first instinct was to bolt, to get the hell out of there as fast as I could. Fuck.

Rolling over in bed, I stare at the wall, fucking pissed at myself for treating her like that. The guilt's gnawing at me, eating me alive. I can't shake the image of her face as I walked out-hurt, confused, maybe even starting to hate me. And right now, I'm right there with her. I fucking hate myself for doing that, for leaving her when she didn't deserve it.

Sitting up, I run my hands through my hair, trying to shake off the weight pressing down on my chest. I need to do something, anything that'll drown out the mess in my head, but nothing seems to work. No matter what I do, her face keeps surfacing—those eyes, that raw look of vulnerability. It's like she's haunting me, and there's nowhere I can go to escape it.

I should've stayed. I should've talked to her, explained how fucking confused I am. But no, I just left her there, exposed and vulnerable, while I ran like a damn coward.

The phone buzzes on the nightstand, and I find myself staring at it, half hoping it's her, half dreading that it might be. But it's just a text from Kit, reminding us that we're checking out of the hotel tonight. I toss the phone aside, ignoring it. I know I need to talk to her, but where do I even begin? What the hell do I say?

I sit on the edge of the bed, elbows resting on my knees, staring at the floor like it has all the fucking answers. The tour bus is going to be awkward as hell tonight if I don't patch things up with Scarlet. There's no way to avoid her on that cramped bus, and honestly, I don't want to. I can't run anymore. I need to face this, face her, and own up to the mistake I made by running away.

Dragging myself out of bed, I throw on some clothes, moving slowly, like I'm gearing up for a damn execution. Every step feels heavier than the last as I head out the door. The hallway outside my room is blindingly bright, too normal for what I'm about to face. My mind races, but all I can think about is what the hell I'm supposed to say to Scarlet. But no matter how hard I try, nothing comes. Every excuse I run through in my head sounds weak as fuck, and I know I need to do better than that.

The moment I arrive at her door, my stomach tightens. I know I've got to do this, but I've no fucking idea of what to say. I stand in front of her door for a second, just staring at it, trying to pull my shit together. Then, before I lose my nerve, I knock. The sound echoes down the hallway, and I hold my breath, waiting.

Nothing. I knock again, a little harder this time, but still—nothing. Maybe she's avoiding me. Hell, I wouldn't blame her if she was. I stand there like a fool for a minute, feeling the weight of my mistakes, before finally turning and walking away.

As Xander steps out of his room, his gaze meets mine as I stand awkwardly in the hallway. His eyebrows furrow, and a deep frown forms on his forehead when he notices me. "Hey," he says, his tone cautious, like he's not sure what to make of me just standing there. "What are you doing?"

"Not much," I reply, forcing a casualness into my voice, even though my insides are twisted in knots. "What about you?"

"Just heading down to grab a bite before going to pick up Poppy and Alex," he says, a grin spreading across his face at the mention of their names. He's been buzzing with excitement about Poppy and Alex flying in.

I nod, struggling to summon some enthusiasm of my own.

"You heading down to grab something to eat?" he asks.

I hesitate for a moment, shooting a quick glance at Scarlet's room, but then I decide to hell with it. Maybe spending some time with Xander will help clear the shitstorm swirling around in my head. "Yeah, sure. Let's go."

As we make our way to the all-you-can-eat breakfast buffet, Xander keeps the conversation light, effortlessly chatting about random topics. "So, how'd things go with your sister last night?"

I let out a heavy sigh, the weight of our conversation washing over me again. "It was... intense. There's just so much to unpack. We had years to catch up on, and it all came rushing back at once."

Xander nods, his expression turning serious for a moment. "Did you manage to talk through everything?"

"Yeah," I reply, running a hand through my hair. "She had a rough time in that house too. I don't want her going through it alone. I'm thinking I'll be there when she comes out and sets the record straight. We should face it together, you know?"

As we head into the restaurant on the second floor, I take in the chill atmosphere. There are only a few tables occupied. Toward the back, I spot Scarlet and Theo at a table for four, deep in conversation. Xander leads the way, my stomach twisting at the sight of her. I can't help but wonder if Theo knows what I did last night.

As Xander settles into one of the empty chairs, I watch Theo and Scarlet look up. Scarlet's face lights up with that warm, radiant smile of hers. "Hey, Xander," she greets him, her voice filled with warmth. Then her gaze shifts to me as I approach, and for a brief moment, I feel a wave of relief wash over me, hoping maybe she's not pissed at me for last night.

"Hey, Ace," she says, her voice steady, but there's an edge of something else there. Just as quickly, her eyes dart away, and she focuses on her breakfast, pushing the food around on her plate.

That small gesture hits me like a cold splash of reality. It's clear things aren't okay between us. Sure, she spoke to me, but that's just Scarlet—always polite, even when everything is a mess. It serves as a stark reminder of how different we really are.

I slide into the seat next to Xander, trying to play it cool, but the tension in the air between Scarlet and me is thick and palpable. Theo sits there, silent, sipping his coffee while keeping a close eye on the two of us, as if he's expecting the whole thing to blow up at any given moment.

Xander kicks off a light conversation about meeting up with Poppy and Alex, but I can barely focus on his words. My mind is fixated on Scarlet—on the way she won't even glance in my direction. It's gut-wrenching. I know I need to say something, do something to break this suffocating silence, but nothing feels right. Every word that comes to mind feels like it'll only dig the hole deeper.

"So, uh... you sleep okay?" I finally manage to ask, my voice coming out weaker than I wanted it to. It's a lame question, I know, but it's all I've got in this moment.

Scarlet glances up, her expression unreadable, like I'm staring at a closed book. "Yeah," she replies, her tone flat, devoid of any warmth. "You?"

"Yeah, I guess," I lie with a nod.

She goes back to pushing her food around on her plate, and the silence stretches out, thick and awkward.

I can feel Theo's eyes darting back and forth between the two of us as if he's trying to figure out what the hell is going on.

It's awkward as fuck, and I can see him getting restless like he's on the verge of asking what's going on.

After a beat of awkward silence, Xander pushes his chair back and stands up.

"I'm gonna hit the buffet," he says, casting a quick glance my way.

I follow him, anything to break the stifling tension between Scarlet and me. We grab plates, and while Xander starts piling on food, I just stand there for a moment, staring at the spread of options in front of me.

"What's going on?" he asks, glancing at me with that concerned look, a spoonful of eggs hovering over his plate.

I hesitate, struggling to find the right words. What the hell do I even tell him? I glance down at the food under the warm lights, feeling a knot tighten in my gut. There's no way I can look Xander in the eye when I spill this. "She told me she loved me."

"Fuck," he says. "And I'm guessing you couldn't say it back to her?"

I glance at him, shame washing over me. "No, I didn't do anything except fucking bolt. I didn't know what the hell to do."

He goes back to piling food onto his plate. "I get it, man. It's hard as hell to open up." He looks back at me, like he knows exactly what I'm wrestling with. I can tell he wants to dig deeper, but I step away from him, cutting off any chance for him to press further.

I grab a few random things, not really caring what I end up with. Scrambled eggs, bacon, a couple slices of toast—whatever. By the time we make our way back, Theo and Scarlet have already left the table. The sight of the empty seats causes my stomach to twist with unease.

While waiting for Poppy and Alex, Xander and I are chilling in a quiet corner at the airport, a welcome escape from the bustling crowd. I can see the anticipation radiating from him. The way his eyes sparkle with excitement as he practically vibrates with energy. The way he constantly glances toward the arrival gate, reveals just how much they mean to him—these two are his whole world.

On the way here, I figured Xander would bring up the shit that happened with Scarlet, but to my surprise, he hasn't said a damn word about it. Maybe he knows I'm not ready to unpack that mess yet, or maybe he's just too caught up in his own excitement to care. Either way, it's a relief not to have to dive into that shit right now.

"Daddy!" Alex's voice slices through the air before I even spot him. He comes barreling toward Xander, jumping into his arms with a squeal of delight.

Xander holds him in a warm embrace, and it strikes me once more just how profound Xander's world is. It's as if he's crafted this perfect little life, a whole universe that belongs solely to him. Watching this moment unfold makes me acutely aware of what I've been missing in my own life.

Poppy strolls toward us, a smile beaming from ear to ear. She's rolling a suitcase behind her, nothing too big, just enough for a few nights on the road. This is Alex's first time staying on the tour bus, and before all the shit hit the fan, he had challenged Theo to a Mario Party showdown. Knowing Theo, he's probably been practicing nonstop, annoyed as hell that a kid can kick our asses every damn time. The thought makes me smirk.

"Uncle Ace!" Alex shouts as soon as he spots me standing next to Xander. Xander sets Alex down and strides over to Poppy, his face lit in an adoring smile.

I crouch down to greet Alex, flashing him a smile and feeling grateful for the kid's infectious energy. "Are you ready for some fun on the tour bus?"

But my eyes can't help but shift to Xander and Poppy. The way Xander pulls Poppy close, their kiss is intense and full of passion, like they're in their own little universe. For a brief second, I'm reminded of what real love looks like, and it hits me hard, twisting my gut. They have this connection that feels unshakeable, a bond that makes my own shit with Scarlet seem even more complicated.

When Xander finally pulls away from Poppy, they walk over together, Xander wheeling her suitcase. As soon as Poppy spots me, her face lights up with a smile, and she steps forward, pulling me into a hug.

"Hi, Ace," she says, her voice overflowing with genuine warmth. It feels nice, like a little reminder that not everything is heavy and complicated.

I can't help but marvel at how things have changed. Back in school, Poppy was the girl everyone overlooked, but now she's grown into this incredible woman. Less than a year ago, she was raising Alex on her own, fighting through every challenge with a strength that's damn impressive. I regret not getting to know her back then; maybe if I had, I'd have seen the amazing person she is sooner. She's made Xander happier than I've ever seen him, and that's something I'll always appreciate. It's like she breathed life into him again, filling in the cracks with love and laughter.

Walking towards the exit, Alex's small hand holds mine tightly as he chatters excitedly about everything and nothing. Poppy and Xander walk close behind, their fingers entwined, lost in their own conversation.

"Where's Uncle Theo?" Alex asks.

I glance down at him, giving him a smile. "Uncle Theo's back at the hotel. He knows you're coming today. He was talking about you earlier this morning, saying he can't wait to see you, buddy."

Alex beams up at me, clearly pumped about reuniting with Theo. "I can't wait to beat him at Mario Party," he says, practically bouncing with anticipation. It's clear Theo's gaming challenge is the highlight of his day.

Neil leads us out to the car, and we climb in. Poppy and Xander take the seat together, while Alex and I settle across from them.

Poppy glances over at me, her smile warm but her eyes filled with concern. "How are you holding up, Ace? With all that media mess from the interview. Are you hanging in there?"

That's Poppy—no beating around the bush, just straight to the point.

"Yeah," I say, forcing a smile. "I'm getting there."

As the car moves forward, Xander reaches out and threads his fingers through Poppy's. My eyes follow the simple, intimate gesture, causing a knot to tighten in my chest. I've done that with Scarlet a few times, felt that connection, that grounding. As I lift my gaze, I observe them, engrossed in each other, speaking softly, creating a bubble where only the two of them exist.

A question lingers at the back of my mind: Can I ever have this with Scarlet? That ease, that certainty. The thought is heavy and unshakable. It's a reminder of everything I risked by running away from her, and now I'm left wondering if I'm just too fucked up to let anyone in.

Why can't I let my walls down like him? Xander and I were both broken assholes who've come from fucked-up childhoods, but while he's managed to climb out of that pit, I'm still trapped in it. I need to change how I deal with shit. I need to let someone in, just like he let Poppy in all those years ago.

The thought eats at me. I watch Xander and Poppy share a laugh, their eyes sparkling with something real and unguarded. It seems as if they have established a fortress of trust, a refuge where vulnerabilities are safe, and it evokes a sense of longing in me. What would it take for me to break down my own barriers? To stop hiding behind my anger and fears?

Alex's voice breaks through my thoughts, pulling me into his world.

"Have you been to the pool, Uncle Ace?" he asks. "Mom says I can go for a swim when we get there."

"Nah," I reply, forcing a smile. "Haven't been there yet."

His eyes, so much like his father's, lock onto mine. "Will you come for a swim with me?" he asks, the simple question bringing a smile to my face.

"Yeah," I say, nodding at Alex. "I'll come for a swim with you."

At least this way, it'll give Xander and Poppy some alone time together. Knowing Xander like I do, he's probably itching to get her alone for some private time.

Plus, having Alex around, it'll keep me from drowning in my own thoughts.

The car comes to a halt in front of the hotel, and as we exit, Alex is right beside me, chattering away about the pool and all the fun he plans to have. His enthusiasm is infectious, but as we walk past Scarlet's door, my mind drifts. I can't shake the thought of her being just on the other side of that door. My pace falters for a moment, my hand instinctively clenched, but I force myself to keep going.

Alex finally breaks away, darting into the room with his parents. His chatter fades as the door clicks shut behind him. I head to my own room, the silence pressing in as I prepare for our trip to the pool. It's a small escape, but right now, it's the distraction I need.

A few minutes after I've changed into my swim trunks, I hear a knock at the door. My heart skips a beat, hoping it's Scarlet. But when I open it, I see Xander and Alex standing there. Alex, with a towel slung over his shoulder, is practically bouncing with excitement, dressed in his swimming trunks, floaties strapped to his arms, and swimming goggles perched on his head.

"Thanks for taking him, Ace," Xander says, his grin wide, clearly eager to get back to Poppy.

I grab my towel, and step out of the room, closing the door gently behind me. Alex waves goodbye to his dad, and we make our way toward the elevator.

When we reach the pool area, I spot Theo lounging in one of the chairs. His hair is still damp, and he's sprawled out, looking completely at ease.

The moment Alex sees him, he bolts forward, a huge grin on his face.

Theo's expression transforms in an instant. A warmth spreads across his face, making it impossible to miss. He rises from the chair and strides over to Alex, his smile widening as he kneels down to greet the kid. It's a simple yet profound moment, and it hits me just how much our lives have changed over the past year.

Alex has changed everything for us. He's brought a new kind of joy and connection, especially between Theo and himself. I can see it clearly now—how their bond has grown, how Theo's face softens whenever Alex is around. It's a different Theo from the guy I knew before.

"Hey, buddy!" Theo says, scooping Alex up into his arms. Alex giggles as he's lifted off his feet, his little arms wrapping around Theo's neck.

If Theo's here, then Scarlet has to be nearby. I scan the area, searching for any sign of her. There's no escaping it now—it's time to face the music with her.

"Are you finally coming for a swim, old man?" Theo shoots me that grin, the one that used to drive me crazy back in the day. But now, for some reason, I actually welcome it.

I lift my gaze and spot Scarlet standing there, looking fucking incredible in a red bikini. Her tattoos are on full display. Our eyes lock, and I'm momentarily speechless, completely captivated by the ink on her sexy body. It's impossible to focus on anything else—I don't even realize Theo and Alex have already moved back to the chairs.

I know I need to talk to her. There's a shitload of stuff I need to say, but right now doesn't seem like the best time. Not with her looking like that, her body all hot and distracting. And definitely not with my damn dick practically begging for attention, especially not in front of Theo and Alex. But my feet move on their own, as if my body's taken control. I make my way to the side of the pool where she's standing, drawn to her like a moth to a flame.

She drops her head, focusing on something around her feet, and I can't help but let my gaze wander down those long, fucking legs. I see the nerves flickering in her posture, and damn, I'm right there with her. I've played to eighty thousand people, but right now, I'm a fucking mess of nerves. Nervous because it's her, nervous because I have this gnawing feeling that whatever we had is slowly slipping away.

"Hey," I say, trying to keep my voice steady, but it comes out a bit hoarse.

When she looks up, her eyes lock with mine, creating a moment where everything around us seems to vanish. It's just us. It feels like we're the only ones that exist.

After a long moment, she looks away.

"Scar," I say, my voice rough and almost hesitant. "We need to talk."

She meets my gaze, and I see the heat in her eyes—a mix of frustration and something else I can't quite pinpoint. "You don't need to say anything, Ace. Your actions spoke for you."

She steps aside when Alex and Theo approach, and I watch her crouch down to chat with Alex, her focus entirely on him. As she gets lost in conversation, I feel Theo's gaze on me. The second I look at him, I realize the bastard knows exactly what went down between us—how she told me she loved me and I fucking ran.

# CHAPTER 28

## Scarlet

Since I expressed my love to Ace, I can feel a shift in the air around us. Everything between us is so fucking awkward now, like we're both walking on eggshells.

Even though Ace hung around by the pool for a while, trying to act normal, I couldn't help but feel a wave of relief when he finally headed back to his room. If it weren't for Theo keeping Alex entertained with his endless goofy games, I'm sure even Alex would have picked up on the tension between us.

Despite how unbearable it feels, I don't regret telling Ace how I feel, because it's the truth. I love him—love him in a way I've never loved anyone before. But the one thing I know for sure now is that Ace can never love me the way I need him to.

I can't keep letting myself get caught in the same cycle, where every ounce of reason disappears the moment he touches me or gives me that look—the one that makes me feel like I'm the only thing in his world. For the sake of my own sanity, I need to break free from this. It's time to move on. And that's exactly what I plan to do.

In the green room, I pass the time scrolling through my phone, pretending to be absorbed in it, as we wait for Walter's band to finish their set. My brother's text from earlier—wishing me luck, telling me to kill it tonight—feels like a lifeline, something grounding in the midst of all this. Theo and Alex are off in their own world, laughing about something I can't make out, while Poppy and Xander sit close, wrapped up in each other. It leaves Ace and me in this uncomfortable silence, an invisible line drawn between us. I can feel his gaze on me, relentless, like I'm the only thing that matters right now, even with everyone else around.

I don't even need to look up to know that Ace is heading my way. My nerves go haywire, my heart pounding faster with every step he takes toward me. He sits down on the couch next to me, and it takes everything I've got not to turn and look at him. I force myself to keep my distance, even though every damn part of me wants to close the space between us.

"Scar," he says, his voice low and smooth.

I hate the way my body betrays me, a shiver running through me at just the sound of my name, even though I wish it didn't affect me like this.

I pause my scrolling, my fingers hovering over the screen as I slowly lift my gaze to meet his. A strained smile tugs at my lips.

"Are we good?" he asks, and there's something in his voice—just a flicker of uncertainty. He's uneasy, clearly struggling to find the right words.

"Yeah, Ace," I say, pushing myself to sound sincere as I force a genuine smile. "We're good."

Our eyes meet, and for a split second, it feels like he's about to say something—something that might finally cut through all the tension hanging between us. But instead, he hesitates, his gaze wavering as though he's lost, searching for the right words but coming up empty. His jaw tightens, and I catch the way he swallows, a flicker of vulnerability breaking through his usual confidence. He runs his hands over his jeans, almost like he's grounding himself, trying to find his footing before he looks back at me, the silence stretching just a little too long.

"Well, I'll let you get back to it then," he mutters, nodding toward my phone. He stands up, lingering for a split second, and then heads back the way he came, leaving me sitting there, torn between wanting to call him back and letting him go.

I feel the weight of someone's gaze and turn my head, only to find Poppy and Xander watching intently. I quickly drop my gaze back to my phone, trying to lose myself in the screen and escape the awkwardness of the moment.

Within seconds, Poppy slides onto the couch beside me, her presence a comforting distraction. "Hey," she says, her voice warm and inviting.

"Hey," I reply, putting my phone away and giving her my full attention. I'm curious about what she wants to talk about. She's always been polite, but we've never really had a private conversation before—there's usually a crowd around. This one-on-one feels unexpected.

"Hang in there," she says, and for a moment, I'm not entirely sure what she means. The confusion must show on my face because she quickly clarifies, "I'm talking about Ace."

"Oh," I reply, the weight of her words hitting me.

Poppy leans in closer, lowering her voice to create a more intimate atmosphere. "I went through something similar with Xander," she begins. "He knew he loved me but didn't really understand it at first, so he tried to push me away. It wasn't until years later that I discovered everything he was feeling."

She glances over at Ace for a moment, her expression serious. "Ace is a lot like Xander. They've both faced so much over the years that they build these walls to keep everyone out. I can see he's torn and unsure of what to do. When you told him you loved him, it might have opened his eyes to feelings he's never considered before."

"Oh God, does everyone know about that?" I mumble, covering my mouth in embarrassment.

I know Theo is in the loop because I told him, but now that Poppy is bringing it up, it's clear that Ace has said something to Xander. My cheeks flush in embarrassment.

Poppy laughs, letting out a little snort before quickly covering her mouth, which makes us both laugh. "Don't worry," she says, her smile reassuring. "It'll all work out in the end. The Ace I know wouldn't have bothered coming over to you if he didn't feel something. Trust me—he wouldn't give a shit otherwise. There's definitely something there, and both Xander and I can see it. He just hasn't figured out what it is yet."

Despite my instinct to push him away and shield myself from more pain, Poppy's words light a tiny spark of hope inside me. Maybe, just maybe, Ace really is starting to change. The guy who once drifted from one girl to the next seems different now. If he's struggling with his own feelings, then something's definitely shifting. And that thought, as fragile as it is, gives me a sliver of faith that this might not be the end after all.

"Just give him time," Poppy advises. "Ace has probably never heard those words before, and he's struggling to make sense of it all."

"Thank you," I reply, genuinely grateful that she reached out. I've always known Ace was closed off, and it's been a battle for him to lower those walls. But hearing Poppy say she sees the changes in him—that he's never acted this way before—makes me believe that maybe, he feels something for me. Yet deep down, I know this doesn't change everything. Just because he's struggling with his own feelings doesn't mean I'm going to make it easy for him. I've been through enough to know that I can't settle for anything less than what I truly deserve.

If Ace wants this—wants me—he's going to have to show it. He'll need to break down those walls and prove that I'm not just another woman to use and discard. I won't give in until I see that he's ready to fight for us, just as I've been fighting for us in my own way.

The door opens, and Kit steps into the room. "Hey, guys! You're on in ten," she announces.

Alex jumps up immediately, rushing toward the door, and Kit greets him with a bright smile. Then she turns to Poppy.

"Is it okay if I bring Alex with me?" she asks.

I watch as Alex glances back at his mom, his eyes sparkling with hope.

Poppy gives him a gentle nod and smiles. "Sure, go ahead. I'll come out and grab him when I'm ready to watch the guys from the side."

With that, Alex eagerly heads toward Kit, and they slip out together, shutting the door behind them.

Theo leans back on the couch, a cheeky grin spreading across his face. "I tell ya, that kids got everyone wrapped around his little finger. I might have to get him to spill the secret."

Xander walks over. "The difference is, he's cute. You're... not," he says, grinning.

Theo doesn't skip a beat, his trademark smirk widening. "That's not what you said in bed last night, babe. If I recall correctly, you were all over me."

Xander rolls his eyes, taking a seat on the couch beside Theo, trying to keep a straight face.

Theo chuckles and gives Xander a playful nudge. "Hey, don't be shy, babe. We both know the truth."

"Fuck off," Xander mutters, but the hint of a smile tugging at the corners of his mouth gives him away, undermining his fake irritation.

The night's been a blast. The crowd's energy was electric, spilling over into the merch signing. It's such a relief to see the guys more relaxed now, enjoying themselves—Xander and Theo are laughing, tossing around their usual smart-ass comments. It feels good, especially knowing I was the one who stirred up all that tension between them before. But Ace? He's off tonight, and it's not just me he's distant with. Something is gnawing at him, a weight he can't seem to shake. When Theo initiated their guitar challenge, Ace didn't bring his usual intensity. He seemed different, almost distracted, and as a result, Theo ended up taking the win. Ever since we got back to the green room, Theo's been riding that victory wave, boasting about it non-stop. Honestly, I'm starting to wish he'd just shut up.

As the night wraps up, a wave of relief settles over me, and I head for a drink. There's something satisfying about finishing up early—it means getting back to the tour bus sooner, maybe even grabbing a few precious hours of uninterrupted sleep. I'm beyond exhausted, having spent most of last night tossing and turning, replaying the moment Ace walked out of my room. This early end feels like the perfect chance to unwind and finally shut my mind off for a while.

As I pour myself a drink, I feel Ace close behind me. His presence is impossible to ignore, like a magnetic force pulling me in. As he reaches for his own drink, our arms brush—just a brief touch, but it sends a jolt through me, stirring up emotions I desperately want to bury.

I can feel his eyes on me, the weight of his gaze almost tangible. It's as if he's trying to pull me back to him without uttering a single word, and each second stretches into eternity.

Every instinct in me screams to turn around, to give in to the pull that seems to draw me toward him. It would be so easy to let go, to let myself get lost in him again. But I can't. Even as my heart aches, I force myself to stay grounded, refusing to let him pull me under.

Finally, I gather the strength to walk away, and it feels like a physical ache deep in my chest. The hardest part is making myself move away from him when all I truly want is to be close, to feel that undeniable connection we once shared. But I remind myself that I need to be strong.

Walter and his band have already left the greenroom, leaving just our band, along with Poppy and Alex. Exhausted, I collapse onto the couch. As Ace moves across the room, I make a conscious effort not to watch him.

We're over halfway through this tour, with still eighteen more shows ahead, and I have no fucking clue what's next after this. Will this experience change anything for me, or will it be the same old story—always living in Nate's shadow? The thought of auditioning and facing rejection time and time again is infuriating, and the idea of returning to that reality fills me with dread. But then again, this has always been my life: surrounded by men who only want to fuck me, who want to use me for my brother's connections, and of course, me constantly feeling utterly frustrated by the lack of opportunities for my music career.

I down my drink just as Theo approaches, checking to see if I'm ready to head out to the bus. With a sigh, I push myself off the couch, toss my plastic cup into the recycling bin, and follow him toward the door. I know it won't be long before the rest of the band piles onto the bus, but for now, the thought of retreating to my bunk sounds inviting—just a chance to escape and gather my thoughts until we arrive at the next venue.

# CHAPTER 29

## Ace

Fuck this shit. Her constantly ignoring me is driving me fucking insane. That fake-ass smile she throws my way whenever I try to interact with her, I fucking hate it. I want the real one. The one that lights up her face and tells me I still matter to her. The one that makes me feel like maybe I'm not as fucked up as I think I am. I need to fix this, to set things right, and soon.

All day, ever since I returned from the pool, I've been caught in a battle between doing what's right and pursuing what I truly want. Maybe I should just let her go. Perhaps that's the best choice for her because, let's be honest, I'm a fucking mess. All the broken pieces of me will only drag her down. Yet every time I entertain that idea, the thought of losing her feels like someone has shoved a dagger through my heart.

How the hell am I supposed to do any of this?

Scarlet and Theo left for the bus before I even had a shot at talking to her. So now here I am stuck on this fucking bus, slouched on the couch, half-listening to Xander and Poppy's conversation, barely pretending to care about whatever bullshit they're talking about. Theo's on the phone with Nate, going on about their usual shit. Alex is out cold in one of the bunks at the back of the bus, and though I haven't seen Scarlet since we boarded, I assume she's back there too, keeping her distance.

It's late, and we've been sitting here for hours, talking about pointless shit. But I can feel it—the damn elephant in the room. Everyone's tiptoeing around it, trying to figure out how to bring it up without pissing me off. But no one's got the guts to say it. Not yet, anyway.

I down another beer, barely tasting it, and nod at something Xander just said. If he were to ask me anything right now, I wouldn't have a fucking clue what he was talking about. My mind's too far gone, wrapped up in thoughts of Scarlet. All I can do is watch him and Poppy and wonder how the hell he does it—how he manages to keep her happy, make her smile, and not some fake ass smile but a genuine one. The kind that lights up the whole damn room, not like the fake-ass smile Scarlet's been throwing my way lately. It's killing me, knowing I'm the reason for that.

My eyes dart to the door as Scarlet stumbles out, looking all sleepy and absolutely fucking adorable. She glances around, offering everyone a smile—a real one this time. The kind that isn't forced or hiding behind a wall of bullshit. That fake smile? That's reserved just for me, apparently. Her hair's a mess, exactly the way I like it, but I can't help feeling disappointed that her loose-fitting t-shirt covers too much of her body. Still, those long, perfectly tattooed legs captivate me like a magnet, and I can't resist letting my eyes wander down them.

"Nate says hello!" Theo shouts out to her.

"Tell him I said hello back," she replies with a soft smile.

Poppy glances at her, "Did you want to come join us?"

"Thanks, but I just came to grab a bottle of water," Scarlet says, moving toward the mini fridge. "Then I was going to head back to bed."

The idea that she might be avoiding me—avoiding being in the same room as me—fucking stings.

As she moves to the fridge, I down the rest of my beer, trying desperately to distract myself from the ache in my chest.

Leaning forward, I add the empty bottle to the collection on the table, a silent testament to my futile efforts to dull the pain. Each bottle represents a little piece of me I'm trying to drown, but nothing seems to work.

"Ace," Poppy's voice slices through my thoughts, pulling me from the chaos in my head.

I glance over to find her and Xander watching me, his arm draped around her protectively. There's a knowing look in their eyes that makes my stomach twist.

"Go talk to her," Poppy urges, her tone gentle yet firm.

I shake my head, my voice barely above a whisper. "I don't know what the fuck to say to her."

"Anything will be fine. Trust me on this," Poppy insists, her eyes soft but filled with determination. "Please."

With a deep sigh, I push myself off the couch and make my way toward the kitchen area, slipping past Theo. My heart hammers with each step, feeling heavier as I get closer.

She's bent over, digging through the fridge, and my gaze drifts to those tiny sleep shorts that hug her ass perfectly. My cock reacts instantly, reminding me just how much I fucking want her.

With a bottle of water in hand, she straightens up and closes the fridge door. When she turns to face me, her eyes widen slightly, as if caught off guard. For a split second, we just stare at each other, the air thick with everything unsaid.

"Hey," I mutter, hating how weak it sounds, but it's all I can manage right now.

Every word I want to spill gets stuck in my throat. I'm not even sure what the hell I'm supposed to say, but one thing's crystal clear—I want her. I crave this connection we've got, no matter how fucking complicated it may be.

Her tired eyes meet mine, silently questioning what I'm doing. I sense her walls beginning to build up, and it fucking kills me.

"Can we talk?" I ask, feeling the weight of every word.

I know whatever comes next has to mean something; it can't be the same old bullshit we've been dancing around.

"I'm tired, Ace," she replies, and I can hear the exhaustion in it—like she's just done with all of this, done with me.

She's sick of the small talk, and honestly, so am I.

But I can't let it end here. Not like this.

I step closer, closing the distance between us. My heart's pounding like a fucking drum, but I push on. "I get it," I say quietly. "You're tired of this, tired of me not having my shit together. But I need you to hear me out because I don't know how to do this, how to be what you need... but I'm trying, Scarlet. I'm fucking trying because I can't stand the thought of losing you."

Theo's voice fades into the background, and I'm vaguely aware that he, Xander, and Poppy are all watching. But in this moment, none of that matters. Scarlet's the only thing I can focus on.

She looks up at me, her eyes searching mine, and I take a deep breath, letting it all out. "I'm just gonna say it." I pause.

*Just lay it out, asshole, before you lose the best thing that's ever walked into your life.*

"You're the one thing in my world that makes sense when everything else is so fucked up. I don't know how to do this right, but I want to. I want to figure it out—with you."

She stares at me, and I can't tell if she's about to laugh, cry, walk away, or a combination of the three.

So I do the only thing I can think of. I reach into my pocket and pull out the small, worn piece of paper I've been carrying around since she said she loved me. It's nothing fancy—just a scrap I tore from one of my notebooks.

I stare down at the words I've scrawled on the paper, my heart racing as my eyes run quickly over each line.

*Scar,*

*I'm a fucking mess, and I know I've hurt you. I see it in your eyes, see it in your smile, the way you've started to pull away. But here's the thing: when I'm with you, I feel something real—something I can't shake. It's like you've pulled me out of a dark pit I've been stuck in, and I don't want to go back.*

*You make me want to face my own bullshit, to be better, to fight for something that matters. You've shown me what it means to give a damn about someone else, and that scares the fuck out of me. I'm so sorry for the way I've treated you, for all the times I pushed you away when all I wanted was to pull you closer.*

*I can't pretend anymore. I love you, Scar. I really do. It's terrifying to say it out loud, because everyone I've ever loved has walked away. And I know you deserve better. Better than who I am.*

I glance back up at her. "I wrote this," I say, my voice a little shaky. "It's all the shit I can't say out loud because I'm too fucked up to get it right. But it's real, Scarlet. Every single word."

I hold it out to her, and she hesitates, eyes flickering between me and the note.

When she finally reaches for it, her fingers brush against mine, sending a jolt through me. For that fleeting moment, everything feels like it could be okay, like maybe we could find our way through this together.

She turns the paper, her eyes skimming over the words I poured my heart into, and I hold my breath, hoping like hell this is enough. That I'm enough. I need her to see just how much she means to me, even if I'm a total fucking mess when it comes to expressing it.

Then she glances up, and I catch the glimmer of tears in her eyes. "You love me?" she asks, her voice barely a whisper, like she can't quite wrap her head around it.

I nod. "Yeah, Scar. I do."

She takes a shaky breath, my words clearly hitting her hard. "I—"

I cut her off, stepping closer and pulling her into a fierce, unyielding kiss. My hands slide to her back, holding her as tight as I can. It's a kiss filled with desperation and devotion, a promise of all the things I can't put into words. When our lips finally part, I keep my forehead pressed against hers, my gaze locked onto hers with a fierce intensity.

"You're mine, Scar," I say, my voice low and full of heat. "You're all I fucking want."

When she smiles that genuine smile, it's like a beacon of light that shines on her face, and I feel a swell of pride, knowing that I am the source of her joy. Suddenly, we both realize we're not alone and turn to face the couch. Xander's sporting a shit-eating grin, like he just witnessed the greatest show on earth. Poppy has her hand pressed to her heart, her eyes glistening with emotion, as if she's about to burst into tears over some grand romantic gesture. Theo's watching us with a thoughtful look, holding up his phone. At some point during all of this, he switched the call to video, and now Nate's image is on the screen, his eyes glued to us.

I should feel embarrassed by our uninvited audience, but honestly, I couldn't give less of a fuck. All that matters is the way Scarlet's looking at me and how right this moment feels.

"You better fucking mean it, bro," Nate says through the phone.

I look over at Scarlet, my gaze steady and full of resolve. I take her hand in mine, feeling the warmth of her skin against my own. "Yeah, I fucking mean it," I say, my voice rough with raw honesty. "I'd tear down the whole fucking world just to make you smile. You're everything to me, Scar."

If we didn't have an audience right now and we were alone in a hotel room, I'd show her just how much I love her, reveal every filthy thought running through my mind. I'd have her sprawled out on the bed, fucking her, licking her, making her come on my cock just to seal this promise. But for now, instead, I take a deep breath, feeling a wave of relief wash over me, feeling lighter than I've felt in a long time—like the weight of the world has finally lifted because I've claimed her as mine.

Since I finally pulled my head out of my ass and told Scar how I feel, things have only gotten better. It's been a week now, and she's been in my hotel room every night since. I feel lighter, like I can actually breathe, and there's a real connection building between us. Every conversation peels back another layer, and I'm sharing parts of my past that I never thought I'd tell anyone. The mind-blowing sex. That's just the icing on top. The way she comes, the sounds she makes—they've got me completely hooked. Tonight, after another killer show, I can't wait to take her back to my room and ride that high all over again.

As Scarlet stands beside me in the elevator, it takes every ounce of willpower not to reach out and grab her ass, but with Xander, Theo, and Neil squeezed in here too, I resist the urge. I keep reminding myself that in just a few minutes, I'll have her sprawled out on my bed, exactly how I want her.

Strangely enough, the usual groupie scene on this tour has been almost non-existent. Now that I'm officially off the market, it's like the chaos just faded. I can tell Theo's missing his fuck buddy; he still turns on the charm whenever there's a girl around, but I'm not even sure he's hooked up once this entire tour. The whole vibe's different now—quieter, more toned down.

Things are moving fast with Scarlet, and despite my earlier doubts about where we're headed, it's not freaking me out the way I thought it would. Last night, I almost said those three little words, wanting her to hear them straight from me instead of reading them on a piece of paper. They were right there, sitting on the tip of my tongue, but I couldn't make myself say them. I can't figure out why it feels so terrifying. I know she'd never laugh or make me feel small, but letting down that guard—it feels like the hardest thing in the world. How fucked up is that?

Two nights ago, I had a video call with my sister that lasted until the early hours of the morning. It was a bit disappointing that Scarlet had dozed off in the bed next to me, as I didn't get to indulge in my favorite thing—her. But on the bright side, I finally got to meet my three nieces. Seeing them together brings back memories of Daisy in her youth.

Daisy and I finally discussed setting the record straight about all the lies our mother has been spreading. Even though her story isn't making headlines like it did a few weeks back, the term "abuser" keeps popping up—especially on social media. Kit's been deleting endless comments just to keep the negativity at bay.

Kit made all the flight arrangements for me and Scarlet to join Daisy for an interview with Jerry Goldman tomorrow. I'm fucking nervous about diving back into that dark place and reliving it all. But I keep reminding myself that I owe it to that little boy—the one who suffered through all that pain—to make things right for him.

After that, my plan is to fly back and regroup with the guys for the next part of our tour—New York. I asked Scarlet to accompany me, and honestly, I don't know if I'd get through this without her. She gives me the strength to be better, to be kinder to myself, and to see myself in a new light. She's right—it was never my fault that I had fucked-up parents. I just wish I'd figured that out sooner.

The elevator doors slide open, and even though I'm dying to get Scarlet to my room, we hold back, letting Neil check the corridor first. Once he scans the area and gives us the all-clear, Xander and Theo step out, and then Scarlet and I follow.

As we walk, I pull her close, wrapping an arm around her waist and planting a soft kiss on the top of her head. It's something I find myself doing more and more lately. Not too long ago, being this close would've sent me into a tailspin, convinced that letting someone in would set loose things I wasn't ready to face. But now, with her by my side, it feels like each kiss is helping those fears melt away, bit by bit.

Neil waits in the hall as we each say our goodnights and head into our rooms. I close the door, and any restraint I had left vanishes. I pull Scarlet close, pressing her against the door, my lips crashing into hers with a hunger that's been simmering all night. Feeling her warmth, her steady presence, drowns out everything else—any worries about the future, any shadows of the past. At this moment, she's my anchor, grounding me, and I can't get close enough to her.

She smells fucking divine, and that soft moan of hers sets my whole body ablaze with desire.

Her head tilts back, a soft, breathy sigh escaping as I trail my lips down her neck, savoring the warmth of her skin. My fingers find the button on her jeans, quickly flicking it open before tugging down the zipper. But of course, she's wearing those damn jeans—the ones that cling tight and take forever to peel off. It's maddening and exhilarating all at once.

"Don't move," I command, dropping to my knees, my gaze locked on hers. I can see the anticipation in her eyes as I slowly slide off her shoes. When I finally peel her jeans from her thighs, she steps out of them, revealing her black lace underwear hugging her curves. The sight alone stirs a deep groan from me, my mouth watering as I take in the soft lace, knowing just how close I am to her bare skin.

Fuck, this girl gets me going like no one else ever has. I look up at her, desire burning in my eyes, as I tap her ankle to widen her stance.

"Spread them," I command, kissing the inside of her thigh, savoring the softness of her skin. When she obeys, I run my tongue along her thigh, coaxing soft, desperate noises from her, like she's my instrument and I'm drawing out every sound of pleasure. "Now take off your shirt and bra," I urge, my voice dripping with need. "Let me see those perfect tits."

While she strips off her clothes, my tongue inches up her thigh toward the place I crave, where I know she's aching for me to taste her. The moment she tosses her clothes to the floor and I get closer to her pussy, I hear her breathing change. I see her head drop back against the door, her eyes fluttering closed, lost in the pleasure building between us.

"God, you're beautiful," I murmur, my breath hot against her skin as I inch even closer.

When I reach her panty line, I tease her with my tongue along the edge, not bothering to break that barrier just yet. I want her to beg for what she craves. I can tell I'm getting to her by the way her palms are splayed against the door, as she fights for control.

"Ace," she gasps, her voice all breathy and filled with need. "You're killing me." I can hear the frustration lacing her words, and it only drives me harder, eager to push her over the edge.

I press a kiss to her hip, smirking as her body shivers beneath my lips. Every little reaction tells me I'm getting her right where I want her, coaxing her to let go. She's grown so much bolder with sex since those early days, when we first started fucking months ago. But now? She's right there with me, her confidence matched by an intensity that drives us both wild. Ever since she took charge that day, something shifted between us. Now it's no longer just a way to get off; it's about savoring every second, drawing out every thrill until we're both on the edge, ready to tip over together.

I slide her panties aside and run my tongue through her folds, giving her a quick flick of my tongue over her clit. Fuck, she tastes so good. The moan that escapes her lips sends a jolt of desire straight to my cock, making it harder than ever. I pull back, trailing kisses along her thigh, and when she drops her head to look at me, her eyes wide with confusion, I can't help but grin.

"If you want it, you have to tell me you fucking want it," I taunt, my voice low and teasing. "Beg me to give it to you."

She lets out a deep sigh, her eyes boring into me, like if she didn't need it so badly, she'd tell me I was an asshole for doing this to her. She pauses, watching me, and I can't help but move my face closer. I blow hot air over her already aching skin, teasing her with the promise of what's to come. A smirk pulls at my lips as I take in her reaction, and just to make it even harder for her, I flick my tongue out, landing a quick, tantalizing swipe against her clit.

When I pull back, she grabs my hair, yanking my head up to meet her gaze. I love this side of Scarlet—so desperate to get off, so demanding. "You're going to get me off with your fucking mouth, asshole." Then, with a softer tone, she adds, "Please."

I reach up and rip her panties from her body, tossing the scraps aside so she's completely bare and ready for me. Leaning forward, I give her what she craves, my tongue dancing over her, coaxing moans from deep within her with every swipe, every flick, every teasing pressure on her clit. Her fingers tighten in my hair, pulling me closer, and when her hips start to move, grinding against my face, it's the hottest fucking thing I've ever seen. I can't take my eyes off her, watching her take what she wants in the most mind-blowingly erotic way.

I slip two fingers inside her, pumping them in rhythm with my tongue, and as I find that sweet spot, she becomes loud and explosive, just the way I love her. The thought of anyone walking past our door in the corridor, hearing her lose control, sends a thrill through me. Just the idea of fucking her against this door turns me on even more. She's mine, and I'm going to make sure she knows it.

I can feel the pressure building inside her, the way her pussy throbs with need, begging for release. She's so close, and I love how she's losing herself in the pleasure I'm giving her. Every throb of her clit against my tongue drives me wild, and the urgency in her movements makes it clear she's on the brink.

Her breaths come in desperate gasps, each one a sweet invitation to push her over the edge. She's losing control, and I'm utterly captivated by the sight of her crumbling before me. The soft, pleading sounds spilling from her lips make me pick up the pace, my fingers curling just right as I stroke that sweet spot deep inside her. I can't help but growl against her, savoring every delicious note.

"Come for me, baby," I murmur against her, my voice low and husky. "I want to feel you."

She's so close, so damn close, and I can feel it in the way her body reacts—tightening, pulsing, begging for release. I can't wait to watch her unravel, to see the moment she lets go completely, surrendering to the pleasure coursing through her.

And then it happens spectacularly. She cries out, a melody of pure ecstasy that fills the room, and I drink it all in—her pleasure, the way she quakes beneath my touch, her essence flooding my mouth. I'm fucking hungry for more, each drop igniting a fire inside me. I savor her, letting her pleasure wash over me, feeling every wave of her climax ripple through her body as she holds onto my head, her grip tightening as she rides my face, trembling with every pulse of her release. Each throb of her clit against my tongue sends a rush through me, and I'm consumed by the intoxicating blend of her pleasure and the need to keep her spiraling into ecstasy.

As her body quakes with the aftershocks of her orgasm, I pull back, a cocky smile spreading across my face. I love knowing I just gave her that kind of release, the kind that leaves her breathless and wanting more. I run my tongue over my bottom lip, savoring the sweetness of her orgasm lingering there, every taste reminding me of how badly she needed it—and how much more I want to give her.

Standing up, I watch her lean against the door, breathless, her chest rising and falling rapidly. She's still caught in the haze of her orgasm, her skin flushed, her body trembling. Seeing her come completely undone like this drives me wild. I can't wait any longer. I need to be balls deep inside her, feeling every inch, like it's the only thing that matters right now.

I strip off my clothes in a rush, my cock hard and throbbing with need. Grabbing a condom from my pocket, I roll it on quickly. Every second I'm not in her is unbearable. I step forward, lifting her with ease, her back pressing against the door as her legs wrap around me. My cock brushes her entrance, the heat of her making me grit my teeth, and I angle myself just right, teasing her for a heartbeat before I slide into her, filling her completely in one smooth thrust.

The moment I'm inside her, her warmth surrounds me, and I let out a low groan. She feels incredible—tight, wet, and perfect.

Her nails dig into my shoulders, her hips pushing against mine, urging me deeper. I pull back just enough to thrust into her again, harder this time, and the sound she makes—fuck, it goes straight to my cock.

Her legs tighten around me, her body meeting every thrust as I slam into her, setting a rhythm that has her gasping. Each time I drive into her, I feel her pulse around me, her pussy clenching as if she doesn't want to let go. My hands grip her hips, guiding her, fucking her against the door as she moans my name, her breath hot against my neck.

The sounds of our bodies colliding fill the room, her back thumping softly against the door with every thrust. Her head falls back, her eyes half-closed, and all I can think about is how fucking hot she looks, lost in the pleasure I'm giving her. I lean forward, my mouth finding her neck, kissing, biting, tasting her as I fuck her harder, feeling her getting closer to the edge again.

Her moans become louder, more desperate.

The sound of her voice as she says my name, is raw and needy, pushing me to fuck her even harder. The wet slap of our bodies echoes through the room, dirty and obscene, and I know anyone walking by would hear everything—the filthy rhythm of us fucking, her loud moans, her breathy whimpers. But I don't care. I'm too lost in the way she feels wrapped around my cock, so tight and hot, her body quivering as she chases another orgasm.

Her head falls back against the door, her lips parted, and I can see that look in her eyes, the one that tells me she's close again. The way her pussy grips me is almost unbearable, the heat of her making it harder to hold back. I thrust into her with everything I've got, driving her closer. I dig my hands into her hips as I pin her against the door.

"Ace... I'm gonna—" Her voice breaks off into a moan, and I feel her body tense as her orgasm crashes over her.

But I'm not done with her. Not yet.

"Fuck," I growl, gripping her hips harder as I fuck her through it. The way she's coming again makes me push deeper, faster. Her moans turn into gasps, her legs trembling as I keep driving into her harder, my cock throbbing inside her. The door rattles under the force of it, and every noise she makes just makes me wilder.

I'm barely holding on, the feel of her too fucking good to stop. I slam into her again, harder this time, feeling the slick heat around my cock. The need for release builds up, my body tightening, every thrust pushing me closer to the edge.

Her fingers claw at my back, her nails digging into my skin, and I feel her pussy flutter around me as she starts to come again, her body giving in to the pleasure. That's all it takes. The way she grips me, the sound of her falling apart, it sends me over the edge. I give her a few more brutal thrusts before my own release explodes, my cock pulsing deep inside her as I come hard.

The pleasure hits me like a wave, and I keep fucking her, feeling every second of it, every squeeze of her pussy as we ride out our orgasms. Her gasps and my groans mix until we both collapse, spent and breathless, against the door.

I can feel her body clinging to mine as we both catch our breath. I breathe her in, burying my face in the curve of her neck, inhaling her scent—a mix of sex, sweat, and something purely her. The warmth of her, the softness of her skin against mine, is intoxicating, and I can't bring myself to pull away just yet.

Her fingers trace lazy patterns down my arms, and I can hear the soft rise and fall of her breathing, still coming down from the high of everything we've just done. I press my forehead against her collarbone, taking a moment to soak in the feeling of her against me.

When I finally pull back, I meet her gaze, a slow smirk spreading across my face. Her eyes are heavy, lips parted as she breathes, still drunk with pleasure. I kiss her neck one last time, nipping at her skin before I push us off the door, holding her tight as I carry her toward the bathroom.

# CHAPTER 30

## Ace

I tossed and turned all night, barely catching any sleep. The thought of today's interview weighed heavily on me, dragging me down a dark path. My fucked-up childhood kept resurfacing, haunting me. The only thing that kept me from spiraling was Scarlet, her back pressed against my chest as she slept. I held her close—no; I fucking clung to her, as if she were the only thing keeping me from sinking into the abyss and losing myself entirely.

Even though it's morning and sunlight is streaming through the curtains we forgot to close last night, my mind's still a mess. The thought of facing that asshole Jerry Goldman today, digging into my dark past to clear up shit that was never my fault makes my stomach churn. How the hell is this considered entertainment? And why the fuck am I the one who has to fix it? It's all because of the fame, the way the paparazzi twist the truth to make headlines.

Scarlet turns in my arms, her face just inches away from mine. She's smiling, and seeing her like this—happy, content—wipes away every bit of dread that's been clawing at me. She's stunning, and every day, I'm still in awe that she's mine—mine to love, mine to hold. I know the way guys look at her and every filthy fucking thought that goes through their heads. Even last night, when those fans were eyefucking her, I had to force myself not to walk over and lay them out for even thinking they had a shot. But I kept my cool, my fists clenched at my sides, because reacting would just feed into the bullshit rumors my mother started—painting me as some violent monster.

I reach out, gently brushing a strand of hair from her face.

"You're so beautiful, Scar. Beautiful in every way," I murmur, the words spilling out easier now like a truth I can't keep inside.

The second my fingers graze her face, she closes her eyes and leans into my touch. I love that I have that effect on her, as if she's drawing comfort from me. When she opens her eyes again, she leans in and presses a soft, caring kiss to my lips. It's brief but carries a tenderness that makes my chest tighten in a way I can't quite explain. As she pulls back, her brows furrow, and her gaze sharpens, like she's trying to read me, to unravel the thoughts I haven't shared.

"You're worried about today, aren't you?" she asks.

"Yeah," I admit, still amazed at how she can see right through me. "I've been struggling with all of this... and now having to bring it all out in the open... it's just something I'm not sure I'm ready for."

She lifts her hand, cupping the side of my face with a touch that's both gentle and firm. "You don't have to justify anything, Ace. Not to anyone. If it's too hard, then fuck it all. Screw what your mother said. She's the one at fault here, not you. You're the one left with all the scars because of her. If you can't go through with this, then don't."

I nod, feeling the weight of her words settle in. "I know. But it's something I need to do. I know that it's going to be tough, diving back into that headspace. But I have to be there with Daisy."

She snuggles into my chest, and I hold her tighter. "I can't wait to show you around New York tomorrow, once we get there," she murmurs against me.

I'm relieved by the change of subject. I've told her before that, despite touring all over the world, I've barely taken in the sights. That's why she's so keen to share all her favorite spots in New York. I'm already planning to take her out on a date, hoping that once this interview is behind me, I can organize something special just for us. It's the least I can do after everything she's done for me, and I want to make sure she knows how much I appreciate her and our time together.

Fuck, listen to me—I've turned into some sappy guy, but I can't help it. I'm loving this openness between us. All the walls I spent years building around my vulnerability are gone, and for the first time, I'm not scared of her seeing the real me—the broken parts, the messed-up shit. The way she looks at me, like all my flaws and scars are just parts of who I am.

By mid-morning, we're in a town car, heading toward the airport, and I can feel the tension tightening in my chest. Daisy's agreed to meet us in L.A. at the studio for the interview, and after that, Scarlet and I will catch a flight back to New York to join the guys for the next five shows. But right now, all I can think about is the interview ahead, hanging over me like a storm cloud I can't shake.

Six grueling hours later, we finally touch down, and the moment we step out of the airport, I'm barely holding it together. Scarlet's warm grip on my hand calms the storm brewing inside me. It's like this relentless worry is coursing through my veins, a dark energy pulsing under my skin. I can't help but wonder after all these years why my mother still has this effect on me. Or maybe it's not just her—it's the thought of revisiting those painful memories, dredging up the past that left its mark. With each mile closer to the studio, my anxiety twists tighter, coiling like a knot in my gut.

When we arrive at the back entrance of the studio, I spot Daisy right away, nervously biting her nails as she waits. Her anxious energy radiates off her, and it's clear this is hitting her just as hard as it's hitting me. The urge to shield her kicks in—she's doing all this for me, willing to step into the spotlight and dig up painful truths just to set things straight, to finally lay everything bare.

"Are you okay?" Scarlet asks, just as the driver steps out and approaches our door.

I shift my gaze from Daisy to Scarlet, and the worry etched on her face hits me hard. I know she'd rather I walk away if this is just going to open old wounds, and that makes me love her all the more. But the truth is, I'm already carrying the weight of this pain, whether I confront it or not. Facing it head-on might be brutal, but it's something I need to do if I'm ever going to find some peace.

"Yes," I say softly as I lean in to kiss her on the lips. Just the feel of her warmth makes everything a little less heavy. If she wasn't right here beside me, I know this would be so much fucking harder.

Stepping out of the car, I automatically extend my hand to assist Scarlet, a gesture that has become second nature for me recently. Once she's out, our fingers intertwine as we walk towards Daisy.

In the past two weeks since reconnecting with Daisy, we've been talking every couple of nights, and that old childhood bond is starting to resurface, bridging the years and distance between us. It's like we're slowly piecing together what we once had, finding familiarity in each other all over again.

Daisy flashes me a smile, and I can't help but return it, even though my cheeks ache from the effort.

That's another thing I can't quite wrap my head around—I'm actually smiling more these days. The grumpy asshole I used to be seems to be fading away, and I know it's all because of the woman standing beside me. Scarlet. She's broken down the walls I used to hide behind, and, somehow, I'm starting to believe it's okay to let this happiness in.

I let go of Scarlet's hand and stride over to Daisy. The moment I'm in front of her, I pull her into a tight hug, holding her close as if I can absorb some of her tension.

"It's going to be okay," I whisper, trying to convince myself as much as her.

"Yeah, I know," she replies, her voice steady. "We'll get through it."

With Daisy by my side and Scarlet right behind us, we enter the studio. The place has that all-too-familiar, clinical vibe—cold, bright lights glaring down and an overwhelming silence hanging in the air. A few crew members mill about, setting up equipment. A young girl clutching a clipboard approaches and asks us to follow her.

Once we're ushered into a private room, the tension in the air thickens. I sink into a chair, and Scarlet sits beside me, her hand resting gently on my knee. But I can't bring myself to look at her; the anxiety is gnawing at me, coiling tighter with each second, dragging me inward. It's like there's this restless beast clawing from the inside, making it harder to breathe.

Daisy sits in the chair opposite, her leg bouncing up and down like she's trying to shake off the nerves.

The room feels too small, too stuffy. Then, the door creaks open, and a woman walks in, holding two small microphone packs.

"Hey, I'll get you both wired up," she says, her smile practiced but failing to reach her eyes.

She starts with Daisy, clipping the mic to her blouse and adjusting it until it's just right. Daisy shoots me a nervous glance, her hands clenched tightly in her lap.

When the woman turns her attention to me, I force myself to sit still as she attaches the mic to my shirt. Her hands are quick and efficient, but she keeps talking, her voice fading into the background as my focus drifts elsewhere—on what's about to happen and the messy reality we're about to step into.

"There you go," she says, stepping back to admire her work. "You're all set."

I nod, afraid that if I speak, I'll lose control. My mind races with a million thoughts, and all I can do is hold onto the hope that I'll keep it together long enough to make it through this.

A few minutes later, a crew member pops into the room, giving us a quick nod. "Follow me, please."

I take a deep breath and stand up, squeezing Scarlet's hand one last time, needing that connection before we step into the unknown. Daisy falls in step beside me, while Scarlet hangs back, her worried gaze lingering on me as we begin to walk.

The harsh lights hit me the moment we step onto the set. Everything is blindingly bright, and the layout is typical of every talk show—simple, pristine, crafted to make you feel utterly exposed. My eyes settle on Jerry Goldman, already perched at the big desk with that smug expression glued to his face. But then I look to the side—and freeze.

Sitting to Jerry's left is the woman responsible for all my pain—my mother, with her wannabe biker husband beside her. She's perched there like she belongs, and my breath snags in my throat. No one warned me she'd be here. No one mentioned she'd be part of this. The thought of facing her through all this twists something deep inside me.

A crew member guides Scarlet to the side where she can watch the shit that's about to unfold.

"Go ahead and take a seat," the same crew member says, approaching Daisy and me, snapping me out of my thoughts. He gestures to the two empty chairs on Jerry's right, and I feel Daisy's hand slip into mine.

She gives me a gentle tug, guiding me toward the seats. I let her lead, my eyes still darting between my mother and the man beside her. Each glance only heightens the knot of anxiety in my stomach.

When we finally reach the chairs, I sink into the one closest to Jerry, while Daisy takes the seat next to me. I can't tear my gaze away from my mother, the questions and raw anger churning violently inside me like a storm ready to erupt. This wasn't how it was supposed to happen—this wasn't the moment I envisioned. But here we are, trapped in this nightmare, and there's no turning back now.

She sits there with a chilling casualness, that smug smile etched on her face as if she's relishing every second of my torment. It's a smile that twists my insides, igniting a deep, consuming rage that threatens to break free. Just seeing her makes my skin crawl, every beat of my heart pounding with fury and betrayal I've kept buried for far too long.

The studio lights are blinding, and the noise around me fades into a low hum as the crew finishes setting up. I try to focus on anything but the fact that she's right there, watching me. My fingers dig into the armrest, gripping it tight as I fight to stay grounded. I feel Daisy shift beside me, her discomfort palpable as she glances at our so-called mother.

The crew moves around us, barking quick instructions and adjusting equipment as they prep for the show. A producer steps into my line of sight, holding up a hand and counting down with their fingers—five, four, three, two, one. The countdown looms like a dark cloud, and I brace myself for the shitstorm about to hit.

The red light on the camera flicks on, and Jerry Goldman's voice slices through my thoughts.

"Ace Roberts is a name millions around the world recognize, not only as the guitarist and founding member of Broken Oasis, the biggest band on the planet, but also as the man who has recently dominated headlines for a very different reason. With their latest album hitting number one worldwide, Broken Oasis continues to take over the music scene, but Ace has found himself in the spotlight for reasons that go beyond his music. Many of you have seen the footage—Ace stepping out of his car, visibly frustrated, grabbing a paparazzi's camera, and throwing it to the ground when they refused to move out of the way. It was a moment of anger that sparked widespread debate. Adding to the controversy, Ace's mother, Gloria Fletcher, recently gave an eye-opening account of what life was like with her son, describing it as 'living with a ticking time bomb,' which has led to many difficult questions about the pressures and challenges behind his rockstar persona. Tonight, for the first time on television, Ace Roberts sits down with us to tell his side of the story. Joining him is his sister, Daisy, to provide her own perspective on the man behind the headlines and what it's really like to grow up alongside one of music's most iconic figures." He turns his head to look over at me. "Ace, Daisy, welcome, and thank you for being here."

I force myself to meet Jerry's gaze, but I can't resist glancing back at my mother one last time.

The way she sits there, so damn confident, just pisses me off. Her husband sits next to her, silent and smug, like he's got a front-row seat to a fucking train wreck.

"Well first of all why did you decide to go public," he says, his tone oozing with that slick, rehearsed charm.

Is this asshole for fucking real. His people have been hounding Kit, day in and day out for this interview. I take a deep breath, ignoring what I really want to say to this fucker, and keep my tone casual.

"I want to set the record straight."

"Have you seen the footage of you throwing that camera?" Jerry's voice is sharp.

I clench my jaw and force myself to nod. "Yeah, I've seen it. I'm not proud of how I acted that day. I—"

He doesn't let me finish, his voice barreling right over mine. "There's been a lot of talk lately, especially concerning your mother, Ace. I think it's only fair we address some of those rumors head-on, don't you?"

My pulse quickens, and I feel all eyes in the room turn toward me, waiting.

Daisy's hand slips under the desk and finds mine, her fingers gripping tight, a lifeline in the middle of this storm. I focus on that small connection, trying to ground myself as the weight of the moment presses down hard.

Across from me, my mother leans back in her chair, that same damn smile plastered on her face—like she's already won, like she's waiting for the cracks to show.

"Ace, your mother has made some serious accusations about you being a violent and abusive person. Can you tell us your side of the story?"

I take a deep breath, fighting to keep my hands steady even though every nerve in my body is screaming. "These allegations are completely unfounded," I begin, my tone more controlled as I push through the anxiety. "My mother's claims are nothing but a desperate attempt to cash in on my success. She's always had her own issues, and now she's trying to use a mistake I'm ashamed of—the camera I threw—as a way to turn that narrative against me. I shouldn't have done it, I know that. But it wasn't out of violence, it was out of everything piling up—Nate's accident, the tour, the pressure. I snapped in a moment of stress, not in violence or to hurt anyone."

My eyes lock onto Jerry's, daring him to challenge the truth in my words. The studio lights burn against my skin, making everything feel more intense, more suffocating. I wait for him to interrupt me but he doesn't so I continue. "Throughout my childhood, my mother had her own problems with drug abuse. I've never been abusive or violent to her or anyone for that matter. Not once." I pause, the words choking in my throat because I know what I have to say next will tear open old wounds. "The truth is... I endured the abuse—cruel, relentless abuse—from the men she brought home. And she never cared enough to protect me. Or my sister, Daisy, for that matter." I swallow hard, forcing down the lump in my throat. "Now, she's seen an opportunity—a platform—to twist the narrative, to turn my pain into her payday. And that's what this is. It's a quick money grab, nothing more."

The words hang heavy in the air, my heart pounding in my chest.

"Ace, Daisy," Jerry says, his eyes flicking between the two of us, "I just want to play a little clip." He glances off to the side, signaling someone.

My eyes follow his, and a screen flickers to life. A second later, my mother's face appears, and I know it's from her interview. Her voice echoes through the studio. "Even Ace's father and his sister Daisy left, because they had to get out of the house—it was too toxic."

The clip ends, and the room is silent for a beat, before Jerry's voice fills the space. "Daisy, what do you think about that statement? What's your perspective on these accusations?"

Daisy stiffens beside me, and I can see her struggling to hold it together. "Well, our childhood was far from normal," she begins, her voice steady but strained. "It's true—our mother was a drug addict, and the men she brought home were abusive."

Jerry, of course, cuts in before she can say more. "How long did you put up with this abuse?" His tone is clinical, detached, like we're nothing but just another story.

Daisy swallows hard, her grip tightening around my hand. "I remember being the one to look after Ace when he was just a baby—"

"Where was his father?" Jerry interrupts again, leaning forward with that annoying glint in his eyes.

"He was never around," Daisy says, her voice firm. "He left when Ace was only a year old."

Jerry seizes on that immediately, a hint of triumph in his voice. "Let me get this straight—so Ace's father didn't leave because of these so-called violent outbursts?"

"No," she says sharply. "He left because he didn't want the responsibility. Not because of anything Ace did, and not because of any 'toxic environment' my mother claims."

The weight of her words hangs in the air, and for the first time in this whole mess, I feel like we're finally pushing back.

"Ace was just a baby," Daisy continues. "None of what she's saying has any truth to it. Like Ace already stated, it's just a desperate attempt to cash in on his fame." Her gaze shifts toward our mother, a fierce intensity in her eyes. "And that's all she's doing now. She never cared about us, never bothered to protect us from what the guys she brought home did."

Jerry raises an eyebrow, clearly intrigued. "But your mother claims you left because you couldn't stand it there due to Ace's violent behavior?" He glances briefly at my mother before redirecting his focus to Daisy.

Daisy lets out a bitter laugh that echoes in the tense air. "Yeah, I suppose she would say that, given the kind of stories she's been spinning." Her expression hardens as she presses on, her voice steady yet layered with emotion. "The truth is, I had to leave because of the men who tried to come into my room. It was a nightmare, and it broke my heart to leave Ace behind, for him to face that cruelty all alone." She turns to me, her eyes glistening with unshed tears. "It's my biggest regret—that I left him there to endure all of that by himself. I wish I could've done more to protect him."

Jerry's gaze shifts back to my mother, his expression scrutinizing. "Gloria, we've heard Ace and Daisy's side of the story. Can you clarify the specific incidents they're referring to? The men you would bring home. The conditions in which your children were living? Daisy raising Ace when she was just a child herself?"

Each question hangs heavily in the air, amplifying the scrutiny directed at her.

Gloria's smile falters, and she clears her throat, her discomfort palpable. "It's not easy to recall exact specifics..."

Jerry leans forward, his tone sharp and probing.

"Come on, Gloria, you've made some serious accusations here. Surely you can remember the incidents Daisy and Ace are talking about. Or are you suggesting that they're both fabricating their stories?"

Gloria stammers, her confidence visibly crumbling. "It's just... I recall some incidents where Ace was... aggressive."

Jerry doesn't relent, pressing harder. "And yet, you can't provide specifics or any evidence to support these claims? We're talking about some serious allegations here."

The studio lights seem to intensify, making Gloria's discomfort more obvious as her face pales. She starts fidgeting, glancing away like she's searching for an escape. The silence stretches, her growing hesitation speaking volumes, highlighting the fragility of her accusations. Each passing second adds weight to the tension in the room, and I can feel the momentum slowly shifting in our favor.

Jerry shifts his focus, his tone sharp and probing. "There's one more crucial detail in these allegations—take a look."

He turns back to the screen, and I follow his gaze, to see my mother's face reappear on the monitor. "There was an incident when he was seventeen. His stepfather, Larry," she glances at the scumbag sitting next to her, "tried to protect me, and Ace didn't take it well. There was this moment when he grabbed me and wouldn't let go. That was the day I genuinely feared for my life, truly believing it could be my last. A boy should never lay a hand on his mother like that. I just can't understand where I went wrong, raising a son with so much hatred in his heart. If Larry hadn't been there, I don't know what I would've done."

The clip ends abruptly, leaving a heavy silence in its wake. Jerry faces my mother, his tone shifting. "Gloria, you claimed that Ace's stepfather—"

"He was never my stepfather," I interject firmly, cutting Jerry off.

Jerry glances at me briefly, then redirects his attention back to my mother. "Gloria, you've stated that Ace was violent towards your boyfriend. You even made that claim right here on this very show. Can you explain that?"

The man beside Gloria looks uneasy, shifting in his seat as if he's trying to shrink away from the scrutiny. "I—well, there were incidents..."

Jerry presses on, shifting his questions to the dickhead beside my mother. "Incidents? Can you be more specific? What exactly happened? And where's the evidence to back up these claims?"

The man's face reddens as he glances nervously at Gloria, who seems to be struggling to hold it together under the mounting pressure. The tension in the room thickens, the truth becoming harder and harder to mask.

The old biker wannabe shifts again, his hands fidgeting in his lap. "I—he was always aggressive. I was attacked by Ace, and it was unprovoked."

Jerry's attention snaps back to me, his gaze intense and expectant. "Ace, what's your take on these claims?"

"That's not true at all. He came at me first. I was just seventeen, and he had me pinned to the wall with his hands around my throat. Xander Williams was there-"

"Xander Williams, the lead singer of Broken Oasis, was there?" Jerry cuts in, his curiosity piqued.

"Yes, he was there. He can confirm I was not the aggressor." I feel the fire in my chest blaze hotter as I recount the truth, knowing it's my only weapon against the lies being spun.

As I sit here, facing my mother, I think about all the years of fear and intimidation my mother instilled in me now seems misplaced. I've been haunted by this woman who, in reality, is nothing more than a sad, desperate figure clinging to whatever she can get. The anger and hurt I've carried for so long feels almost laughable against her pitiful attempts to cash in on my fame.

"Will Xander Williams confirm the truth of this story?" Jerry asks, bringing me out of my thoughts.

"Yeah," I reply firmly. "He was there. He knows exactly what happened." I can feel the weight of the moment, each word cutting through years of silence and fear. I won't let her spin this narrative anymore. I won't let her control my life.

The fucker beside my mother looks increasingly uncomfortable, his earlier smugness now replaced by unease. My mother drops her gaze, her facade cracking. The shaky foundation of her accusations is now crumbling under Jerry's relentless questioning.

Jerry turns his attention to Daisy. "And was this man one of the men who tried to get into your room, Daisy?"

"No," Daisy shakes her head firmly. "I've never met him. I didn't see him until he started spreading lies about my brother."

Jerry's expression grows skeptical as he looks at Gloria. "It seems there's a significant discrepancy between the claims being made and the evidence provided. Gloria, are you sure you have a solid basis for these accusations?"

Gloria shifts uncomfortably in her seat, her earlier confidence now wavering under Jerry's intense scrutiny. "I... I just know what I've seen over the years," she stammers, her voice losing its edge. "Ace has always had a temper. He's always been violent."

"Violent?" Jerry interjects, his tone sharper. "You keep using that word without providing any proof. You've made serious claims about your son, but when pressed for specifics, you falter. Are you suggesting that Ace is lying, or are you simply using his fame to push your own agenda?"

The spotlight on her grows harsher, exposing the cracks in her story. She fidgets, avoiding Jerry's sharp gaze, and I can see the wheels turning in her mind as she scrambles to craft a response that might save her claims.

"I... I don't know. It's just—" Gloria's voice trails off. She can't even muster the strength to defend herself against the truth, and I feel a surge of vindication as those watching witness her unraveling.

Jerry then turns back to me and Daisy, his tone shifting to a more conclusive note. "It appears there's a clear gap between the accusations and the evidence. Ace, Daisy, thank you for sharing your side of the story and clarifying the situation."

He leans forward, talking to me. "But people will watch this who have seen you lose your temper, Ace. They'll be trying to work out where the truth lies. I think, at the very least, you've been portrayed as someone who doesn't care—someone painted as a crazy person who could explode at any given moment. So, to those watching us now, to those who still doubt you, what do you want to say to them?"

I turn my head to the camera, my heart racing as I meet its gaze. "I am not a violent man. I never have been. This is just a twisted attempt to exploit me for money." My voice steadies as I speak, each word a declaration of my truth.

"Ace, Daisy, thank you very much," Jerry says, then faces the camera with an authoritative nod. "Believe it or not, but from what it appears, the real story here seems to not be about Ace Roberts but maybe the issues within Gloria's life."

The camera's cut off and Jerry stands up, stepping away from us. I glance at Daisy, who meets my gaze with a smile. Despite the lingering pain, I'm grateful for her support and for this chance to finally set things right.

To the side, our mother and that wannabe biker fucker are already yanking off their mics, eager to make their escape. The tension between them is palpable as they move swiftly toward the exit. They don't spare me a glance, and I don't care. I have no words left for them, and their retreat only reinforces my resolve to leave the past behind.

As a crew member comes over to remove the microphone from me, I barely register the movement. My focus is entirely on Scarlet as she walks toward me. Every glance at her during the interview felt like a breath of fresh air, cutting through the weight that's been pressing on me for so long. Confronting my mother and reliving those painful memories has drained me, but having Scarlet here makes it feel a little more bearable.

It's as if she's the missing piece that makes my world fall into place. For the first time in ages, the world feels like it's tilting in a better direction, and the burden of the past is beginning to recede.

# CHAPTER 31

## Scarlet

I'm so proud of Ace for confronting his demons head-on like that. After the interview, we spent some time with Daisy, just hanging out and killing time before our flights. We grabbed dinner at the airport, and I could see the heaviness lifting off him bit by bit. It's good to see him like this—smiling a little more—even though the shadow of everything he'd just been through still lingers.

When I saw his mother sitting there in the studio, I honestly thought Ace was going to lose it. The way he froze the second he saw her—I braced myself for a meltdown. But he held it together. Every accusation against him was torn apart, exposed as nothing but lies. To everyone who called him an abuser and waved those hateful signs—fuck you. I can't help but smile, knowing the "hero" you defended was nothing but a fraud.

In the moments before boarding, Xander, Theo, and Nate all called Ace to check-in. I love how these guys look out for each other. It hurts to think that just a few weeks ago, they were at odds because of me. I never want to be the reason for any more tension between them.

By the time we arrive in New York and the cab pulls up to the hotel, it's late. The doorman's warm smile welcomes us as we step through the grand double doors and into the lobby. Ace takes my hand, and we walk through the refined space, the quiet hum of late-night activity surrounding us. We grab the envelope Kit left at the front desk and head down the long corridor.

As we wait for the elevator, Ace turns toward me, his eyes softening. He just watches me for a moment, and I can tell he wants to say something, but it's like he doesn't know how to get the words out. Before he can even try, the elevator doors slide open, and just like that, the moment is ruined.

Stepping into the elevator, the doors slide shut with a soft hiss, and Ace turns to me with a tenderness I've never seen in him before. He pulls me into his arms and presses his lips to mine in a soft, lingering kiss.

When he pulls back, his eyes are softer, vulnerable in a way that speaks louder than any words. He doesn't say anything, but that look—the raw, genuine side of him—tells me exactly how much I mean to him. In that silent moment, it's as if he's letting me see the part of him he keeps hidden from the world.

He takes a deep breath, swallowing hard, his brows knitting as though he's wrestling with something deep inside. "I... I love you," he says at last, his voice barely a whisper. "I fucking love you, Scar."

A rush of emotions overwhelms me, and tears well in my eyes as I struggle to keep them from spilling over. The depth of what he's just said—the sincerity in his voice—touches something deep within me.

I look at him, my vision blurred by tears, and smile. "I love you too," I whisper.

Finally, a single tear escapes, rolling down my cheek, but I don't bother to wipe it away.

Instead, I let it fall, feeling both vulnerable and utterly cherished.

Ace reaches out, gently brushing a tear from my cheek with his thumb. The moment feels timeless, and I can't help but feel that, in this quiet, intimate space, we've both discovered something incredibly precious and real.

The elevator doors slide open and we step out, our fingers still entwined, the warmth of his hand a comfort against mine. The warm, buttery glow of the sconces along the hallway bathes us in a gentle light, creating a cozy cocoon just for us.

As we step into our room and the door closes behind us, the world outside fades away, leaving only the two of us in this intimate haven.

Ace's gaze locks onto mine, his eyes blazing with intensity. He steps closer, the heat of his body sending a spark through the space between us, electrifying the air.

Time seems to stand still, and in this moment, nothing else matters but the love we've just confessed.

His touch is both gentle and commanding as he cups my face, his thumbs tracing along my jawline, sending shivers through me. He leans in, and our lips meet in a slow, teasing kiss that quickly ignites into something urgent and wild.

He pulls me in closer, our mouths moving together like we're desperate to meld into one. Each stroke of his tongue sends fire racing through my veins, lighting me up from the inside. I can feel his need against me—hot and hard—his cock straining as he presses against me, heightening the urgency of every moment.

My fingers thread into his hair, holding him tight, like I'm afraid to let go. The kiss is full of everything we've been holding back. Every touch, every breath, only drives me deeper into him. The need between us is unbearable. I need him. All of him.

He grips the edge of my shirt and, without hesitation, pulls it off in one swift motion, along with my bra. I gasp as he takes my nipple into his mouth, each touch sending waves of pleasure rippling through my body.

In seconds, he unbuttons my jeans and slides them down my legs, leaving me fully exposed.

"Christ," he breathes, his eyes burning with desire as they roam over my naked form. His fingers trace the curve of my breast, gliding over my skin until they rest possessively on my hip. "You're so fucking perfect, Scar."

I tug at the waistband of his jeans, urgency thrumming in my veins. "Get these off now," I demand, my voice low and filled with need.

A sexy grin curls at the corner of his mouth as he replies, "I love it when you fucking take control. I love it when you're so fucking dirty." He lifts me up effortlessly, guiding me toward the bed, then sets me on my feet.

"Lay down," I command, gesturing to the bed.

He lifts his hands, tugging his shirt over his head, then leans back on his elbows, his eyes fixed on me, watching my every move.

I undo the button and zipper on his jeans, sliding them down slowly along with his boxers, revealing his hard cock as it springs free, lightly grazing his stomach.

Lying back, he threads his fingers behind his head, his gaze intense and unwavering. I can't help but admire the ink sprawled across his chest, the designs trailing up over both shoulders. The intricate patterns and musical notes are mesmerizing, each telling a story that only he knows. But my eyes always gravitate to the skull in the center of his chest, its bony fingers wrapped around it, obscuring its eye sockets. It feels like a haunting symbol of his past, a reminder of the battles he has endured.

I've always wanted to ask him about it, to understand what it means, but I hesitated, not wanting to bring up painful memories. Now that he's more open and facing his demons, I decide to take a chance. "Is this the pain you've carried?" I ask, my fingers softly tracing the long, bony fingers of the tattoo.

When he doesn't answer, I glance up and catch him watching my fingers glide across his skin, his gaze intense. I can feel the scars beneath the ink—each one a reminder of his past struggles, like the cigarette burns on his arms he tries so hard to hide.

"Yeah," he finally replies, his voice low and raw. "It's how I've always felt. Like no matter how hard I tried, those fingers always probed into my thoughts, dragging me back into that dark world."

As my fingers trace down his chest, I notice goosebumps rising under my touch. I slide my hands lower, exploring his abdomen, then wrap my fingers around his cock, giving him a soft stroke. Feeling bold, I lean in closer, my tongue flicking out to taste the milky drop on the tip. The moan that comes from him sends a thrill through me, fueling my desire.

His hands lower to his sides, fingers clenching tightly as if he's battling the urge to tangle them in my hair and command me to open my mouth so he can fuck it. I watch his nostrils flare as I repeat the teasing action.

"Fuck, Scar," he breathes, his voice dripping with affection.

A surprised squeal escapes me as he suddenly pulls me on top of him, his lips crashing against mine in a scorching kiss. The heat of his mouth sparks a hunger inside me, one I can't ignore. I bite his bottom lip softly, urging for more. His kiss grows deeper, intense and commanding, his fingers splaying against my neck while the other hand grips my hip, holding me still as he takes what he craves.

A gentle pinch on my nipple makes me gasp, urging me to grind against him, lost in the heat of the moment. I'm so aroused that I could scream. Gasping for air, I pull back from the kiss and whisper, "I need you to fuck me, Ace. Fuck me now."

"You don't have to ask, just take it, Scar," he growls, his voice thick with desire. "It's fucking yours whenever you want it."

His words make me grind across his hard cock. Oh, my God. Every bump and vein is perfectly designed to drive me wild with pleasure.

"Christ," he breathes, his voice low and filled with lust. "Your pretty pussy is drenching my cock." The heat in his eyes sharpens as he reaches down and grips himself, his gaze locked on me. "Rub it on your clit," he commands, his voice rough.

Wrapping my fingers around him, I take control, savoring the power I have over him. His eyes drop, fixed on my hand. "That's it," he whispers, teeth clenched as I trace the sensitive area.

A moan slips from my lips as I indulge further, getting lost in the sensation.

"Fuck, I bet that feels good," he says.

"So fucking good," I moan, but it's not just the sensations of his cock and piercing that have me entranced. It's the way he watches me, his eyes dark with desire, lips parted just enough to reveal his hunger.

I quicken my pace, rubbing his cock against my clit, the overwhelming pleasure building inside me. I'm so incredibly wet, teetering on the edge of my release.

"Fuck, I can feel you throbbing on my cock," he breathes, tilting his head back, eyes closing as he loses himself in the moment. His hands grip my hips hard, anchoring me to him.

And now I want it even more. I need him inside me like I need my next breath. "I need your cock in me when I come," I confess, the words spilling from my lips with desperation.

He snaps his eyes open and sits up, pulling me closer with an arm wrapped around my lower back. His deep, husky voice does something to me when he whispers, "I want my cock inside you too."

Goosebumps ripple across my skin. Our eyes lock as he slowly enters me, stretching me to accommodate every hard inch of him.

"Fuck, you feel so good," he murmurs, sliding his thumb down to tease my clit while I ride him.

His feral kiss ignites something in me, each thrust is pure bliss. Then it happens spectacularly. The orgasm hits like a tidal wave, crashing over me in a rush of intense pleasure. Fuck it feels so good. I gasp, pleasure erupting, my back arching, and every nerve-ending screaming. "Oh my God," I gasp, lost in the overwhelming pleasure.

A deep growl rumbles in his throat as my pussy tightens around him. His forehead rests against mine, his strong chest rising and falling, as if he's just experienced his own release. In a blissful haze, I lean into him.

He wraps his arms around me, pulling me so close that there's no space left between us. The intensity of what I'm feeling is almost overwhelming. His breath brushes my skin, warm and inviting, as our foreheads remain pressed together. I can see his restraint etched on his face, the way his fingers tangle in my hair.

My heart races as I take in every detail of his face.

The sharp angles, the heat radiating from his eyes, and the palpable torment etched into his features. It's clear that holding himself still, while buried deep inside me, and not moving is a battle he's barely winning. Yet, despite the struggle, he fights against the overwhelming urge, determined to satisfy my every need.

I lean in closer, my lips brushing against the shell of his ear, my breath a sultry whisper. "I need you to fuck me."

That's all it takes to shatter his restraint.

His hands grip my ass, desire blazing in his eyes, and abruptly withdraws, leaving me breathless and aching from the sudden emptiness.

In an instant, I'm lying on my back, and the look in his eyes transforms into something primal—like a predator closing in on its prey.

"Spread your fucking legs," he commands.

The moment I obey, he leans in, his skilled tongue finding its way to my most sensitive spot, drawing soft moans from me. His fingers slide up my body, then teasing my nipples, sending shivers of pleasure through me that almost make me purr. It's as if he knows my body intimately, every pleasure point mapped out in his mind.

With a playful touch of his tongue, he circles my clit. I grow impatient, instinctively grinding my hips against his face, desperate for more.

"Ace, please, just fuck me," I beg, my voice thick with need.

With a wicked grin that spreads across his face, he lets out a chuckle. "In a fucking minute," he replies, his tone low and seductive. He's teasing me, making me work for it, and I can feel the heat rising in my core.

Frustrated, I let out a groan.

His laughter sends pleasurable vibrations through me as he kisses my pussy, and I bite my bottom lip, my gaze locked on him. I can't focus on anything except the way his tongue circles my clit and his fingers thrust deep inside me.

"You're so fucking wet," he remarks, pulling his hand away and aligning the tip of his cock with my entrance. "Take a deep breath," he whispers, leaning down to shower tender kisses along my stomach.

Then, with a swift thrust, he enters, filling me completely.

"Oh, fuck," I gasp, my mouth falling open in surprise.

Rising onto his knees, he grips my hips with a firm, possessive hold. I shiver with anticipation as he pulls back, then thrusts into me, each movement driving deeper. His hold is so tight, I can already feel the promise of marks left behind. The way he moves, the way he takes control, leaves my legs trembling.

"Ace," I whisper, my hand reaching out to him, overwhelmed by an insatiable longing I can hardly comprehend. All I know is that my desire for him eclipses anything I've ever craved before.

His gaze is intense, utterly captivating, locking me in its grip. The depth of his stare does something to me.

With each thrust, as he drives into me again and again, the rhythm builds, and the pleasure intensifies, making my toes curl with every movement. I lift my hips, eagerly meeting his deep thrusts, enhancing our fiery dance. With each penetration, I surrender to the rhythm, completely losing myself in the sensation. My hands glide down his back, reveling in the strength of his muscles as they flex and ripple with every thrust.

"Ace," I moan, the sound spilling from my lips like a desperate plea, urging him to push deeper, to take me higher.

Each time he thrusts into me, I feel myself coming apart, his presence sinking deep into my core. He's never fucked me like this before; it's as if he's starving for my touch, yet can't fully satisfy his craving.

As my fingers trace the stubble on his jawline, admiring his breathtaking beauty, his gaze meets mine, burning with an intensity that takes my breath away. He's not just physically inside me; this goes deeper, so much more profound. It's everything I've ever wanted—this undeniable bond between us. Ace Roberts doesn't just fuck me; he worships me with every part of him, and I can feel the weight of that devotion.

As our fingers intertwine, he lifts my hand above my head, pinning it there with a possessive grip. His other hand roams between us, teasing my sensitive clit with tantalizing strokes. Every deep thrust pulls another whimper from me, sending me spiraling closer to the edge.

I part my lips, desperate to plead for a moment's respite, but instead, a sultry moan escapes me. I bite down on my bottom lip, trying to stifle the sounds pouring from me, but it's pointless. The tension builds within me, my orgasm looming on the horizon.

"Fucking hell," he groans.

His next deep thrust catches me by surprise, his piercing hitting that perfect sweet spot inside me, shattering the fragile thread of control I've been holding onto. I tumble over the edge, a wave of pleasure surging through me, my primal moan filling the room as I drown in the intensity of my orgasm.

Then, Ace suddenly freezes, concern flickering across his face. "Are you okay?" he asks, his voice filled with worry.

I pant, breathless and overwhelmed, struggling to find the words to express just how incredible I feel. Instead, I can only manage a blissful smile, my eyes sparkling with unspoken joy.

He thrusts back in and out of me, and I watch as pleasure twists his features, each shudder signaling the oncoming storm of his release. With each deep thrust, he picks up the pace, fucking me with an urgency that makes my body ache for more, as if he's desperate to drown himself in every inch of me. I feel him throb inside me, and then he finally comes, his release filling me.

As he collapses against me, I feel his hot breath against my chest, and I lovingly thread my fingers through his damp hair, pulling him in closer, craving his warmth. He grips me tightly, unwilling to let go as he catches his breath, savoring the moment we've just shared, our bodies still entwined in a haze of raw desire.

His hand glides over my ribs, teasingly grazing the curve of my breast before settling over my heart, which thunders beneath his touch.

"Who knew a woman named Scar would have the power to heal my fucked up scars," he murmurs against my skin.

He presses a soft, lingering kiss right over the place where my heart races, sealing the moment with his devotion.

# CHAPTER 32

## Ace

As the early morning light, soft and golden, slips through the blinds, I reach out, brushing a strand of hair away from Scarlet's face. She's asleep, completely at peace, and for a second, I just take it all in.

Everything is clear now. I love her. Probably have for way longer than I even knew. But saying it out loud last night? That shit changed everything. There's no going back now. Not after this.

For the first time in my life, I've let someone in. Really fucking let them in.

I laid it all out for her—the shit I never thought I'd say aloud, let alone to anyone else.

And the crazy part? It felt right. No hesitation, no second-guessing. She's the one for me. I get that now. No one else will ever get this close, not the way she has. It's terrifying, sure, but fuck, it's the best feeling I've ever had.

I pull her into me, careful not to wake her just yet. I need to hold onto this. Hold onto her. It's just us, no more chaos. I'm hers, and she's mine. That simple truth makes everything feel... lighter.

She stirs, her eyes fluttering open, and when those big, sleepy eyes land on me, I can't stop the smile tugging at my lips.

"Good morning," she murmurs, her voice soft and raspy.

"Morning," I reply, leaning down to kiss her, slow and gentle.

Her smile widens against my lips. "I've got the perfect day planned for us. I'm going to show you all my favorite spots in New York."

"I can't wait," I say, smirking as my voice dips low, "but you know I'd prefer to keep you in this bed all day."

She flashes that wicked grin, her fingers trailing down my chest, sending a spark through me. "Oh, really? You think you can handle me in bed all day?"

She laughs, slipping out of my hold, and I let out a frustrated sigh.

"I've got the whole day planned," she says.

"And I've got other plans in mind," I say, grabbing her wrist, pulling her back to me. My lips brush against her ear. "You better make it worth it, 'cause I'm this close to saying screw your plans and just keep you here."

Her laugh is light, but there's fire in her eyes. I'm tempted to lose myself in her right here and now, but the idea of her sharing her favorite things with me draws me in just as much.

With one last heated kiss, I let her go, watching as she heads toward the shower, my eyes roaming down over her tight body.

I'm about to follow her when my phone rings, and Xander's name lights up the screen, stopping me in my tracks. I pause, torn between going after her and taking the call. With a frustrated sigh, I swipe to answer and lift the phone to my ear.

"Hey?" I say.

"Just checking in. I wanted to see how you're holding up after that interview yesterday," Xander says.

I glance toward the bathroom, hearing the water running, and smirk. "Everything's good. Better than good, actually."

An hour later, disguised and ready, we plunge into the bustling chaos of New York City. The streets pulse with bright lights and towering buildings, an overwhelming mix of car horns, bursts of laughter, and the mouthwatering scent of street food that makes my stomach rumble. This place is a circus—way more intense than Los Angeles.

Our first stop is a cozy little coffee shop tucked away near Central Park. Scarlet's eyes light up as she orders two steaming cups, the rich aroma wrapping around us, adding a warmth that feels almost intimate. We settle by the window, letting the city's pulse wash over us as we watch the world buzz by. The soft hum of conversations and the clink of cups create a laid-back atmosphere, but all I can focus on is her. She talks about all the previous times she's come here over the years, her voice filled with stories and memories, and I can't help but be captivated, completely drawn in.

Sitting here with her, it really sinks in just how far we've come. This isn't just another day in New York—it's us, building something real, something solid that's been quietly growing between us for a while now.

I take a slow sip of coffee, but my eyes stay fixed on her, captivated. I get lost in the way she speaks, how her hands move with each story, and the way her face lights up with every word. It's these little moments, so genuine and effortless, that pull me in deeper and make me fall even harder.

Afterward, we stroll through Central Park, surrounded by vibrant green trees and a gentle breeze brushing against my face. The future doesn't feel hazy anymore—it's clear, almost within reach. I can sense it in the sweet scent of blooming flowers, feel it in the warmth of the sun filtering through the leaves. It's like I'm watching our life come together, piece by piece, with Scarlet and me building something lasting, something real. In this moment, I'm absolutely certain of it. She's my safe haven, my anchor in this vast, unpredictable world.

"What are you gonna do once the tour's over?" I ask, keeping my tone casual, though inside, the thought of not seeing her everyday hits hard. The idea of her not being there, of not being able to reach out and touch her or watch that smile light up her face—it feels like a punch straight to the gut.

"I don't know," she says, her voice trailing off into silence. As we head back toward the bustling city street, I watch her carefully. "I guess I'll have to find another band that needs a drummer."

"It should be easier now that people know your name and how kick-ass you really are," I reply, trying to reassure her.

She glances at me, her expression thoughtful. "Yeah, I suppose. But some will still try and use me for the connections I can make."

I fucking hate hearing that. The thought of someone using her, taking advantage of her just because of her last name. It doesn't sit right with me at all. I want to protect her from that, to make sure she knows her worth is more than just who she's related to. She deserves to shine on her own, not in someone else's shadow.

We leave the park and wander through the city, stopping by a quirky little bookstore she loves—the kind that smells of old paper and fresh coffee. Then there's the rooftop garden she once stumbled upon—a hidden oasis high above the concrete jungle that is New York. The moment we step inside, we're wrapped in the intoxicating scent of blooming flowers and fresh herbs. Tiny fairy lights hang around the space, their soft glow sparkling in the sunlight, adding a hint of magic. Each spot offers a glimpse into her world, and with every stop, I find myself even more captivated by her.

As we sit together in the silence, I know we need to head back to the hotel before soundcheck at three. But for the first time, I don't want to leave for my music. I don't want to break this closeness, this moment we're sharing. It's not like me—music has always come first. But right now? All I want is to stay here with her, wrapped up in her world.

Then it hits me, clear as day. I finally understand what Xander meant when he said he'd give it all up for Poppy and Alex. I thought he was crazy when he said that to all of us. But with Scarlet here beside me, it makes perfect sense. She means more to me than any stage or spotlight ever could. And this feeling... It's stronger than any high I've ever chased.

The fans' cheers, a deafening roar that echoes through the venue, fill the air as we wrap up another killer show. But all I can focus on is the smoking hot chick who's been killing it on the drums—yeah, the one who's mine. Watching her pound those drums with everything she's got has my pulse racing and my dick straining against my jeans all night.

I even caught Theo sneaking glances at me a couple of times while I was watching her. Ever since that little incident on the bus, the asshole's been a bit more relaxed about us. Even Nate has eased up about me being with his sister. Of course, they've both made it crystal clear they'll kick my ass if I ever hurt her. But honestly, they don't need to worry—I'd never fucking do that to her.

As we walk off the stage, Scarlet stops in the wings and waits for me. The moment we're together, I wrap my arm around her shoulders, pulling her close. It's funny—at first, it felt weird having the guys watch me do this, their eyes glued to my every move, but now? I don't give a flying fuck. If I want to touch her, I'm gonna do it. And right now, all I want is to have her close, no matter who's watching.

Xander and Theo, ramble on with their usual bullshit as they lead the way down to the green room. Before entering, Xander ducks into another room to change his sweaty shirt, and while we wait, Theo just stands there, staring at us with this odd look on his face, like he's got some secret agenda. I'm half-expecting him to drop a smart-ass comment or some snarky remark. But no, he just stands there with this weird ass grin. What the fuck is he playing at? It's creeping me out, like some new pet that won't stop staring at you while you sleep.

Xander comes back out, and Theo, like some kind of loyal sidekick, falls in step with him as we head into the green room. Disturbed and Twisted are already in there, knocking back drinks and soaking up the aftershow buzz. Jack and Walter are sprawled out on one of the couches, nursing their drinks, and I can't help but notice the way they're totally eyefucking their bass guitarist. Yeah, there's definitely something going on there.

It makes me wonder if these guys are like Theo and Nate, sharing more than just a tour bus and a stage. I haven't seen them with any of the groupies this whole tour. Maybe they're keeping their hookups under the radar, or maybe they're just not into that kind of scene.

Xander tosses Theo a water bottle, then hands one to Scarlet and me. The three of us crack them open and take a long swig.

Kit walks into the room. "Okay, guys," she says, eyeing Walter and Jack and then shifting her eyes to the rest of their band. "I've got extra tables set up so you guys can sign stuff with Broken Oasis for the fans."

I glance over at them, catching the stunned look on their faces, realizing we've just made their night. Usually, it's just us signing autographs for fans, but with the band's growing popularity, Xander suggested incorporating Walter's band into the session. Seeing the excitement on their faces takes me back to the frenetic energy of our first tour with the hottest band at the time. That moment when we joined them for signings felt like everything.

Within seconds, Kit ushers us into a room across the hall, and I can already hear the buzz of fans waiting, practically vibrating with excitement to meet us. Behind the screen doors, I catch snippets of conversations—guys talking about Scarlet—and it makes my blood fucking boil. Those assholes. If any of them so much as think about touching her tonight, they'll have to deal with me. I won't hesitate to shove my fist right into any prick's face who crosses that line. No one's laying a hand on what's mine—I can fucking guarantee that.

Kit sets us up at the table, black Sharpies ready in hand. Scarlet is at the end, with Jack next to her, and I'm right beside him. Jack was a total asshole when we first met, but he's chilled out since then. We've had drinks and bullshit sessions in the green room, and after Theo and I laid into him, he's kept his distance. I don't expect him to try anything with Scarlet again. Besides, he's probably figured out we're together, especially since I made a point of holding her hand when we walked in.

"So, how many pairs of tits do you get to sign at these things?" Jack asks, grinning like a kid in a candy store.

I chuckle, thinking back to the time when Theo and I were just as excited doing our first signing. "Quite a few," I reply, still laughing.

Jack's eyes light up, and he grins wide. "I don't think that'll ever get old. If a chick wants to flash her tits, I'm all for it. The more, the better."

"I hear ya," I say, laughing. Scarlet leans forward, shooting me a look that could melt steel, and I can't help but grin. The jealousy in her eyes is kinda fucking adorable.

"Asshole," she mouths, turning her head away.

The doors swing open, and the fans come charging in, nearly tumbling over each other to reach the roped-off section Kit set up. I watch them, eyes wide and starry, as they scramble to line up.

Scarlet's the first one in line for signings at the table, and I spot a girl at the front, her friends racing behind her. She's holding one of the new posters Kit had printed with Scarlet on it, and watching Scarlet sign it—rather than having to scribble her name on Nate's image—makes me grin like an idiot. I can tell this is a huge deal for her.

"Thank you. You're awesome," the girl says before moving on to Jack.

The look in her eyes heats up as she checks him out. He's decent enough—not a pretty boy like Xander—but I bet the chicks will still go fucking nuts for him. As soon as he drops that Aussie accent, it's like she fucking melts. He gives her a wicked grin, and his lines roll off his tongue smooth and flirty, just like Theo's.

Fuck me, I have to stop myself from laughing. Jack's charm with that accent is off the charts. I can already picture the chaos if he and Theo teamed up on the prowl—those chicks would be losing their shit. With Theo's effortless swagger and Jack's smooth-talking Aussie vibe, they'd turn every room they walked into a full-on frenzy.

When she finally pulls herself together, she saunters over to me. Even though she's still in that gooey, Jack-induced daze, she manages to flash me a smile.

With a grin, I take the poster from her and sign it, then hand it back, and watch as she shuffles off to the next person in line.

I spot a girl standing right in front of Jack, flashing her tits in his face. His eyes go wide, and he's grinning like he just won the lottery. He tries to act casual, but it's pretty obvious he's loving every second of it. I can't help but laugh at the ridiculousness of the whole thing. Jack glances at me and says, "Fuck, I love this job, man."

Still wearing that stupid grin, Jack signs the girl's tits before she struts over to me, her top still pulled up, flaunting her assets like it's no big deal. I scribble my name on her skin, and she thanks me before walking off. These groupies are fucking wild. But now that I'm with Scarlet, they don't have the same pull they used to.

We keep pushing through the crowd, signing tits and moving merch. After a while, everything starts to blur together.

About twenty minutes later, Jack shoots me a look, his face twisted with concern. "Something is going on with Scarlet."

I lean forward, my stomach twisting into knots as I spot a guy standing in front of Scarlet, his hand clamped around her wrist like a vice. She's tense, struggling to pull her arm free, but the asshole just tightens his grip, a smirk on his face.

That sight ignites a fire in my veins, rage surging like a tidal wave. I shove my chair back, the screech of wood on the floor ringing out like a battle cry. There's no way I'm letting this asshole think he can lay a hand on her without consequences. My blood is boiling, and I'm ready to march over there and make it painfully clear that he's crossed a line.

# Chapter 33

## Scarlet

I'm still buzzing from the rush of seeing my face on the posters and signing my first autograph on something that's actually mine. The crowd's energy has me floating, like I'm on top of the world.

But then, slicing through the noise like a razor, I hear a voice that stops me cold. My heart kicks into overdrive. I look up, and there he is—Beck, my ex. Standing right in front of me.

The noise of the room fades into a dull hum as panic rushes through me. He's not supposed to be here. Not now. My first instinct is to run, but I'm rooted in place, frozen by the fear that he's here to finish what he started.

Before I can react, his hand shoots out, clamping around my wrist, trapping me. My heart hammers in my chest, a chill slicing through me as his twisted gaze meets mine. That smirk on his lips—it's smug, taunting, a sick satisfaction that tells me he knows exactly the effect he's having on me, and he's savoring every moment of it.

"Hello, babe," he murmurs, his voice laced with a dark edge that cuts through me. "Long time, no see." His grip tightens, not enough to hurt but enough to make his threat clear, like he's daring me to pull away. That twisted glint in his eyes churns my stomach, feeding off the fear he's stirred up. It's not just my wrist he's holding—he's dragging me back into all the dark memories I've fought hard to bury. And the worst part? He knows exactly what he's doing.

I yank my arm, desperate to break free, but his grip is unyielding, fingers clamped around me like a vice. Panic claws at my chest, stealing my breath. "Let go of me!" I gasp, my voice trembling, but he doesn't flinch. Every time I pull, he tightens his hold, pain shooting up my arm, each struggle fueling his twisted satisfaction. It's like he's feeding off the control, enjoying every ounce of fear he's forcing through me.

Then it happens in a blur. Someone steps in front of me, and before I can register it, Beck's ripped away, a hand around his throat, yanking him back with brutal force. I gasp, my heart pounding in my ears, as I look up and see Ace, his face twisted with rage, inches from Beck's. His voice is cold, lethal. "Let her fucking go."

The crowd's chatter vanishes as every eye snaps to the scene unfolding. Beck's face twists in panic, his wide eyes full of fear as he chokes on whatever words he might've dared to say, but Ace's iron grip silences him completely. I stand frozen, my heart still pounding from the sudden shift, caught in the gravity of Ace's fierce protection.

Theo's there in an instant, right beside Ace. "That asshole is her ex," he spits, his voice a low growl, the barely contained rage simmering in his eyes, like he's ready to explode and make Beck pay for everything he's done.

"So, you're the fucker who hit her?" Ace's voice is low and deadly, his grip tightening around Beck's throat.

The room stays eerily still, the weight of the moment hanging thick in the air. Everyone's frozen, watching, waiting for what's about to go down.

Xander steps in, gripping Ace's arm, and tries to pull him back. "Not here, Ace," he says, his tone calm but laced with urgency. But Ace doesn't budge, his gaze fixed on Beck with an intensity that crackles in the air, his hand still gripping Beck's throat like he can't bear to let go. Every second stretches as Ace's fury remains unshaken, refusing to back down even a step.

"Time to go, asshole," Ace growls, dragging Beck toward the door we walked through earlier.

I need to stop this, to do something—anything. But before I can take a step, Theo steps in front of me, his jaw set and his eyes narrowed, a look that leaves no room for argument.

"Let him handle it, Scar," Theo says, his voice calm but firm. "He's just doing what Nate and I would've done."

Xander strides over, concern written all over his face. "You okay, Scarlet?"

"Yeah," I manage, swallowing hard, trying to shove the fear back down where it belongs. He gives a quick nod, silent but reassuring, before turning to Kit.

Kit steps in, her presence commanding as always. She clears her throat, cutting through the hushed murmurs. "Alright, listen up, everyone!" she calls out, her tone sharp and authoritative. "We're getting back to the signings. Let's keep it moving. One asshole isn't going to ruin the night."

Her words snap the crowd back to focus, and the tension in the room starts to ease.

I slide back into my seat next to Jack, who gives me a sympathetic smile, leaning in just enough to be heard over the noise. "Fuck me, is this shit always this tense?" he asks, shaking his head slightly.

I manage a small smile in return. "No, only when assholes show up."

He lets out a low chuckle, but my eyes shift back to the crowd. The fans are gradually falling back into their excited chatter, the tension loosening its grip, yet I'm still rattled by what just happened. As the line inches forward, my heart's pounding, and my mind is a storm of worry and adrenaline. I force myself to focus on the faces in front of me, signing posters, making small talk—anything to drown out the lingering dread and the unsettling reality of whatever's unfolding between Ace and Beck.

Every time I sign my name or muster a smile for a fan, my mind slips back to whatever's unfolding beyond those doors.

Is Ace all right?

What if Beck tries something else?

The questions spiral, twisting tighter and tighter, making it harder to hold up the mask of normalcy.

I'm on the verge of a full-blown panic attack, as the last fan leaves the room, and Ace is still nowhere to be found. As we all head back into the green room, my heart pounds louder with each step. As I enter, my gaze instantly falls upon him, slumped on the couch, a cold beer in his hand.

But it's his fists that grab my attention. Swollen, bruised, the skin cracked and raw—there's no mistaking what happened. As soon as I sit beside him, I can't stop the words from tumbling out. "What did you do, Ace?"

Theo stands beside me, but Ace's gaze never leaves mine. There's a cold edge in his voice when he speaks, low and steady. "I did what I had to," he says, his expression hard. "Just know, that asshole isn't coming near you again."

"What if he presses charges?" I ask, my voice shaky, worry gnawing at me more than anything else.

"He won't," Ace replies, calm but firm.

"You don't know him like I do, Ace. You should've just left it alone."

He lifts his battered hand, his fingers grazing my cheek as he tucks a strand of hair behind my ear. The tenderness in his eyes catches me off guard, offering a brief moment of calm in the chaos.

"He hurt you," he says. "Not just in that room, but those fucking bruises he left on your face. I had to look at them for days—almost a week. That asshole had it coming."

I can still see the simmering anger beneath Ace's calm exterior, but there's also something more—determination, fierce protectiveness. He's not just trying to reassure me; he's trying to protect me from everything I'm afraid of.

"He's okay," Ace says, his voice firm but soft, like he's trying to steady the storm inside me. "A bit roughed up, sure. But don't forget what he did to you—how he touched you when he had no fucking right. I told him if he even thought about going to the cops or coming near you again, I'd make sure his career in the music industry was over. Neil handled the rest, got him in a car, and sent him home."

Ace leans into me, his lips pressing softly against mine. His kiss is a promise, full of reassurance and raw intensity. "You never have to fucking worry about him again."

As the tour continues, days blend together, the cities spinning past like a blur on a never-ending carousel. But somehow, in the midst of the chaos, Ace and I find our rhythm, settling into a routine that feels unexpectedly natural. It's strange to think that just weeks ago, I was wishing for the kind of love Poppy has with Xander. Now, I can't help but realize that I've found it—with Ace. Who would've thought that Ace Roberts, with his rough edges and guarded exterior, could love with such fierce, raw intensity?

Every time he looks at me, every time he touches me, it's like he's burning away all the doubts and fears I've ever carried. And in those moments, I realize that this—us—is everything I never knew I needed.

We never spoke of Beck again after that night, as if it had become an unspoken rule between us. Still, I knew Nate had called Ace after Theo filled him in. I didn't ask about their conversation—I didn't need to. According to Theo, Nate had actually thanked Ace for doing what he couldn't.

Nate got his cast off today, and in the coming days, he'll be flying out to join us on tour. Theo's pumped and the rest of the guys are just as excited to have him back. I miss my brother, but there's this strange feeling creeping in. Having Ace around Nate... it's going to be different.

Nate has always been the one looking out for me, the constant protector. But now, things have shifted. Ace has taken up that role, in his own way, and I can't help but wonder how Nate will handle it. Seeing us together, especially after everything that's happened... It's going to be a delicate balancing act. I don't know if Nate's ready for this change, or if he'll be okay with how things have evolved between me and Ace. But one thing's for sure—this isn't something that's going to be easy for any of us to navigate.

Since our time in New York, Ace and I have practically been living together, and I can feel something has changed in him. It's hard to pinpoint exactly what it is, but maybe it's because he finally faced his mother and confronted the demons that have been haunting him for years. There's a softness in him now, a warmth that wasn't there before, and he's become more affectionate, even around the guys. It's like he's shedding some of his old armor, letting me see the side of him that used to stay hidden. And, for once, it feels like we're both in this together, fully.

Although it is still a bit strange when the guys watch us—especially Theo, who smirks at every opportunity. I can't quite figure out if it's because he's never seen Ace like this and wants to tease him, or if he's genuinely enjoying seeing how happy Ace makes me.

Tonight, on our night off in yet another new city, Ace told me to be ready by seven in something fancy. He knows my wardrobe inside out—he's practically seen everything I own and has definitely undressed me in most of it. But nothing I had felt right for whatever he has planned, so I ended up asking Kit for help. I hate doing that. Kit's wonderful and always willing to lend a hand, but she has enough on her plate without playing stylist for me too. The dress she sent, though? It's stunning—beautiful and sexy, just the right mix of elegance and allure. It hugs my curves in all the right places, and as soon as I slip it on, I feel like I'm stepping into something unforgettable.

Ace isn't here with me in our hotel room—I haven't seen him all afternoon. He mentioned he had something to take care of but didn't elaborate. I've been waiting, sitting on the bed, my mind running in circles, trying to figure out what's going on. Then, I hear a knock on the door. I get up and walk over, half-expecting it to be Theo. We've been speculating all day about Ace's plans for tonight, and if Theo's here to ask me again, I might just lose it. My nerves are already frayed from the waiting, and the last thing I need is another round of questioning.

I open the door to find Ace standing there, looking absolutely irresistible in a sharp suit. His dark eyes brim with nervous excitement, and his tousled hair strikes the perfect balance between messy and hot. He holds a big bouquet of flowers, their vibrant colors popping against his sleek outfit.

I can't help but notice how his gaze slides over me, his tongue flicking out to wet his bottom lip. He clearly likes what he sees, and I struggle to restrain myself from yanking him into the room and begging him to fuck me, to pleasure me just as much as I want to pleasure him. The way he looks at me makes it clear that if I make that move, we'll end up lost in each other all night—because that's usually how it goes.

"Hey," I say, instead.

As I meet his gaze, I notice a shift in him. The intense, sexual look has vanished, replaced by a sweet yet slightly nervous smile. He shifts from foot to foot, looking downright adorable and unsure, as if he's still figuring out this whole "dating" thing.

"I'm not sure if I'm doing this right," he admits, a hint of vulnerability in his voice. "I've never been on a date before."

I can't help but laugh; his nervousness is kind of cute. I step aside to let him in.

"You're doing great," I reassure him. "Trust me, you're doing just fine."

His face lights up with a relieved smile as he hands me the flowers. "I hope you like them," he says, nerves lacing his voice. "This is my first time buying flowers for a chick."

"They're perfect," I reply, my smile warm and sincere. "Thank you." I take the bouquet, my fingers brushing against his as I look up at him, a wave of affection washing over me. Turning away, I walk across the room, carefully placing the flowers on the table. Before placing them down, I lift them to my nose, inhaling their sweet scent. "So, where are we headed?" I ask, glancing back at him.

"You'll have to wait and see," he replies.

I grab my purse, curiosity piqued. I can't help but wonder if one of the guys helped him put this together. Ace has to have gotten changed somewhere, and since Theo didn't have a clue, I'm guessing Xander might be in on it. He's likely the one who helped Ace organize this date.

As I walk over to him, still standing just inside the door, the look in his eyes catches me off guard. It's one of deep admiration and love, a gaze I've longed for and dreamt about for years. Having him look at me as if I'm his entire world stirs something inside me that I can't quite put into words.

As soon as I reach him, he turns and opens the door for me, a gesture that makes me smile. I step out into the hall, and he follows closely behind. We make our way to the lobby and slip out through the back entrance to avoid the throng of fans waiting out front.

We ride in silence, the hum of the car and the soft glow of city lights reflecting off the windows. The streets grow quieter as we leave the lively downtown behind, giving way to older, more quaint buildings that exude character. When the car finally slows to a stop, I glance out the window, catching sight of a sign: Rooftop Revel.

Even as I take in the name, I'm still completely in the dark about where we're headed.

I glance at Ace and catch the smirk tugging at his lips, clearly savoring the fact that tonight's a complete surprise for me.

The car door swings open, and he gets out first, offering his hand with a knowing look in his eyes. I take it without hesitation, my fingers slipping into his. Lately, he's been doing this more often, reaching for me, touching me without a second thought, not caring who's watching.

We step into the building, and my curiosity deepens as we approach the old-fashioned metal grate elevator. Ace pulls down the grate with ease, the smoothness of his movements making it look effortless. He presses a button, and the elevator jolts to life, its old mechanisms creaking as it begins to ascend. I stand beside him, my mind racing with questions, still completely in the dark about what's coming next. The anticipation is almost unbearable but in the best way possible. Every moment of this night feels like a small mystery unfolding, and I'm more than ready to see where it leads.

When the elevator stops and Ace opens the doors, the scene before me takes my breath away.

We step onto the rooftop, and the noise of the city fades away, replaced by the tranquil ambiance of a restaurant. The soft, golden glow of fairy lights threaded through delicate latticework along the edges of the roof, casts a dreamy, almost ethereal light. Lanterns flicker in the evening breeze, their gentle glow creating shadows that dance and shift across the floor.

As I take it all in, a smile tugs at my lips.

I instantly recognize why he brought me here. Back in New York, I told him how much I missed the rooftop coffee shop I'd shared with him, and this place—so enchanting, so serene—feels like a beautiful tribute to those precious memories.

It's as if Ace has somehow captured that feeling and turned it into this perfect moment.

In the center of the rooftop, a table for two is dressed with meticulous care. Crystal glasses catch the light from a flickering candle. To one side, a small fire pit crackles softly, surrounded by a cozy loveseat and a plush rug that beckons invitingly. The entire space feels impeccably private, and I know without a doubt that Ace has arranged for us to have this place all to ourselves tonight.

I turn to see him watching me, hardly believing the lengths he's gone to for me tonight. The effort he's put into creating this perfect evening overwhelms me.

"Is it okay?" he asks, his voice tinged with vulnerability. "I wasn't sure; I thought you'd—"

"Yes," I say, stepping closer and cutting him off with a kiss. His response is immediate; he wraps his arms around my waist, pulling me possessively against him. This man, with his tenderness and intensity, is going to be the end of me. "It's perfect," I murmur against his lips. A smile spreads across his face, relief and joy shining in his eyes, as if he's been waiting for confirmation that he got it right.

A middle-aged lady approaches us with a warm, welcoming smile. "Welcome to Rooftop Revel! It's a pleasure to have you dining with us tonight. Would you like to start with a drink by the fire or begin with your meal?"

I glance at Ace, who meets my gaze, waiting for my decision. "How about we have our meal first and then sit by the fire afterward," I suggest.

He nods, and the lady leads us to our table.

We are soon seated, choose our meals from the menu, and have our drinks placed on the table. I take in the surroundings, noticing tiny details I hadn't before. When I glance back at Ace, I catch him watching me, a soft, almost tender look on his face.

As I lock eyes with him, my mind races toward the future. The tour ends in a week, and I'm staring into the unknown—no idea what comes next. What jobs will be out there for me? I don't know where I'll end up or what will be waiting for me when I get there. And as much as I want to know what the future holds for Ace and me, I don't have the answers. I need to talk to him about it—about what's next for us.

He loves me. He's told me every day, and tonight, with everything he's done for me, it's clear he means it. But the thought of pushing him too hard, of talking about something too serious and scaring him off, keeps me quiet. Ace has never been in a serious relationship before, and I don't want to be the one to complicate things for him, especially when everything between us feels so right.

He lifts his beer, taking a slow sip, his gaze steady on mine. When he sets it down, I can tell he wants to say something, but instead, he looks at the glass, his fingers tracing the condensation.

"Does this feel weird for you?" I ask. "Planning a date like this? Do the guys know what you had in mind?"

"Yeah, it's weird. I had no clue what the hell I was doing—didn't know if it'd be too cheesy or if you'd hate it. But Xander said Poppy loves it when he does stuff like this. And judging by your face when we walked in, I'd say I got it right. No way in hell am I telling that asshole he was right, though."

I smile, seeing that softness breaking through his usual tough exterior, like a flower pushing through concrete. That tenderness he shows is only when it's just us, while the hardness stays firmly intact around the guys.

He grins. "I didn't tell Theo. That dickhead never keeps his big mouth shut and would've ruined the surprise." He takes another long sip, then hesitates, glancing down at his beer. "There's something I wanted to ask"

"What's that?" I ask, taking a drink.

He swallows, clearly unsure. "I was just wondering what you're gonna do after the tour. You said you'd need to find a new band, but... do you think you could do that from L.A.?"

I smile. "Yeah, I was thinking of staying out there anyway."

"Look, Scar, I don't know how to say this, so I'm just gonna come out with it." His fingers tap nervously against his glass, the sound a small rhythm of his anxiety. He's clearly struggling to find the right words, and I can feel the weight of the moment in the air between us. "I want this... whatever we have between us. I want it to keep going."

His eyes meet mine, searching, like he's waiting for me to confirm what he's feeling, to assure him that this isn't something he's imagining. And I can see it in the way he's holding himself, how vulnerable he looks. For all his strength and confidence, Ace is putting himself out there in a way that feels raw and real.

He wants this. He wants me

"I want that too," I smile.

The lady brings over our meals, and we settle into a comfortable rhythm of conversation—talking about Nate's upcoming visit, joking about how Theo might change once Nate's finally in the same city as us, and discussing how Ace feels now about reconnecting with his sister. It's the kind of easy conversation that flows without effort, the kind that makes me realize just how much I've come to depend on these quiet moments with him.

As he talks, I can see how much Daisy's return has affected him. For the first time, I get a sense of how much healing he has left to do—not just with her, but with himself.

And as I listen, I realize that despite the uncertainty of our future, moments like these are what I want to hold on to. The rest will figure itself out.

Once we finish eating, Ace stands and offers his hand to me. I take my drink and let him lead me to the cozy fire pit. The crackling flames cast a warm glow around us as we curl up on the loveseat, a soft blanket draping over our laps. I lean back, gazing at the serene stars above, feeling perfectly content in this moment with him.

Ace leans in, his breath hot against my ear. "Do you think they'd mind if I fucked you right here, right now?" His voice is low and rough, carrying a dark promise. The playful smirk on his face contrasts with the fire in his eyes.

When he kisses me, it's with such intensity that his tongue claims my mouth. For a moment, when we pull apart, I'm breathless. He smirks, clearly satisfied with the effect he has on me.

I feel the heat pooling in my pussy, the desperate need to have this man right here, right now. He looks at me, and as if reading my mind, his fingers trail up the inside of my thigh, heading straight for my throbbing core. I'm not even sure if anyone's around, but I don't fucking care. All I care about is feeling him, wanting his touch.

He kisses me again, this time slow and filthy, his tongue teasing as he deepens the kiss. His fingers slide under the edge of my underwear, teasing as he touches my pussy. When he discovers just how wet I am, he groans—a low, primal sound that sends a delicious shiver through me. I arch into his touch, begging for more, but he holds me in place, a wicked grin spreading across his face. His fingers circle my clit, pushing me closer to the edge.

"I want you to come," he growls in my ear. "I want to hear you scream my name."

"Ace," I whimper, feeling the pressure build, taut and electrifying. He's relentless, his fingers work their magic, teasing, probing, circling with just the right pressure, pushing me closer to that sweet release.

"Louder," he urges. "Let me fucking hear you."

I can't help but obey, my voice rising as the pleasure intensifies, each stroke sending me higher and higher. The firelight flickers, casting shadows as I surrender to the pleasure, letting my voice spill out. "Ace! Oh God!"

He lets out a soft chuckle, clearly pleased with my reaction, his fingers quickening, more demanding. He leans closer, his lips grazing my ear. "That's it, baby. Let go. Come for me, Scar."

With each movement of his fingers, I feel myself nearing the brink, the world around us blurring. Then, with a final wave of pleasure, I shatter, my body quaking as his name escapes my lips, swallowed by the overwhelming ecstasy that takes me over entirely.

# CHAPTER 34

## Ace

I was a bundle of nerves planning that date, running everything by Xander to make sure I had it right. He told me women love that romantic shit, and the sex that follows is always off the charts. He wasn't wrong. Last night, when we got back to the hotel room Scarlet blew my mind. This morning, in the shower, I tried to recreate that intensity, my hand moving fast on my hard cock as I relived the feeling of her.

Nate's flying in today, and Scarlet's not here with me. She and Theo went to pick him up at the airport. I'm worried about how things will go with Nate around.

Even though he thanked me for handling Beck, we haven't really talked much since.

I'm not sure if he's still pissed about me being with his sister. If he brings it up, I'll set the record straight. I don't give a damn if my feelings for her are out in the open. They're as clear as day, and I know exactly what I want—her.

If I have to prove I'm different with her than the guy Nate thinks I am—the fuck-them-and-leave-them type—I'll do it. I'll show him, day after day, that I'm not like that with her.

We're heading to the stadium right now for sound check, and Xander's with me. He's on the phone with Poppy, clearly missing both her and Alex.

My phone vibrates in my pocket, and I pull it out, a small smile tugging at my lips when I see it's Scarlet.

**Scarlet:** We just got here. You close?

I fire off a reply, my fingers flying across the screen.

**Ace:** Yeah, just pulling up now.

I shove my phone back into my pocket, open the door, and step out. I wait as Xander slides across the seat, still on his phone. Once he's out, I shut the door and we head into the stadium.

We make our way through the long corridors, me leading the way. As soon as Xander hangs up with Poppy, he catches up and falls into step beside me.

"You ready to face Nate?" he asks, clearly concerned about how things will go when I see him again.

"Yeah," I mutter.

"Just be straight with him, Ace, no matter how hard it is. He'll see it's different this time, that you're different with her. We've all seen it."

"Fuck, you're making me sound like a giant pussy," I groan, not even sure where this real talk is coming from between us. We used to joke about women, comparing who gave the best head or who could fuck better. We were naive assholes back then, and yeah, I sometimes miss the cocky little shits we used to be. But I don't want to go back to that broken mess who kept everyone at arm's length. Hiding behind walls was easier, but fuck that—Scarlet's worth every bit of this vulnerability. So, yeah, maybe it's different now; maybe I'm different now. If it means letting her in, then I'm all for it.

I shove open the door, and Xander and I step into the green room. Nate's sprawled out on the couch between Theo and Scarlet, both caught up in whatever bullshit Theo's spouting this time. The second they hear us, their heads snap our way. My eyes immediately land on Scarlet, and that smile of hers hits me. I can't help the grin that spreads across my face. She gets up and walks over, wrapping her arms around me like she's been waiting for this all day. As I pull her in, I notice Nate and Theo watching us, until Xander steps in front of them.

"Hey, how's the shoulder?" Xander asks.

Nate pushes himself up from the couch, and I can tell his movements are still a bit stiff. He extends his arm and pulls Xander in for a brotherly hug. "Getting there," he replies, his voice steady, even if his body hasn't fully caught up yet.

I move over to Nate, knowing I need to face him, leaving Scarlet by the door. When Xander steps back, I pull Nate in for a hug, careful not to hurt him.

As soon as we're close, he whispers in my ear, "We need to talk." He's quiet enough that no one else hears, and I know he's serious.

I nod, acknowledging that we need to clear the air about everything that happened when he first found out about me and Scarlet.

I take a step back, giving Nate some room. Xander stands beside me, his arms crossed, and the tension starts to ease as the conversation shifts. Nate scans the room, that familiar spark lighting up his eyes once more.

"Man, I've missed this," he says. "Being away from this is driving me crazy. I can't wait to get back out there. It'll take a while, though…I can't keep up with the fast stuff yet. My shoulder's still a little stiff. But I'll get there."

Scarlet moves to stand next to Nate, her smile soft as she links her arm with his. "You will. Just take it slow. You'll come back when you're ready."

Nate nods, but a hint of frustration lingers in his eyes.

Theo chimes in, his tone playful but blunt. "So, you can still fuck, right?" he asks with a smirk. "Because I haven't hooked up with a chick this whole tour, and I'm sick of having my cock in my hand."

Scarlet rolls her eyes. "Theo, for fuck sake, no one wants to hear about you jerking off. Especially not me."

Theo smirks. "Hey, cut me some slack. My dick's been benched this whole tour."

I laugh at the look of disgust on Scarlet's face as she walks away shaking her head. She wanders over to the fridge and grabs a bottle of water.

While the guys talk, I walk over to her, hands shoved in my pockets. Normally, I wouldn't care what Nate thinks—he's been around for all the women I've been with, from when we hit it big to those weekend parties when we were still nobodies trying to make it in the music scene. But with him watching me now, I feel a bit nervous as I approach Scarlet.

As if sensing me, she turns around, and I can't help but let my eyes devour her. The top buttons of her shirt are undone, her tits pushed up, practically begging for my attention. I know I shouldn't be fantasizing about getting lost in them with her brother right behind me, but fuck, all I can think about is coming on those perfect tits.

"Hey," she says, unscrewing the cap off the bottle. "Did Nate say something to you?"

I think about lying, but I want to be honest with her. No secrets between us. "Yeah, he said we need to talk."

Catching a flash of anger cross her face, I reach out and take her hand. "Don't stress. The two of us do need to talk."

She frowns. "I don't want this to turn into some bullshit drama, Ace. Nate and Theo always think they can control every aspect of my fucking life."

I squeeze her hand, trying to reassure her. "They won't. I just need to talk to your brother, lay it all out, and let him know where we stand. I've got to make sure Nate knows things are different with us and that he needs to accept it."

The door swings open, and Kit pokes her head in. "The guys are waiting." She spots Nate and steps into the room.

While Kit chats with Nate, Xander strolls over, grabs a bottle of water, and chugs it like he's trying to drain every last drop. He finishes it in one go and wipes his mouth with the back of his hand.

"Alright, let's get the fuck out there," he says, tossing the empty bottle into the bin.

Scarlet and I follow behind him as he chats with Neil, who's leading the way to the stage. Theo and Nate trail behind us, with Theo animatedly chatting to Nate about Walter's band. Even though Nate's right behind me, I reach out and take Scarlet's hand as we head toward the stage. I couldn't give two flying fucks that her brothers are right behind us.

As we stop at the side of the stage, I catch the look on Nate's face—he's itching to get out there, wishing he could dive into the action.

Xander steps up to the mic, and we all slide into position, getting ready for the set.

After soundcheck, we're back at the hotel. Nate and Theo are waiting for me in the bar downstairs. I know I need to lay it all out and be straight with Nate. I have to make him understand that Scarlet isn't just another quick fuck. I need him to see that.

As I step into the bar, I spot Theo and Nate already drinking in one of the booths, their heads close together in what looks like a serious conversation. I order my drink at the bar, then make my way over, steeling myself for what's about to happen.

As I approach the booth, I can hear the low hum of their conversation fade as Theo and Nate look up, their faces shifting from whatever they were discussing to focus on me. Theo grins, raising his glass in a mock toast. "Finally! I was starting to think you'd gotten lost on your way down here, old man."

Nate's expression turns serious, and his eyes, narrowed slightly, seem to pierce through me. It's clear that whatever's about to be said between us is important. I take a seat across from them; the tension settling over us like a thick fog.

"Alright, let's cut the bullshit," I say, keeping my tone steady. "We need to talk about Scarlet."

"We do," he replies, his expression serious.

"So let's get this shit out of the way." I take a deep breath. "I'm sorry I went behind your back with Scar all those months ago."

Nate's eyes narrow. "You're lucky I found out the way I did. Because if I had been there, you would have been fucked up Ace."

"And now?" I ask, trying to gauge where Nate stands now that he knows about Scarlet and me.

"Look, Ace," Nate replies, his tone serious, "I've known you for years. I've seen all the shit you've pulled with chicks at those apartment parties we used to throw—hell, I've seen you with three women at once. I never want Scar to be just another number, and that's what's got me fucked up about the whole situation between you two."

"It isn't like that with her," I say, making sure he hears the conviction in my voice. "Looking back, I'm pretty sure it never has been. Since the first time Scarlet and I hooked up, I haven't been with anyone else."

"Seriously?" Nate raises an eyebrow, his tone a mix of skepticism and surprise. "Because the Ace Roberts I know would fuck anything with two legs."

I smirk, knowing he's not wrong. A wet hole to get me off was my motto back in the day.

I glance over at Theo, who's sitting there unusually quiet. He's usually the one speaking up to make his point clear, so his silence is throwing me off.

"What about you, Theo? What's your take on this?"

Theo gives me a hard look. "I was with Nate at first; I wanted you to stay the fuck away from her." Then he turns to Nate. "But honestly, seeing Ace with Scarlet? It's like watching him try to bake cookies—messy, confusing, and you can't help but laugh at how far out of his depth he is."

I let his smart-ass remark slide.

A few weeks ago, all I wanted was to hear him bust my balls instead of giving me the cold shoulder.

"But I also see a different side to him," he continues, his tone shifting. "He loves her, Nate. I can fucking see it. It's just like the way we loved Bianca. I never thought I'd see the day Ace Roberts could actually fucking love something, but I see it with Scar. It's in the little things he does and the way he treats her."

I stay quiet, not sure how to respond. The guys don't often bring up Bianca, except for that photo they showed me and Xander—a snapshot of the beautiful girl they lost all those years ago, a picture they both keep on their phones.

"You love her?" Nate asks, cutting right to the chase.

I could easily tell them both to back the fuck off and mind their own business, but instead, I lock eyes with him and stand my ground. "Yeah," I say firmly. "Yeah, I love her."

Nate keeps his gaze steady, and I can't help but wonder what's running through his mind. Then, without a word, he extends his hand. I look down for a moment, then reach out and take it.

"I approve," he says. "But listen up, Ace—if you fuck her over or treat her badly, I'll fucking end you."

I shake his hand, holding his gaze. "And I wouldn't expect anything less," I reply.

With that, Nate takes another sip of his drink, and the tension begins to dissipate. I can see the trust slowly building between us, the kind that makes this whole crazy situation feel a little more solid.

Tonight, as we walk onto the stage, Xander turns to face me, his expression serious. "Don't count us in tonight, Ace. I've got something I want to do first."

I nod, my mind racing.

What the hell is he planning now?

He turns to the stagehands, snapping his fingers and calling out for them to power up his mic and get the curtain moving. As the curtains part, roars erupt from the crowd. The noise is deafening, and the atmosphere is thick with excitement. It's as if the whole place is vibrating with anticipation, and I feel it thrumming through my veins.

Xander spreads his arms, and the crowd instantly falls silent, like he's some kind of prophet about to drop a major revelation.

"Before we kick things off tonight," he begins, "I want to bring someone out on this stage. Someone you all know."

I nod, catching on, and glance over at Nate.

"Someone who hasn't been able to hit the stage with us this whole tour," Xander continues.

The moment the crowd realizes who he's talking about, chaos erupts.

Xander grabs the mic and shouts, "Come on out here, Nate!"

Nate steps onto the stage, a wide smile spreading across his face as he takes in the roaring applause. He raises his good arm to the crowd, soaking up every moment. It's like he's finally back where he belongs, even if it's just for tonight.

The cheers of the crowd are like a welcome home. I'm just stoked to see him here, part of this world he helped create.

Nate strides up next to Xander, a broad smile on his face. They share a knowing grin, a silent acknowledgment of the moment. Nate gives one last wave, letting the crowd soak up his presence before stepping back to the wings of the stage. With the roar of the audience still echoing around us, Xander turns, nodding for me to count us in. I start it off, and we launch into the first song of the night, ready to give it everything we've got.

The night pushes on, and the energy in the arena stays electric. We power through our set, pouring everything into each song. Every time I glance toward the side of the stage, I catch Nate watching Scarlet. He's finally seeing her step into the spotlight, witnessing the magic he's been missing.

By the time we reach the last song, I'm breathless and drenched in sweat. Xander grabs his stool and guitar, and I spot Scarlet getting up from the drums and moving toward Nate. My gaze follows her, curiosity sparking, and I notice Xander and Theo watching just as intently. Scarlet leans in close to Nate, and I catch the smile and nod he gives her before she hands him the drumsticks.

Nate steps up to the drum kit, and Xander and I exchange a look, both wondering if he's pushing himself too hard to make a comeback.

"Are you sure you should be doing this?" I ask, moving closer.

"Yeah, it's slow enough," Nate replies. "I'll be fine."

I glance over at Scarlet, standing on the side of the stage, her face glowing with pride as she watches Nate take his seat.

As the opening notes of "Creep" fill the arena, we glance at Nate to make sure he's holding up. His drumming is steady, with no signs of struggle. He's fully immersed, lost in the rhythm, feeling every beat like he used to.

After getting a text from Nate, calling for a band meeting, I slip out of mine and Scarlet's hotel room.

The message was clear—this one's just for the four of us guys. No Scarlet.

Lucky for me, she's on the phone with her mom, so slipping out unnoticed wasn't an issue.

Walking down the hall, I rake a hand through my hair, feeling the exhaustion weighing me down. My eyes are bloodshot—we went hard last night. It was me, Scarlet, Xander, Kit, and Neil, partying until the early hours. Theo and

Nate bailed early, though. Theo had already set himself up with some brunette for the night's "entertainment," so they didn't stick around.

When I finally reach Nate and Theo's room, I knock and wait.

Theo swings the door open, smirking like he's ready to make some smart-ass remark, but, for once, nothing comes out.

Strange.

I step inside, and the stale scent of cheap perfume hits me—probably from whichever groupie they brought back here last night.

I'm the last to arrive.

Xander's already here, Kit too, which immediately sets off alarms. My gut twists, and my first thought is, what the hell has my fucked-up mother done this time?

As I step in, all eyes turn to me, and I feel the tension hanging thick in the air. My gaze lands on Xander, sitting on the couch with his arms crossed, looking pissed off about something.

Without a word, I cross the room and drop down next to him, sinking into the cushions.

"Alright, what's up?" I ask. My voice comes out rough, but I don't care. Whatever's going on, it's big. I can feel it.

All eyes shift to Kit as she starts talking. "Yesterday, someone reached out to me. They're interested in Scarlet."

"Who reached out?" I ask, already feeling my jaw clench. My mind goes straight to Beck. Don't tell me that prick went to the press after I dealt with him.

"A label."

Nate doesn't even wait a second. "It's not fucking happening," he snaps, storming over to the opposite couch, sitting next to Theo. His eyes are blazing.

"Hold up," I say, running both hands through my hair, trying to catch up with the conversation. I lean forward, elbows resting on my knees, and lock my focus on Kit. "What exactly are we talking about here?"

"Kit's had a call from a label who is looking to put a band together, and Scarlet's caught their eye," Xander chimes in, filling me in on the details.

A smile tugs at my lips as I think about Scarlet finally getting her big break. She deserves this—she's got the talent and drive to go far. But the thought quickly turns, twisting in my gut.

"Why the hell isn't she here then?" I ask. "If they're interested, she needs to know. This could be huge for her."

Kit glances over at Nate and Theo.

"Because it ain't fucking happening, that's why," Nate retorts.

My anger flares, and I fix him with a hard look. "What the hell do you mean it's not happening? That's not your call to make."

Nate's eyes flash, and he leans forward, his tone turning sharp. "I'm looking out for her, Ace. You know how the industry is. It's a fucking jungle. Labels fuck people over to get what they want."

I don't back down. "So? This could be her big fucking break! We took it when it was offered to us. Why the hell would you try to stop her, especially when you know how hard it's been for her to step out of your shadow?"

I can see the hurt flicker across his face, the realization that her struggles have something to do with him. But fuck that. This isn't about him; this is about Scarlet finally getting the chance she deserves. "This is not our decision; it's fucking hers."

The silence stretches between us, thick and charged. I can feel the tension hanging in the air, and for a moment, it's like the room is holding its breath, waiting for someone to speak. I'm not backing down—not now. She's been given a chance, and I'll fight tooth and nail to make sure she gets it.

I shift my attention to Theo. "So what about you, asshole? Are you against this too?"

Theo shifts uncomfortably on the couch, avoiding my gaze. "I don't want her used by a fucking label the way we were. I'm with Nate on this one."

"No fucking shock there," I mutter, shaking my head as I turn to Xander, desperately looking for some clarity. "What's your take on this? Why are we even discussing this shit?"

"Hey, don't look at me," Xander replies, hands raised defensively. "I'm all for Scarlet getting her shot. She fucking deserves it."

"Then why the hell are we even here?" I look over at Kit, my frustration bubbling over. "Why didn't you just take this to Scarlet?"

I know I shouldn't be taking this out on Kit; she's always been great at what she does, which is exactly why we brought her along when we left the label. But my frustration spills out anyway.

Kit stands up, locking eyes with me, her gaze fierce and unwavering, despite being about two feet shorter than me. She squares her shoulders. "You know what, Ace? Maybe you should get off your high horse for a second! I mentioned it to Nate yesterday in passing, thinking he'd be happy that Scarlet got her chance. But clearly, I was wrong—and that's why we're here."

I can't help but smirk at her, respecting the verbal ass-whooping she's handing me. I shift my focus back to Nate and Theo, my resolve hardening. "You two need to get your fucking heads out of your asses. Scarlet deserves this, and I'm not gonna sit here while you try to keep her from her shot. She's ready to fight for it—and so am I."

I take a breath, about to launch into a full-blown argument, ready to go toe-to-toe with them over this. But just as I open my mouth, a sharp knock echoes through the room.

# Chapter 35

## Scarlet

My body's sore from what Ace did to me last night. Hours spent with him taking me hard and then slow, exploring every inch of my body, pushing me to the limits with each deep thrust. Even now, as I walk to Nate and Theo's room, each step sends a delicious reminder of what he did to me.

I have no idea where Ace went, and I'm getting fed up with waiting for him to come back. I knock on my brother's door, and it swings open to reveal Theo.

I step inside, expecting just him and Nate, but the whole band's there—Kit included. I pause, confused. They didn't call a band meeting, but then again, I'm just a fill-in with only five days left on the tour. My eyes scan the room, landing on Ace. He stands with his arms crossed, looking serious, but when our gazes meet, he gives me a smile that makes my heart skip. Still, the tension is thick. Something's going on, and I'm not part of it.

All eyes are on me as I walk toward Ace, and for a moment, I feel a surge of anxiety. Did I mess up? Did the media catch wind of something? Beck. That asshole better not have gone to the press about what Ace did to him. If he has, I'll have no choice but to set the record straight and let everyone know what he did to me. But God, I don't want that out in the open—the ugly truth of it all. I don't want my past with Beck dragging me back to a place I've been fighting so hard to escape.

"You might as well tell her," Xander says, his eyes fixed on Nate.

I glance at Nate, sitting next to Theo, both of them silent as hell. The quiet is starting to get to me, the tension building with every second that passes. My gaze snaps back to Xander, waiting for him to speak up, to explain what the hell is going on. But instead, he looks over at Kit.

Kit steps forward, and that's when the worry really starts to kick in. My heart races, and I feel a tightness in my chest. What the hell have I done to make them all so on edge?

"Scarlet, we've had a label reach out to us," Kit says, her tone a little too serious for my liking.

"Okay…" I reply slowly, still not sure how any of this has anything to do with me.

"They've been keeping an eye on the tour, and they're impressed with how you've stepped into the band. They want to sign you—along with a few others—for a new band they're putting together."

A smile creeps across my face as the weight of uncertainty finally begins to lift. I can feel a spark of excitement starting to build. "Really?" I ask.

"Yes, they reached out to me yesterday," Kit confirms.

"Wow," I reply, my smile growing wider as the excitement settles in. I glance around the room, taking in the hopeful looks from Ace, Xander, and Kit. But when my gaze lands on Theo and Nate, their serious faces pull me up short. The lack of enthusiasm on their part makes me pause, and I can't help but wonder why they aren't as thrilled for me as I am.

My smile fades as I glance back at Kit. "Is there a catch I don't know about?"

She shakes her head. "They haven't given us any details on what they're offering yet, just that they're interested and want you to give them a call."

"Okay," I reply, still feeling a bit unsettled by Theo and Nate's lack of enthusiasm. I glance at Ace, who stands next to me with a proud look on his face. His support is the one thing I can count on right now.

I turn back to my brothers, my curiosity getting the better of me. "What's wrong?" I ask, my voice steady but tinged with confusion. "Why aren't you guys as excited as everyone else? This is a big deal, and it feels like something's off."

They exchange a look before Nate finally speaks. "We were screwed over by our old label, Scar. We don't want that happening to you."

Are you fucking kidding me right now? I finally get a glimmer of a future after this tour, and now they're telling me it's a bad idea.

I let out a sharp, exasperated sigh, my chest tightening with frustration. I fold my arms, shooting a glare at Nate, then Theo.

"Nah, hear us out, Scar," Theo cuts in, trying to smooth things over. "We just don't want you to get taken advantage of like we were."

"For fuck's sake," I snap. "I can't believe you're trying to shut this down before I even get the chance to see what's on the table."

"The label always takes advantage of band members," Nate says. "They work you into the ground, Scar. Trust us, we've been there. We know exactly how much they exploit you."

"So this whole meeting was basically to decide whether you should even tell me about this offer?" I ask, my voice shaky with a mix of hurt and disbelief. The sting of betrayal cuts deeper than I want to admit. After everything I've given these last two months, this is how they repay me? "If I hadn't walked in on this, would any of you have bothered to tell me?"

Nate's expression softens a bit, but his tone remains firm. "We've seen too many bands get chewed up and spit out by these labels."

I shoot him an incredulous look. "So, you think I can't handle it? Is that it?" I glance at Ace. "So, you're with them?"

"No, I'm fucking not," Ace replies, his voice firm and unwavering. He meets my gaze, his confidence giving me a sense of relief. "I told them it was your choice, not theirs." The weight lifts off my chest, knowing he's got my back in this. "As did Xander."

I turn back to Nate and Theo, my anger bubbling when I catch the irritation carved into their faces. It's obvious—they didn't want me to know they were the ones blocking my shot. They took their chance to make a life out of their music, and now they're trying to pull the rug out from under me. Well, fuck that. My fists clench, and I don't give a shit about whatever excuse Nate's about to spit out. I move forward, cutting him off before he can even open his mouth.

"I'm so fucking tired of this shit with you two," I snap, leaning over them. "You think you control my life. Well, I don't answer to either of you. I make the decisions, and I'm the one who gets to choose what happens next. Whether it's joining a band, signing with a label, or who I fuck— it's none of your damn business." I watch as their faces tighten, knowing the last part stung. "So here's the deal: I don't need your approval. Get it through your fucking heads and stay out of my way. I'm living my life, not yours."

I stand upright and shift my focus to Kit. "Kit, could you please forward me the label's contact information. I would like to make the call myself."

She smirks and nods. "Okay."

I turn and walk toward the door, not bothering to glance at anyone in the room. My hand grips the handle, and with a sharp yank, I throw it open. Without a second look, I step through and slam it shut with a resounding crash, leaving the tension behind me

I storm into my room and drop onto the bed, staring up at the ceiling. The anger still simmers, tight and raw, twisting in my gut. My entire life, they've made decisions for me—decided what's best, without even asking what I wanted-ed. How many choices did I never know about because they were too busy controlling everything? I let out a long, frustrated breath, trying to calm the storm raging inside.

The door swings open, and Ace walks in, grinning like a damn fool.

"You know how fucking hot that was, right?" he says, dropping down beside me on the bed. I can't help but let out a breath, the tension in my chest loosening a bit just from his presence.

He shifts, pulling me gently by the waist until I'm lying on top of him. His lips meet mine in a soft, lingering kiss, and I melt into him.

"I don't think those two assholes will be prying into your life any time soon after that," Ace says with a chuckle. "I never thought I'd see the day when Theo was speechless."

I can't help but smile at how happy he is over such a small victory. Resting my chin on his chest, I feel the comforting warmth of his body beneath me. "I swear, sometimes they think I'm stupid, Ace," I say. Ace's gaze never wavers from mine, his hand propped under his head as though he's hanging on every word. "I get that labels exploit you, work you to the bone. But what those two idiots don't seem to understand is that they had their shot all those years ago. I've never had mine—not like you guys did."

"So, you're going to do it?" Ace asks, his fingers lightly brushing a strand of hair from my face.

"Yeah, I want to," I say, my voice a mix of excitement and nerves.

"Good," he replies.

But then a thought strikes me, and I hesitate. "Did Kit mention where the label is based?"

Ace raises an eyebrow. "Nah, why do you ask?"

"I don't know," I admit, exhaling slowly. We touched on the idea of the future that night at the rooftop restaurant, but it feels too soon to dive into it now. I don't want to push him or rush us into something we're not ready for.

"Just say whatever's on your mind, Scar," he encourages, gently.

"Why do you think—"

"Because I can tell," he interrupts. "Like how you get this little crease in your forehead when something is weighing on you."

I take a moment, trying to piece everything together. Finally, I look up, meeting his eyes. "What if it's back in New York? What if we never get to see each other?"

I lower my gaze, feeling the weight of uncertainty settle in. Long-distance relationships are never easy, and I can't shake the fear that, eventually, he'll grow tired of waiting for me.

Without saying a word, he rolls us in the bed, positioning himself on top of me. My legs instinctively wrap around his waist, and he gently cradles my face in his hands. His eyes lock onto mine—intense and filled with passion.

"So what if it is? There's something I've been wanting to talk to you about anyway," he says firmly.

I start to wonder what could be making him so serious, the shift in his demeanor making me worry.

"Scar," he starts, his voice thick with raw emotion. "You're my fucking everything. I don't want anyone else but you. If you end up on the other side of the world, I'll cross oceans to be with you. I want you to chase your dreams with everything you've got, and if that means we're apart for a bit, then so be it. But know this—I'll be right there with you, every single step of the way. I'm not going anywhere, no matter where life takes us. I promise you that there's no way in hell I'm letting you go. I'm all in, and I'm not backing down. I fucking love you, Scar. Like I've never loved anyone else in my life. You're my everything, my fucking life." He takes a deep breath, a hint of vulnerability in his eyes. "And I want you to move into my house with me. Let's make this real, Scar. No more doubts, just us."

My heart pounds in my chest as his words hit me like a wave, knocking the air out of me. He's so sure, so raw, and it feels like everything inside me is being pulled toward him. I blink, trying to process the weight of his confession, of the intensity in his eyes, the love and devotion etched in every syllable.

"Are you serious?" I breathe out, my voice barely a whisper, the question hanging between us.

He nods, his grip tightening on me, but there's no hesitation in his touch. "More than I've ever been about anything."

At that moment, all my doubts and fears dissolve into nothing. What remains is the unwavering certainty of his love and the unspoken promise of a future together—no matter the distance between us.

My heart races as I stare at the number on my phone, my thumb hovering over the call button. The seconds feel like an eternity. The label—Neon Records—is right there, but the fear of what's about to come holds me in place, frozen in uncertainty.

"Just do it," Ace encourages, echoing his words from the last two times I hesitated.

I meet his gaze, the fire in his eyes grounding me as I take a steadying breath. This is it. With a burst of determination, I press the button.

The call connects, and I hold the phone to my ear. Ace's gaze never wavers from mine as I hold my breath. With each ring, the pressure mounts, my heart beating louder with each passing second.

"Neon Records, how can I help you?" A smooth female voice says on the other end of the call, and a jolt of adrenaline rushes through me.

"Hi, I'm Scarlet Reynolds," I say, my voice trembling slightly at first but steadying as I continue. "I'm calling to speak with Tony Montgomery. He asked me to give him a call."

"Hold, please. I'll connect you," the woman replies.

As I wait, my heart races. I can't help but glance at Ace, who gives me an encouraging nod.

The line goes dead for a moment before a deep voice comes through. "Scarlet. This is Tony Montgomery."

"Hi, Mr. Montgomery," I reply, forcing myself to sound calm.

"I've been following your progress with Broken Oasis," he says. "You've made quite the impression, stepping in and holding your own. It's not easy to fill those shoes."

"Thank you," I respond, feeling a rush of pride. "It's been a wild ride."

"I'm putting together an all-female band, and I think you'd be a perfect fit."

My breath catches in my throat. "An all-female band? Really, that sounds incredible!"

"This is a big opportunity. You've got something special, Scarlet. I want to offer you a chance to thrive in a new setting, with a group of women who share your passion for music."

"That sounds incredible!" I can't help but smile.

"I'm glad to hear that, Scarlet," he replies. "In a few days, my secretary will reach out to set up the contract for your lawyer to review. If everything looks good, we can start putting the band together and get this project off the ground."

"Thank you so much!" I can hardly contain my excitement as I hang up the phone, a wide smile stretching across my face. "He's sending a contract!"

Ace's face lights up with excitement. "I knew you could do it, Scar!"

"I can't believe this is really happening!" I say with a smile as I look over at Ace. This is it—a new chapter, a chance to finally step into the spotlight I've always wanted.

# CHAPTER 36

## Ace

I couldn't help but feel a surge of pride when Scarlet stood up to Nate and Theo. Watching her put those assholes in their place was straight-up badass. Honestly, I'm surprised she didn't do it sooner, but that's just Scarlet—always too damn nice and trying to keep the peace. It's the complete opposite of me; I'm the guy who has no problem telling someone to shut the fuck up. Maybe that's why we work so well together—we balance each other out, bringing out the best in each other even with all our differences.

I didn't give a damn which label it was—even if it had been our old one, Victory Records.

All that matters is that Scar is finally getting the chance to live her dream after this tour. She's everything to me, and I'll always have her back, no matter what.

The contract came through two days later, and I could see the relief on her face when she found out the label is based in Los Angeles.

Honestly, I felt the same damn relief. But let's be real—I would've followed her anywhere if it meant she was happy. That's all that matters to me now—her happiness. Watching her light up with real joy... There's nothing like it. Knowing I'm part of that happiness... It's everything. I've never experienced anything like it before—the pure satisfaction of making someone else so incredibly happy.

And let me tell you, it's fucking contagious.

As we wrap up the last night of the tour, there's this bittersweet feeling that won't leave me. It's not just the tour ending—it's the thought of not having Scarlet here anymore, not hearing the way she pours her heart into those drums like she always does. These last sixty days... They've turned my world upside down in ways I never saw coming. This tour wasn't just a series of shows or about the music we played—it's been a fucking journey into the depths of my soul.

It's this tour where I finally faced my demons—where I confronted all the shadows from my past that had been clawing at me for years. Each show, every moment we shared, brought me closer to the surface, forcing me to reckon with all the shit I've kept buried deep inside. Even now, those shadows linger, whispering doubts in the back of my mind. That scared little boy who hides in the dark is still there, reminding me of the battles I've fought and the ones I'm still fighting.

But through all of it, Scarlet has been my light. She's the reason I found the courage to open up, the reason I felt safe enough to show her the real me. Now, as this tour winds down, I can feel that emptiness creeping in. I never thought I'd find someone who could understand me the way she does, and the thought of losing that connection... well it scares the shit out of me.

Every day, I remind her that I love her, that she's everything to me, and it's incredible to see the effect those words have on her. It's crazy how something as simple as "I love you" can change the way someone carries themselves, like it sparks something deep inside. And when she says it back to me, I have to fight the urge to doubt it, to question if I truly deserve that love. Those harsh words from my mother—those voices from my past telling me I'm unlovable—don't have as much of a hold on me as they once did.

Despite the doubts and insecurities that were drilled into me as a kid, I'm finally starting to believe I'm capable of being loved. It's a revelation I never thought I'd reach, and it's all because of Scarlet. She's shown me a side of love I didn't think existed, a kind of love that heals rather than hurts.

With Nate sticking around for the remainder of the tour, constantly chasing after every groupie he and Theo can fuck, Scarlet and I have been stealing more moments together. Every night, Nate takes the stage for the last song, but tonight, he told Scarlet to stay on the drums and perform the final song herself. I couldn't be more stoked that he gave her that chance. She's earned it. She deserves to show the world just how fucking talented she is.

As I glance over at her behind the drum kit, our eyes lock, and she gives me a smile that's full of emotion. The stage lights catch the tears shimmering in her eyes, and I can see just how much this final night means to her. It's the end of this chapter, but I'm confident in what lies ahead for her. The future is wide open, full of possibilities, and I'm beyond excited to see where her dreams take her. This is just the beginning, and I know she's destined for greatness.

The final note hangs in the air for a beat before the crowd erupts into cheers, a deafening roar that shakes the entire stadium. Xander raises his hands in the air, his face lit up with a grin of pure triumph. I rip my guitar off, following suit as Theo does the same beside me. We exchange a brief glance, before stepping toward the front of the stage. It's time for our final goodbyes.

As I walk up, my eyes catch Scarlet rising from behind the drum kit. She steps forward, joining us at the front of the stage.

Xander steps back up to the mic, his voice cutting through the ambient buzz of the crowd as they start to quiet down. He glances at Scarlet, a proud smile tugging at the corners of his mouth, before turning to face the audience.

"Thank you, everyone, for being here with us tonight," he says. "It's been an unforgettable ride, and none of it would have been possible without all of you."

The crowd roars, their voices crashing together in a wave of pure, electrifying energy that pulses through every inch of the stadium.

"I want to take a moment to give a massive shoutout to someone who's been absolutely crushing it these past two months," Xander starts, the crowd instantly quieting, eager to hear what he has to say next. "Let me tell you without Scarlet stepping in, this tour wouldn't have happened. She's not just a stand-in; she's proven herself to be one hell of a talented drummer." He pauses, his gaze locking onto hers, pride radiating from him. "Scarlet, you've got something in you that the world needs to see. This is just the start for you, and I know you're gonna do amazing things." He turns back to the crowd. "You all need to keep an eye on her because this girl's got big things coming. When she starts with her new band, she's gonna blow the fucking roof off." He turns back towards Scarlet. "So, from all of us up here, thank you, Scarlet, for everything."

The crowd erupts into cheers again.

Scarlet's smile lights up her face, and I can see the glimmer of tears in her eyes as she nods her head toward Xander.

I step closer, wrapping my arm around her shoulders and pulling her into a tight squeeze. I press a kiss to the top of her head. I'm so fucking proud of her—for everything she's done for us and for our label. All those assholes who said we couldn't pull this off. Well, fuck you. We didn't just do it; we fucking nailed it. And a massive part of that is because of her.

I lean down to whisper in her ear, my voice low but full of emotion. "You've earned every bit of this, Scar. You're a fucking star." She looks up at me, her eyes shining with unshed tears, and her smile widens as if she can't believe it either. But she should. Because she is.

"Until next time," Xander says into the mic, his voice echoing across the crowd. We all wave one last time at the audience, Theo, Scarlet and I wait, expecting to follow our usual routine—Xander walking off first. But then he gestures for Scarlet to go ahead, giving her the spotlight one final time.

As she walks across the stage, my eyes can't help but lock onto her ass. She's mine now, and I'm not about to waste a single fucking minute with her. Every second counts, and I intend to make the most of every moment we have together.

When she reaches Nate at the side of the stage, he pulls her in tight, wrapping his arms around her like she's the most precious thing in the world. I can't catch the words he whispers in her ear, but the way she nods, that small smile playing on her lips, speaks volumes.

Despite their ups and downs, their bond as siblings is unbreakable. There's a loyalty between them that runs deep, and moments like this make it crystal clear.

As they pull back, Theo steps in next, wrapping her up in a solid hug of support. It's about damn time these two overprotective assholes started giving her the space to take charge of her own life.

When Theo finally lets go, Xander steps in and places a hand on her shoulder, giving it a firm squeeze. "Thanks, Scarlet," he says, his voice carrying a rare sincerity that breaks through his usual stoic exterior. It's no surprise that Xander skips the hug—that's just not his style. He reserves that kind of warmth for Poppy and Alex, keeping things a little more guarded with the rest of us.

As soon as Xander steps back, I can't hold back any longer. I step in and wrap my arms around her, pulling her close, breathing in the scent of her hair mixed with the faint hint of sweat from the night's performance.

"I can't wait for us to get home," I say, and the words roll off my tongue. The thought of Scarlet living with me, of having her there every day, feels so damn right. We've practically been living together for the past month, and the idea of not having her beside me in my bed—feeling the warmth of her body next to mine—is something I can't even bear to think about. My house was built as an escape from everything I left behind—the poverty, the brokenness, the feeling that I had nothing to offer. A few months ago, the idea of being with the same woman every day would've terrified me, but now? The thought of my place without her feels like the worst fucking nightmare.

I lean in and kiss her, pouring every ounce of my heart into that moment. It's raw and intense, a desperate attempt to claim every bit of her joy as my own. I want her to know how deeply in love I am with her, how she's become my everything.

When we finally pull away, I can't help but grin like an idiot, my heart racing like it's the first time I've ever felt this alive. This is it. This is everything I've ever wanted, and it's just the beginning. I can see the future stretching out ahead of us, bright and full of promise, and I'm ready to dive in headfirst with her by my side.

# Epilogue

## Ace

## One Year Later

As I sit in this cramped little room, a backstage pass weighing heavy around my neck, the memories come crashing down on me, relentless and sharp. It's been years since I've thought about those days—when we were just the fucking opening act for one of the biggest bands in the world. That gig was the turning point. It didn't just change the game; it catapulted us from obscurity to the top. And now, as I get ready to watch Scarlet's band, I feel it deep in my gut—they're on the brink of that same kind of explosion. They're not just good—they're fucking incredible. There's no question in my mind that they're about to take over, just like we did.

But sitting across from me... This fucking guy. The lead singer's boyfriend, who's been glued to his damn phone the entire time he's been here. Not a single ounce of interest in what's happening around him, no excitement in his eyes. It's like he doesn't even grasp how huge tonight is for his girl. It pisses me off—how clueless some people can be when they're right on the verge of something that could change their whole fucking life.

Each of the band members were only given one backstage pass for the night. Tomorrow, Nate will be Scar's plus one, and the night after, it'll be Theo. What she doesn't know, though, is that the guys are already sitting out there in the stadium, dressed in their ridiculous disguises, ready to lose their shit cheering her on from the crowd.

As I sit here, waiting for someone to take us to the wings of the stage so we can catch the show from the side, my eyes wander to the massive bouquet of flowers I brought with me. A smirk tugs at my lips, and I shake my head. I remember a time when I thought guys who bought flowers were either completely fucked up or just plain pussy-whipped.

But damn, if that isn't me now. And you know what? I don't give a shit. Not one bit.

I'd do anything for Scar.

If that means this tattooed, rough-around-the-edges asshole is walking around with a bouquet of flowers for his girl, then so fucking be it. She's worth every second of it.

Hell, anyone who's got a problem with it can catch a fist to the face. That's where I'm at now. She's mine, and I'll do whatever it takes to show her that—every damn day.

My phone vibrates in my pocket, and I pull it out, already knowing who it is.

**Nate:** How is she?

I quickly type back my answer, my thumbs moving fast.

**Ace:** Good. She was fucking pumped. They're gone now, so the show should kick off soon.

I can practically picture them now, sitting there like a couple of dickheads, waiting for the show to start.

Nate with his black wig, doing his best to look incognito, and Theo, of course, rocking that ridiculous seventies pornostache, like he's about to start the next big trend.

The guy's a fucking trip. He doesn't care about the weird stares or whispers—hell, he thrives on it. Always has. That's just Theo.

The door swings open, and this young guy strolls in, looking like he's just walked into the holy grail of backstage moments. He's got one earbud in, clipboard clutched in his hand like he's managing the damn Grammys. The second he spots me, his face lights up like I'm Santa Claus about to drop off his Christmas gift.

"I'm here to take you out to the wings so you can watch the show. But first, can I snag a photo with you, Mr. Roberts?" He's already heading my way before I've even got a chance to respond, phone out, ready for his moment of glory.

The douche sitting across from me finally lifts his head from his phone, his brows pulling together as he tries to figure out who the hell I am.

"Yeah, sure," I say, standing up from the couch.

"I'm a huge fan of your band," the young guy says, tilting his head toward me for the selfie. He snaps the photo, quickly tucking his phone back into his pocket with a grin. "Thanks, man," he adds, then motions for us to follow him. "Alright, this way."

I fall in step behind him, the bored douchebag reluctantly following along.

I know damn well I could find my way to the stage on my own, but tonight isn't about me—it's Scarlet's night. It's her show, and I'm here to support her.

As we make our way through the narrow corridors, crew members spot me. Some shout my name, others give quick fist bumps or nods.

"So, you're in a band?" the douchebag finally pipes up, walking next to me.

I glance at him, raising an eyebrow. "Yeah. Something like that." My tone is flat, dismissive. I'm not in the mood for a conversation with this guy. Earlier, when Scarlet left and I was bored, I tried to make small talk—he ignored me, glued to his phone. Now that he thinks I'm someone important, he suddenly wants to talk. Fuck that. I channel my inner Xander, giving him nothing. Let him take his fake interest and shove it. I'm not here to boost his ego.

He doesn't stop with the questions, probing relentlessly about who the hell I am, but I shut him down with short, disinterested responses. By the time we make it to the stage and the clipboard guy leaves us in the wings, I'm already losing my patience.

"Listen, asshole," I snap, my voice low but cutting. "I'm here to watch my girl and enjoy the show, not answer twenty fucking questions. So, back the fuck off."

He blinks, clearly thrown off, but I don't give him the chance to reply.

My focus is already back on the stage, waiting for the only person who matters to step into the spotlight.

And then I see her—drumsticks in hand, sitting behind the kit—everything else fades away.

The idiot beside me. The background noise. It's just her and this moment, the one she'll remember for the rest of her fucking life, just like the four of us do.

As Scarlet sets up behind the drums, she looks towards me in the wings, her eyes locking onto mine. I catch a brief flicker of nerves, but it's gone in an instant. She takes a steadying breath, and when I give her a nod, I see the small, reassuring smile on her lips.

That look. It says everything. She's about to give it her all, and I know she will. I've seen her step in and crush it before.

As the lights dim and the guitarist counts them in, I watch Scarlet take one last deep breath, steadying herself. I know she's got this. She's played in front of eighty thousand people before. This smaller venue should be a fucking breeze.

********

**Book  Three — Seven Lost Summers, is out September 15th 2025 — visit your favorite retailer for details.**

## About The Author

Eve Campbell writes steamy romance novels that capture the excitement of love. Her books feature broken characters and draw readers into a world where even the most damaged hearts can find passion and healing.
Join my Facebook Readers Group – Or find me on Social Media to keep up to date with any new releases.

Sixty Days Of Summer – ISBN – 9781923416055